John Pritchard was born NHS career began with Casualty receptionist in his local hospital, after which eye-opening introduction he worked in administration and patient services, and currently helps to manage the medical unit in a large hospital in the south of England. *Angels of Mourning* is his second novel and follows the highly successful *Night Sisters*.

JOHN PRITCHARD

Angels of Mourning

HarperCollins*Publishers*

HarperCollins Paperbacks
An Imprint of HarperCollins*Publishers*
77–85 Fulham Palace Road,
Hammersmith, London W6 8JB

A Paperback Original 1995
1 3 5 7 9 8 6 4 2

A catalogue record for this book
is available from the British Library

ISBN 0 00 648013 6

Set in Sabon

Printed and bound in Great Britain by
HarperCollinsManufacturing Glasgow

ACKNOWLEDGEMENTS

A large number of people have inspired, informed and added flavour to this story, in their many different ways. They include *All About Eve*; Luis Enriquez Bacalov; Simon Boswell; Giuliano Carmineo; Stelvio Cipriani; Giuseppe Colizzi; Sergio Corbucci; Guido & Maurizio di Angelis; Veronique Duverge; Beth Elgood; Sergio Endrigo; *Fields of the Nephilim*; Christopher Frayling; Gianni Garko; Enzo Girolami; Mario Girotti; Lallo Gori; Romolo Guerrieri; Bob Johnson; Sergio Leone; Joe Millard; Ennio Morricone; Indra Morris; Mike Oldfield, Gianfranco Parolini; Huw Pryce; Carlo Rustichelli; Jean-Paul Sartre; *The Sisters of Mercy*; Laurence Staig; Richard Stanley; William Terry; Luigi Vanzi; Thomas Weisser; Tony Williams; and Michael Wood. I'm very grateful to them all.

Thanks are also due to:
Geraint Lloyd Davies, Rene Hogguer and Fabrizio Li Perni (for keeping me in Spaghettis)
Eira & Max (for hospital anecdotes and the unwitting loan of their house)
Brenda, Lesley & Rebecca (my first ever fan club)
Barbara B (for chocolate hobnobs and making life interesting)
Marie and Sheila (for nursing advice)
Viv (for her unfailing cheerfulness, enthusiasm and for not sacking me)
London Walks and the Museum of London (for deep background)
Rachel G (And Why Not?)
and
F.M.E. (not first, nor last, but always).

Any similarity between characters in this story and real police officers or units is certainly not intended! Nor is Rachel's workplace based on any one hospital.

To
Veronique and Huw
For all their sense and humour

PART 1

The Mercy of Angels

Chapter 1

I remember waking up on that first, awful Friday, and thinking how good it felt to be alive.

I'd come to the surface in my own sweet time. No need to grope for my alarm clock through the darkness – nor meet my pasty-faced reflection in the bathroom mirror, the window beside it still black from the night outside. No call to venture out into the pre-dawn city chill.

No more Earlies for me this week. I wasn't on until one.

So I just lay where I was, content and clear-headed from a full eight hours, and soaked up the duvet's warmth. With bed and bedclothes all to myself, I'd snuggled deep into a cosy little nest: the hardest sort of all to quit. And maybe I'd started building it when I should have still been sharing – at least if Nick's usual complaints were anything to go by.

But Nick was long gone now; out before six to catch his shift-change. His turn to tiptoe to the bathroom, and dress in the dimness, and let himself out into the darkest hour.

I hadn't woken.

Sleep – at long, long last – was somewhere I felt safe.

The light through the curtains was pale and flat; they were going on about snow on the radio news. But it didn't really register until I'd gone through, yawning, to open the front door – and couldn't find the milk bottles.

The doorstep was a shapeless heap; our street was blanketed. I started delving – then stopped again to listen to the hush. It seemed unreal: like the sallow, sick-rose pink of the sky above the rooftops. For a moment I just knelt there, not feeling the chill that came gnawing through

3

my nightshirt. Knelt, and stared in wide-eyed wonder, and couldn't stop the grin spreading over my face. Because I've always loved the early-morning snow: loved the way it can turn a dreary winter city to another world. From back when I was a girl growing up in the Midlands, to now, in drab North London, the magic hadn't changed. It still made me want to play snowballs.

Even the prospect of the chaos I'd face getting in to work didn't dampen my mood.

A note on the cork board caught my eye as I came back in with the bottles. *Raitch. I'll get some more bread on the way home. Love, Nick.* Which probably meant he'd finished the loaf; no wonder there were all those kisses at the end. I blew him one back, and carried the chilled milk through into the kitchen.

After breakfast, with a couple of hours left to kill, I wandered round the house for a while. Some stray bits of dirty washing to be rounded up (*Nick!*); a few fastidious flicks of the duster. But it had been a lived-in sort of place from day one, which was what I really liked about it. Overlooking Clissold Park: two bedrooms – one damp – and it had cost us. But it was ours now. A place of our own. A place we'd begun to call home.

Ours. Something special: something shared. Something to make the past seem very far away.

Sometimes.

And sometimes it seemed like yesterday. Three crowded years just fled away, and the dark was so close it made me catch my breath. But such moments were more fleeting now; much fewer. I might still dream the dreams, but I couldn't recall them. And they didn't wake me, sobbing, in the night.

Ready to go – bag packed, and travelcard ready in my purse – I wrapped up warm, and picked my way out into the silent street. The snow was slick and icy underfoot – I almost slipped – but there was a narrow, gritted gap down

4

the middle, like the safe path through a minefield, and I followed it carefully towards the main road. This was busier, and already mostly slush. A queue of people were waiting by the bus-stop, and I'd joined them just long enough for my cheeks to start stinging when the number 73 came rumbling into view.

I rode the bus as far as King's Cross, then changed to the tube for the rest of the journey; watching the snow melting off my boots as we banged and rattled southward, from tunnels into canyons open to the slaty sky.

Someone was waiting for me at the other end.

Coming up out of the station, I found him right in my path – huddling on the stairs like a survivor of Stalingrad. A beggar wrapped up in a hospital blanket, his stubbled face pinched tight with the cold. His grey eyes hungry.

And survivor he was, I thought numbly: straggling in retreat from an undeclared war. A man defeated. But I was the one who spread my mittened hands, as if in surrender.

'Sorry, mate . . . No change . . .'

He'd asked as I said it; the appeal stayed frozen to his face. And all I could do was pass him by, my helpless hands still empty; giving him a small, regretful smile.

Big help, of course. But with shock still thumping dully in my chest, it was as much as I could manage. Hardly his fault, poor bloke – but some things still brought the worst of it back. And try as I might, I couldn't keep my nerves from reacting.

After a moment I raised my face again – and the hospital was there before me, looming up like a tenement block; sombre as stone. But its windows leaked light and warmth from the world within: a place protected from this bitter day. A refuge in refugee city.

I waited for a gap and crossed the road: hunching my shoulders against the cold.

Finished scribbling the last detail, I looked up from my notebook. 'That it?'

Sue nodded, and I glanced quickly back over what I'd written. Six patients handed over, in varying degrees of recovery. I glanced out through the office door, and the pages of notes were transformed into six exhausted bodies, hemmed in with machinery and monitors. The nearest ventilator hissed steadily. Intensive Care was nearly a full house.

'Oh . . . we had some lost property handed in . . .' Sue added, as I clicked my pen. 'I locked it in the drugs cupboard . . .'

'What, from relatives?'

She shrugged. 'Cleaner found it. Some sort of toy or trinket. Doubt if it's valuable . . .'

The rest of the shift were already stirring. The phone at the station rang again, and Jez led the way out to answer it. Sally was helping Jean turn Mr Hall. The next eight hours began here and now.

I stood, and tucked away my notebook. Beyond the blinds and windows, the grey sky looked like porridge; it made our lights seem all the brighter. I could almost feel the chilly wind against the glass; sense the mess of slushy streets below us. But winter couldn't reach us here.

I'd come to this hospital with my ENB 100 under my belt, and my mind on a fresh start; but it had been a bit like a homecoming as well. London was where I'd trained: where I'd grown from girl to woman. I always knew I'd return one day. The ITU qualification had been my ticket back.

Intensive Care. A whole new ballgame after A&E, but no less demanding. I'd been one of the Sisters here for nine months now – and all of them on days.

I'll not be working nights again.

Not ever.

'Do you want me to change Joe's infusion?' Sue asked, already glancing in that direction; still smoothing her polythene pinny.

6

I glanced down at my watch; the time had flown. She should have been gone an hour ago.

'No, you get off home now. And thanks, Sue. I mean that.'

She gave a tired little smile – which flickered to a frown. 'Oh, yes . . . That lost property. I was meaning to give it you . . .'

'Look, don't worry . . .' I began, but she was already going over to the wall cupboard. The red light above the door came silently on as she unlocked it, like a warning sign. And that was how it struck me, for no good reason – even though I'd seen the like on every single working day. Red for danger: a glowing, bloodshot eye.

Then the softer yellow light of the interior bathed our faces.

'Here. I didn't seal it.' She handed the envelope across, and I took it, peered inside – and curiously drew the object out.

It was the oddest thing: like a die on a small metal stalk. Something you'd spin like a top, I realised; see which side finished uppermost. Except that the sides were all the same.

All aces of spades.

I felt the faintest frown across my forehead.

A trinket from someone's Christmas cracker, probably. Hardly worth handing in. I turned it over in my fingers one more time; then slipped it back into the envelope. And after just a moment's hesitation, I licked the flap and sealed it.

'Thanks. I'll get it sent down during supper.' I smiled then, in a mock-resigned sort of way. 'Assuming we get any.'

As it turned out, we didn't. The bomb went off just after half past six.

Jez and I were queuing for supper in the canteen, and heard it there. A dull but distinctive *boom*. The darkened windows rattled faintly, and were still.

7

I felt a cold little knot drawing tight inside me. Still balancing my tray, I turned to Jez – but Jez was already peering out into the night. I craned my head in turn, but there was nothing to see: no flicker of flame to tell us where.

'Oh God, not another one . . .' I muttered.

He grunted. 'Sounded big. And not too far.' His eyes came back round to me. 'Bastards . . .'

I knew who he meant, of course. After the past fortnight, no one needed it spelled out.

Bombs in London: big deal. That's how I used to think. But then I came to live here. Then I started travelling on the Underground. And then, two weeks ago, the year's first bomb blew a tube station apart.

There'd been no warning; no caller with a helpful Irish accent and recognised code word. Just a suitcase load of semtex at St Paul's. The place had been demolished, starting a fire that the underground wind had sucked deep into the tunnels. At least we hadn't had another King's Cross, thank God; it had been late, just the last train left, and the platforms and stairs had been almost empty.

Five people died.

And then the next bomb, and the next: set off completely at random, as though someone was playing battleships with an *A to Z*. One in an Oxford Street restaurant at Saturday lunchtime, leaving it a burned-out shell. One in the City, breaking windows at the Barbican. We'd waited, shaken, for the admissions – the *claims* – we knew were coming.

But they hadn't come. There'd just been silence. And not of guilt or shame, for all my wishful thinking. Just an absence of human contact: an eerie *emptiness*. And then another awful bomb.

I could hear sirens now, reaching us fitfully through wind and windows; already wailing their despair. The lump of ice in my stomach grew sharper edges as I pictured the chaos out there. The snow would only make it worse, of course. And the night would make it far more frightening.

Disasters at night always haunt me the most. From the Tay Bridge to the *Titanic*, they give me the shivers. All those people lost and screaming in the dark . . .

'Think they'll come to us?' Jez asked; but I saw I wouldn't need to guess. An ambulance crew was sitting at the nearest table, and the bloke was already fiddling with his radio handset. His companion watched pensively, biting her lip. They were still wearing their green and yellow anoraks, the reflective stripes aglow under the canteen lights. They'd hardly had a chance to touch their coffee.

The radio crackled into crosstalk. Too distant for me to hear; but after a moment the crewman met my eyes, as if expecting to find me watching, and raised his voice.

'Liverpool Street.'

'*Shit*,' from Jez. I shared the sentiment – but saved my breath.

I guessed I'd be needing it soon enough.

It wasn't certain that they'd come to us; just bloody likely. If this was a big one, with lots of casualties, the units all around would be receiving. Even as we finished loading our trays – the hot food sandwiched by paper plates to keep it warm – our own A&E would be gearing up and clearing the decks. And I knew we'd need to follow suit.

'Who can we move?' Jez asked, as we retraced our echoing steps along the corridor.

'Mrs Hickson, probably . . . if we're pushed. But let's see what Murdoch says.' I turned to back in through the unit's swing doors, held them open with my heel while he followed me through, then led the way over to our rest room. A glimpse of faces glancing round as we passed the relatives' room; but I'd given up feeling embarrassed. Even angels eat chips.

Lucy looked up from the sagging chair into which she'd sunk. 'Rachel, did you hear –'

'Yep. Liverpool Street.' I was still looking round for somewhere I could leave my supper to get cold. 'Any details?'

Lucy – who'd worked overtime this week, and looked it – just spread her hands. No worry. Dumping my tray, I left her to her well-earned break, and went on down into the unit proper. The lights were low, now: the glow of readouts seeming brighter in the dimness. Fuller lighting was on around two of the beds, where procedures were underway – and at the desk, where Johann Meier was listening intently to the phone.

I went over and waited; a bit keyed-up, and trying not to show it. Johann's eyes found mine, and said hello. Like most of the ITU medics he worked in shirtsleeves, and I could see sweat stains in the armpits.

After a moment he spoke again – his English calm and precise – and the conversation ended.

'A&E are expecting two,' he told me, hanging up. 'One will probably go straight to theatre. The other comes to us as soon as he is stable.'

We'd get them both in due course. 'So who's going?'

'Mrs Hickson. She is still under the physicians, so Murdoch is talking to them. And that is us full.'

Again. The second time in three weeks we'd closed the doors. We had the beds for more, of course; but not the nurses.

I turned away as he dialled again; reaching up into my short uniform sleeve to scratch my shoulder. Staring unhappily at middle-aged Mrs Hickson, inert on her bed. She'd improved steadily since she came off the ventilator; Dr Murdoch had been pleased with her progress on the teatime round. But she could have done with another day here. Just to be safe.

Which made me think of something else: how safe I felt in here. Well settled now – and getting real satisfaction from helping to run a specialist unit: a world within a world. A place whose informality and instant crises concealed a secret order – of patience, skill and common purpose. It had boosted my confidence no end. Even the long dark winter evenings didn't depress me any more.

I still turned my back on the windows, though: avoiding them like eyes. Even in this overheated room, they seemed to radiate cold. As if the effort of holding the night at bay had turned them into sheets of hard black ice.

Mrs Hickson was transferred on out; the first of our two bomb victims came in to take her place. He was dead within the hour.

I knew we were on a loser from the start; it didn't need a nurse's intuition. He'd been close to the core of the explosion, his body dreadfully burnt. But as long as a glimmer of hope remained, we fought to save him.

Even as we struggled, a part of me found time to watch how well the team was working. Dr Murdoch – our consultant in charge – mucking in with his sleeves rolled up; another anaesthetist at his elbow, still wearing his theatre pyjamas. Michelle and I busying ourselves with drips and drug infusions, setting them up as fast as the medics could put them in. Others hovered round us; came and went. Someone's ventilator alarm started bleeping at the far end of the room, but the problem was corrected quickly. Jez had the rest of the unit well in hand.

Our nameless – faceless – patient's output was fading all the time. Murdoch kept at it, his own face stern with concentration; but the damage done had been too great. The spark of life grew dimmer; dwindled. Died.

We lost him. Let him go.

And kept right on working. No time for a breather. Just fenced off the bed with mobile screens, and turned our attention to the living. Oh, the frustration lingered on of course: I felt its weight inside me as I phoned down to Haematology for some more bloods. And the handset felt much too bulky as I set it down again, and turned – to find a uniformed young copper standing rather nervously behind me.

'Er . . . evening, Sister. I've got the relatives of one of the bomb victims. James Baxter. Casualty said he'd come up to you . . .'

'Oh, God.' I glanced past him. They were clustered in the corridor outside, not speaking. 'Couldn't you have rung?'

He gestured helplessly: looking more out of his depth by the moment. 'They tried, but all your phones were engaged. I thought I'd better . . .'

'All right. Don't worry . . .' I grabbed Lucy as she passed, and told her to shepherd our new arrivals into the now-empty waiting room. Then turned back to the PC. 'It's just that he's . . .' I crossed myself '. . . and we haven't had a chance to clean him up yet.'

'Shit. They know he was critical, but . . .'

But someone was going to have to tell them the worst. Murdoch had gone off somewhere with the casenotes; and Johann was busy. Which – as per usual – left it to me.

Afterwards I went back into my office and sat at my desk: resting my mouth against my hands for a minute's dull silence. I'd remembered to bin my soiled pinny before going in to see them – only to have them notice my cheery unofficial trappings (smiley lapel badge, and teddy bear pen-top) as I broke the news. They took the tidings numbly; and after I'd explained all the procedures – and dissuaded them from seeing him just yet – I quietly withdrew, and left them to it.

Some things you never get used to.

After a pause – and without really thinking – I leaned back and opened the top drawer. The envelope with its lost property was there where I'd left it, amid the peppermints and paper clips. And I couldn't have licked the flap thoroughly enough: it was coming unstuck.

I picked it up, and peeled it fully open. The little top came out into my palm. I rolled it thoughtfully between fingers and thumb. The faces of the die looked worn, as if many people had done as much before me.

Something that came up ace of spades, every time; the card of ill-omen. It wasn't a toy, I'd realized that. There was something altogether too grim about it: almost grotesque.

Something that abruptly made me put it back, and close the drawer. And wipe my hand – so recently scrubbed clean – right down my dress.

I'd phoned home to say I'd be late, and not to worry; but Nick was out in the hall to greet me before I'd fully locked the door.

'Hiya.' Quick kiss. 'You must be knackered.'

'You bet I am.' I went through into the lounge and flopped down onto the sofa; and suddenly it seemed I'd never find the strength to rise again.

'Hang on, I'll get you a drink. What'd you like?'

'Um. Horlicks, please. Lots of milk.' I rested my head against the cushion, and turned towards the TV. Some film or other. From the spread of books and notes by his chair, Nick had been doing his homework in front of it. Naughty boy.

Still, looking at all those weighty tomes on *The Criminal Law*, I guessed they needed some diluting. Just like nursing textbooks did.

Nick came back from the kitchen a few minutes later, and passed me my mug; watching with some concern as I took a first, grateful sip.

'You got some of those from Liverpool Street, then?'

I nodded; drank again. 'Two. One died. The other was still in theatre when I left . . .'

'It was on *News at Ten*: the bomb was down in the Underground. Four dead, and more than fifty injured, they said . . .' He shook his head. 'They're just scum, Rachel: they really are.'

He seemed to be expecting a response to that. When I didn't oblige, he sat wearily down beside me, slipping his arm around my shoulders.

13

'Come on, Raitch. I know you want to believe there's good in everybody, but it isn't true. Some of the people we deal with are just plain *evil* . . .' His tone was gentle, persuasive; inviting me to see reason for myself. 'The ones who've been planting these bombs – they're past forgiving.'

I shrugged: still staring at my drink. 'Oh, don't worry – I think they're *scum* as well. I'm just trying not to be judgmental . . .'

'Nothing wrong in judging,' he came back evenly. 'It's what the bastards need. Christ, they even had the gall to make a statement *denying* it was their people doing it. That was on the news as well . . .'

I could see our old capital punishment argument looming up again. Enjoyable enough when I was in the mood – and just the kind of debate that had first brought us together, in the pub following a fund-raising five-a-side match. But tonight I really wasn't up to it. Besides, with the eyes of five grieving people still wide in my mind, I just wouldn't have been objective.

'One of your lot brought the relatives in,' I said, rather obviously changing the subject. 'Still wet behind the ears.' I glanced across, and managed a faint grin. 'Reminded me of someone . . .'

'Gerroff,' he grinned back, and squeezed my shoulders. His clean-cut features were boyish enough, to be sure; but Nick had been on the beat quite long enough to know his business.

'Oh, yes . . .' he said, as I finished my drink. 'Someone rang for you earlier. From your church. Wanted to know if you could help with the soup run tomorrow night.'

I pulled a face, I couldn't help it. 'Well . . .'

'Don't worry: I said you probably couldn't. Pressure of work and all that.'

'Thanks,' I murmured; not even trying to feel guilty.

'Come on,' Nick added brightly, getting up. He turned and took my hands, his grin fading to a knowing little smile.' "*Time for bed*," said Zebedee. BOINGG!'

Which succeeded in giving me the giggles – and so left me completely at his mercy.

And so I ended up where I'd begun – as though this long and gruesome day had never been. Deep under the soft duvet, with Nick cuddling me close: a warm, safe refuge from the night. And yet my mind just would *not* rest. Even after I'd screened out all the evening's traumas, it kept on niggling.

That strange little thing: that gizmo. For some reason I couldn't get it out of my head. Could almost feel its coldness in my fingers.

That windy night I hardly slept at all.

Chapter 2

A flick of my fingers and thumb and it was off again —
veering over the desktop in a black-and-white blur.

I watched it, mesmerized, chin in hand: my pen laid aside
on the sheaf of Off-Duties; the requests ledger forgotten
at my elbow. My turn to do the rosters this month, a
chore at the best of times — but this was more than just
distraction. The thing had virtually found its own way
to my fingers; they'd itched to make it move. There was
something morbidly compelling about its inevitable
progress: it held my attention like a hook.

It spun like an ordinary top at first; then with the weird,
wobbling motion of a gyroscope, leaning out at forty-
five degrees for longer than I'd thought was possible.
But finally it fell, and rolled, and came to rest in front
of me.

The Ace of Spades, of course.

So what game of chance could you possibly play? No
matter how you spun it, you'd never beat its bias towards
bad luck.

I halfway reached for it again — then changed my
mind, and let it lie. It almost felt like a test of my resolve:
being able to leave the bloody thing alone. In (and out
of) my desk five days already, and I still hadn't got round
to handing it in. No one had rung to enquire, but even
so . . . This afternoon, then, I decided. This time I won't
forget.

Maybe my fingers just needed something to keep them
busy; maybe it was nerves. Like when I sometimes caught
myself fiddling with the rings on my fingers, or the cross
round my neck: an unconscious, edgy reflex.

The sort I knew I'd shown this morning, while I listened to Lucy weep.

It's not just the relatives who need a quiet cry sometimes; the stress can wear the best of us down. I've needed a good, hard hug myself before now. But poor Lucy had more than the workload or the death of a patient on her mind. She'd just lost one of her friends.

Quite horribly.

I hadn't known the girl myself: she'd worked over on one of the surgical wards, and our paths hadn't crossed. Anna Stubbs, her name was. And yesterday she'd got into her car, just round by the nurses' home; turned the ignition – and been burned alive.

No warning: no hope. The car had been a fireball in seconds. We'd known nothing at the time – all sirens sound the same on a busy day – and it wasn't until I got home and saw the TV that I realised where the commotion had been coming from. There'd been a fleeting clip on *South East News*: the gutted hulk that had once been a trim Mini Metro. '... *a tragic accident*,' according to the voice-over '*claimed the life of a young nurse in London today*...' And watching, I'd lost my appetite completely.

How much worse for Lucy, who'd been sitting on a birthday present, ready-wrapped, for Anna's twenty-third: next Thursday. She'd come in this morning with a brave enough face, but couldn't hold it. And when I suggested a quiet chat in my office, it wasn't long before she let herself go completely.

In between sobs and sniffles she'd tried her best to talk it all out – and I'd done my best to help it come. An awful, awkward job; but one I felt oddly at ease with. Perhaps because I knew just how she was feeling.

'Really I do,' I'd insisted, while she watched me miserably, and wiped her reddened eyes. 'I mean ... I lost my parents when I was just your age. That was an RTA. And then ... a couple of years ago ... my flatmate was ... was murdered by her boyfriend ...' And oh, there'd been more to it than that, of course. Much more. But it was enough to sit her up, quite startled – then sympathetic herself.

'Oh, Rachel. I'm so sorry . . .'

I shrugged, and quickly steered the conversation back to her. Her problems. I felt guilty dwelling on my own.

And really didn't want to.

But they'd already started stirring again, at the back of my head. The memories of darkness, and burning, and bloody death. Stuff it had taken me months to get over; and years to begin to forget. As Lucy talked on, her voice getting slowly stronger, I fingered my crucifix – feeling its ends digging in under my nails – and tried very hard just to follow her words.

'Did you . . . ever get depressed or anything?' she'd ventured after a while; having said all she'd felt necessary on her own account. Ready to listen in turn now: the first step back up the ladder. I was grateful for that, at least.

'Well . . .' I hesitated. Then: 'Yes, I was – for quite a while. Reactive depression, you know?' And she nodded, the term familiar to us both. Except that mine had been the reactive depression more commonly associated with surviving fires or train crashes. The sort that gives dreadful dreams – and waking weeks of utter hopelessness. I'd been fine for a while, too – coping really well, or so I'd thought. Then the tears from nowhere had begun. The conviction that getting up in the morning would not be worth the trouble. The thoughts of suicide.

Not active suicide, of course: not really. More the passive variety. Like, if a car had mounted the pavement, out of control, I wouldn't have bothered getting out of the way. Suicide with a clear conscience, if you prefer.

And I still think the only thing that kept me going through it all was Jenny. Her face in my dreams. Jenny, who'd been my best and closest friend. Jenny, who'd died before my own nightmare even began.

Jenny, who'd reached out from her grave to save me

18

from a fate far worse than death. And in all the weeks that followed, I'd felt her with me still: even in the darkest, longest nights. Beckoning me on towards the breaking of day.

I'd met with her murderess, too: the witch-like woman who'd risen from her deathbed to strangle her. We'd faced each other in an overcast cemetery, over Jenny's last resting place – and the old woman had just smiled a toothless smile, and gone her way. Perhaps to find a resting place herself; but maybe she was out there still.

Whatever, it was an end between us. I'd sensed that much, that day.

And so life had gone on, as it always must. And as I moved on too – new job, new town, new home, new friends – so the past had faded into the background. But sometimes, even now, I'd feel an emptiness: the strangest yearning for what was gone – like someone who's been somehow left behind.

Oh Jenny. What about me?

'Penny for them, Rachel,' Murdoch said quietly.

I came back to myself with a start – to find him in the office doorway, watching me. Dressed in a charcoal-dark suit, as always: it gave him a sombre aspect, despite his crimson tie. His long, thinly-bearded face could often look severe, as well – which made his smile now all the more engaging.

'Oh . . . It'll cost you a good deal more than that, Dr Murdoch,' I said airily – already feeling just a little better. And Murdoch's smile grew wider.

'I'll be starting the round in a moment: any problems?'

I shook my head. 'Nope. They're all being very good. Jez'll go round with you.' Even Murdoch called him that now. I guessed only his mum still called him Jeremy.

'Good. I'll speak to you later.' He gave me a courteous nod and went on towards the station. I sat back, still smiling myself. Some of our anaesthetists were temperamental

as hell: perhaps it went with the territory. But Murdoch –
though one of the youngest – was probably the calmest of
them all. And the softest-spoken.

Which, when he did get angry, made his rages all the
more unnerving. They were cold: controlled. I'd got on the
wrong side of him once, and he didn't even raise his voice
– but left me shaking.

I hadn't made the same mistake again.

But today he seemed in sunnier mood – which brightened
up mine in turn. As a unit we worked well together: we
got on. Sue had once even ventured the opinion that Murdoch was 'kind of a handsome man'. And added (a few
drinks later) that 'he could put me under any time' –
politely ignoring our cheerful, pop-eyed stares of disbelief.

Well, now. Sue could go on the Early with Jean. Jez had
requested a day off. So who could I put on the Late? I
pondered – or tried to. But the real question was, could I
find an excuse for not doing the soup run again this week?

Getting into bad habits, and I knew it. Knew, and didn't
much care. Not that it had ever been my favourite way
to spend a cold winter's evening: doling out soup to the
street-sleepers. The temptation to let it go had always
itched beneath the surface. But there was something more
than apathy or mere distaste involved this time. I'd really
had a fright.

An awful shock.

And all in the mind, as I'd realised soon enough. A last,
stray echo of things left well behind me. But still – sitting
here, pen poised – I could feel the way my guts had *clenched*
inside me. I wasn't about to go through that again.

It had been a fortnight ago; we'd been bringing soup to
an enclave of the homeless near Waterloo. Quite a crowd
had gathered round our van, to slurp from steaming
beakers in the dimness. I'd started out by making conversation – and ended up quite absorbed. Chewing the fat
with a wryly funny Scotsman not long out of a psychie

unit – and a well-spoken accountant type, who'd ended up on the street with what sounded like petrifying suddenness.

'Gissa hand, will ye?' the Scots bloke asked at length, taking a fresh beaker in each hand and jerking his head towards the people still crouching in the shelter of the nearby bridge. 'Some o' yon lads're too tired to bloody stand . . .'

I nodded, grabbed a couple more helpings of oxtail and followed him over. Hands reached up gratefully from the foxholes of cardboard and blankets. I glimpsed someone sitting apart from the others, almost submerged in the deeper gloom beneath the arch, and made towards him with my last beaker.

I was only a few feet short when I suddenly stopped dead. So suddenly that the soup slopped out, scalding my wrist between sleeve and glove. So dead, I scarcely felt it.

The person ahead of me was squatting with their back against the brickwork: wrapped up in an old black great-coat. A battered, wide-brimmed hat was pulled right down to cover the face beneath; black as the coat, but smudged and smeared with ashy grey.

I suddenly felt like a knife was being pushed into my belly. Pushed and twisted. My skin grew instantly cold. I took a tiny step backwards.

The bowed head never moved.

'. . . one over here, lassie . . .' the Scotsman said cheerfully. He sounded a long way off.

The shadow-shrouded figure didn't stir. Probably asleep, of course. Exhausted, hungry, and about to miss his chance because of my ridiculous unease. Yet all I could do was back away, my heart now racing like a drum-roll.

The Scotsman had to clap me on the shoulder to snap me out of it: the casual grip of his grimy hand was more welcome than I'd have ever dreamed. With a last, wary look towards the shape beneath the bridge, I turned towards the faces I could see, and made an effort to return their smiles and quirky greetings. But all the time I could feel the chilly sweat of that moment: trapped under my clothes, and slowly soaking in. And even after I'd got home, and showered, and scrubbed it all off, my jumpiness remained. My stomach felt sick and sore. Even though I told myself, again and again, that it couldn't have been her. It *couldn't* have.

And of course, it hadn't been: I surely knew that now. Not Razoxane.

Because Razoxane was dead and gone – to Hell.

Three years ago, I found out what *Hell* meant.

I'd been just another nurse; an A&E Night Sister getting on with her job. Then *she* had come in off the street, and Hell had followed with her. I'd thought she was a psychie case at first, which was scary enough – but then she'd revealed the magic in her madness; opened my startled eyes, and made me *see*. Comfortable certainties had crumbled to dust. And then she'd dragged me into her feud with a firm of Physicians as evil and old as she was: and the blood-bags really hit the fan . . .

I found the top was in my fingers once again: I'd fished it up from my drawer without thinking. Turning it over in my free hand, I put Michelle down for the Late – then gave in to the temptation, and set it spinning one more time.

Maybe I should just tell them I can't spare the time, I thought glumly, watching it move. Maybe I'll even manage not to make it sound too selfish . . .

Maybe.

The little top toppled, and spiralled to a stop before me.

Ace of bloody Spades.

Chapter 3

The next day I passed a uniformed policeman in the downstairs corridor: a bag of sandwiches from the foyer shop in one hand, a coffee in the other – and a huge black revolver in a holster at his belt. He seemed not to notice my startled double-take. So I was left to speculate – until Jez broke the news at the gossipy tail-end of Report.

'Heard who they've got down on Ortho? Only one of those bloody terrorists . . .' You could tell he was pleased with our reaction: his freckled face lit up. 'Under armed guard. One of the porters was telling me.' Which made it gospel, of course.

'I heard it was some gang leader or someone,' Lucy countered equably. 'Got shot, and they've had to give him armed protection.' She hesitated. 'Or maybe he was stabbed . . .'

The hospital grapevine was obviously working well. I smiled to myself, still writing.

'Well he wouldn't be on Bones if he'd been stabbed, would he, Lucinda?' Jean pointed out beside me: putting on her most sententious tone. The sort with nearly thirty years in nursing to back it up. And I, with less than twelve, might be Sister to her Staff Nurse – but it still sometimes felt like she was the headmistress, and I was just head girl.

Most of it was just an act, of course – though her sense of humour was too dry for some people, who took it all seriously. But Lucy knew the score, and they got on well. No one else would dare call her Lucinda: she *hated* that.

'Now, Mr Clarke,' Jean continued, fixing Jez with shrewd grey eyes. 'If you would be so kind as to expand upon your information . . . ?'

23

He was glad to. 'Well, according to Bob, he was brought in after the Liverpool Street bomb: leg and back injuries. But something about him didn't fit. The cops who interviewed him got suspicious. Now they reckon he probably *planted* the damn thing, and didn't get clear fast enough . . .' His smile had faded now. Like the rest of us who'd been on that night, he was clearly recalling the mess that bomb had made of two hapless human beings.

The second victim had survived his emergency op, and come through to us in the small hours of the following morning. He was still with us now: still struggling. Scarcely a square inch of his skin visible between the bandages, IV sites and ECG electrodes.

'Bastard,' Sue muttered, with a glance towards the bed. Hardly an original sentiment; but a sincere one. I added a rider, something about them probably not being sure yet. But I knew it lacked conviction.

I taxed Nick with it when I got home; he confirmed Jez's version in a roundabout sort of way. Terrorist suspect under guard. There'd been nothing about it on the news as yet. But give it time, I thought.

What most unnerved me was the thought of armed police around the hospital – for all that they were trying to keep the profile as low as possible. I couldn't forget the look of the pistol that PC had carried – strapped snug into its holster, but still full of latent threat: seeming much bigger and heavier in real life than the guns you see in films. I'd stepped much further aside than I'd needed to let him pass; but while one part of me had shied away, another had stared in morbid fascination.

It would have to be loaded, of course. Live ammunition. And what would happen if someone made a try for their charge? Would they draw those guns in a hospital ward, and start to shoot, with helpless patients all around (and nurses, come to that)? It almost made me shudder just to think it.

So I was glad I had other – happier – things to occupy my next day off. Besides, it was worth it just to see Nick's face when he walked drowsily into the kitchen to find me having breakfast with a giant yellow teddy bear.

'. . . *who's* it for?' he asked again, still eyeing it warily while he poured his coffee. Propped up in the chair at my elbow, it seemed to stare affably back at him through its cellophane wrappings.

'Sandra. You know, that girl we had in with us the other week. Meningitis . . .' I had another spoonful of cereal while he came and sat down. 'She's still in the kids' ward, and . . . I don't know, I just wanted to brighten her day.' Which was the only way I could express it, really. I'd been thinking about her a lot of late; and buying this had suddenly felt *right*.

'Fair enough.' He made a show of leaning forward, face set, as though intimidating a suspect. The bear remained unfazed. 'Got a name, has he?'

I shrugged, grinning.

'Utilising his right to remain silent, eh? I know his type . . .' He snorted; then reached across to take my free hand, and squeeze it. 'That was a really nice idea, Raitch. I hope she loves it.'

'Me too. She's a nice kid.'

He gave me a half-suspicious look. 'Not getting broody, are we?'

'No, we are not.' I raised my eyebrows. 'Any more questions?'

'Are you wearing anything *at all* under that shirt?' he asked conversationally.

'*Nick*. I'm having breakfast.'

'So. We can improvise.'

'Sod off.'

He met my smile with a look of injured innocence; then sighed dramatically, and spread his hands.

'Well, then: can I interest you in some toast?'

*   *   *

25

At least his hope for the afternoon was realised; and mine as well. Sandra liked her present lots.

I sat back in the bedside chair and watched her hug it — pressing it up against her cheek. It looked about to smother her.

'Oh, Rachel . . . he's lovely. Thanks ever so much.'

'Thought you'd like him,' I murmured, feeling almost as delighted as she looked: enjoying the glow of warmth that grew inside me. Nothing to do with broodiness, despite Nick's suspicions; just the simple, heady buzz of making somebody's day. Someone I'd seen at death's door, and helped nurse back to health. She was still a little pale, but her fine brown hair had its sheen back now — and her eyes their sparkle. She looked like an eight-year-old girl was supposed to look: carefree, and full of fresh life.

And I'd been her age once, of course — but I couldn't imagine it. Not any more. Couldn't dream of seeing the world with such unclouded eyes.

I felt my smile becoming wistful, and glanced away: around the bed-bay. The colour scheme was insistently cheerful — bright paint backing up an agreeably scrappy wallpapering of kids' drawings. Toys and televisions vied for attention. All trying — against the odds — to make the place a little bit less scary; a little more like home.

It still smelled like a hospital, though. And no child's bedroom was ever this clinically clean.

'Has your mum been in to see you today?' I asked, looking back at her. And Sandra shook her head, still cuddling her present.

'Not yet — she's coming tonight.' She said it quite matter-of-factly; but I saw her squeeze the bear a little tighter as she spoke, as if seeking reassurance.

I knew what the problem was, of course. Her dad had walked out years ago, leaving her mum to manage on her own with three small kids. So the poor woman had to work her guts out to make ends meet. I'd learned as much when Sandra was in with us – her mother almost frantic with worry, yet unable to spare the time she wanted to: time that was money her family needed. It had taken me a lot of quiet talking to convince her she was leaving her daughter in safe and loving hands; and a whole lot more to persuade her that she needn't feel so *guilty*.

Now that Sandra was back on the ward, I'd taken to visiting her regularly: trying as best I could to fill the gaps when her mum couldn't make it. It would take more than giant teddy bears to manage that, of course; but she was always glad to see me, and the feeling was mutual.

'Did you see the snow?' I asked her, looking over towards the window. It was tall, and much in need of cleaning; the rooftops I could see through it were more grungey grey than white.

'Oh yes. We can't see much from up here, but Nurse Janet told me all about it. She promised to let me throw a snowball at her . . . if it's still here when I go.' Her small face fell. 'But I bet it won't be.'

Someone had appeared at the end of the bed: a sandy-haired young man with a serious, bespectacled smile. He acknowledged me with a nod, then turned his attention to the patient, and leaned forward to examine the bear. 'Hello, Sandra. Is this your new friend, then?'

She stared up at him, eyes narrowed in childish suspicion. 'Yes, he is. Are you a doctor?'

His smile widened. 'I certainly am. Look . . .' He unslung the red stethoscope from round his neck. 'And this is my badge, see . . .' It was pinned to his check shirt. 'My name's Dr Miller.'

She didn't appear convinced. 'You're not a *proper* doctor, though. You haven't got a white coat.'

Dr Miller glanced at me again. I just rolled my eyes.

'When mum takes me to see Dr Hughes,' Sandra went on firmly, 'he usually wears a suit, but sometimes he's got his white coat on. So I know he's a *proper* doctor.'

So much for the medics on the kids' ward not wearing white coats in an effort to make the place seem homelier. I grinned, and got to my feet.

'I'm sure he's a proper doctor really, Sandra: he looks like one to me. So I'll leave the two of you to have a chat . . .' Dr Miller winked gratefully; he'd already unhooked the clipboard of charts from the bed-end. I leaned down and ruffled Sandra's hair.

'Listen, I'll try and drop in tomorrow, okay? Take care. Say hello to your mum from me.'

She nodded brightly, and gave me a wave. As I left, I could hear her proudly introducing Dr Miller to her very newest friend.

I was still smiling as I left the children's unit: off the ward, past reception and out through the double doors. They swung closed again behind me – and I heard the automatic locks click into place. There was a keypad next to them for staff, but otherwise it was admission via intercom only. You can't be too careful these days.

Well, that's your good deed done for the day, Rachel Young. And now there was the shopping to be thinking of – and getting home before the rush-hour started. I paused in the corridor to plot my course: idly scuffing at the lino with the toe of my boot while I thought the options through. After the brightness of the ward, it seemed very dim out here: no natural light for a dozen yards. The corridor's whole length would be well enough lit come nightfall, of course; but it was daytime now, and electricity could still be saved. Energy policy and all that. I'd seen a memo somewhere . . .

So: Safeway or Sainsbury's? I turned pensively towards the distant lifts. There was a cleaner mopping the floor half-way along the corridor, working in a pool of wintry sunlight from the nearest window. I'd taken the first step in her direction when I realized someone was behind me.

There'd been no sound; not even a shifting of air. Just

that sixth-sense tingle you sometimes get, when some prankster tries tip-toeing up.

I turned round quickly.

The corridor was empty.

I stood quite still for a moment: puzzled. I'd been mistaken . . . and yet the nape of my neck was still cool and itchy.

The gloom was deeper in this direction: the corridor leading to an unlit stairwell. The paint on the walls – already cheerless – had been sullied by shadow, like a coating of dirt. Even the air seemed grainy and begrimed.

But no one was there. I could see that much, at least.

Even as I stared, I felt *unease* creep up, and slip its arms around me. Despite myself, I almost squirmed – then turned sharply on my heel, as if to shake it off completely. But it clung on by its fingernails, and dogged me all the way back down to the lifts. The cleaner smiled a greeting as I passed her, and I managed one back – but it was just my face going through the motions. Something – out of nowhere – had spoiled my mood: some hidden concern, intruding to cast its shadow. Now, of all times. I could almost taste my disappointment.

That, and something else: something much more bitter on the back of my tongue.

Just before I got to the lifts I glanced over my shoulder one more time: I couldn't help it. Beyond the cleaner in her splash of sunshine, and the signs announcing *Paediatric Wards*, the corridor lay in dingy silence. A hospital thoroughfare like any other.

Of course. But it still took an effort to turn my back on it again; and a still greater one to stop thinking of all that *darkness* between myself and Sandra's cheery smile.

Through the rest of the afternoon it kept on coming back: that queasy, churned-up feeling in my stomach. Sometimes so acute that I even began to wonder – hopefully – if it wasn't just something I'd eaten. Or some other easy explanation I could cope with.

But as I trailed round Sainsbury's, trying to focus my mind on budget and bargains, I couldn't out-think the other possibility. I prevaricated for ages over which washing powder to go for; read and re-read each label in turn; but it didn't help. Words just failed to sink in: my head was far too full of grimmer matters.

I knew I was . . . *sensitive* to certain things around me: I'd found that out before. A common gift, apparently – but in my case strong enough to give me revelations: dreams and nightmares; and the awareness – sometimes – of presences not seen.

It wasn't a gift I'd ever wanted. After . . . the last time . . . I'd studiously ignored it: tried to school it out of my head. And as time had passed, I'd even started to forget it – and put my occasional flashes of insight down to female intuition. Or whatever.

But what I'd felt this afternoon had been something more than that.

So the hospital's got ghosts. So what? It's an old enough building . . . I made for a mental shrug, and – as usual – plumped for the Persil.

By the time I got off the bus at the bottom of my road, I was feeling better. Still a bit delicate – the prospect of cooking tea aroused no enthusiasm at all – but my leaden mood had lifted somewhat. Maybe it was just tiredness, after all: things had been pretty hectic of late. I reckoned I could do with an early night.

I let myself in, and lugged the two full carriers through to the kitchen; not bothering with lights, although the place was awash with winter dusk. I was back on home ground now: familiar territory, made more intimate by shadow. Here even the dimness had its comforts. But I liked the way the glow from the fridge spilled out around me as I loaded the shelves.

I checked the kettle and clicked it on, then wandered

30

back into the hall. The house was quiet: Nick wouldn't be back until late. I was just shrugging out of my coat when I noticed the footprints.

Smeared grey footprints, on my freshly-hoovered carpet: leading upstairs, and out of sight.

For what seemed like a minute I studied them in silence – but that silence was full of all the sounds I'd just been making, coming back to me in waves: the rattle of the lock, the opening door; my tired little sigh, and footsteps through to the kitchen. Each mundane noise magnified a hundredfold by the knowledge that someone else had heard them too: that *someone was in here with me*.

Nick, I thought, and opened my mouth to say it. But the dusky air flowed in and dried it up. My throat as well. Suddenly I couldn't even croak.

Because I knew it wasn't Nick, of course; knew before the thought had barely formed. A stranger's boots had made those marks. And even as I stared upstairs – and strained my singing ears against the hush – a fist of foreboding closed inside me.

A burglar. Still here. I've surprised him. Upstairs.

My eyes flicked to the phone on the wall. The overfull pinboard beside it seemed almost insultingly cheerful.

So how fast could I grab it and dial 999? Faster than a shadow could come racing down the stairs towards me? And how long after that would a police car turn up? How many minutes?

A minute's a long time in rape. A *very* long time.

I took a quiet, cautious step back towards the door – the one I'd closed so noisily behind me. All my attention was on the motionless murk at the top of the stairs; but as I passed the doorway to the front room, something just grazed the corner of my eye – and clicked in my mind a moment later. My head snapped round.

A woman was sitting on the sofa, hunched uncomfortably forward: watching me from the dimness with cold, dark eyes.

I rode the bitter wave of adrenaline, and just stood there staring back. She looked about my age: her face pale and taut. The eyes stayed steady; but they couldn't belie the wariness – and hostility – in her expression.

After an awful pause – a dozen painful heartbeats – she opened her mouth and said: 'Rachel.'

I swallowed. '. . . What?'

'You've no need to worry. Listen . . .' Her voice was low, and carefully emphatic. There was an accent there, but my mind was still too slippery with shock to grasp it.

I wavered; her obvious edginess was hardly reassuring. Whoever she was. I made to ask the obvious. She cut me off.

'Just sit down a minute, why don't you?' She was rising even as she said it. Shabby donkey-jacket, I noted; worn black jeans. And for all her attempts at a conciliatory tone, she was still watching with eyes as intent and unforgiving as a beggar's.

'All right . . .' I murmured meekly, glancing down – then made a lunge for the front door. The lock, which Nick was always promising to oil, seemed to stiffen under my frantic fingers – stiffen and jam. I was still fumbling with the sodding thing when she grasped my collar, hauled me back hard, and sent me lurching off into the breakfast room. I turned around, teetering – and found she was pointing a *gun* at me. A pistol, held out at arm's length. The face behind was livid.

'Sit *down*,' she hissed; and now I caught it right enough. Her accent – thick enough to slice.

Sit *doyne*.

Oh . . . shit shit shit.

I took a helpless step backward – and once more had that spine-tingling feeling of somebody behind me: close enough to kiss my neck. I spun around. And this time there really was.

She was watching from the kitchen doorway; I'd been in and out and missed her in the dusk. All the time I'd been filling the fridge, she'd been one of the shadows behind me, muffled in her long black greatcoat – her face masked with gloom beneath the brim of her hat. But the hat was in her hands now, her close-cropped head uncovered, and her face stood out as bleakly as a newly-risen moon.

'Hello, Rachel,' said Razoxane softly. 'Welcome home.'

Chapter 4

I might have fainted then – but my body refused to opt for such a cop-out.

Razoxane straightened up from her slouch against the door-jamb: smiling thinly. I flinched, and swallowed a moan, but couldn't step back: not with that gun behind me. All I could do was gawp.

She hadn't changed a bit. From the state of her clothes she hadn't changed those, either. Maybe she looked a little paler; and thinner, to judge by the hang of her scarecrow coat; but still not a day over twenty-five or so. And the smile was all Razoxane: all razor. It cut me to the quick.

My hand crept up to cover my mouth. I made a small, scared sound behind it. No point protesting I was seeing things, hallucinating horrors; still less in wondering how she'd got here – because here she was before me.

Flesh and cold blood.

The day outside was almost dead – but she still wore those shades of hers, the lenses cupped like goggles to the sockets of her eyes to exclude all trace of sunlight: the light she couldn't stand. I tried to return her blindwoman's gaze, but it was hopeless: like trying to out-stare a skull. Dusty-mouthed, I glanced aside; and realised I'd begun to shake.

'Jackie's right,' came Razoxane's voice. 'You look like you could do with a good sit down.'

It was the edge of dry amusement in her tone that brought my head back round – and pushed fear past the flashpoint into anger.

'For Christ's sake leave me alone!'

The words came out like a stream of spittle. I've even

heard that spit can drive back demons – but perhaps it's the vehemence behind it that counts; the *hate* that really matters. And hate was what I tasted now: it filled my mouth like bitter medicine. Hate for the past I thought I'd left behind me. And hate for Razoxane – who'd brought it with her.

Not being a demon, Razoxane stood her ground – and clicked her tongue in mild admonishment.

'Rachel. Is that any way to greet your long-lost sister?'

'You're no bloody sister of mine . . .' I managed grimly.

'Not in this life, maybe.' Her thin smile hadn't faltered; it was still so horribly *knowing.* 'But we still belong together, Rachel. Believe it. We've walked apart too long.'

I almost choked. 'Listen, I'm not following you *anywhere* . . . *ever* . . . *again.* All right?'

Behind me, the Irish girl shifted impatiently. Unsettled. '*McCain.* You said we could trust her . . .'

That lifted the hairs on the back of my neck: made me think of twitchy trigger-fingers, and bullets in the spine. I swallowed so hard it hurt my throat.

Razoxane looked past me. 'She's had a shock; it's only to be expected. Thought I was dead, didn't you Rachel?' (*Hoped,* I thought back viciously, still glowering.) 'Listen, give us a few minutes alone: I'll talk her round.'

I risked a glance behind me; the girl met my eyes suspiciously, before lowering her pistol with exaggerated slowness. There was a message in the gesture as much as in the gaze: a barely-veiled threat.

Jackie. That's what Razoxane had called her. I found a moment to wonder if that everyday name – this young, unsmiling face – was one of those behind the atrocities of recent weeks. The thought was dizzying. I really hoped she wasn't.

And was really afraid she was.

Then Razoxane was beside me, her hand on my shoulder: her bloody hand – however many times she'd washed it.

I didn't even try to shrug it off. Suddenly I didn't have the strength.

So we went upstairs to our bedroom – Nick's and mine: retracing Razoxane's dirty bootprints to the place I'd once felt safest. Once inside, I went straight to the window and just stared out – at the cherry-red streetlamps coming on, and the ashen sky beyond them; stared, while our bed creaked behind me. There were kids still playing, down there in the park: scampering and shouting through the gathering grey.

I left it as long as I could; then let go of the outside world, and turned reluctantly around.

She was reclining comfortably against the pillows, her booted feet crossed on our nice clean duvet. The black leather was withered and grey with grime; her jeans were tucked into the tops. The grubby combination of her greatcoat and her grin made me think of some Victorian ragamuffin in a long-faded photo.

'I was quite looking forward to that cup of soup, you know . . .' she said, reproachfully.

'Why'd you come back?' I hissed. It sounded almost petulant: the last stab of someone who's lost the argument already. Which of course I had.

Razoxane shrugged. 'It's a round world, Rachel. Even if we walk away, we always end up back in the same place.'

I mulled that over dully for a moment, then ventured: 'You . . . cheated the Void, then?'

She nodded. 'In the end. It almost had me . . .' Her gaze slid away as she said it, her voice growing raw. She paused, and her silence spoke the rest – or some of it.

I waited nervously.

'Melphalan got out,' she continued after a moment, her unseen eyes now roving the room. 'Bastard. I couldn't hold him . . .' The shades fixed me once more. 'But you stopped him, Rachel. You really did. I was impressed.'

An image of cremation lit my mind – and filled my nostrils with its stench. I grimaced, instinctively rubbing my fingers over my pinched-shut lips. Then something else occurred to me, and almost froze them into place there.

'But . . . If you got out . . .'

Her smile was back again, still faint; she shook her head. 'The other two didn't. They hadn't the strength: they hadn't the *will*. They'll still be sinking now, Rachel. The Void goes on forever.'

And you almost dumped me there, didn't you?

Another pause. She'd returned her attention to her hat: was turning it idly between her fingers. I noted the circlet of old, discoloured iron pushed down around the crown.

'So what do you want now?' I asked.

'Your help,' she answered simply.

'*What?*'

'It's true,' she insisted. 'Believe me, Rachel, if I didn't, I'd have left you in peace. You've already been through enough.'

I could agree with her on that, at least. More than enough. Again I waited.

'I've things to do in this city,' Razoxane said slowly. 'Things you don't want to know about . . .'

'Oh, God,' I blurted. 'Not *more* Clinicians?'

She shook her head. 'Not this time. My business with them is finished.' She settled herself back. 'I'll say no more about the wherefores: it's best you don't know. But it's work I've recruited some help for.'

I thought of the restless woman downstairs; could almost picture her pacing up and down in the hall. 'That girl – Jackie or whoever. She's . . .' I hesitated, half-aware I was stating the obvious. And half afraid to. 'She's a terrorist, isn't she?'

'That's an emotive word,' said Razoxane mildly.

'*Razoxane*. Jesus!' I could feel my frightened outrage beginning to seethe. 'What the *hell* are you doing, bringing her to my house?'

'I thought it would cut out some of the small talk,' was

37

her unperturbed response. 'Explanations and such. Much easier to let you see for yourself.'

'I'm living with a *policeman*, for God's sake.'

'Well, she doesn't know that, does she?'

I found I was hugging myself. Gripping my shoulders tight. 'All those bombings . . . Liverpool Street and places. You did those?' My voice had sunk to a disbelieving whisper.

'Not personally, no. But I'm involved. There are reasons, Rachel.'

I stared back at those uncompromising shades. The face below had hardened; like the voice.

Open-mouthed, I just shook my head. Fractured images of mutilation seemed to rattle round inside it. And then all the rest came crowding in; the other injuries and deaths. The tearful faces. The creeping fear we'd all begun to feel – and our revulsion for the people who made us feel it.

One of whom was staring at me now.

'No reasons, Razoxane,' I said, still whispering. 'Not for that . . .'

'You'll understand them someday,' she told me evenly. 'Some fine day . . .' She paused then, and glanced back down at her hat; picking her next words carefully. 'But in the meantime, one of my . . . co-workers has managed to get himself injured. He's in your hospital, under guard. We need your help to get him out.'

Just run that by me again is one of those Americanisms I pick up from time to time. I almost used it then.

Instead I just said, incredulously, 'Fuck *off.*'

'Language, Rachel,' she chided amiably.

'Just go *away*,' I snapped, not looking; my fingers sliding up into my hair to grip my skull and squeeze it. As if that would somehow stop the pounding in my head. 'Please, Razoxane . . . whatever you're up to . . . for Christ's sake leave me out of it.'

'I'm sorry: it has to be done. This isn't something

primitive like politics, Rachel; it's much more serious than that.'

'Razoxane. I don't want to be involved.' I stressed it like a string of full stops.

'But you're already involved,' she pointed out softly. 'You've seen her face, now: one of my terrorists – as you call them. An excitable young woman, as you'll have noticed. If she finds you won't co-operate . . . Well.'

I felt my stomach lurch, and looked up quickly. She was fingering the occult-looking amulet she wore at her throat; her pale smile had grown sly.

'What if she was to find out you sleep with a policeman?' She glanced over at the dressing table. 'That him, is it?'

There was a photo of the two of us in a frame there. Nothing fancy; just a snapshot by a friend. Nick in a chair and me sitting in front; his hands resting gently on my shoulders.

I nodded wordlessly.

Razoxane's smile grew chilling. 'What a very nice couple you make.'

My eyes were suddenly stinging wet: tears of sheer frustration as much as anything. She'd do it, all right – and nothing I could say would stop her. I was past feeling scared for myself now; but fear for Nick yawned inside me like a bottomless pit.

'Please . . .' It came out sounding like a sob.

'No need to get upset,' she murmured. 'It's all so straight-forward, Rachel. No risks. I just need you to find out the layout of the ward he's on; where the guards are. That sort of thing. All right?'

I sniffed, and managed a reluctant little nod.

'Excellent. I knew we could count on you.' And with that she clicked on the bedside lamp, and turned her attention to the bookshelf beneath: the things I sometimes browse through on the downslope to sleep.

I rubbed my sleeve across my cheek, and watched her study the selection. I tried to focus my frustration into rage again, but it wouldn't gel. I was too demoralised for that. All I could think of was house and home and happiness now balanced on a knife-edge: the steel of her razor smile . . .

'Glad to see you've still got both feet on the ground,' she remarked drily, pulling out a book to read the back. *The Radical Tradition*; I recognised it from here. Saints standing up for the poor. Most of my religious books were the same sort of thing. Social awareness; justice and peace. None of that trite evangelical stuff.

'Still believing in saints then, Rachel?'

I nodded again, feeling the smallest spark of defiance inside me. But it wasn't kindled. Her smile was thin, but not mocking.

'And guardian angels too?'

'Maybe, Razoxane,' I said dully. 'Maybe. But you're not one of them.'

She shrugged, and picked another book.

'Ah, yes . . .' There was satisfaction in the word. 'Mother Julian of Norwich. The visionary. The Anchoress.' She looked at me again. 'You know her story, then?'

Once more I nodded; warily now. 'She walled herself up inside a church – to meditate on God. A lot of people did things like that in the Middle Ages. Hermits and such . . .'

'So they did. Withdrawn from the sight of the living . . . that's what the name meant. Anchoress. Anker. *Ankerite* . . .' There was an edge to the way she pronounced that last word, but I couldn't grasp why; and Razoxane just went on thumbing through the book.

'Cheer up,' she said a moment later: her smile sardonic. 'See what she says here, Rachel. *All manner of thing shall be well.*'

She had, too. All manner of thing. But right now I couldn't believe it.

After a pause I said: 'Your . . . terrorists. They don't know what you're doing either – do they?'

She put back the book, still smiling. 'Not entirely.'

'So what . . . ?'

'They've got fire-power in all its forms: I need it to finish this work. I need their bullets and their bombs. But most of all I need their *blindness*. Once someone's started killing for a cause, they're so easy to use. So easy to snare and to seduce. I promised them power, in the context of their sordid little war; they came scuttling to me for what they thought they could get. And now they're *mine*.' She flicked dust – or ash – from the brim of her hat, and watched it filter downward through the lamplight; then raised her sombre gaze to me. 'We're going to put the terror back into terrorism. Believe me, you're well out of it.'

'Will I be, though?'

'Yes, you will. One small favour, and then you can forget you ever met us.'

'Witch's promise?' I asked bitterly.

Razoxane grinned.

I swallowed. 'And what if they realize . . . ?'

'They won't: at least, not in time. And a little more time is all I need.'

My mouth was still dry, but I found the saliva somewhere. 'I might tell them.'

Razoxane's smile grew almost fond. 'Yes, Rachel, you might. But I wouldn't recommend it. Not unless you want your vocal cords cut.'

I didn't. So I shut up.

When we came back downstairs, the girl – Jackie – was waiting in the hall, her pistol out of sight again and both hands in her jacket pockets. She hadn't turned on any lights, and her face was smudged with dimness, but I could read the impatience written there – and the unease.

'All right?'

'Sure,' said Razoxane calmly. 'No problem.' She turned to me. 'I'll be in touch, Rachel. Soon.' Her smile showed up palely in the shadows. 'Keep the faith till then.'

I almost hit her.

Jackie opened the door – so easily, after all my struggling – and peered out into the street. The air that wafted in smelt of frost. After a moment she glanced back at Razoxane.

'Okay.'

Her gaze switched to me – a mistrustful parting shot – and she slipped out. Razoxane followed. I shut the door behind them.

Silence fell.

I listened to it for what seemed like ages: the stillness of a truly empty house. Then I went slowly into the unlit front room, sat gingerly down, and just waited for the rising night to swallow me whole.

Chapter 5

I felt suddenly — absurdly — afraid to turn the page, but only for an instant. Then, with a rustle of paper, it was done — and the entry leaped to meet me.

Johann's dog-eared copy of the British National Formulary: I'd picked it up from where he'd left it on the desk, without thinking, and started browsing morbidly through it, towards the page I used to dread. Perhaps today it would help me get a grip: seeing the word again in black and white.

Razoxane.

Just a drug-name; one of God alone knew how many aliases she'd used (like McCain, which I'd known her as first, and which — it seemed — her terrorists called her still). Its very sound was viciousness enough; but it was appropriate for other reasons too. Because razoxane's a chemo drug, one of those for people with cancer. Cytotoxics, as they call them. Cell-killers.

Kill or cure.

The last time our paths had crossed had been like one of those operations which succeed at the cost of the patient's life. She'd come on like a medieval doctor — bleeding and butchering in her hopeless quest to *heal*. I scarcely dared think what she might be up to this time.

So don't, I told myself grimly. *Don't think. Just do what she wants and forget it.* I did feel a twinge of guilt at the prospect of helping a terrorist escape — but only a twinge. The cold, unpleasant instincts of survival quite eclipsed it.

It would happen anyway, and what could I do? Tip off the police? Tell them the current round of atrocities had been unleashed by an eighteenth century witch, who

43

believed she was a reincarnated fallen angel? Oh, yeah, that would *really* go down well.

Besides, whatever they thought, they'd never catch her. And she'd cut much more than my vocal cords next time . . .

A sudden quick shudder went through me: the sort you might get if you linger too long on a whiff of vomit, and your body starts coming out in sympathy. Still grimacing, I glanced up – and found Sue leaning over the upper worktop, watching; mouth nervously half-open.

I reshaped my expression as fast as I could, but discouragement was there in hers already. I could have kicked myself. Because Sue had something on her mind, I knew it: something that had been troubling her for days. And just then she'd seemed on the brink of broaching the subject.

She didn't now. Just swallowed, and asked me to crosscheck Mr Jackson's next drug infusion with her. I did so, waiting for her to try again even as I compared label and drug-chart. But she didn't; and in another moment the rhythm of the unit had drawn us apart again, with different nursing matters to attend to.

I wondered what was up. Boyfriend trouble? Or something more work-related? I didn't think it was that poor girl's death: Lucy's friend in the burning car. Sue had been preoccupied before that happened. Quieter than usual; sometimes snappier, too. Something was there inside, and wanted out.

Another job for Sister.

It wasn't one I'd shrink from. Like Lucy, she was a friend as much as a member of my staff. I wanted to see her smiling again; I'd be happy to listen and advise – when she was ready.

When I got back to the station, the BNF was still lying there open: almost mockingly. I closed it on that awful word, and glanced down at my watch. Nearly ten to one: it would soon be time for break, and a well-earned breather.

And a wander, on some vague pretext or other, to the Orthopaedic wards.

They were trying to be less obtrusive. I'd gathered there had been complaints about armed policemen parading around. But the situation was obvious enough — a uniformed copper in an unzipped anorak sitting boredly outside the side-room door. The window-curtain was drawn behind him. A rather superfluous note sellotaped against it advised all-comers not to enter without seeing the nurse in charge — a form of words more commonly used on the wards to convey the discreet message *There Is A Dead Body In Here.*

But not this time. At least (oh, Razoxane . . .) not yet.

I'd been through two Ortho wards already; it was getting difficult to keep my cool. I was in full uniform, of course — laminated ID badge and all. No one had given me more than a glance (a guilty one in the case of a Care Assistant I'd found gossiping in the corridor). But I still felt unnervingly exposed; as if the eyes of every patient and nurse I'd passed had turned to watch me.

Pure paranoia, of course. The walk down that last long ward had felt like half a mile, but the two girls doing the drug round only looked up long enough to judge, from the briskness of my stride, that I knew where I was headed. Beyond them, another nurse was perched on the paper-strewn desk, the phone tucked under her chin as she scrawled out a note. We'd exchanged a casual smile; she kept on talking. I kept on walking.

The adjoining ward was empty.

I guessed it had been shut a while ago; perhaps they were even getting round to painting it. The beds had been stripped to their metal bones, looking doubly bleak in the grey daylight. But there was a fluorescent on at this end of the room, just beyond the entrance doors. Peering cautiously through the porthole, I saw the copper sitting there.

No Entry said a hand-printed sign above the window. A bit difficult to miss, but still . . .

The PC glanced round as I came on through, his expression dour. 'Sorry, this bit's closed.'

'Oh . . . right,' I said, and nodded dutifully: trying to ignore the thudding in my chest. 'Still at it, eh?'

He grunted, but amiably enough. 'Yeah – but not for long. Shift change in half an hour . . .' His eyes narrowed slightly. 'You don't work round here, do you . . .'

Oh God, he's got his wits about him, this one. I felt my smile slipping.

'Er . . . no. Just passing through. Shortcut . . .'

'Thought I hadn't seen you. Anyway, I'll not be sorry to get going. Hate hospitals. Don't know how you nurses stand it . . .'

Just an idle enquiry, that's all it had been. A bored young man just making conversation. I swallowed.

'Being good, is he?' I ventured. Somehow it managed to come out sounding casual.

'Who, him?' He jerked his head towards the door behind him, the curtained window. *Please speak to Nurse in Charge before entering.* I couldn't quite get the ominous connotations of that phrase out of my mind.

'Good as gold,' the copper was saying, a sneer on his thin young face. 'Not much choice, really, has he? Sod . . .'

My heart was still steaming away. I was convinced I'd betray myself if I lingered for another minute. But I also knew I'd never have the nerve to try this again; and people would get suspicious if I did. I had to get everything I could in this one go.

'You never know . . .' I smiled (hoping it *looked* like a smile) '. . . he could be making a rope out of sheets right now.'

He snorted. 'Nah. Brian's in there with him. And not to read him bedtime stories, neither.'

I nodded; but my eyes had found his revolver now, the

46

butt peeping out from under his anorak as he bent forward, and I couldn't keep them off it.

He didn't notice; he'd been picking up his paper. 'There's a lot of crap in the *Sun* these days, too,' he muttered, folding it back onto the crossword. 'I went down to get the *Mirror*, but they'd sold out . . .' He sat back, and the gun was out of sight once more. The ease with which he ignored it only made its presence seem more menacing.

Two of you, then.

'I'd best be getting on,' I said quickly. 'Have fun.'

'I will. I'll see you, Sister.' With a grin, he got back to his puzzling.

I supposed if I'd been an ordinary member of the public he'd have called me 'Miss'; a courtesy that always seemed to come out sounding cold. But uniformed professions can meet on equal terms; and trust each other. Oh, yes.

Retreating – walking off the ward and back towards the lifts – I hoped against hope that he was wrong: that the two of us would never meet again.

And that he wouldn't be on duty when Razoxane came visiting.

Nick was late home; it was gone eleven when I heard his key in the door. More than a little relieved, I called hello – but if he answered at all, I didn't hear it. When he came into the front room, his expression was wan and strained.

'You're not going on any more of those soup runs,' he said, without preamble.

I blinked. 'What?'

'You heard me, Rachel. It isn't safe.'

I was curled up on the sofa, watching *Question Time*. Comfortable and half-asleep – until a second ago. Now I sat up, frowning.

'What *are* you on about?'

'Listen a minute, will you . . .' He saw my frown deepen towards a scowl, and spread his hands. There was a can of beer from the fridge in one of them. 'For your own

47

good, Raitch. Something . . . bloody terrible happened this evening.'

The TV seemed suddenly too loud. I fumbled for the remote and flicked it off. Then drew my knees up under me and waited.

Nick took a long swig, and swallowed it down. Wiped his mouth, still watching me. Then started to talk.

'There was a fire-bombing over in Kentish Town – just after nine o'clock. Wasn't it on the news . . . ?'

I shrugged; I hadn't watched it.

'Well, it was a squat, and someone burned it down. Two people were trapped inside. Died inside.' He paused for another gulp of beer. 'Three managed to get out: two dossers, and some woman we think was a charity worker. Shelter or whatever. They'd all had the crap beaten out of them, and . . .' He paused again there, but not to drink. Just shook his head. There was a look like helplessness on his face.

I felt my heart-rate speeding up.

'And we'll never get to hear what happened, Rachel. Not from them. Because . . . *Jesus* . . . whoever did it gouged their bloody eyes out – and cut out their tongues. All of them: even the ones who burned . . .'

I almost flinched back from him; almost mewled in disgust. But now he'd started talking, he had to finish.

'Some neighbour came to see if he could help – so the bastards set dogs on him, Rachel. Bloody Dobermans, from the state he's in. Poor sod's in ribbons. And there I am, just looking forward to booking-off time when I get called to attend *that*. Blood everywhere, and . . . screaming. Faces, *screaming*. And they wouldn't stop. Not even the ambulance men could make them stop . . .'

I just sat there, numb, both hands to my mouth. Strands of hair had fallen into my eyes; I didn't even think to brush them clear. This had been a cosy room a minute ago; now – in just my loose T-shirt and leggings – I suddenly felt freezing.

Nick took a deep, tired breath.

I clambered up quickly, and started towards him. His words alone had given me gooseflesh; but he'd seen *sights*. Such awful sights. There'd be counselling available, and colleagues to talk to – but right now, I knew, he needed holding. It was as much a nurse's instinct as a lover's.

Oh, Nick.

'Still don't believe in evil people, then?' he asked me sourly; and even through my sympathy, I felt the barb in that: it hurt.

'Well they're out there anyway, Rachel. And that's why you're not going on any more soup runs.' His tone was flat, and categorical. 'End of story.' He turned back towards the kitchen.

And of course, if he'd put it just a bit more reasonably, I might even have agreed. Would probably have jumped at the chance not to go out and get my hands dirty again – especially with Razoxane now lurking in those grimy shadows . . .

But to *tell* me what to do like that, and turn his back, had just the opposite effect. Sympathy went up in smoke. Abruptly I was bloody furious.

'Don't you talk to me like that, Nick Mitchell,' I snapped, going through after him. 'And don't *ever* tell me what I'm going to do.'

I caught up with him as he was getting a second can out of the fridge; the kitchen lino felt clammy under my bare feet. I grabbed his sleeve. 'Look, you can lay off that, as well . . . *I'll* decide if it's safe for me to go out and help the homeless, all right?'

He shrugged me off. Blocked me with his back while he cracked the can open.

'All right?' I repeated, and he turned.

'Sorry, Rachel, I forgot. You have to be a socially responsible member of society, don't you.'

I couldn't stand the edge of sarcasm in his voice. Suddenly I tasted tears. 'Just sod off, Nick.'

'. . . or maybe it's just your Christian bloody duty.

Always the bloody same. God, you're never alone with a Catholic . . .'

I just gasped aloud at that. He walked past me, gulping beer, and I wheeled.

'Well, thank *you*. I'm bloody *living* with you, aren't I?' And yes, I did get guilt complexes about it sometimes — but that was something I could live with too.

He went back towards the lounge: I followed. The argument went round and round. Shouting didn't help, but we shouted anyway. It struck me at one point, as I paused for breath, that this was the best row we'd had in ages — one for the archives. Perhaps he should get his bloody camcorder out, and tape it. The thought brought a moment's bitter pleasure. Then I laid in once more.

The end, when it came, was quite sudden. Without any warning the fires went out, and left us there weak and winded; I had the same sick feeling I remembered from school sports day, at the end of a gruelling race. I turned my face away long enough to wipe my arm across my eyes, then glanced back at Nick. He didn't look too far from tears himself.

'Oh God, Rachel, I'm sorry . . .'

I sniffed.

'I'm so sorry,' he repeated, almost whispering. 'I'm worried about you — that's all. Couldn't *stand* the thought of that happening to you . . .' He reached tentatively out; I slapped his hand aside. After a pause he tried again, and so did I, but he caught my wrist, and then my other — and I felt my strength and anger melt like wax. I didn't resist as he clumsily embraced me; and after a moment I was hugging fiercely back.

'Oh, Rachel, Rachel . . .' he whispered into my hair, as I finally let the floodgates open. 'I love you. Love you so much . . .'

We finished up in bed together: a reconciliation on equal terms that sweated the last of the bitterness out.

Afterwards, I just snuggled up against him, with sleepy satisfaction. No thoughts left now, only feelings – and the sense of a timeless moment here in the dark: a refuge between tomorrow and today. I was probably still smiling as I floated into sleep.

And found my worst nightmare waiting.

Chapter 6

The feel of it came first: a slick and clammy dampness on my skin. I tried ignoring it for as long as I could, lying there in the murk – but enough of my mind had surfaced for me to realise that I wouldn't make it to the morning – not now. I was soaked in fresh sweat: fever-sweat, like the onset of flu. And sooner or later I was going to have to peel myself off the bedclothes, pick my way through to the bathroom and wash it off.

So it might as well be sooner, I decided glumly; waited another few minutes, and finally forced myself upright. And with that movement, the scales fell from my eyes.

Daylight filled them; but a dull, damp daylight, like the reflection from wet pavements. And everything was gone: the bed from beneath me, the bedroom around. I found myself out in the rain, beneath a bleary sky – cold droplets striking my startled face, and rolling down like tears.

I was in the middle of a building site: a field of grey earth and gravel against the city skyline. The downpour had turned much of it to mud. The nearest buildings were all gaping shells; whether half-built or half-demolished I couldn't tell. The rain pressed home the atmosphere of this unfinished place: the sense of dripping desolation.

Pools and puddles were swelling in the mire around me, bubbling beneath the downpour.

I clambered breathlessly up, already sopping wet. There was no one in sight, but that didn't reassure me; my stomach felt as hollow and sore as if I'd fasted for a week. This place looked like a war-zone – a killing ground in Eastern Europe – and it felt like one as well. Those tread-marks in the mud had been left by bulldozers, of course;

but the watchful sniper-silence of the buildings was not so easily shrugged off. I backed away from them, stumbling; shivering – and then a sound came rasping through the stillness, and I swung around to look.

Still nothing to see, but the noise came again almost at once: a grim, metallic scrape. It sounded like a shovel. Like someone digging, just over a rise in the ground to my right.

For a moment I just stood there, getting wetter; gnawing nervously at my thumb. The shovel-sounds continued in a broken rhythm – and at least they meant that somebody was working in this waste ground.

So why didn't I want to even see him?

But the buildings were giving me the creeps as well; I was becoming convinced that someone was lying up in one of them, and staring balefully out at me.

It was that thought that finally drove me up over the rise. Better the devil you see than the one that you don't . . .

The digger was there on the other side – and closer than I'd thought: head-down over the shovel. Dressed all in soiled and sodden black, like a vagabond undertaker. And it was Razoxane.

I gasped – and her head snapped round.

The scene winked out before her face had fully registered – but as I dropped back through the dark towards my sleeping body, the palest after-image of her expression followed me down. No more than what I'd glimpsed; but I sensed a dreadful anger there – as though I'd stumbled onto something I was never meant to see.

I almost whimpered with fear . . . and realized I was back in my bed. My nice warm bed. The shock was almost physical – as if I really had plunged from a dizzying height, with only the mattress to break my fall.

You'll come down to earth with a bump, my girl: that's what Mum used to say when she scolded me. *One of these days . . .*

I tried to open my eyes. They wouldn't.

'Jesus, we're losing her . . .' someone snapped.

There was sudden consternation all around me: a frantic sense of movement overhead. Even as I lay there, helpless, I heard that voice and others overlap; the words seemed frighteningly familiar. Then someone's fist slammed down onto my chest, and my eyes sprang staring open.

Even in that first, winded moment I knew I was in hospital – but not as a nurse. Not this time. The glare of striplights was mostly blocked by overhanging bodies, and faces peering down at me; a tight-mouthed doctor to the fore. But I was the one in bed now. And as the crushing pain continued, and filled my chest, I realized I was dying.

The doctor put his hand on my heart, pressed his other palm down over it, and began compressing – hard. It *hurt*. Cardiac massage means squeezing the heart between sternum and spine, and now I knew just what that felt like. I wanted to groan out loud; I found I couldn't even grimace. Not a muscle of my face would move.

Someone else – the anaesthetist? – forced my slack mouth wider, and shoved an airway deep into my throat; I almost gagged. The pumping went on. I felt a needle pierce my arm, as sharp as a wasp-sting – but the pain was nothing compared to the panic. My chest was still on fire; there was the bilious foretaste of vomit in the back of my mouth. But worst of all was the icy feeling that I had only seconds left to live . . .

'. . . defib . . .' someone said; then: 'Clear . . . ?' The figures drew hastily back even as I felt the cold metal paddles – slick with jelly – pressing down against my smoothed-out breasts. Then the defibrillator buzzed.

And the agonising jolt brought me fully awake.

At last. At last. I was gasping tearfully for breath – and drenched with sweat. Nick had woken, and his arms were round me, holding tight. And as his instinctive, sleepy mumbling grew clearer and more comforting, so at last I let myself relax. My heart kept up its whamming for a minute or two longer, but that was almost a joy: proof positive that it wasn't going to stop.

'God, Rachel . . .' I sensed his smile then, in the dark. 'You were making more noise than when we were awake . . .' He brushed the damp hair off my forehead. 'Bad dream?'

Very bad. I gave a quick, wordless nod.

I let him cuddle me for a while longer, then peered over at the alarm clock. Just gone five. No chance of any more sleep this morning; I'd be getting up anyway in an hour. And I wasn't about to lie here, cold and greasy, and count the minutes.

'I'm just going to take a shower,' I whispered. 'Sorry I woke you.'

He murmured something, his hand sliding down my back as I got up. I heard him settling down again as I went through to the bathroom, and shut myself in with its hot, bright bulb.

For more than a minute I wavered between the shower and the toilet bowl. My stomach felt close to overspill, and even the short walk across the landing – naked in the dark – had sluiced it round some more. I waited until it was fully settled before venturing behind the plastic curtain. Then I just turned and turned the tap, until the spill became a downblast.

I stayed under it for ages. Soaped and scrubbed; shampooed and soaked. And little by little I felt myself becoming clean. But when I closed the tap again, and the roar of water dripped and dribbled into silence, the ghost of Razoxane's face was still there in my mind. And so was the fear of her rage in my belly: as indigestible as lead.

Oh God, I didn't mean it, I found myself thinking even as I reached for my towel. *I didn't want to see. And now I'll forget it, Razoxane: forget it ever happened. Promise . . .*

And maybe she heard my thoughts: sensed them from wherever she was now, out there in the night. But even if she did, I knew she wouldn't believe my promise. Because neither, of course, did I.

* * *

I was still a bit shaken by the time I got to work – but a busy morning helped fix my mind on the here and now. Routine stuff, but plenty of it: infusions to change, effusions to aspirate and measure, observations to record. I wrote up my nursing notes in a stark spill of light from the X-ray box as Murdoch – just out of Theatre – discussed fresh films with his juniors. Then it was on to the unit round, providing casenotes and commentary as each patient's progress was reviewed. Our newest, a bloke in his sixties, was still distressed and disorientated; not least because the ventilator patched into his throat left him unable to speak. I took time to comfort him as best I could; trying hard to understand and answer his gaspy, voiceless questions.

All of a sudden it was nearly half-past twelve.

'Doesn't it just fly when you're enjoying yourself . . .' Jean observed drily, on her way to the sluice to empty a bedpan. I couldn't help a wry little smile at that; but it was true enough.

And after lunch, in the slacker time of shift overlap, I'd be doing Sue's appraisal: a review of her professional development. Something else to get my mental teeth into. And maybe we'd get round to discussing whatever it was that was bothering her, as well. Someone else's troubles to consider, for a change.

'Sure there's nothing else?' I asked casually. I knew I was nearly there.

In my office with the door closed, we'd started off formally enough – but after an hour of honest, friendly discussion, we'd both relaxed a lot. I found I'd drawn both legs up under me where I sat, almost without realizing. And Sue's initial apprehension had largely faded. But still she hesitated at the question; not quite meeting my eye.

'Fancy a Polo?' I prompted, reaching into my drawer. I felt for the packet – and found that metal spinner waiting there. It chilled my fingertips; but I managed to keep my smile in place, and fumbled out the mints.

She nodded, and reached over to pick one. Still smiling, I watched her face: and wondered. Like me, she was clearly trying to put something dark behind her; but whatever it was still kept her awake at nights – I guessed as much from the weary pallor of her features. She looked like she hadn't slept for days. This afternoon she'd made an effort: done herself justice, and come over well. But even then, there had been moments when her mind was somewhere else again.

She wanted to talk, I knew; and didn't want to. An equal balance. It was down to me to tip it.

'I'm always happy to listen, Sue,' I told her quietly. 'Professional or personal, it doesn't matter. And sometimes it helps to talk, it really does.'

Sue shrugged. There was a pause.

Then, still looking down, she whispered: 'Rachel, I'm so *scared*.'

Whatever I'd been expecting, it wasn't quite that. Domestic problems, perhaps, or money worries – but not fear. I leaned forward, frowning: concerned. '*Suzy*. Scared of what?'

A few suggestions skittered through my head even as she paused again. Unplanned pregnancy. Positive smear test. Even unprotected sex with a stranger. I didn't much fancy coping with any of those.

She swallowed. 'I have to tell someone, Rachel. I have to. And . . . maybe you'll understand . . . Being religious and all . . .' When she glanced up at me again, she looked on the verge of tears.

I waited.

'We were just fooling around,' Sue continued, her voice still low. 'Me and a few of the girls on my corridor. We'd been to see a show, we got back late . . . we were talking. Just sat around in the top-floor common room, talking. About ghosts and things like that, at one in

57

the morning. And then ... just for a giggle ... Gill suggests we have a seance.'

She paused again, uncomfortably: watching for my reaction. I just nodded her on.

'Well ... we'd had a bit to drink, and we thought, why not? Safety in numbers, and all that. So: we laid out one of those ouija board things, with a glass and all, and ... Have you ever tried one of those, Rachel?'

I shook my head quickly.

'No, well, you're lucky. Anyway, we all put a finger on the glass, like you do, and we started ...'

Something cold had started creeping up my back, towards the nape of my neck; but I managed to keep my expression neutral — like a good Samaritan. I knew Sue lived in one of the old residential blocks annexed to the hospital; I could almost see the scene before me. Everyone sitting round the table in that upstairs room, the empty mugs and cigarette-stubbed saucers cleared away. Just the circle of makeshift letters in their midst, now — and the upturned glass.

'It moves, you know. By itself. It really does.' She was suddenly insistent — as though pre-empting any show of scepticism. She needn't have bothered, though; and I think my face told her so, as much as my nod did. I believed her right enough.

'So anyway ... we were asking questions, and it was spelling out answers — really slowly. And then, while we were thinking what to ask next, it started to spell a word of its own.'

She stopped.

'Which was?' I ventured, against my better judgement.

Sue hesitated a moment longer. Then: 'Wampir.'

I blinked. 'Spelled ...?'

She spelt it out almost cautiously, as though afraid someone would hear her through the door. Or the wall. And I leaned back, still frowning — but beginning to see a glimmer of light now. A glimmer of hope.

'Listen, Sue . . . You're sure it wasn't one of your mates winding you up?'

She shook her head – quite calmly. 'Oh, I'm sure, Rachel. Because as soon as it had finished, it started again. Only harder.'

The glimmer began guttering.

'And then again, and again, just the same word. Wampir. More and more violently, as if something was coming closer all the time.

'And then the glass just shattered.'

I was so absorbed by this point I actually winced.

'And that really freaked me out, Rachel,' Sue finished quietly. 'Well, all of us, actually. And now . . . I just keep thinking, what did we really do? And what might happen next?' She'd managed to keep the threatening tears in check through all of this, but the catch in her voice now showed how close the dam was to bursting.

'Oh, Sue, Sue . . .' I reached out for her hand, and took it tightly in my own. 'How long have you been bottling this up for, then?'

She sniffed. 'About . . . a week.'

'Well listen . . . The best thing you could have done was tell me about it: not just let it fester inside you. We can look at it together, now.'

I could feel her returning my grip: it's a good job nurses have short nails. She moistened her lips, looking like a girl fifteen years younger than me, rather than just five. 'Do you . . . believe what they say about . . . evil spirits and things getting out during seances?'

'Um . . .'

Yes.

'. . . I think it might have happened sometimes,' I said carefully. 'But I *don't* believe anything like that can really hurt you, Sue: not unless you let them. And the very fact that you're worried means you don't want that.'

She gave her head a miserable little shake.

'You're right to think it's dangerous,' I went on. 'But I

think you've been lucky. I'd tell your friend Gill the same thing, if I were you.' She had let her eyes drop, and I freed one of my hands to lift her chin up and meet them again. 'It's all right, Sue. Really. I'm glad you told me – and you'll feel better for it. You wait.'

She smiled damply back; and I felt a moment's inner satisfaction at the sight. Hardly your average appraisal session – but it had achieved its objectives nonetheless.

I tried to ignore the lingering discomfort between my shoulder blades. Damp patch. Cold spot. An awareness of what *might* have happened, when Sue and her friends had started to unpick the edge of darkness . . .

'Do you . . . think it could have been a real vampire?' she asked after a moment; a bit more objective now. Interested, even.

I smiled faintly. 'No, I don't. I don't believe at all in vampires, Sue. Whatever it was you picked up was just trying to scare you, that's all.'

'Well, it bloody well succeeded.' She gave a final little shudder, and settled back. Some of the weight had lifted already, I could tell. 'Thanks ever so much, Rachel. I really needed to talk.'

'No trouble.' I gave her hand another squeeze before letting go.

We tied up the interview's last loose ends; already preparing to get back to the hands-on business. But at the door she paused, with her hand on the handle, and glanced back once again.

'Rachel . . . Could you give us a thought tonight?'

I nodded once. 'I will.' And she went on out.

A shabby Victorian nurses' home; a high winter night. She'd need to know she wasn't alone: that someone else's thoughts were with her in the silence.

I knew it was the closest she'd go to asking for a prayer.

Time for me to re-emerge, too. Back into the fray. But not quite yet. I sat looking down at the word that I'd doodled, and imagined – though I struggled not to – a voice without a throat, speaking out of the darkness. Slurred and distorted by the distance and dead air.

Wampir. Wampir. *Wampir.*

Chapter 7

In the crisp afternoon sunlight, even the grey streets behind King's Cross had a certain glamour about them. Patches of melting slush flashed bright reflections; the tarmac glistened. The drab pavements looked as if they'd been gilded.

Fool's gold, and we knew it. Both of us. Me on the Sunday afternoon soup-run, and the bloke I was talking to, who hadn't slept in a bed since last September.

'Not that I believed all that stuff,' he insisted, taking another sparing sip. 'A city's a city; this one's the biggest, that's all. You think, there's got to be some kind o' work here *somewhere* . . .' He shrugged.

'Preston, you said you come from?'

'Aye.' He smiled quizzically. 'And you: Birmingham, right?'

I shook my head. 'Coventry.'

'Nearly right.'

I gave him a look – and grinned.

'Well we're all in the same shit-hole now.' He glanced around him; past the parked minibus and its straggling group of customers, to the sombre façades that hemmed us in. The two huge stations loomed above and beyond them, to the west. King's Cross, with its vaulted canopies; and St Pancras, towering and gothic. St Pancras Cathedral, I always wanted to call it: a real pile.

The sun hadn't made it any warmer; hunks of dirtied, frozen snow still lingered in the gutters. I hunched my shoulders up inside my coat as the wind changed again – and almost felt guilty for the gesture when he did the same, with only his threadbare bomber jacket to keep it out.

62

'Mind you don't get cold now,' he murmured, without irony. He sounded quite concerned.

'Don't worry . . .' I assured him; and wondered how Nick would take it, if he knew.

Which he didn't, of course. After we'd argued to a standstill the other night, the subject had been left lying. But I think he reckoned he'd had the better of it – and made me see sense at last.

So I'd volunteered to go on this afternoon's run partly for the private satisfaction of doing what *I* saw fit. Partly. But there was a particular reason why I'd opted to go with the King's Cross group, as well. A reason to do with the dream.

It was one of the few real details I remembered: something seen smudgily through the downpour as I'd breasted the rise. St Pancras Cathedral, off to the west; like a gloomy castle rotting under the rain.

The thought of using the landmark, and actually seeking out the waste ground, had appalled me when it first occurred; and grown increasingly fascinating thereafter. My reasoning mind had tried to shake itself free: warned of tempting fate – of tempting *Razoxane*. But all to no avail. My dream had picked up on something secret, I knew that much: something she wanted no one else to see.

So perhaps if I saw . . . and even partly understood . . . it might give me some kind of leverage against her. Something I could use, if push came to shove. Which, knowing her, it would.

I realised the others had started packing up; the ragged gathering around us was beginning to disperse. The bloke from Preston downed the last of his soup.

'Listen . . . you ain't got a fag, have you?'

'Sorry – gave up a while back.' Regretting it sometimes, too.

'Very wise, flower. Wish I had the will.' He gave me a worn-looking smile. 'Thanks for the soup.'

I nodded, and watched him wander aimlessly off. A couple of older men – much further down the road to dereliction – passed behind him, snarling at each other. Jim Stanley's touch on my shoulder made me jump.

'All aboard again, Rachel.'

I turned my head. 'No, it's okay: I'll stop off round here. I've . . . got to check some train times.'

'We'll drop you, then. King's Cross . . . ?'

'No, no . . . Really. Five minutes' walk is all it is.'

He looked doubtful. 'You sure, now? It's not the sort of area you want to hang around in. Not on your own.'

He was right of course: I didn't want to. Not one bit. But the impulse had its hooks in now, and I knew there'd be no denying it. Just a brisk little wander was all it would be: looking over towards St Pancras, trying to line it up with my memories. Never straying too far from the busier main roads.

Work on the rail link was well underway now; open-cast construction sites spreading out behind the stations like mismanaged bed-sores. Old buildings – slums and store-houses – were being cleared away, and new foundations laid. So I knew pretty much what I was looking for. I just had to find my particular field of mud.

'Don't worry. I'll be fine.'

I smiled, but said it firmly, and Jim knew me well enough to leave it at that.

'Okay then.' He hesitated just a moment longer: a pleas-ant-looking bloke, with his thoughtful eyes and greying ginger beard. Then raised his hand, palm outwards. 'We'll see you, then, Rachel. Good to have you along.'

I nodded, and watched him get in behind the wheel. Others waved from inside; I waved back. And then the minibus was off, and heading back down towards Pen-tonville Road, its exhaust pipe smoking in the cold.

The empty street seemed very quiet when it had gone. Most of the dossers had already withdrawn: fading back into the shadows like a phantom army. I was on my own now.

Digging my hands deeper into my pockets, I glanced uneasily around; then started walking. The rattle and clank of an incoming train drew my attention, but it was lost to sight behind buildings. I mentally followed it south to the brooding towers of St Pancras. Was this the angle I'd dreamed it from? I paused.

Perhaps.

Moving back onto York Way, I turned north, towards the main excavations. Even this main road was relatively quiet – just sporadic Sunday traffic swishing by. The building sites themselves were silent and deserted. Coming to the first, I peered curiously in between rusting railings – but mounds of churned earth blocked most of the view. There were old sleepers and chunks of masonry mixed in with the spoil. A little further on I had a tiptoe glimpse of derelict goods sheds, and nettle fields hedged with brambles.

None of which left me any the wiser. I paused again, not sure what I should do next. Something was nagging at the back of my head. I couldn't quite place it; but plain common sense suggested I head west into Camden as soon as I could. This was hardly the most salubrious of districts, especially for a woman on her own. It wasn't just the prospect of kerb-crawlers or aggressive addicts that was nibbling at my nerves, though. And a moment later, I twigged what my subconscious mind had already noticed.

The trickle of traffic had stopped completely. No cars at all had passed for several minutes.

Frowning, I peered both ways: the road was empty for as far as I could see. Almost as if it had been blocked somewhere.

The thought of the area being sealed up with me inside it was hardly likely, but it finally lost me my nerve. Quickly I retraced my steps to where the road branched westward, and turned along it. *Goodsway*, said the signs on sooty brick. The walls were high and grimy on both sides; but a set of gates on the right gave a view of the canal.

Still no traffic passing.

A building on the far bank caught hold of my attention. It looked like a ruined warehouse; the roof was missing, the windows glassless. Scaffolding braced the crumbled upper levels, and snagged at the sky. The place had a sinister, lowering air. At four or five storeys, it seemed as imposing as a fortress.

Something squeezed my heart like an iron hand.

It was nothing I could justify with eyes and ears; just a horrid sensation of being watched from those lofty ramparts. As if Razoxane herself had made her roost there.

Spooked, I looked away and pushed onward – round the corner and downhill: putting the wall back between us. I passed the old gas works, its girders standing out against the sky like the ribcages of giants. And then a car appeared, cruising steadily up towards me . . . followed by another. I felt an irrational upsurge of relief.

St Pancras Cathedral hove slowly into view.

There was more clearance work going on near the foot of the hill, but I wasn't going to hang around investigating that. I made straight for the junction under the railway bridges. The afternoon sun was sinking fast, and the triple span cast a long deep shadow, soaking the road. A glimpse of the westering glow beyond made it seem for all the world like a gateway out of hell.

With a sentinel on sombre watch beside it.

I slowed almost to a stop; the impression was quite unnerving. Then I realized it was a policeman waiting there.

I felt a rush of reassurance; but only for a moment. As I drew closer, and took more in, I saw details that unsettled me afresh.

He wasn't a beat PC: oh no. Not with that short black

carbine across his chest – cradled lightly in the crooks of his arms. A weapon as real as the ones I'd seen at work, and twice as ugly: I couldn't stop staring – not even when he turned his head to watch me pass. His eyes were flat and unfriendly beneath the peak of his cap. A black muffler covered his mouth against the cold, its ends tucked into his turned-up collar. I could see the in-the-ear headphone he wore, wired up to the handset beneath his coat.

I wondered what was up. A crackdown on the crack dealers, perhaps. Or maybe this was part of the anti-terrorist response we'd all been promised: more police on the streets, with the wherewithal to finish the job.

I sensed him follow me with his gaze as I walked on into the gloom. Heard him murmur something to his radio, and I knew he was talking about me. And even as my ears began burning, my stomach shrank towards the opposite extreme. In all my innocence, I realised I felt guilty. Suddenly I'd have preferred any number of building-site 'appreciations' to that quiet, clipped report.

The dimness I'd walked into was damp and smelly, but the sunlight beckoned beyond it. A rhythmic clunk of sleepers overhead, and then I was out; the bridges behind me, and their dour guardian too. I could have sighed with relief.

There was a big police transit up ahead, parked with its wheels on the pavement; its bodywork like gleaming bone beneath a patina of grime.

I closed the distance slowly, curious now. Perhaps I'd get to see an operation underway; the sightseer in me felt a flash of anticipation at the thought. But the waiting vehicle still left me uneasy, like they always did: not just for its cold, aggressive bulk, but for its grimmer features – the wired-in lights, and the riot shield racked up above its windscreen like steel mesh shades. Community policing kissed goodbye; the riot sections rode in things like this. And the firearms units too: coppers with guns, like the one back there under the bridge.

God, Nick. Stick with your squad car. Stay smiling.

The side and rear windows were ambulance glass: I couldn't see whoever was inside. I knew they could see me, though. I could almost feel the watchfulness coming through those black panes as I passed.

The driver was in his cab, and gave me an unsmiling glance. He made me feel like a potential criminal as well. I lowered my head and kept going.

'Excuse me, Miss . . .'

I wavered – that *guilt* again – and then turned towards the man who'd spoken. He was already crossing the road towards me, a radio in one hand. Wearing one of those high-visibility yellow jackets over his uniform, the reflective stripes like ribs. There were silver pips on his epaulettes, I noticed. He'd be an Inspector or something.

'May I ask where you're going, please?' Quite politely – but some reckless part of me still wanted to mutter *No, you may not*. The sort of witty riposte that gets you a night in the cells if you're not careful.

'Camden Town,' I answered, sensibly; trying to appear all calm and unruffled. 'I've been helping with a soup run by King's Cross.' Trying to seem the interested citizen too as I added: 'Is this to do with the bombings, then?'

He looked like he hadn't had more than two nights' sleep in seven: his face pale, and shadowed with stubble. But his smile, when it came, was genuine enough: it widened his light blue eyes, and made him handsome. I guessed he was a little older than me; but even after all he must have been through these past few weeks, there was still something almost youthful in that wry expression.

'Afraid so. We had some information . . . but it's come to nothing.' His tone was low and pleasant, with just a hint of exasperation. I found myself beginning to warm to him. With some people, things just click.

'You . . . look like you've been on the job a while,' I ventured.

'Too bloody right.' He scratched absently at the rough-
ness of his cheek. 'Surveillance stubble, you could call
this . . .' As he turned his head to glance upstreet, I saw a
neat receiver tucked into his ear, too, its wire leading down
into his collar.

The transit behind us started up, and sat there ticking
over.

The Inspector lifted his handset to his mouth. 'All units
from Whisky Oscar One . . . Back to the transport, we're
moving on.' He lowered the radio, and smiled at me again.

'Best be on your way too, Miss. It's not the safest area
to be on your own in . . .'

I nodded; though it still felt safer than the one I'd left
behind me.

Walking on, I couldn't help wondering if they'd caught
a whiff of Razoxane's terrorists: somewhere round here.
Or maybe Razoxane herself. If their information had really
been correct, they'd have had a result, all right: a total
blood-bath. No prizes for guessing who I thought would
walk away. And I'd shared a smile with that bloke while
knowing what I knew.

This time the twinge of guilt was real.

I'd walked a hundred yards or so when the transit passed
me, cruising. I glimpsed the Inspector sitting up beside the
driver. They reached the intersection just ahead – and came
scrunching to a stop.

Give Way said the sign; but nothing was coming. The
intersection stayed deserted, like the street. But the transit
just sat there – its brake lights all the brighter now that
the day was losing colour.

For no obvious reason, I began to slow my pace.

And then they were off again, tyres rasping over tarmac
as they turned north, and put on speed, and were quickly
lost to sight.

A personable bloke, that Inspector; but something told
me he knew his stuff. As did his men, if the one I'd seen
was anything to go by.

Well, Razoxane, I thought, resuming my thoughtful walk. *I'd watch my bloody step if I were you.*

Maybe the outcome of their encounter wouldn't be such a foregone conclusion after all.

Chapter 8

According to the *Know Your Medics* notice on my office pinboard – a classic fifth-generation photocopy – Consultants can clear tall buildings in a single bound, walk on water and give policy to God. But when Murdoch put his head round the duty-room door, it was only to ask if we were all okay for transport next Thursday evening.

'I've room for two more if not; three, if you count the roof-rack . . .'

We assured him that we'd manage, and were looking forward to coming – which was true. Sickness and workload had conspired against the unit's Christmas meal out last month, and it had gone by the board; an act of surrender that had left us feeling pretty flat. He'd picked up the vibes – and quietly organized a party at his own house. I don't know about the others, but that gesture had really warmed me inside. Some Consultants stay aloof; but Murdoch, medic and manager, was very much one of our tightly-knit team.

It promised to be fun: a night off we all needed. I just hoped I wouldn't be the spectre at the feast . . .

'Well if there's nothing else, I'll be wending my merry way homeward . . .' He glanced down at his briefcase. 'I've got my mobile, if anything interesting crops up.'

I smiled goodbye, and listened to his footsteps click away towards the exit; then looked round at the others.

'Really nice of him, isn't it? The party, I mean.'

Johann (*Senior Reg: clears short buildings with a favourable wind, and talks to God*) leaned back, grinning. 'He has these aberrations sometimes.'

'I couldn't have imagined it when I came here,' Lucy

murmured, from the depths of our comfiest chair. 'Him throwing a party. I was really scared of him to start with.'

'You are not alone,' Johann said, with a wink at me. 'I think even Rachel is afraid of Dr Murdoch.'

'Good God, yes,' I agreed cheerfully, tucking my feet up under me. 'Bloody *Godzilla* would be scared of Murdoch when he's in one of his moods . . .'

'His wife's meant to be very nice,' Michelle put in. 'She's a nurse, isn't she?'

'Used to be, I think. What's her name, too . . . ?'

'Mrs Murdoch.'

'*No.* Her proper name.' I gave Johann a withering look; he beamed it back at me.

'It's not an other-halves do, is it?' This – without enthusiasm – from Lucy, who was currently unattached.

Michelle shook her head. 'Members only.' Which was what most of us preferred. I quite liked showing Nick off on occasion – but there were times when we needed to be together as a group. It had been the same in A&E, and on other wards before it. The things we'd shared between us forged a special kind of bond.

'You and your bloke well settled now, Rachel?' Lucy asked me.

'Mm.' I smiled. 'My parish priest was asking how my "significant other" was, the other week. Always teasing me about it, he is.'

'You haven't managed to drag him along to Mass, then?'

'He keeps threatening to mention that I'm on the pill. Rotten sod. Don't know why I put up with him, sometimes . . .'

'Do we know who's bringing what to this bash?' asked Theresa, which brought my head round: I'd half-suspected she'd nodded off. She'd been the doctor on call last night, and it was obvious.

SHO: *makes high marks on wall when trying to clear short buildings; is sometimes addressed by God . . .*

'I said I'd do some sausage rolls,' I told her, ignoring the look of mock-panic that passed across Johann's features.

'Right. I think I'll do something veggie, just in case ...'
She stifled a yawn.

It was almost time to get back to it.

I felt at ease in here – unwinding from a dismal afternoon. The hours of routine graft hadn't been enough to
distract my thoughts from the man in that empty ward
down on Orthopaedics; still less from Razoxane, and whatever she was planning. Break, in this comfortable room,
had provided a welcome refuge from all that, with everyday
friends relaxing around me. But all good things must come
to an end.

'Okay, folks,' I said, unfolding myself and reaching for
my shoes; and the others sighed and complied. Even
Johann: because Senior Reg is just no match for Sister.

*Lifts buildings and walks under them. Freezes water with
a single glance. She IS God.*

It had rained hard during the evening: a sour, spiteful noise
against our darkened windows. I'd tried to ignore it,
hoping it would somehow have cleared by the time I
knocked off – and when I finally emerged from the front
entrance, I was pleased to find it had done.

The road was a river of lights: white and red and orange
all reflecting from the glistening surface and shimmering
in puddles. I thought it looked quite pretty. The air felt
cleaner, too – freshly-scrubbed of its fumes; the City grit
dampened down. And up above my head, seeming not
much higher than the hospital's grey gables, the moon was
unravelling the clouds.

So I kept my brolly furled, and walked on down towards
the tube station with a damp breeze in my hair. It was
turning chilly now, and my long nurse's raincoat wasn't
thick enough to keep it out, so I didn't hang around. A
brightly-lit bus hissed past; a whirring taxi. Then enough
of a gap for me to cross the street, and hurry in under the
reassuring glow of the *Underground* sign.

That bloke in the hospital blanket was waiting there again. Perhaps this was his pitch now: I'd seen him a couple of times since that first day of snow. He sat just inside the entrance, his back to the wall; both knees drawn up in an almost foetal huddle. He'd had an emergency haircut from somewhere, and the result made him look more like a refugee than ever.

Deliberately he met my gaze – and extended his hand.

Hungry and homeless said the cardboard sign beside him. *Please help*.

I was already fumbling out my travelcard; my purse was there before me in my open bag. I still managed to walk right past him. Perhaps it was the particular grimness on his face this cold, wet evening that made me turn on my heel.

His slaty eyes blinked, but showed no other emotion as I went back towards him. I knew that if I gave in to him now, he'd expect it again – looking for one friendly face amid the daily flood of blank expressions – but what the hell. I fished out 20p even as my eyes strayed to the blanket to see if it was one of ours: we'd had enough of them nicked. Then I stooped, and offered him the coin.

He made no move to take it; just looked from it to me – and grinned with all his teeth.

'That's kind of you, Rachel,' he murmured drily. 'But I'd much prefer it if you offered me a drink.'

I just stood there, arm extended. Staring.

'You've gone terrible pale, girl,' he continued after a moment, sounding amused: the grin had dwindled to a sombre little smile.

That accent: Scottish – right? Please?

'C'mon.' He began getting to his feet; I backed away a step. 'There's a coffee van just down the road. Just so's you can make sure I'll not be spending it on booze an' all . . .' The irony in his tone only made the accent richer; and it wasn't Scottish.

People were brushing past me all the while. I heard muttered imprecations, but not a word of them sank in. All I could do was grip my bag – clutch it close to my tight chest. I knew I'd lost colour, all right: I could feel my bloodless cheeks becoming cold.

Grey eyes. Metal eyes. They made his dirty face seem all the bleaker. And now the smile had faded in turn, and he was watching me without expression. It struck me then that – under the soiled and trailing blanket, and the cast-off clothes beneath it – he must be carrying a gun. Something he'd use without a scruple, if the need arose.

Something he'd use on me.

'Let's go.'

A jerk of his head and he was off and walking. It took me a moment to unfreeze myself – and then I was hurrying to catch up, the bright, bustling haven of the station falling behind me. Not that I was keen to leave it, of course; just scared to death of putting a foot wrong.

'Don't look so bloody nervous,' he muttered, as I stumbled into step beside him. 'You're buyin' me a coffee, remember. Out o' the kindness o' your heart.' Walking with my head down, I sensed his sidelong glance. 'So *smile*, and *say* somethin'.'

I swallowed, forced a ghastly grin, and said, 'Are you . . . really living rough, then?'

He grunted. 'For the moment. What better cover in this shit-city of yours? I'm just another fucking Irish drunk.' The irony was all gone now; his words had the same dull, steady bitterness as the evening's rain. I guessed that whatever prejudices he already held against the English had surely been redoubled by his experience of the streets.

I wondered what he'd have done if I hadn't spared some change tonight. Maybe come after me; accosted me on the platform. Dragged me back up top again . . .

'At least you offered,' he went on, his tone a little softer. 'And without knowin' who I was, to boot. Like I said, that was kind.' He glanced at me again – and now that he'd cleared some of the sputum of resentment from his chest, he seemed to really see me for the first time. Including the uniform I wore.

'It's not usual, y'know: people from your kind of profession supportin' the cause. They can't see past the violence . . .' From his pensive tone, I couldn't even tell if he was admiring my vision – or just regretting the fact that even nurses could get dragged into his dirty little war.

Either way, I almost shuddered with disgust.

The snack van was up ahead: an unhygienic-looking trailer selling burgers and hot-dogs as well as drinks. I went ahead and bought two beakers of muddy coffee, avoiding eye-contact throughout; turned to hand one to him – then followed him on round past the vehicle.

To where Razoxane was waiting. I nearly dropped my drink.

She was leaning against the corner, nursing a beaker of her own in both shabby gloves. Spots of rain still glistened on the brim of her hat, where the street light fell upon it; the face below was all in darkness.

The Irishman walked over; I baby-stepped unhappily after him. And Razoxane raised her unseen eyes.

'Evening, Rachel.' A stripe of orange light showed up her smile. 'How's it going?'

I didn't deign to reply.

'This is Frank,' she went on calmly, nodding to my companion – and once again I was thrown by the ordinariness of the name. Maybe I'd expected him to have been called Seamus or something.

Frank took a swallow of coffee. He looked about twenty-five, and tough: like the sort of bloke who'd start a pub fight. The press, police and politicians had poured out all their rage and frustration against a faceless enemy – but I'd looked him right in the eye. And her as well: that Jackie. Both close enough to touch. And smell . . .

Razoxane tipped her head up: studying the hospital

across the road. I followed her gaze towards its glowing windows – and for the first time felt like an outsider myself. Excluded. Looking in from the cold.

'What have you found out for us?' she asked.

I told her, in a flat reluctant voice. The empty ward, the room, the guards. I'd seen a copper by the lifts, as well; another in the main foyer. When I'd finished, I just took a swig of coffee. Quite tasteless, but the heat scorched right down into my belly and made me grit my teeth.

'When's the best time?' Razoxane wanted to know.

'Um . . . To get to him, you mean? Probably the Late/Night handover . . . nine o'clock. The nurses next door will all be in Report. Out of the way,' I added emphatically.

Frank had finished his own drink, and was putting together a roll-up; but every few seconds he glanced up the street, and down it. A wary reaction rather than a nervous one, perhaps; but nervous was what it made me.

Razoxane drained her beaker, and flipped it casually towards the nearby litter-bin. 'Think they might transfer him?'

I hesitated, keeping my face towards the wall. 'It's possible, yeah. Somewhere more secure . . .' I forced down some more coffee – fighting the chill.

'We'll come tomorrow night, then. What shift will you be on?'

'Late again, but . . .' I stopped. Then, uneasily: 'Why?'

'Because first you'll have to get hold of some hospital clothes,' she explained patiently, 'and then meet the *visitors*, and show them up to the ward . . .'

'Oh no I *won't*,' I blurted back, my breath still steaming from the coffee. 'You asked for information, I gave it to you, now sodding well leave me alone.'

Razoxane seemed to absorb that in silence; the hiss of tyres on wet tarmac was very loud in the pause that followed. Beside her, Frank licked and sealed his crumpled cigarette, his gaze not leaving me now.

Then Razoxane said: 'Remember what we agreed –

77

about our mutual friend? I'd really hate to come between you.'

I knew she meant Nick, of course. The way she said it made me think of a falling shadow, a guillotine blade — but of course it would be more horribly mundane than that. A ring on the doorbell, perhaps; his footsteps going through to answer it. I might be in the kitchen, or reading a book. And then . . .

I'd have thrown the last of my coffee in her face if I'd thought it would do any good.

'Something for two people to wear,' her cold voice persisted. 'White coats, theatre pyjamas — whatever. Find them somewhere to change. Then up to the ward . . .'

She was sucking me in again, and I knew it. Deep into her dark whirlpool of madness and terror. I should have bloody realised from the start.

'Agreed?'

I managed one convulsive nod. It probably looked about as agreeable as a head-butt.

'Got a light?' Frank asked.

I simply turned to him and stared; it was Razoxane — of all people — who fished in her pocket and brought out a book of matches. Frank stooped, and lit up from the flame she'd struck; straightened a moment later with a murmur of thanks.

Razoxane kept staring at the flame.

It quivered and grew bluish in the restless air; she cupped the glow, and her glasses caught it. Even in my sick, numbed state, I registered surprise.

The shades weren't for show, I knew that much. Whether as a consequence of the witchcraft she'd used to prolong her life, or just the centuries she'd spent delving into the darkness, she hated light: it *hurt* her. But still she watched the burning match.

Then the night breeze snuffed it out.

Her head half-turned towards me, as if to catch me watching. The gesture re-awoke the fright of my dream and I looked quickly – guiltily – away, across the road.

When I looked back, she'd moved in close: I had to swallow down a shudder before it set all my muscles off. Frank was smoking, over by the kerb: still watchful – but not quite within earshot.

'It's all part of the same favour,' Razoxane said quietly. 'I meant what I said before. I don't want you involved this time.'

I stared helplessly back at her; this icy, evil woman who treated me as she might a younger sister. And suddenly a question was rising to my mouth, as irresistibly as vomit. Something that – involved or not – I knew I had to ask.

'Last week . . . There was a fire-bombing up in Kentish Town. People with their . . . eyes and tongues cut out.' I swallowed; the question's bilious taste remained. So I spat it out. 'Please tell me that wasn't you.'

Razoxane smiled faintly. 'It wasn't me.'

I felt a tiny flicker of relief.

'It was someone looking for me,' she added softly.

Chapter 9

'What's up with her ladyship today?' I heard Lucy mutter – unaware that I was there, outside the storeroom.

'Who, Rachel?'

'Yeah. Five minutes late, that's all, and she really bites my head off. Cow.'

I know listeners never hear good of themselves, but her tone still hurt a lot. It didn't sound like a friend talking: not even a frustrated one. More like someone who's bottled up her feelings for far too long.

And I'd thought we got on well, the two of us. Her cross, unguarded whisper made me wince. On top of everything else – all the weight on my mind – I had the sudden, scary thought that maybe *no one* cared for me, not really; that all their smiles were just for show. Suck up to Sister and keep her sweet . . .

At that moment – still only half-way through this dragging afternoon – the sense of no one left to turn to almost broke me down in tears.

'I think she's just tired, that's all,' came Jez's voice. 'She didn't mean to snap . . .'

'Yeah, I *bet* she's tired. I think she's got a bloke on the side somewhere, and it isn't working out . . .'

Oh you *bitch*, I thought; but more in misery than anger.

'. . . my last Ward Sister was the same. She'd have maybe five blokes going at once, and whenever she'd had a bust-up with one of them, she just came in and took it out on us . . .'

Biting my lip, I walked quickly on down to my office – no longer caring if they heard my footsteps. I could picture their reaction back there: a shared, sniggery glance of mock-horror. Sitting down at my desk, with the door safely closed, I felt a salty stinging in my eyes and nostrils: creeping up like a gathering sneeze.

Being Sister is often a lonely job, of course; and sometimes a thankless one. But even its most isolated moments couldn't compare with the awful solitude I felt now.

And there were still six hours to go.

I'd counted nearly sixteen out already; I hadn't slept a wink. All through the night I'd squirmed and wriggled, trying to get comfy while Nick just snored. Trying and failing. The bedside clock had crawled on through the small hours: at half-past three, the rain began again, wet and sullen against the windows. Lying with my face pushed into my pillow, listening to the streaming black night, I just hoped she was out there somewhere – and getting very wet.

I pretended to be asleep when Nick got up for his six-to-two, though. I couldn't bear the thought of sleepy small talk on this of all mornings. Not when I was nerving myself to betray two of his colleagues, and help put a murderer back on the streets. His gentle parting kiss on my bare shoulder almost made me sob.

From then on, things got slower: time became treacle. It was like all the worst waits of my life rolled into one. Interviews. Exams. Even my driving test. I felt breathless and gutted. When I finally got up, I couldn't face the thought of breakfast. Slouching in my nightshirt on the sofa, trying to browse through the paper, I felt just like I had before my last interview. Could practically see myself, dry-mouthed and dressed to the nines, nervously crossing and uncrossing my legs. Skimming through a copy of *House & Garden* that might as well have been in Russian.

But that had been a bit exciting, too: a challenge. This was like waiting for an execcution – without hope of a reprieve.

It might have been better if I'd known this was some

meticulously planned operation, weeks in the preparing: something that might go without a hitch, and no one hurt. But what I'd been roped into was a rush job, made up almost as it went along, and the potential for disaster was appalling. Of course the sheer nerve of the thing was a crucial factor; spontaneity and single-mindedness might yet succeed against the odds. But if they didn't . . .

The thought of *terrorists* shooting their way out of a sleeping hospital turned my stomach inside out.

And just to put the lid on things, there was Razoxane's chilling little comment to contend with. What she'd said about the Kentish Town atrocity. *Someone looking for me* . . .

She'd told me I didn't want to know her business, and she was right. But she'd still involved me, up to my neck; and ignorance was no defence against whoever might be on her heels – as that poor woman from Shelter had discovered. Whatever she was up to, someone (or *something*?) in this city was ready to mutilate and burn without mercy in its efforts to track her down.

And they'd come by night before; but what if they'd got wind of me, and were already on their way? Right now? A few grey streets away, and getting closer . . . ?

What if, what if, what if?

Feeling physically sick now, I forced myself to take a long, hot shower. And then I dressed, with almost fatalistic care. Everything clean and fresh, from knickers and slip on out. *In case you're in an accident*, they say. As if the thought of them stripping clean clothes off your lifeless body is supposed to make you feel a little better . . .

Someone scratched at the door – and brought me back to my office with my jolt. I turned my head and swallowed. 'Come in.'

It was only Jez, his smile seeming casual enough. Perhaps he hadn't heard me walk away; or maybe he had, and was trying to gauge my mood. I felt the worm of paranoia begin to wriggle again.

'We're running low on shrouds,' he said brightly. 'Thought I'd let you know.'

Oh, brilliant. Thank you, Jez.

He'd leaned in around the door-jamb, and was just swinging himself back out again when I saw him hesitate, almost teetering. 'You okay?'

Did I look like I'd just been crying? At least the betraying streaks of tears were gone – soaked up by the tissue now lying crumpled in my wastebin. I managed a sore-eyed smile.

'Yeah, I think so . . .'

'You look whacked,' he persisted seriously. 'You really shouldn't push yourself so much.' The concern in his face was friendly and genuine, and it gave me a lift I really needed. I felt my smile becoming warmer.

'I won't, don't worry. I've . . . got some time owed from Monday: I'll go off at half-eight, if you're happy to do handover.'

'Sure, no problem.' He grinned encouragingly, and was gone.

My smile dried up and withered on my face.

One more step towards the point of no return – if I hadn't already passed it. I'd told Razoxane I could be waiting at the door downstairs with half an hour to spare: and that was now confirmed. Jez hadn't seemed surprised, either, even though I didn't often bother to take time back. Usually I'd be here to the bitter end, reluctant to cut and run – for reasons that lay somewhere between a sense of duty and a sort of superstition . . .

Maybe he saw it as a measure of how tired I really was.

Not that I'd be getting any rest tonight, of course; I wondered if I'd ever sleep again. My system was sick and singing with adrenaline now, and my shift not half-way over.

Half-past eight, then. The fire-doors nearest the loading bay. That's what I'd told them last night. The outside lighting was poor round that side of the hospital; the door itself was not alarmed.

Scrappy NHS security: I'd complained about it enough times in the past. Raised it direct with management when my own locker got broken into. Nothing had been done. Well, they'd had their chance . . .

Less than six hours, now. I knew I'd be measuring them out in minutes as I went through the motions.

And at some stage – probably my supper break – I still had to steal those bloody clothes.

It was just gone half-eight when I started down into the cold bowels of the building. Feeling smaller and less confident with every step.

Ours was one of the oldest hospitals in London: a great, rambling Gormenghast of a place – just like in those books I'd read at school. Each specialty held its corner, its enclave of wards, supported by a warren of clinics and kitchens, laundries and labs; all linked by lifts and stairwells and long, haunting corridors – a labyrinth you could easily get lost in.

But this real-life citadel had its dark side too. The brightest light couldn't keep its dinginess at bay. The leap from sterility to seediness you got, coming out of our hi-tech unit, always came as a jolt. And down in the nether regions, beyond the public gaze, the decay was even further advanced.

All depressing enough at the best of times; but tonight I really felt like I was going down to the dungeons.

I had the clothing with me. Getting hold of it hadn't been hard: not really. I'd put it off long enough to start getting panicky, but in the end all I'd had to do was raid a linen skip in the corridor outside. Two sets of loose blue pyjamas, the hospital's name stencilled boldly on the backs. They were used, but not obviously soiled. I'd glanced around and grabbed them, stuffing them into the yellow plastic rubbish sack I'd brought along. Back on the unit,

I'd helped myself to a spare white coat as well; there were a couple hung up in the office. None of the others gave me a second glance as I came and went; we're bagging up waste all the time. When I finally took my leave, it just looked as if I was taking a sackful down to the doors. Jez waved goodbye from a bedside. I faked a smile.

The presence of the bag down here would be a bit harder to explain, so I hoped I wouldn't run into anyone. But the Lates wouldn't start filtering down until after nine-fifteen, so if I was lucky . . .

Then again, if I was lucky, I wouldn't have got caught up in all this in the first place. Would I?

The corridor was bare, and bleakly lit; I hurried down it. I hadn't left stuff in a locker since the break-in – and after a nurse was attacked down here last year, I hadn't used the changing rooms at all. Certainly not at the end of a Late. Even wearing my uniform on public transport, which sometimes got me ogled and even pestered, was preferable to that.

It was quiet down here. Echoey. My footsteps bounced ahead of me. My throat was tight and dry by the time I got to the fire-door.

There was no one out there.

Swallowing, I leaned down on the bar – and the door clanked loudly, stiffly open. The damp night air swilled in. Silence from the nearby backstreet; a faint swish of traffic from round the front. I drew back, my heart hammering.

For maybe a minute, nothing happened. Maybe more than a minute. The yard outside lay motionless in the half-light of a white sodium lamp. Then a shape detatched itself from a stand of metal wheely-bins and walked quickly over, closely followed by another.

I drew even further back as they came through. The first was a man of about Frank's age, with brown hair and beard; he looked me full in the face for an unsettling moment, then past me to check the corridor. I could tell at once that he was nervous. The second was the girl called

Jackie; she didn't look too keen on this herself. Both of them were scruffily dressed, and smelled of the Underground: that dull, distinctive odour. They'd probably spent the last few hours down there, haunting the platforms, sheltering from the rain. Psyching themselves up.

'This is Brendan,' Jackie introduced grudgingly. I just nodded, with inbred politeness – and noticed the short, thick bundle he carried under his arm, wrapped up in a Sainsbury's bag.

'Er . . . what's that, please?'

I said it just like a nurse: one who's caught a patient trying to hide an illicit food parcel. Jackie almost sneered.

'Flowers for the patient; what d'you think?'

'God . . . Listen, you're not going to start shooting in there, are you?'

'Not if no one gets in our way,' she answered flatly. 'Now let's get ready.'

I hesitated, feeling really wretched; then handed over the pyjamas, and led them back down to the changing rooms. Brendan put his head cautiously around the Male door, and slipped inside. I led the way into the Female.

Empty, thank God.

The lights above the aisles of lockers were bright and stark, but the annexe of toilets and showers lay in dimness. I ventured warily over to check they were all unoccupied. They were; but one of the shower heads was still dripping slowly in the gloom of its stall, as if it hadn't long ago been used.

Jackie made straight for the nearest toilet, and gestured me in after her. Unwillingly I followed, closed the door and put my back against it. With my arms grimly folded, I watched her start undressing.

The claustrophobic space gave it all a stifling intimacy; closing me in with her sour-smelling coat and sourer stare. The clothes beneath looked like jumble sale rejects: ripped and grubby. Frank was right, they were ideal cover. People would look right through her – go out of their way to

86

avoid her eye. And all the time she'd squat there, smiling inside; her pistol pushed snug into the waistband of her jeans.

She drew the weapon now, and proffered it. 'Hang onto that a second.'

I stared at the thing; practically hugging myself now.

'Go *on*, then,' she hissed, so sharply that I flinched. Unthinkingly I took the gun. The weight almost dragged it from my fingers. Beads of sweat popped up across my back.

She allowed herself a smile: still stripping. I peered down at the ugly hunk of metal in my hands, and wondered how she could ever bear to touch it. How she could bear to do any of the things she did . . . My mind's eye was suddenly clogged with the blackened mess of her Liverpool Street victim.

This is what the bombers did. To a human being.

A silver crucifix – like mine – was glinting in the hollow of her throat.

Down to her underwear now, she stepped into the pyjama trousers. I leaned miserably back against the door: straining my ears for any sound beyond it.

Nearly ten-to.

'Not used to this side of it, are you?' she asked tersely.

I shook my head.

'Well it's deeds we need, not words. Words're cheap . . .' She pulled the smock on. 'It's time people like you . . . stood up to be counted . . .'

I wondered dully just what Razoxane had told her. That I was an armchair sympathiser, probably: playing up the fact I was a Catholic. Maybe even someone who owed their awful cause a favour.

What the hell had she got me into?

Jackie sat on the toilet bowl to retie the laces on her grubby trainers; I hoped no one was going to notice those. Her street clothes went into the bag I'd brought. 'You make sure these get *burned*,' she told me, straightening up.

I made an affirmative sort of noise, and passed her the lab coat. She shrugged herself into it. 'Right, give us that . . .'

I relinquished the pistol. She grasped it with a familiarity I found quite chilling, and set about examining the coat. It didn't take her long to find the standard slit behind the pocket. She pushed gun and fist inside it – and drew them smoothly out.

My mouth was so dry I almost had to peel my lips apart to talk. 'I can't go up there . . .'

A cold glance. 'You bloody will.'

'People will see me with you. How the *hell* . . .'

'Tell them we accosted you or somethin'. Held you at gunpoint.' And with that she pulled at the pistol in her hand. It seemed to unlock and slide apart; then snapped together like a trap. I knew that meant she'd cocked it.

For a moment I glimpsed something flicker behind her dour, determined stare. It was gone again before I had it fixed; but I knew that it was fear.

A human response to what was coming: it should have reassured me. But all it did was accentuate my own.

'Go check on Brendan.'

I turned, and eased the door open. The changing rooms were empty. I scuttled across to the main door, rubbing my palms down my uniform: trying to wipe away the pistol's oily feel. Brendan was already waiting outside: ready to hand me his street clothes. The V-neck of his scrub top revealing matted hairs on his chest. The stubby bundle he carried was now wrapped in an old towel.

The twin muzzles of a sawn-off shotgun stared vacantly out from between its folds.

I pressed the call button for the lift: it lit up beneath my finger. Somewhere, floors away, machinery began to move.

I stepped back, peered up at the indicator. Watched the lights come counting down towards us. Anything to avoid looking at the others. Anything.

After all these hours of waiting, we were down to the last few minutes. I'd half-hoped my adrenal glands would have worn themselves out by now, but they clearly hadn't. I felt clammy and short of breath; my heartbeat punching through my chest.

The silence was tense: icy. They knew I wasn't one of them – and that I might prove a hindrance, screw things up somehow. If things went wrong, they'd probably shoot me first. At point-blank range.

I've had to reason with violent people more than once – especially when I worked in A&E. Sometimes they'd had knives. Almost always they'd been drunk, on drugs, or just mentally disturbed. But this pair carried guns; and whatever else they might be, they were stone cold sane. Killing me would be a swift, pragmatic act; the outcome of a tactical decision. And no amount of reasoning would stop it.

The lift arrived. The doors rolled smoothly open. In we got.

I waited until we were on our way up before finally mustering the nerve to say: 'Please don't hurt the coppers.'

Jackie glanced at me. There was the faintest sheen of sweat on her pale forehead; wisps of her fringe were growing damp.

'Depends if they behave.'

I looked to Brendan. He stared back, his face unfriendly. The lift came smoothly to a stop.

We were one floor short.

The doors slid open to reveal a middle-aged couple – obviously visitors, although chucking-out time should have come and gone. 'Going down?' the woman beamed.

'Going up,' I countered, already reaching for the button. It came out sounding like a croak.

'That's all right; we might as well take the tour, eh George?' They came in across the threshold before I could say anything more. And though I'd held the button down, the door was going to close in its own sweet time.

Jackie had rather obviously turned her face away, and was staring hard at the wall. Brendan looked down at the toes of his scuffed shoes. All I could do was gaze out down the corridor into the Surgical Unit. It was empty, apart from a nurse at the far end.

'Busy day, love?' the woman asked me kindly.

I managed a non-committal smile.

'They should double your pay,' she added, with great sincerity. 'You're angels, you really are . . .'

Come on, close, you bastard.

The door finally obliged; we lurched and continued upward. Next stop Orthopaedics. With a murmured goodnight, I led the way out.

The corridor here was empty. No sign of a guard.

I let my breath wheeze out as I got my bearings. We were starting where I'd finished last time; the closed ward was just along the corridor. I looked down at my watch. Between five and ten past nine now. Most of the nurses would be in Sister's office for handover. And the coppers, into the last hour of their shift, might just be caught napping.

Another linen skip had been left here for emptying: the bulging laundry sack topped off with a couple of pillows. Brendan checked both ways, unwrapped his shotgun and pushed it in between them. I stiffened my muscles against a shudder.

His face was quite immobile now: a mask cemented into place. Watching him, I felt Jackie close behind me – so tense that my bare nape almost tingled with the static.

A thought fled through my mind, then – and blazed into a horrible conviction, like a spark setting off a blasting charge.

They've come to kill him.

No wonder they hadn't discussed what they might do if he was bedridden, in traction, immobile. No talk of borrowing a wheelchair, or hijacking a trolley. They were here to stop him talking. Shut him up.

And me? Shut me up too? I stared wide-eyed at Brendan as he wheeled the trolley forward; nodding to Jackie as if I didn't exist.

Jackie prodded me in the ribs. I jumped, swung round. Her other hand was buried in her coat's false pocket.

'C'mon.'

Instinctively I complied, walking on to the next set of fire-doors and pushing them open; holding them for the trolley even as I tried out-thinking my own mind.

That's mad. They're here to free him. He's their friend . . .

Ward closed, said the sign ahead. *No entry.*

'You go first,' said Jackie in my ear. 'Say we're here to check on the patient; anything. Just give us the chance to get close . . .'

I came to the ward doors. The guard was there beyond them, under the light. Not the one I'd talked to; this bloke had ginger hair. We'd caught him napping right enough: he'd nodded off. Just slumped there, chin on chest; arms loosely folded.

I eased the door open; the trolley slid through. One of the wheels was squeaking, but it didn't rouse him. Three yards, two, one . . .

And Brendan grasped the topmost pillow and lunged, clamping it over the copper's face. Shoving the dozing man back upright, his shotgun jammed into the soft white mass – and in that moment I knew for sure there'd be no quarter: just one stifled blast, and the poor bloke's brains all over the wall. I opened my mouth in horrified protest, sucking in air for a shout . . .

It seemed to clog in the back of my throat. The taste was warm and rancid. Suddenly I wanted to gag, and spit it back out. Instead of which, I *saw* – and almost spewed.

The policeman's arms had dropped to his sides; he'd made no other move. Between the open flaps of his anorak, a clotted crimson slime was bulging outward. A chunk of it broke clear even as I gawped, and plopped to the polished floor like a stewed tomato.

Brendan reacted like a man electrified: standing rigid for a stupefied moment – then flinging himself clear, still grasping the pillow. The side that had pressed against the copper's face was already dyed bright crimson. The mouth and nose that had soaked it were streaming blood now; the rest of the face as pale as sallow cheese. The eyes had rolled right upward: two sightless, sour-milk slits.

Jackie recoiled past me, knocking me to one side. Her own eyes stared like saucers.

The policeman's corpse began at last to overbalance.

I felt a blow against my spine: it sluiced fear through my stomach in the moment before I realised I was up against the wall, beside the darkened office doorway. With my hand clutched tight across my bile-filled mouth, I watched the body topple to one side. Watched it fall, and strike the floor. The impact burst its belly like a blister; visceral pulp, held in place by the sheerest film of tissue, came slopping out across the lino. The smell was *awful*.

Even as I swayed – head swimming – the side-room door began to move.

Maybe the body had brushed it as it dropped; or maybe the heavy, soggy *thud* had set it swinging of its own volition. But all I could do was stand there, as if nailed to the wall, and wait for something in that room to come shuffling out.

The door creaked slowly open . . . and what I saw on the bed, albeit for just a second, sent horror crashing through me like a breaking wave. I simply fled.

Jackie had already bolted, back towards the lifts; Brendan followed, panting, at her heels. But in my panic I went the other way – deeper into the unlit ward. My momentum had carried me half-way down the long, hollow room before I realized my mistake, by which time it was far too late. The empty beds closed in on either side, looming out of the gloom like lurking skeletons. Almost whimpering with fright, I reached the toilet at the far end, and fairly fought my way inside; dragging it closed and locking it. It felt like a cell; a coffin on end. Darkness spiked with disinfectant. But I didn't dare reach for the light switch. All I could do was stand there, shivering; both hands pressed hard against my mouth.

I knew I mustn't be sick. I really mustn't. Because someone would hear, and smell it, and come smashing in through the door to rub my face in it . . .

Oh Mary – oh Mum – pray for me.

I couldn't see a thing. But my mind's eye stayed fixed on the ghastly mess I'd glimpsed, lying on the bed in that overlit side-room. Fixed and staring. I couldn't close it.

In the course of my nurse training, I'd learned that the human body contains nearly nine pints of blood, and has intestines twenty-eight feet long. *Well fancy that*, I'd thought.

It hadn't meant a thing before tonight.

Time might have raced or crawled; in the silence and blackness I couldn't tell. The acrid smell of hospital bleach filled my nostrils. Compared to the stench from the far end of the ward, it was a perfume.

A footstep sounded then, outside the door. The squeak of a shoe on the lino.

I waited, hands across my mouth; eyes huge. Trying not to tremble. Not even to breathe.

Silence.

Then a sudden flurry of gibberish from the other side of the panel – a hissing, distorted voice that sent a fresh bolt of panic through me. There was something eerily ethereal about it, as if the speaker was a gulf away.

As I listened, with tears on my cheeks, the shoes creaked again; I heard the bathroom door across the way easing open. Another hiss came – wordless this time. A crackle and pop of static.

And suddenly I realised it was crosstalk on a two-way radio. A police radio. Oh thank Christ.

I was about to fumble for the lock when something inside me said: Don't.

I hesitated.

More footfalls. The door of the toilet next to mine swung open; its unoiled hinges squealed.

I had a cold flush then: it bathed me like melted snow and almost sent me into spasm. My reasoning mind, still insisting I should open the door and let him lead me back to safety, was suddenly choked. In uncomprehending dread I waited; and his radio squawked again.

He murmured something in response.

More twisted words from out of the ether – and a moment later I heard him pass my door and walk back down the ward, his shoes clicking and squeaking into silence.

Policeman. That's all he was. An ordinary copper . . .

I closed my eyes against the darkness, and lowered myself shakily down onto the toilet bowl. And for the next hour, while all sorts of consternation came and went in the corridors outside, I just sat there, with my head in my hands, and silently wept.

Chapter 10

The long, heavy blade came up slowly, and caught the light – reflecting it sharply back at me. I managed not to flinch. Taking another sip of strong tea, I kept my eyes on the screen; even when Nick leaned over the back of the sofa to stroke my hair, running his hand down inside my dressing gown collar.

'Sure you're up to tonight?' he asked quietly.

I nodded – absorbed in the news conference; watching the solemn-faced man hold the machete gingerly up by its handle and tip. The spokesman beside him looked grimly back into the cameras.

'We believe a weapon similar to this was used: a machete, or possibly a butcher's knife of some description . . .'

'Jesus, what their wives must be going through,' Nick murmured. His fingers tightened to a stop on my shoulder; then resumed their gentle squeezing. I drank again, the mug held tight in both my hands. Still peering warily over the rim.

'. . . *the actual weapon?*'

'No, the weapon used has not been recovered as yet,' the policeman responded heavily. 'Our conclusions have been drawn from the pathologist's report. All three victims died from severe lacerations compatible with . . .' His mouth kept on going through the motions; his strained face told it differently. Behind the formal language – the forced dispassion – I glimpsed his pent-up anger and disgust; the effort of keeping it inside him turned him white.

Two coppers killed in the line of duty: gutted like fish in a busy, *British* hospital. The atmosphere under the TV lights was tripwire-taut. We could almost feel it seeping out into the room.

Even if I hadn't seen the carnage for myself, the shock would still have numbed me. Partly because the police we take for granted aren't supposed to get killed: it breaks the *rules*. And partly — of course — because of Nick. To judge by the photos they'd shown, both men had been his age. Imagining his sheepish mug-shot in their place was far too easy.

When I'd finally emerged from my hiding place last night, the floor had been alive with stunned police-men; dark uniforms offsetting bleached, tight faces. The ones I ran into by the stairwell established who I was as politely as their outrage would allow, and ushered me along. I was finally nodded out through the front doors at nearly half-past ten, leaving the hospital lowering behind me.

Night castle. Black fortress. Staring after me with its hundred blazing eyes . . .

The reporters on TV were demanding theories. The spokesman spread his hands.

'We can confirm that the hospital patient was in police custody. We believe the murderer or murderers were primarily interested in him . . .'

'. . . *Is it true he was a terrorist suspect . . . ?*'

'I cannot comment on that at this time . . .'

'Thank Christ he wasn't in with you,' Nick said softly; from the tone of his voice, he was as unnerved on my behalf as I was on his. This sort of horror in hospitals was against the rules as well. Was out of *order*.

He didn't know the half of it.

The next item of news came on, and at last I leaned my head back. His face was close to mine, and full of concern. I smiled faintly.

'I'll be okay tonight, don't worry. Been looking forward to it . . .'

'Just ring when you're ready to come away from there.'

'No, don't wait up. I'll call a cab . . .'

'You *ring* me, right.' His hand closed firmly on my shoulder. 'Please, Rachel. There's some bad bastards around at the moment.'

I wouldn't dispute that, either. The murders at our hospital had made such a splash (sorry: wrong word) on the evening news that other items had been pushed aside; but as I'd listened to GLR while doing my cooking this afternoon, the local news had provided a grisly little snippet of its own. A prostitute found hanged in a bedsit near King's Cross. The police didn't reckon it was suicide.

And whoever had done it had used piano wire.

We could have done without that detail; the very thought set my teeth on edge. Learning that the body had hung undiscovered for several days didn't help, either. Maybe she was already dead and dangling when I'd made my abortive recce of the area. Maybe I'd passed quite close, and never known it . . .

'What time's your friend coming?' Nick asked, straightening up. I glanced at my watch. Nearly six-fifteen.

'Seven.' Which was plenty of time. I'd had my bath already; washed and dried my hair. Now I could spend ages deciding what I was going to wear.

I was determined to enjoy myself tonight; leave all my cares behind me. If that meant drinking lots of wine, then well and good, but I had other reserves to draw on too. Like a nurse's ability to distance herself from dreadful things she's had to deal with. And – after all I'd been through three years ago – a survivor's resolve to keep on going forward.

Besides, for me the war was over. Surely. I'd done all that Razoxane had asked of me; it wasn't my fault that someone got there first.

. . . *someone looking for me* . . .

Her dry, remembered words made my stomach lurch; but that was pure reflex. I was out of it now. Whatever she might be pitting her wits against this time, it was no concern of mine.

So it was curiosity as much as anything that made me ask if there'd been any progress with the Kentish Town fire-bombing.

Nick shrugged. I'd wandered through to watch him prepare his supper; ever ambitious, he was doing beans on toast.

'Nothing definite, not yet. The bloke who got savaged by the dogs is the only one who can say anything, and he's still pretty shocked. Not making much sense at the moment . . .'

He paused to add what seemed a suicidal amount of West Indian Hot Pepper Sauce to the beans; then glanced back over his shoulder.

'One word that keeps coming up is "Wiking", apparently.'

'What, with a W?'

'Yep; it's a bit confused . . . But there's an offshoot of the BNP round there who call themselves the *Vikings* . . . silly buggers . . . and the gentleman was coloured. So we've pulled a few of them in for questioning.'

That threw a new light on things. I straightened hopefully up from where I'd been leaning against the wall. 'And the others – the people in the house. Were they black too?'

'No; all white. But we thought we'd give these bastards a going over anyway.' He grinned and turned back to his beans; not seeing the flicker of hope on my face snuffed out again.

Someone looking for me.

Wiking.

I shook the words right out of my head, and went hastily upstairs to choose my clothes.

Not wanting to get too giggly (or go to sleep), I'd decided to take it easy with the wine. Just a glass or two of white, to keep me cheerful. But halfway through my third or fourth, I just thought, belatedly, sod it; and let Murdoch top me up again.

It was going well, though: I was glad I'd come. The house, up in New Barnet, was lovely – wide white rooms, deep carpets and the sort of chairs you could doze off in. Mrs Murdoch – Emma, she insisted – had prepared a delicious hot-and-cold buffet, to which we added our various contributions; Michelle and I helped her lay it all out on the long dining table. Going back through to the lounge, I'd glimpsed two young kids peering down at me through the banisters at the top of the stairs. Grinning, I gave them a little wave. The little girl returned it shyly; her brother stayed politely serious. Already very much his father's son, I mused.

Still smiling, I thought of Sandra, who I hadn't been able to visit for a while. I hoped she'd be safely home soon as well; and that I'd have a chance to say goodbye before she went.

With the ice pretty much broken by the warmth of our welcome, the evening unfolded smoothly. We ate, drank and talked at length and leisure. Sitting on the lounge carpet, next to a hi-fi system as imposing as some of the life-support equipment we worked with, I felt like someone snapped out of a trance, brought back to the land of the living. In the midst of this cheerful gathering, the dread of the past few days seemed quite unreal, like something I'd dreamed. Even the ghastly sights of yesterday were wholly dislocated from the here and now. Madness, terrorism, murder: it was all sealed off as safely as the night beyond the curtained picture windows.

Maybe people coming out of schizophrenic episodes felt just like this.

I took another sip of cold, sweet wine. The background music – something light and classical – blended softly with the conversations round the room; the readouts on the CD player beside me rose and fell like biorhythms.

Most of the team had made it tonight; those who'd drawn the short straw to cover the Late and Night shifts would be guaranteed their place next Christmas. I was quite sorry Jean wasn't here: her deadpan anecdotes were always a treat.

I wouldn't have minded watching her tease Lucy, either.

That was me being bitchy, but I couldn't help it. Looking across at Lucy now, I almost instinctively found fault: saw sulkiness in her smile, heard smugness in her voice. And knew this was going to get addictive if I didn't watch out . . .

'You're very quiet tonight, Rachel,' Emma Murdoch said lightly, easing into the unoccupied chair behind me. I glanced back at her with a smile, relieved at the distraction.

'I'm always quiet.'

'Enjoying yourself, though.'

I nodded vigorously. 'Very much, thanks. It was a gorgeous meal. And I love the house.'

'It is nice, isn't it? We've been here three or four years, now . . .' She paused. 'I'm glad it's going well. John said you all needed the break. I hear your hospital's . . . been quite busy recently.'

She said it carefully, trying to sound casual; but I could tell from the undertone in her voice what was really on her mind. As a former nurse, the thought of murder and mutilation in a hospital would have shaken her as much as anyone. But the fact that it was the hospital where her husband worked brought the horror right home onto her doorstep.

It suddenly felt like we were both sliding over a frozen black lake – spiralling in towards the thin ice at the centre. She didn't want to talk or even think about what had happened, I guessed that much; yet still some fascination drew her in – and tugged me with her.

With an effort I steered the two of us back towards the bank.

'Never stops, does it? But you'll remember that . . :'

She took the opening gladly. 'Don't I just? My first job was on a really understaffed surgical unit, and it was absolute hell. And the discipline was still so strict, too, with Matron and all. Whereas nowadays . . .'

I gently mimicked her Yorkshire accent. '. . . nurses today don't know they're born, right?'

And smiling she broadened it herself. 'Aye, lass. Sheer *luxury* these days. Now, when *I* were a nurse . . .'

We chatted on; stepping almost subconsciously back off the ice and onto solid ground. She reminded me of Judith, a Sister I'd worked with in my last job. I'd burned a lot of bridges when I'd moved, but the two of us still kept in touch. I owed her a letter, come to think of it.

Emma decided she'd better circulate, and moved on. I joined Sue in a raid on what remained of the desserts. 'Okay?' I asked her quietly as we made our selection, and she gave a quick, grateful nod. Coming back into the lounge with a piece of Black Forest, I joined the nearest conversation. And Jez glanced round with a smile.

'How about you, Rachel? Would you prefer to be buried or cremated?'

Ouch.

People discuss the oddest things at parties, and that one caught me unprepared. For a moment I was out on the midnight lake again, and sensing the chilly depths beneath the ice. Then back on balance – with soft, firm carpet under my shoes.

I shrugged. 'Dunno. Don't really mind.' I forked in a mouthful of gateau, and forced myself to chew. Rich chocolate and cherries – as tasteless on my tongue as cotton wool.

'Any preferences about the send-off?' Theresa asked brightly.

I thought about it, still chewing. Swallowed. Then shrugged again.

'I wouldn't want it to be all miserable. I mean . . . it's not as if it's the end of things or anything.'

'And what would you want played?' Jez wondered. 'I'd quite like *Jerusalem* myself. Not that I'm religious or anything; I just like it.'

I thought again. 'I'd like to have the Hymn of St Patrick, please. Or maybe *Be Thou My Vision*. I love those two. Old Irish hymns . . .'

He grinned delightedly, and nudged me in the ribs. 'Bejesus, Rachel, 'tis the Catholic in ye.'

'Shush!' I elbowed him back. 'No . . . I went on a trip to Ireland when I was in school, and we went to see Patrick's shrine, and where he was buried and everything. There were some pilgrims singing his hymn by the graveside, and I found that really moving. Stayed with me for a long time afterwards.' I shook my head. 'Don't knock it, Jez. It's a beautiful country.'

I'd been twelve, but I still recalled it: standing on the very top of Slieve Patrick Hill with the wind in my hair. Overlooking the sea, with the hills of the Lake District seeming maybe twenty miles off; and nothing behind me but wide green fields, fading back into the haze of the oncoming rain.

That had been a special holiday; a memory I treasured. I still couldn't marry up that countryside, those friendly people, with the violence and hatred we saw so often on the news. The mismatch just made it seem surreal. But now the killers and haters had met me face to face, like all my fears made flesh and blood.

And no sooner had I glimpsed them than they'd gone. Back into the dark, with their forgettable faces and their nondescript names. Like a coffin-ship passing in the night. An evil *Flying Dutchman* . . .

The talk had already turned to other things; and finding my feet I followed. The spasm of discomfort in my stomach slowly faded; my fears were fading likewise.

It was finished.

Listening to Sue's hair-raising anecdote about the ENT surgeon with Parkinson's, I just giggled with the others, and had another drink.

Chapter 11

'I am *not* hung-over,' I assured Jean firmly. 'I just didn't get much sleep.'

'Of course, Sister,' she nodded, her expression grave.

I gave her a suspicious look – there was just the hint of a twinkle in her eye – and went back to sorting through the envelopes the porter had just left. Path. results, mostly; a couple of get-well cards. A folded sheet of paper stapled and labelled *Sister in Charge, ITU*, and a couple of re-used envelopes addressed to me personally. One was marked *Private & Confidential* with a self-important flourish – which usually meant some thrilling communication from the RCN rep. I slid that one to the back.

Sue was eyeing the chocolates again.

They were sitting there on the worktop – a tempting Belgian boxful, brought in by one of our former patients as a way of saying thanks. He'd admitted to having doubts about it; worried we might be 'thinking of our figures'. We'd quickly assured him that our figures could look after themselves.

The top tray was disappearing fast; poor Sue hadn't had much of a look-in. And now here she was, gloved-up ready for a procedure, hovering by the desk while the doctor finished his preparations.

'Coffee cream?' I asked, smiling, and she nodded eagerly. ''Scuse fingers . . .' She opened wide, and I popped it in.

'Ready, nurse . . .' the doctor said.

Murdoch arrived at that point, pausing for a word with some relatives at a bedside before coming on over. 'Morning, ladies.'

'Dr Murdoch,' Jean said, regarding him severely over her spectacles. 'An unlooked-for pleasure.'

'Well you should have,' he came back equably. 'Anything cooking?'

I gave him a brief run-down on how people were doing; one patient giving cause for concern, but otherwise all stable. He glanced over to where the CVP line insertion was now smoothly underway; Sue and the SHO craning over the green-draped bed.

'Fancy a chocolate?' I asked.

He glanced at the box, then turned a serious face to me. 'Rachel. You should know I never eat on duty.' He paused. 'However . . . I shall suffer bodily nourishment this once.' He selected the last nut cluster, and smiled disarmingly. 'I'll be in my office.'

I watched him stroll away – then gave Jean a shaky little grin as my stomach, which had leaped inside me, settled back once more. He could still catch me, even now. Mischievous bugger. But it kept me on my toes, at least . . .

Someone's infusion pump began to bleep; Jean went over to adjust it. I set about opening my post.

The one addressed to *Sister in Charge* was a round-robin from the Control of Infection Nurse; I put it aside for pinning up on the notice board. Next came a note from the library, letting me know a textbook I'd requested had come in and was ready for collection.

I sat back; selected another chocolate. Ripped open the *Private & Confidential* envelope without enthusiasm or hurry. I'd fully unfolded the single sheet of paper it contained before the heading clicked.

Department of Morbid Anatomy.

In that first moment, all I felt was puzzlement. Even as I read *Request for Post-Mortem Examination*, I thought it must have been mis-addressed.

Name of Patient: YOUNG, Rachel Mary Maureen.

The melting chocolate caught in my throat and clogged it.

Extent of Examination Requested was the next stark section heading; and someone had penned a grisly list beneath it. The writing – full of antique flourishes – contrasted bizarrely with the butchery described.

Every organ was down to be dissected.

My hand went quickly to my mouth – just stifling a gasp. My heart was already thundering. Its motion sucked the blood from my skin, and turned me icy cold all over.

Is there any danger of contamination/infection?

... YES was ringed ...

ATTACH BIOHAZARD LABEL TO THIS FORM AND TO SHROUD.

And one was duly attached: that triple-circle warning sign on vivid yellow. Danger. Infectious. *Unclean.*

My pent-up breath was building to a shrieking head of steam.

The routine bustle of the unit went heedlessly on around me; I dimly sensed its sounds and movement. But all my mind could grasp was the form in my fingers, rustling faintly as my hand began to shake.

They'd see. Jean or Sue or someone would see. My face must be as pale as a dead woman's; it felt as clammy. They'd realize I'd had some dreadful shock, and come hurrying to help.

Suddenly I knew they mustn't know.

Mustn't. Because death was out there, like a black wind blowing round the building: carrying off lives like litter. A psychopath witch with her terrorist familiars – and a shadow called *Wiking.* Even sensing their presence would surely be fatal. I thought of Sue's seance: opening minds to the hungry darkness. Mere suspicion might be as dangerous this time.

I felt unclean, all right: threatening my friends with my very presence.

Lowering my head, I gritted my teeth for a silent prayer: repeating the Hail Mary over and over, until all my swirling thoughts were soaked up by the words, to leave a fragile inner stillness at the centre. Then I swallowed – still winded by the punching of my heart – and cautiously raised my eyes.

Nobody had noticed. Yet.

With a sort of resignation, I turned the paper over.

If you don't want this to happen, you will meet me in the City.

She'd signed herself ℞. Doctor's shorthand for treatment. I guessed the irony was entirely deliberate.

Kill or cure.

She hadn't said where in the City, or when; so all I could do was count the wretched minutes to the end of my shift (all three hundred and eight of them), and then venture nervously out into its noisy, teeming streets.

The afternoon was dismal: even the air seemed grey. Blank-faced people filled the pavements, while the traffic flowed past in strengthening rush-hour currents towards the whirlpool of Bank. Traffic lights and roaring red buses were the only bright spots in the whole grim panorama.

I let myself drift with the current, heading down towards St Paul's; just another pedestrian, with my uniform concealed beneath my buttoned-up mac. The cathedral's massive dome seemed to loom against the sky as I drew nearer, as sombre as a skull. I forced my thoughts clear of the comparison, and glanced nervously around. People, people everywhere, and eyes that looked right through me – but of Razoxane there was no sign.

Normally I liked a wander through the Square Mile. Its older corners interested me – and the energy in its busy streets brought a breezy, upbeat feel. But today, in the midst of the crowds, I felt small and lost and entirely alone. For all the eddies and cross-currents still swirling round me, the working population was going out like a tide – their thoughts already fixed on home and tea and telly. If I were to drop, just let myself go, the next ten people would probably step right over me. By eight o'clock tonight they'd all be gone, and this would just be a glowing, orange city of ghosts.

Would I still be haunting it then?

She could be anywhere. Probably watching me already, enjoying my discomfort. But perhaps she wasn't smiling, not even inside. Perhaps she was nursing a freezing rage.

I stopped short — and something struck me from behind. Scalded by adrenaline, I literally jumped; and the bowler-hatted bloke just jostled by me. 'Why don't you watch where you're going, you silly cow?' he muttered, striding briskly on.

I was too relieved even to take offence. Twisting the strap of my shoulder bag, I turned on my heel to see if I'd been followed. No shadower caught my eye. Even as I hesitated, another man brushed past me; and then a woman, power-dressed. Her sidelong glance was just as sour. I took the hint, and carried on towards Bank.

Everything flowed together there; the streams of traffic and pounding feet. People pouring down into the under-ground drain. There was something remorseless and sur-real about it all. Drawing steadily closer, I recalled the lines of some weird French poem I'd translated in school. *Ant-hill city. City of dreams . . .*

Where the ghosts of the daylight grab you.

'Afternoon,' said Razoxane at my elbow.

I spun around so fast I almost toppled; fighting for my balance as the tide swept by.

She was lounging casually in a doorway, her face pinched with cold but grinning; a tattered, black-clad beggar. Rub-bing her hands together slowly, coaxing blood through the fingers that poked from her flea-bitten gloves. An old rucksack was leaned up against the wall beside her, stuffed to bulging and buttoned tight. Her bedding for tonight, perhaps; some extra layers of clothing. And whatever other worldly goods she owned.

Her sombre coat and hat were smudged with grey; and seeing her at last by daylight, I realized it was ash. It put me suddenly in mind of the Ash Wednesday service in my church; Father Jim in his funereal cassock, letting the pale, fine powder slip through his fingers. Perhaps Razoxane used the like in her own secret ceremonies – anointing herself with dust and ashes.

It was a subject I'd always thought around before: the things she did to keep herself alive. What rituals she must observe. What sacrifices.

What she had to burn . . .

'I knew you'd come, Rachel,' said Razoxane calmly. 'You're a wise young woman.' She hoisted the rucksack up behind one shoulder. 'Let's walk.'

I swallowed (the tightness in my throat felt like rampant tonsillitis), and waited for her lead. She glanced unhurriedly both ways, then turned towards Bank. Together we stepped out into mid-stream.

'It wasn't my fault,' I muttered after a moment, trying – without success – to sound assertive.

'I never said it was,' she came back evenly.

I looked at her sidelong; she was staring ahead. Picking pensively at her teeth with a matchstick. A used one. I was reminded of the other night – how she'd struck a flame and stared at it. As if even its glimmer through her shades was somehow mesmerising.

I'd watched her play with fire once before – and burn a house down. Her grin as she'd struck that match had suggested pyromania, pure and simple; ironically at odds with her fear of the light. I'd assumed it was the power that aroused her; a psychie patient once told me that it felt like turning dragons loose.

But what I'd glimpsed on her face this last time was something else again. A different – strangely haunting – sort of hunger.

Whatever for, I didn't need to know. This meeting was surely just to tie up loose ends.

'So . . . what happened?' I asked, my voice still low.

'We got beaten to it.'

I paused for another few paces, telling myself I could leave it at that. But of course I couldn't. 'Who by?'

There was a reluctant tinge of curiosity in my tone now, I had to admit.

'Someone not nice.'

Well look who's talking, I thought sourly. 'Jack the bloody Ripper?' was what I said.

Razoxane smiled at that: in a sly little way that made me think – absurdly – that I'd made a lucky guess. Absurd or not, I felt my neck start prickling.

She saw my unease, and savoured it. It drew her smile back out into a grin.

'Not quite, Rachel; though we're close to his old killing-ground. Right on the edge . . .' She tapped the matchstick against her teeth. 'But these three lost their guts to someone else. I rather think someone used a Scramasax on them.'

I was going to say, A *what*?; but we'd reached the roaring fringes of Bank now, and I'd have had to raise my voice. Not a good idea, even if the crowd did seem entirely heedless of the individuals in its midst. So I waited until we'd turned north and into Moorgate before asking: 'And what's one of those when it's at home?'

'A Dark Age cutlass,' she said, with undisguised relish. 'A weapon for butchers. The remains of one got dredged out of the Thames a while ago; its blade was still inscribed with the runes of chaos and destruction.'

Charming. My mind was suddenly filled with the memory of blood and guts, like an abattoir drain backing up. I grimaced, and fought it down again.

'So this was, like, a replica, then?'

She shook her head. 'No; a real one. Preserved and handed down for fifteen hundred years. Probably forged when all this was just fields.'

I tried thinking away these streets, these stony buildings . . . but my imagination wasn't up to it. Seeing the modern blocks and towers around here, I was hard enough put to picture what it must have been like before the Germans bombed most of it flat. Even Moorgate wasn't a name I could conjure much from; although the taste of bleakness in it had always given me a vague sense of unease. An echo of that awful crash, perhaps . . .

'*Lundenwic*,' said Razoxane drily.

'Sorry?'

'What the Saxons called this place. The Roman ghost-town they took over . . .'

She'd pronounced it the proper way, I presumed. London Witch.

Appropriate.

I adjusted my bag, which felt like it was full of bricks now; my feet were aching in my sensible shoes. I really needed to sit down. But Razoxane just kept walking.

'How do you know about this . . . sword thing?' I asked, trudging after her. After a moment – chilled – I added: 'It isn't yours, is it?'

Once more she shook her head. 'Just suspicions, Rachel: reasons to believe. But the Scramasax is only one piece of the puzzle.'

I side-stepped an oncoming pedestrian, glanced ahead – and saw a couple of policemen waiting on the next traffic island. They were obviously monitoring the inflow, and had been for some time: both looking bored and cold now, buttoned up in their black anoraks, with caps pulled low. Each carried a carbine slung over his shoulder.

Once more I felt the instinctive flush of guilt, and looked away: as if my cheeks – which must be glowing – would betray me. And Razoxane, whose crimes they'd been posted to prevent, just gave them an unperturbed glance and resumed the conversation.

'The past's been buried. They shovelled two thousand years of dirt down on it. But it doesn't rest . . .'

I stole another covert look at the coppers. So many guns on the streets these days; so few friendly faces. The boys in blue had grown up to be the men in black, and it gave me the creeps.

Yet what if Nick – my Nick – was to come up against a sawn-off shotgun tomorrow? Took the man on with just his truncheon, and got his guts blown out? My own stomach turned a somersault at the thought.

One of the policemen turned his head.

I broke eye-contact at once; and then we were turning west onto London Wall. I didn't dare look back; but something about that copper was niggling somehow. Something not quite right . . .

'You've gone very quiet,' Razoxane said idly, still chewing on her matchstick.

I gave her a grim-faced glance. 'All right, then. What does Wiking mean?'

She was silent for a few paces more; then clicked her tongue. 'Oh, Rachel. A little learning is a dangerous thing, you know. And a lot of it can be absolutely fatal.'

'Well, they say ignorance of the law is no defence,' I muttered. 'And I'll bet that goes twice for whatever the hell you're up to.'

Razoxane didn't rise to that. She was walking with her head bowed now; working the matchstick thoughtfully between finger and thumb.

'You think you need to know, then?' she asked softly.

I felt like someone who'd come blindfold to the edge of a cliff; who can sense the space out there: the void . . .

'I don't know,' I hedged, pulling back from the brink. 'Do I?'

Now she smiled afresh (except there was nothing fresh about it). 'I came here to right a wrong. It isn't done yet; and a lot more blood's going to flow under the bridge before it is.' She tipped her head back, gazing up at the grey sky; then looked seriously at me. 'A man I met on the streets once told me this: that the way things are going, there'll soon be no one left in this city but beggars and killers.' The glint of her smile once more. 'And undertakers, of course. Because the undertakers are the ones who clean up, Rachel. In every sense.'

I dropped my own gaze to the toes of my shoes; afraid she'd somehow see the memory that filled my head. The dream of her digging a grave . . .

Mine? Had it been mine?

'Know what necromancy is?' she asked.

I didn't; but the first two syllables told me enough. Made me think of *necrosis*: human tissue turned black and stinking rotten.

'Something to do with death,' I said warily.

'Raising and communing with the spirits of the dead,' she murmured, nodding.

I felt a cold gush of nausea. It settled in my stomach like slime.

'And . . . is that what you're up to, then?' My voice quavered as I said it; I could feel my forced calm beginning to crack. *She was at it again.* And suddenly I realized there was anger bubbling up beneath my fear: the same scared, frustrated rage I used to get from the news, watching the macho posturing of nations bring us closer to the brink. Suddenly I wanted to snap at her, just as I'd ached to scream at them. *Don't you ever learn, you stupid bitch?*

The audacity of the thought turned me instantly cold.

'After a fashion,' she was saying, unruffled as ever. 'But it's necessary, Rachel. For the good of others.'

I'd heard that one before.

'So what's blowing up tube stations got to do with it?' I wondered sourly.

'As I told you: I have my reasons. Things you'd be better off not knowing . . .'

'Well make up your mind. You're the one who invited me out here.' I gave her a sulky glance. 'Threatening me with your bloody autopsies . . .'

'I never said it would be me who'd do it,' came her mild reply. 'Only that someone would.'

Well, that was reassuring.

We turned south again, heading back towards St Paul's: we'd nearly come full circle. The sound of mainstream traffic grew louder with every step we took. I was just opening my mouth to try and extricate myself from this whole horrid *mess* when I glimpsed a police transit lurking down a side street on the right.

It was a common enough sight; I'd seen one racing to answer a call only a couple of nights back, the coppers inside gripping handsets and seatbacks hard. But after our encounter with the two armed officers back in Moorgate, I wondered if this mightn't be the same van I'd seen near King's Cross. That blue-eyed young Inspector and his team.

I gave it one glance, then carefully ignored it; but my heart had already started to beat harder. These were the tough guys, I'd guessed that much; anti-terrorist branch or whatever. And Razoxane's cool was all very well, but what if they came at us from every side, right now? I doubted even she was impervious to bullets. I knew I wasn't.

'What goes "bang-bang-bang-freeze"?' my old friend Mike had asked me once. *'An SAS man making an arrest . . .'*

Swallowing, I made a show of studying the cathedral ahead.

Razoxane tugged at my sleeve. 'Come on.'

Reluctantly I followed her lead – and found myself crossing the street. With a shrinking stomach I realized she was going to walk right past the bloody thing.

Oh God don't push it, please.

I hadn't the nerve to just cut myself loose and let the tide sweep me away. All I could do was trail in her wake, feeling like someone on her way to the scaffold. As we drew closer, I saw there were two coppers lounging in the cab. The one on the passenger side was my Inspector.

My cheeks were burning now; I felt *ashamed*. I'd pass him in the company of a killer, and he'd never know it. One of the very terrorists he and his lads were working their guts out to protect me from. As we came up to the transit, I shrugged my bag-strap firmly onto my shoulder and kept my head down.

Razoxane stopped beside his open window.

I glanced up again, in startled disbelief; and the policeman turned his head. He was hatless today, his fair hair slightly ruffled. In different circumstances, I'd have thought he looked quite dishy. Some vain little part of me even hoped he'd remember my face.

Razoxane shifted the weight of her rucksack; the gesture was as casual as her tone of voice. 'Well, Inspector: our paths cross again.'

The other smiled faintly – and it struck me then how *hard* those open features looked; how pale those eyes. He was sitting back in his seat, as though lulled by the monotonous crackle of crosstalk from the van radio – but something about him made me think of a cat. Outwardly languid, but inwardly poised: ready to spring when the mouse made its move . . .

'McCain. It's been a while.' Even his voice fitted the picture: a soft, ironic purr. His gaze flicked to me then, as I sidled up behind her; and if I'd still been half-hoping for a flattering spark of friendly recognition, I was rudely disillusioned.

I've had blokes undress me with their eyes before, of course; but not right down to the *bone*.

'How's business, then?' Razoxane asked, as if passing the time of day.

The Inspector's eyes held mine for a moment longer; I found my mouth had gone dust-dry. Then he looked back to her. 'I think we're about holding our own,' he said evenly. 'Yourself?'

'Not too bad . . .' She scuffed absently at the pavement. 'Made a couple of quid.'

'. . . *Whisky Oscar Five* . . .' the radio squawked. I found I was taking in every background detail; still groping for balance after the jolt of his stare.

'Been moved on, have we?' the Inspector asked drily.

Razoxane pushed up her hat brim, grinning.

'. . . *Receiving* . . .'

'. . . *Possible at Aldgate Station needs checking out . . .*'

'Haven't seen Whisky Indigo today,' Razoxane said conversationally.

'Oh . . . He's around,' the Inspector said. There was a rather unsettling satisfaction in the words.

'. . . *Roger. Relocating . . .*'

'We'd best be pushing on,' Razoxane said, while I struggled to avoid catching his eye again – and prayed she wouldn't introduce me as an afterthought.

'See you around,' the policeman said.

'Not if I see you first,' was her amiable response. She touched my shoulder and motioned me on. I complied with unseemly haste, and fell into step again beside her; letting my breath go whooshing out.

'You've got a bloody nerve,' I whispered, once I'd got some of it back again.

'More than you might think,' she agreed calmly, and led me across the road towards the vaulted cranium of St Paul's. I felt a sudden itch to look back; then thought of Lot's Wife, and didn't. On we went, around the back of the cathedral. I was just beginning to let relief sink in when I realized what it had been about that first policeman: what had looked wrong.

The carbine hanging from his shoulder had been fitted with a double magazine.

Oh, I'd seen SO19 blokes on patrol with two clipped together . . . parading around in their blue jumpsuits. But this pair had been scotch-taped for a quick reload. An increasingly familiar sight from war-zones round the world; but not a thing we saw on British streets . . .

A shapeless unease stirred inside me; it brought a small frown to my forehead.

Razoxane came unhurriedly to a halt, and looked at me. Her face unsmiling now; the lenses of her shades like black, unblinking eyes.

'So tell me: you want in?'

I hesitated – my unease washed away by more solid

fears. Fear of being blinded, gutted, burned. And fear of someone who diced with demons, and might lose both our souls . . .

Despite the acid in my stomach, I had to nod.

'Of course I don't *want*. You know I don't. But I'm in already – aren't I?'

Razoxane shrugged.

'So now what?' I asked – surprised that I didn't feel so different, now that I'd just put my life on the line. My soul on the line. I've never thought of faith as a leap in the dark, but that was what I'd made this time. Into the dark. Into the void . . .

She considered me for a thoughtful moment longer; then nodded, as if to herself. 'All right then, Rachel. It's time I showed you what it is we're really dealing with.'

I felt something cold and spidery move against the skin of my back.

'What shift are you working tomorrow?' she asked matter-of-factly.

'I'm not. Day off.' I moistened my lips.

'I'll meet you tomorrow evening, then. Seven o'clock. King's Cross.'

That sent a fresh spasm through my belly. I hoped to God it hadn't shown. 'Where . . . ?'

'Main station. I'll find you.'

Nick was on a Late tomorrow; I'd have all evening free. I nodded.

Razoxane smiled thinly. 'In the meantime . . . You've got something of mine with you, I think. I'll have it back.'

I blinked at her: quite flummoxed. 'Sorry?'

'In your pocket,' she prompted, sounding amused. 'You've been playing with it on and off the whole time we've been walking.'

All I could do at first was gape; even though I really should have guessed. Right from the start.

Razoxane waited.

Slowly I fished it out with my free hand: the Ace of

Spades spinner. I couldn't let it alone these days; half the time I didn't even notice. I'd slipped it into my pocket this afternoon without thinking. Reaching down to find and fiddle with it had become a curious reassurance.

I handed it over; she took it, and closed her shabby fingers round it in a fist. A look of unfathomable satisfaction on her face.

'Someone handed it in,' I said defensively.

'I guessed I'd left it somewhere in your building...' She smiled at my wide-eyed look. 'Just passing through, Rachel.'

I nodded dumbly. Suddenly even ITU didn't feel like a nice safe place any more.

'Right then,' she said amiably. 'Tomorrow at seven. I'll see you then.' She looked casually around; I followed suit, more nervously. 'I'd catch my tube back from Mansion House if I were you,' she continued after a moment. 'Stay with the crowds...'

The way she said it sent a chill through me. I glanced around again – then back at her.

She was chuckling softly.

'What's so funny, eh?' I snapped.

'You and me,' she grinned. 'A nice Catholic girl forced to walk with a witch. An angel of mercy in partnership with the Angel of Death. Even the damned in Hell must be amused.'

I gave her a grimace that hopefully spoke volumes. 'Yeah, sure...' I paused. 'So... what'll we be doing, tomorrow?'

'Going underground.'

'What for?' I ventured weakly; and watched her grin become an eerie little smile.

'A game of ghost-trains,' Razoxane said.

Chapter 12

Nick slid his arms round me from behind and *squeezed*. 'Gotcha,' he murmured against my neck.

Normally I'd have squealed, then squirmed around to kiss him. Normally getting caught in just my underwear felt nice. But today I just muttered, 'Piss off, Nick,' and shrugged myself irritably clear.

He relinquished his hold at once; I could see his surprise reflected in the bathroom mirror. Surprise and hurt. 'You're touchy this morning,' he said after a moment.

'Not really.' I glanced over my shoulder. 'Just don't much feel like mucking around . . .'

He gave a *have it your way* sort of shrug, and went back out. Unlike me he was dressed already; he'd been down to the corner shop to pay the papers. I'd just emerged from a disgustingly late lie-in.

I hadn't enjoyed it, though. Oh, there'd been the usual day-off reactions when I woke: the instinctive glance at the alarm clock, the reluctant stirring – and then the blissful realization that I could stay here as long as I liked. No sweeter moment than that, I sometimes think.

But then I'd remembered what I'd be doing this evening, and who with – which put an end to peace and comfort. All I could do was curl up and brood. Nick had tried cheering me up; I'd fobbed him off as patiently as I could, but he still hadn't taken the hint.

And he'd be leaving soon; out of the door and into the big bad world. Anything could happen out there. He could get beaten up, stabbed or shot just doing his job. I had a sudden, awful image of him gasping in a gutter, unable to focus on anything but my parting scowl.

I'd felt like this before, whenever we'd parted with bad blood between us; seized by the scary idea of having no chance to make things up again. I suppose any copper's spouse must feel the same. But after seeing that other policeman disembowelled, my fears for him this time were far more real.

Quickly I went downstairs. He was in the front room, studying the sports page with a sour expression. This time it was my turn to come up and slip my arms around him.

'Look, I'm sorry I snapped, all right? I didn't mean to.'

He just grunted; but after a moment, he reached absently up to stroke my bare shoulder.

'Reckon you'll be busy?' I asked.

'I know we will. Last time the Arsenal were at home, I lost count of the fights we got called to. It was like a bloody pub-crawl without the booze.'

'Well *take care*, all right?'

'Yes, Nurse,' he said dutifully – and smiled up at me. I was glad to see it.

'I do worry about you, you know. I mean . . .' I hesitated for just a moment '. . . there were firearms blokes in the City again yesterday. Very grim, they looked . . .'

Perhaps it was just my guilty conscience, but they'd still been preying on my mind long after Razoxane and I had parted company. Especially the Inspector. He'd really unsettled me with his stare: like he saw what I nursed inside me. Like he knew. Sat there at the centre of his radio network, like a spider waiting calmly in his web . . .

'Can't afford to let our guard down at the moment,' Nick said, his expression becoming earnest. 'I know you don't like it, Raitch; and neither do we. But what choice do we have, eh?'

'Oh, I'm not disputing that. It's just . . .' I held him a little tighter '. . . *you're* not going to get caught up in any shooting matches, are you?'

He shook his head. 'Nah. Leave that to the lads from

Nineteen. We've got a couple of firearms teams on secondment from outside forces, too; even from the MoD, so one of the lads was saying . . .'

I hoped he didn't feel the soft down bristling on my arms as the words sank in. For all that I'd had no choice, I'd taken sides against these teams of marksmen; I'd be a target as much as anyone if things went wrong. Yet I felt a flicker of relief as well – for Nick's sake. There'd be little chance of him blocking Razoxane's road. For that, at least, I could be grateful.

Giving him a last little cuddle, I straightened up and moved to the door: making what followed look like an afterthought.

'Oh . . . I'm going for a drink tonight with some friends from work. Shouldn't be too late, but don't worry if you're back before I am . . .'

'Oh, I get it.' He grinned half-ruefully, like someone who knows he's been excluded, but doesn't mind. 'Girls' night out, eh?'

I managed a small but perfectly-formed smile. 'Sort of, yes.'

'Want some money for the cab?'

Meaning: you are *not* going to be travelling alone on London Transport. I shook my head. 'I've got enough, thanks.'

'Well have a nice time, be good . . .' His smile became mischievous '. . . and *don't* get yourselves done for D&D, because I am *not* coming down to anyone's nick to bail you out.'

'I'll bear that in mind,' I said lightly, and went on out.

'Paint the town red,' he called after me; an entirely innocent choice of phrase.

It had me wincing all the way upstairs.

I've often heard the theory that moments of fear or grief or violence can somehow be absorbed by the places where they happen, setting up vibrations that last for decades.

It's one of the ways in which people try explaining uncanny atmospheres; unexplained noises. Ghosts.

I wasn't sure about the ghosts; but lingering on this draughty platform, only yards from a place where more than forty people died, I could feel an atmosphere all right. And it was *cold*.

Moorgate. Great Northern Electrics. The end of the line.

At the south end of the platform there were bright-red lamps, and buffers beyond them, and then just a solid wall, cemented over. It showed up palely in the dimness. Apart from that there was nothing to see. No trace of what had happened here twenty years ago; not even a plaque to mark the spot.

It could still come back and haunt me, even now.

I'd just been a little girl when a rush-hour train ran into that wall. I remember how the news had shocked and scared me: the thought of all those people dying in the dark. I imagined them seeing sky for the last time before being sucked under ground and southward to their fate. I'd had bad dreams for months afterwards.

And now here I was, where it had happened, staring at a dark dead end. After a moment, and with a little shiver, I turned my face away.

The platform was silent, almost empty; just the nine o'clock train to come.

Razoxane was sitting on the nearest bench, hunched pensively forward, turning the spinner in her fingers.

I walked back towards her, my hands pushed deep into the pockets of my coat – as if drawing the material tight across my shoulders would somehow make me warmer. But it didn't. I knew it wouldn't. The real cold was all inside.

I was picking things up from this platform. Sixth-sensations; echoes of thought. Nothing I could get a fix on, of course; my eyes and ears stayed unaware. But the tension was tightening my guts like a fork in spaghetti.

Razoxane's spinner turned slowly: rotated by her finger

and thumb. She'd taken her right-hand glove off, and a pentagram ring was gleaming on her finger. Her head stayed bowed in concentration. I found myself reminded of people dowsing for water – and realized that maybe she was doing the same sort of thing. For spirits.

Know what necromancy is . . . ?

Not that she'd bothered to explain all that. After materializing right behind me at King's Cross (and giving me the usual fright, the bitch), she'd just led the way down . . . deep down . . . to the Northern Line platforms, and brought us here to Moorgate. *The site of a disaster's a good place to start*, was what she'd told me. And here we'd been now for a good half-hour. She hadn't said another word.

I wandered slowly through onto the parallel platform; it was just as bleak. Ashen stillness: hard, electric dusk. I could too easily imagine some whispering presence out there in the tunnels, drawing near in response to her summons.

There was no one around at all on this side; I hastily retraced my steps. Razoxane raised her head as I re-appeared beside her.

Her coat was unbuttoned, her long scarf loosely knotted. I could see the amulet at her throat – and an ethnic-looking cross along with it. I clutched at a straw of reassurance . . . then remembered the crosses I'd seen in magic circles. Even sorcerers called on God to bind the things they summoned up . . .

'The trace isn't strong,' said Razoxane drily, lowering her gaze to her gizmo once more. 'Not round here. We need to go deeper.'

'Look . . .' I began; she did, and I almost lost my thread completely. With an effort I found it again. 'What are we . . . looking for?'

'We'll know when we find it,' she answered helpfully.

'But this is where it happened. You can feel it . . .'

'Just the echoes, Rachel. Like the light from a star that

burned out long ago. The souls have moved on.' She gave a faint, grim smile. 'I'm trying to find one that's still down here.'

With that she got to her feet, and nodded me ahead of her. 'Let's go back to the Northern.'

The Northern Line platforms ran deeper here: the next level down. I let the escalator carry me at its own pace, and even that felt too fast. Deposited at the bottom, I turned reluctantly left onto southbound. It might have been just my spooked imagination, but the air seemed staler down here. At least there were a few more people waiting.

Eight minutes to the next train south, according to the indicator. Par for the course.

Razoxane lowered herself onto one of the benches, and gave me what might have been intended as an encouraging smile. If so, it didn't work. Looking up and away from her shades, I found my attention caught by the luminous station sign above her head. The double-O in *Moorgate* made me suddenly think of empty, staring eyes; of mourning mouths. An unsettling reflection of all the echoes the name still held for me.

Razoxane tweaked the axle of her spinner, and began to turn it.

'What *is* that, anyway?' I asked after a minute.

'All sorts of things,' was her preoccupied answer. 'A means of meditation. A key to doorways . . .' She smiled again then: making what sounded portentous seem everyday. 'It's very old. Centuries old.'

'One careful owner, eh?' I murmured, with as much sarcasm as I could muster.

She shook her bowed head. 'It's been handed down; passed through many hands. I had it from a friend.'

'And who was that, then?'

'A master grave-digger,' said Razoxane softly. There was something like affection in her tone.

Not feeling like pursuing that, I went for a glum little walk to the far end of the platform: measuring each slow step. I stopped a little short of the tunnel's mouth, and leaned out cautiously to look. There was no sign of light in the depths; not even a zephyr of air. The gloom was thick and chilly.

Turning on my heel, I walked back towards Razoxane; a little more quickly than I'd come. I glanced behind me twice, as well.

Razoxane's hat brim came up enough to clear her shades; then closed down over them once more.

A gentle wind came wafting down the platform, sending litter rustling ahead.

'Listen, how long is this going to take?' I asked dully; it was already past nine.

'No longer than necessary, Rachel. But it can't be rushed. It *mustn't* be rushed.'

Or else what? I wondered. But rather than voice that uneasy thought, I said: 'You were really pushing your luck with those coppers yesterday, you know that? Well if you want to stick your own neck out, then fine, but don't risk mine as well.'

Razoxane smiled to herself; rolling the spinner between her palms.

The oncoming train arrived at that point, bursting noisily into the light. It rumbled to a halt before us, and sat there, whirring. The doors slid open; hissed and rattled closed. After a moment's pause the motor was engaged and the cars were moving out again, into the tunnel; I turned my head to watch the scarlet tail-lights receding in the darkness. The silence of an empty platform settled in their wake.

'Those weren't policemen,' Razoxane said calmly.

For a moment I was going to say, *oh sure*. Then another grisly thought occurred. After what Nick had said about secondments . . .

'You mean . . . like they're SAS or something?' The idea of her being on such friendly terms with a special anti-terrorist unit was even more surprising.

'Or something,' she agreed drily.

I frowned. 'That Inspector . . .'

'Morris.'

'I've met him before – when I was doing a soup run near King's Cross. He certainly seemed like an ordinary policeman; so . . .' And there my voice tailed off; because Razoxane's gaze had swivelled round.

'There were other people round you?' No trace of amusement in her low tones now.

'Um . . . no. I was . . . on my way home.'

She gave a soundless whistle. 'Rachel. You were walking the razor's edge out there, you realize? All along the line. And so easy to slip, and drop astride it . . .'

The image made me wince; I felt the coolest touch of fear between my legs.

'*They're not policemen*,' Razoxane repeated grimly. 'Not Special Branch . . . or SAS . . . or anything else your state calls sacred. No matter how corrupt your governments get – how much they dabble in shit and shadows – they wouldn't dare use law-givers like these.'

There was a pause. Somewhere out in the darkness, a train ran over distant points on its way to another platform.

'Then . . . who?' I asked faintly.

'Morris calls them his proactive interdiction team,' she answered; irony creeping back into her voice. 'That's a euphemism.'

'For what?'

'A death-squad.'

Standing here on this deserted platform, with its closed-circuit cameras overhead, I felt suddenly exposed. Even as the part of my mind it pleased me to call rational struggled to reject what she was saying, the rest of me was huddling tight inside my coat.

'My friends on the road call them scalp-hunters,' she added, still idly turning her spinner. 'Which just about sums it up. Especially when they take souvenirs . . .'

I gawped at her like a goldfish.

'I know,' she nodded. 'Convincing, aren't they? Uniforms and vans and everything. They just appear out of nowhere, do their business and disappear again. And nobody suspects a thing – because they don't leave anyone behind to tell the tale.'

'But . . .'

Her eyebrows came up from behind the shades. 'But?'

'You were *talking* with him.'

'So I was. I've come up against them before. It's all part of the game of cats and mice. Next time we meet, he'll try to kill me.' She smiled faintly. 'And I will try to stop him.'

Some more people had drifted onto the platform while we'd been talking. I glanced round nervously, but they all looked normal. Then again, what did looks have to do with anything any more?

Swallowing, I looked back at Razoxane. 'So . . . why're they after you?'

She considered her answer – and the spinner – for a moment. I watched the aces turning in her fingers.

'I suppose you'd call them mercenaries,' she said at length. 'But you couldn't meet their price with mere money. Not any more. They kill for a different coin now. Morris holds the purse-strings . . . and he'll only turn them loose in defence of something evil. Something hateful or destructive. His crusade of the broken cross . . .' The pallid smile had died on her face; but now I saw its ghost. 'The wages of sin are death, Rachel. And when they're paid, they always go through with the job.'

Another whisper of wind stirred my hair. Another train on its way.

Razoxane made a fist around her spinner, and let it rest against her mouth. 'I'm still not getting through. We need to move south. Down to Bank.'

Aren't you hateful and destructive enough then? I thought shakily as she rose to her feet. *Aren't you an evil worth defending?*

And if she wasn't: what was?

Turning, I saw the approaching train's headlamp glare out from the tunnel, as if burning its way through the dark.

If I'd felt the faintest glimmer of relief as we'd pulled out of Moorgate, it didn't last. Leaving that haunted station well behind us was little consolation for the grimness of Bank. Stripped paint and crumbling plaster; a dismal aura of decay. It made me think of a piece of old plumbing.

The platform emptied quickly – people getting on as we got off, or walking quickly down towards the exits. In a minute or two we had the place to ourselves.

The only movement came from the dot-matrix indicator: it kept going mindlessly through the motions, like traffic lights at an empty crossroads.

MORDEN 11 mins. Bloody hell . . .

Razoxane began to pace thoughtfully along the platform; the grim crunch of her combat boots carrying ahead of her, and bouncing flatly back. With her head bowed over the business of her hands, she looked like some spectral monk, manifesting in a long-forgotten catacomb. A black friar . . .

Or blacker sister.

Of course I didn't want to follow; but still less did I want to be left on my own. I trailed after her to the platform's end, the tunnel's gaping mouth – and back again.

She glanced at me then, and shook her head.

'Nothing yet. But I know we're getting closer.' There was an edginess in her voice I hadn't noticed before.

Me, I was getting more and more unnerved. This was starting to feel like a catacomb, all right; as morbid and oppressive as if its every niche had been stacked with skulls. Somewhere out there, in the labyrinth beyond the lights, I was convinced some ghostly thing was lurking. Something Razoxane was trying to invoke.

Part of my mind started whispering then. *You're trapped down here,* it told me. *You'll never see the sky again.* An awful twist of thought, like mental self-mutilation. Pursing my lips, I tried silently to shout it down, to focus on the home I knew was waiting: its textures of pine and paper, fridge magnets, books, plants, CDs, *anything*. I thought of Nick, and how he'd smile when I walked in through the door. I thought of *sex*.

Two hours, I told myself. In less than two hours we'll both be in bed, and all this will just be memory.

Razoxane said something.

My thoughts were dragged back underground to join me. I found her taking her hat off, and rubbing her forehead with a grimy sleeve. The thong had dropped down from inside the crown, and she used it to hang the hat comfortably behind her neck; then looked at me.

'Ready, then?'

'Er . . . what for?'

'I said, we'll try the Central Line platforms.'

I pulled a face. 'Do we *have* to?' Whatever she was working at, I reckoned we'd pushed our luck quite far enough.

'One more. Then we'll call it a night.'

I just shrugged, and followed dejectedly in her wake.

Walking down the link passage between the two lines, the cancer in my mind began to chew again. Sure, I could get out of this pit, and taste the cool night air – but what sort of gauntlet would I then have to run to get home?

What Razoxane had told me still beggared belief: even after the creepy feeling those coppers had given me. Their sinister aspect was only to be expected; they were psyched up for guerilla warfare, after all. Out to stop Razoxane in her tracks. So why should I believe her?

Every detail had been right – except those matched magazines. The sight of those had niggled, yes. The Inspector's stare had chilled me. But the more I thought it over, the less possible it seemed. Professional killers disguised as policemen – openly stalking their prey down the City's busy streets.

They'd never get away with it.

Would they?

As we trudged up the spiral steps to the Central Line, I shook my head firmly. 'No.'

'No what?' she asked, sounding interested.

'You're ... trying to scare me. Aren't you? In case I think of telling them.'

'Of course I'm trying to *scare* you,' she admitted calmly. 'And for your own good. Because if you go running to Morris, he'll take you somewhere nice and quiet ... then start the interview by cutting off your feet.'

I tasted bile, and gulped it back. '... don't believe you.'

'You can believe what you choose to believe,' was her unconcerned reply. 'But let me tell you something else about him. When they hit that squat in Kentish Town ... I'd moved on an *hour* before ... they could have killed everyone they found. But they didn't. A bullet through the brain and it's all over bar the grieving – assuming anyone cares enough to grieve. But to mutilate someone and leave them alive ...' She shook her head then; it looked horribly like grudging admiration. 'That way the suffering lasts a lifetime. That way the victim costs your society over and over again. One more straw on the spine of your welfare state ...'

I kept my outburst of frustrated fright pent up while someone passed us; then let it all blurt out. 'But they can't pass themselves off as coppers. It's just ... they *can't.*'

'Why not?' she came back softly. 'Who's going to see them and say different? The man in the street just looks, and looks away. Nobody wants trouble. As for the real thing ... well, they've patched themselves in to the radio network; the police on the ground can't move without them knowing. Notice the crests on their van?'

I blinked at the sudden question. 'No ...'

'Ministry of Defence Police. They've used that cover before. Official secrecy; state security. Your average policeman might not like them; but no one's going to ask too many questions.'

We'd reached the platforms now; they curved around the central stairwell, so sharply that you couldn't see one end from the other. A train was pulling out on the eastbound line; it rumbled and clunked into the distance as we found ourselves a seat.

The last stragglers made the exit, and left us to it.

Razoxane returned her attention to the spinner: fingering it slowly around and around, her face a mask of quiet concentration – as though telling some occult rosary. It really made me wish I'd brought my own.

Hail Mary, full of grace. The Lord is with thee . . .

But the words rang hollow in my head. Try as I might, I couldn't get his face out of my mind; nor the sound of the smile in his voice. Inspector Morris. Twice now I'd stood close enough to sniff his aftershave . . .

A muffled, hissing sigh came out of the tunnel.

I sucked air, and started up – then realized it had just been the points resetting. Gasping, I let myself slump down again.

Razoxane never moved. Apart from her mouth – which smiled.

'How many of them are there?' I asked weakly.

'Twenty-two,' she said.

Oh shit.

'Plus dogs.'

I gave her a stunned glance. She was still busy with her divinations.

'Jesus, what are you looking for?'

'Quiet,' she countered sharply – and I noticed her knuckles had grown white beneath their coating of grime. Bone-white.

I waited, listening to my heart. It was pumping faster now. We were still alone on the platform.

'See that?' Razoxane said then. The words seemed to drop from a mouth as dry as mine.

I turned my head. 'What?'

She was staring off down the tunnel; but apart from the string of lamps that dwindled like eerie fairy-lights towards St Paul's, I couldn't see much of anything.

'Occultation,' Razoxane breathed.

That didn't sound encouraging, whatever it meant. I frowned.

'Again, there,' she said after a pause – and this time I did see something. Saw one of those distant lights grow dim, and disappear.

Then another: closer, this time.

Then another.

Razoxane abruptly stood. 'Rachel, we need to get out of here *now*.'

I sat stupefied for a moment; then stumbled up after her. She took hold of my coat and pulled.

Something was speeding down the tunnel towards us, I realized numbly; preceded by the same ghostly wind that the trains always made. But this wasn't a train; it came without sound or lights. And the wind was colder than I'd ever known it, and darker too.

HAINAULT 6 mins said the indicator blithely.

We didn't quite run for the exit, but we got there very, very fast. Onto the steps, and downward; at that speed it felt like plunging into a red-tiled whirlpool. I was breathless and dizzy when we got to the bottom, but we neither of us paused. Back along the passageway we went, towards the lifts. The chill we'd felt up there on the platform still lingered on my skin. It felt like the sweat had frozen in my pores.

Razoxane turned, and walked backwards several paces; I twisted round to follow her gaze. Our footfalls echoed off the vaulted ceiling, and back around the corner. There was nothing there behind us.

A moment later we reached the lifts. The metal doors were firmly closed. Razoxane thumbed the nearest button, and we waited.

My heart was racing now: exertion and fright had

pushed it to maximum revs. Panting for breath, I glanced over my shoulder; then back at her.

Seconds ticked by.

Razoxane slammed the heel of her hand against the button.

The violence of the gesture almost kicked me into panic; it showed me her frustration – and her fear. And even as I stared, I felt the cold begin to catch us up.

It was as if an eddy of wind from the winter night above us had found its way down into the tunnels, and was sniffing out pockets of warmth. Instinctively I hugged myself tight.

'Emergency stairs . . . ?' I managed hoarsely.

She shook her head. 'No *time*.'

The lift was on its way. The muffled hum of machinery seemed almost mocking: deliberately slow. The squares of light beside the door inched down towards us.

The chill was beginning to cut its way in through my clothes now; and that was the least of it. I knew the cold – like the wind – was just a harbinger for whatever was following.

The doors slid open, bleeping; we fairly threw ourselves inside, and waited for them to close again.

And waited.

'*Jesus*,' I whimpered. Razoxane just braced herself, her booted feet apart, staring out through the open doors. The obsessive *beep-beep-beep* went on and on.

STAND CLEAR – DOORS CLOSING lit up at last; and a moment later the thick steel panels slid across. I felt like sobbing with relief as they closed off the dingy recess outside, and the lift – which now felt like a fridge – began to rise.

Even Razoxane let her shoulders sag at that; but her bloodless face stayed blank and tight. I just slumped back against the side, before my legs gave way completely, and ran a shaking hand into my hair: my damp and matted fringe.

After a few deep draughts of air, I raised my eyes.

'*God*, Razoxane. What the *hell* was that . . . ?'

Before she could answer, the lift's bright lights began to die.

I looked upwards, disbelieving. They were guttering and growing dimmer as I watched – bathing us in the same bleak twilight you get from strip lights firing up. The walls of the lift seemed to move solidly inwards – less a fridge than a freezer compartment now. A smothering claustrophobia seized me.

The lift lurched once, and stopped.

'*No*,' I almost wailed – and Razoxane dragged me forcibly back against the rear doors. The next instant, the lights had gone completely, and it seemed we hung suspended in inky blackness.

I realized then that something else was in here with us.

Before the scream in my stomach could make it to my mouth, her hand closed my lips and sealed them; her fingers digging into my cheeks and jaw as she pulled me close against her. Still staring blindly into the murk, I heard the rustling of her coat – and a metallic rasp and snap beside my ear. I knew at once it was the switchblade that she carried.

Even in this lightless box, the knife flashed a blue reflection – an eerie flare that pushed the gloom back almost to the walls. And by that glow I glimpsed a face; a horror-head craning towards us across the lift.

All that really registered was the mouth, stretched wide in a soundless scream. The rest was disfigurement and shadow, the features twisted beyond recognition. No way of telling if that howl was hatred or despair.

Then the dark came at us again, like a grave collapsing. And that was what it stank of, too: an avalanche of mouldy soil, laced with bits of rotting flesh. The flash of Razoxane's knife grew dim, became a glimmer – illuminating nothing now. And then the shape with which we shared this cell began crossing it towards us – preceded by a pressure-wave of cold.

Razoxane shouted something.

It made no sense; a line of Latin. Sounding somehow garbled and corrupted – a bastard version of the solemn tongue they used to use in church. She brandished her knife; then signed the air with its luminous blade. I felt her spittle graze my cheek as she shouted again.

A freezing stillness followed her words. It might have lasted moments; it felt like *hours*. I could hear her rapid breathing in the dark. The taste of her filthy wool glove seemed about to choke me.

Swallowing, she spoke again – more steadily. I still couldn't understand a word. Nor did I need to, to know that both our lives were hanging by a thread.

A sound like a sigh filled the lift; it made me think of something dissolving in acid. And then – starting with the faintest spark – the lights began to come on again.

I just gawped at them: staring with the same disbelief I'd felt when they'd started going out. Watched them wink, and flicker, and strengthen to a healthy glare – so bright it made me squint.

Apart from us, the lift was completely empty.

Razoxane released me then – so abruptly that I was caught unawares and almost fell flat. Clutching at the wall for support, I saw her features twist with rage.

'*Damn* it.'

Coming from her, even that mild expletive bore its original and dreadful weight. I winced. But some of the rage was directed inwardly, as well; I saw that in her face. A bitter surge of self-disgust.

The lift juddered briefly – and resumed its upward journey.

'Well you really fucked that up,' I managed: surprised at how calmly the words came. I reckoned I was probably in shock.

'So, nobody's perfect,' she muttered, folding her knife away.

I let myself slide exhaustedly down onto my heels, still

watching her. I could feel the cold sweat soaking in all over now; as if I'd taken a bath and dressed without drying myself first. And the wetness on my cheeks felt suspiciously like tears. I wiped them hastily off with my sleeve.

'For Christ's *sake*, Razoxane,' I asked at last. 'What was it?'

Razoxane leaned back against the opposite wall, and lowered her sombre gaze to mine.

'An Ankerite,' she answered drily.

The image of an entombed medieval hermit made me want to cringe. Bracing my elbows on my drawn-up knees, I pressed my fingers to my mouth.

'And yes, I . . . miscalculated with that one,' she went on grudgingly. 'It was stronger than I'd thought . . . and angrier too. Apologies.'

I never thought I'd hear her say that; although the word was as empty as the smile she gave me then.

The lift reached the top, and opened up. I got stiffly to my feet and followed her out. Down a low-ceilinged passageway, whose skin of plaster had been peeled away in parts, revealing its sinews of wiring and pipes. Through the ticket barriers, up the steps, and into the fresh, cool night.

Surely resurrection felt like this. *Up from the grave we arose*. I wanted to go dancing off across the orange-lit road – but contented myself with leaning over a crash barrier, and filling my lungs with slow, steady gasps.

Razoxane patted my shoulder. 'We can't hang around. Not with our friends on patrol.'

I straightened up at once. 'Oh shit . . .'

'We've got some leeway,' she added, glancing round the junction; the emptiness at this hour seemed positively eerie. 'I needed them drawn away from Bank tonight, so my . . . colleagues . . . left a bomb at London Bridge. They'll have swarmed over there like flies.'

I pulled a face. 'Just a decoy, right? I mean . . . with a warning and everything?'

'Warnings cut down on the confusion,' was her flat response. 'And confusion's what we need to stay ahead.' I opened my mouth in helpless protest, and she leaned coldly forward to curtail it. 'This is *my* war, Rachel. One without winners or losers. Just those who survive it, and those who don't . . .'

'What're you *doing*?' I asked plaintively. The thought of yet another bombing had left me shamefully unmoved; I was still too full of what we'd left behind us in the vaults.

'I told you: I'm righting a wrong.' She paused to put her hat back on; settled it comfortably. Then looked at me once more. 'Proclaiming sight to the blind, and release for prisoners – just like your Bible says. There are Ankerites under London. Under its stones. I'm here to set them free.'

PART 2

The City of Crows

Chapter 13

And it was night.

Try as I might to lose it somewhere, the Biblical quote kept coming back; turning up in my thoughts like the proverbial bad penny. I knew it was one of the Gospels; St John or someone. *Judas went immediately out. And it was night.*

It was night here now as well; with a wintry wind blowing sleet against the windows. But the fear that swilled inside me as I listened was far blacker and more bitter. That sombre line brought all its context with it: all its echoes of blood money and betrayal. I thought of the people who'd suffered and screamed already, caught up in Razoxane's war. I couldn't rid myself of the conviction that I'd sold them down the river with my silence.

Nick was still working through his block of Lates; I had the house to myself. A whole evening to brood on what I'd been through – and what must surely lie ahead. So here I sat, by candlelight: gazing blankly at the flame while the darkness rose inside me like a tide.

The last time I'd broken out the candles had been our anniversary; I'd cooked Nick's favourite meal with my own fair hands, and we'd eaten in that cosy golden glow. The romantic touch had seemed all the nicer alongside down-to-earth details like Sainsbury's plonk and me burning the pudding. We'd got really rather slushy, with lots of holding hands and gazing into eyes. I remembered it had been a lovely evening.

It might have been a million years ago.

Tonight I'd lit the flame for other reasons. Votive ones. Turning lights on through the house had brought no comfort; just made me feel naked and exposed. But the light of this single candle was oddly calming – even though cobwebs of shadow still clung to every corner. I suppose it reminded me of church.

My eyes strayed to the mantelpiece, and the plastic statue there. One of those horrendous saintly souvenirs; a cheap Madonna and Child. Nick had bought me it on our holiday in Spain, just to wind me up. And strangely enough I'd quite taken to it – and left it on view to irritate him in turn. Its shiny surface caught the glow now, looking more serene than ever I'd known it. And more real a reminder.

God knew, I needed one. The black bile of fear had reached my throat, and felt about to choke me.

Terrorists. And scalp-hunters. Littering London's streets with their maimed and murdered victims. The bomb at London Bridge had been spotted, the area cleared – but not quickly enough. When it went off, a young WPC had lost her sight. And I was caught in the crossfire as much as anyone, but I still felt as guilty as hell – as if knowledge alone was complicity. As if I could somehow speak out now, and stop it all.

But of course what really scared me was what had come after us from the Underground at Bank.

I'm here to set them free, she'd told me. Jesus.

Resting my chin in both hands, I watched the candle flame stroke the darkness; its length growing ghostly at its highest reach. It was mesmerizing, like a live thing – ever-changing; never changing. I thought of the light that always burned above the altar. The light of life.

But the dark of death had come up from the depths last night, and *breathed* on me. It had felt cold enough to snuff the brightest fires out.

Razoxane had offered nothing further. 'Just sleep on what you've seen,' she'd said grimly. 'I'll be in touch.' Which of course set my frightened thoughts freewheeling. And needless to say, I'd scarcely dared to shut my eyes.

An *Ankerite*, she'd called it. Like some demon visionary, sprung from its cell. I knew what necromancy meant now, all right. And maybe she hoped to bind such awful things, and draw power from them – but it had nearly gone wrong. So very nearly. Even the memory of that icy lift was enough to make me shudder.

I knew without doubt she'd go on trying.

Oh Mary. Oh Mother of God.

I didn't like to think what was out there beyond the curtain and the veil of rain. The lamps were on in our street – but what of the next one, and the next? A gruesome impression was growing in my head: one of living on the edge of an unlit medieval city. A warren of streets and buildings in utter darkness, resting on a network of catacombs and cells. And something ancient stirring in the murk . . .

I looked down at my watch. He'd be *hours* yet.

I raised my eyes again, towards the ceiling.

TV tonight would be an insult; even the companionable kitchen radio couldn't fill this silence. I needed something my mind could really chew on. Some of my books would fit the bill – but they were all in the bedroom. And the weight of shadow and stillness up above seemed suddenly so great that I half-expected the ceiling to give way.

I'd been scared of going upstairs as a child; we'd lived in a high and gloomy house, with my bedroom near the top. Two flights of stairs, and a minefield of creaky floorboards. Bedtime had been a race for the safety of my room; I'd sometimes been convinced I wouldn't make it. As for the empty attic-flat above me, I'd been certain that was haunted. Not even daylight could have tempted me higher up.

The sum of all those fears came oozing back to me now.

So I could sit here all night and soak them up – or make a move. I chose the latter, and took the candle with me. It would have been so easy just to switch on lights; but I found I didn't want to relinquish the living flame. Up the stairs I went, as resolutely as I could, and round to our room.

The candlelight warmed it as I slipped inside, softly pushing back the dimness. I went first to the dressing table, and left the candle there next to the little icon in its stand-up frame. A Russian Madonna from Camden Market: solemn and mysterious. That one I'd chosen myself.

Nick teased me about it from time to time, but I didn't mind. He wasn't to know, after all. I'd never told him about what I'd gone through before; and why faith – and even superstition – had been so important to me since.

From the window I could see the lights of London, like a glimpse of a galaxy. A city still very much alive.

Going over to the bookshelf, I pulled out the paperback that Razoxane had browsed through before me. Julian of Norwich, anchoress. She'd been a visionary as well: immured in stone. Her thoughts had helped me over many things, these past few years – but I wondered if even she could give me comfort now, with other dreamers breaking down the walls. Shadows with nightmares to share. Hermits of hatred and destruction . . .

She was mad. Razoxane was mad. No one could think of invoking such things unless they were mad.

I'm here to set them free.

Going back over to get the candle, I paused again at the window. The lamplit street was empty. Central London and the City lay a long bus ride south of here, but of course the lamps would be burning there as well. This was a modern metropolis, after all; not some shanty-settlement about to be devoured by the Black Death.

But the feeling wouldn't go away; that sick sense of another age encroaching. An older, darker age. Trying to grasp the reassurance of reality didn't help, for all my efforts. Because Razoxane was real as well. And so was that demon under the City; and the death-squad that prowled its streets.

And it was night.

Chapter 14

'Shh,' said the staff nurse gently. 'She's sleeping.'

Well I was glad someone was.

Sandra lay huddled up, her face towards us; looking wan and worn-out. I gathered she'd picked up an infection of some sort, which was why they'd kept her in. I tried not to think of her waiting miserably for a visit this long past week, and nobody coming.

'She was really upset this morning,' staff continued, still staring towards the bed. 'Someone let slip about what had happened to . . . Janet.' She glanced at me then; looking far from happy herself. 'One of the girls. You heard, I suppose?'

I hadn't, and said so.

'Oh. Well . . .' She paused, sniffing. 'Jan was Sandra's key nurse; they really got on well. She was found dead in her flat yesterday. Blocked heating flue, they said . . .'

I grimaced. 'God.'

'Sandra asked where she was, and we told her she was sick . . . but we were all in a bit of a state, as you'd imagine, and in the end it came out . . .'

'Poor girl,' I murmured: meaning either of them – or both. I'd met Janet Nicholls once or twice – an RSCN who'd liaised with us over Sandra's transfer. She'd been really nice.

'Anyhow . . . I don't want to wake her. But you can sit with her a while if you want.' She nodded at my uniform. 'You on a Late?'

'Yeah. But I've got ten minutes yet . . .' I touched her arm. 'I'm really sorry about your friend.'

'Thanks. It's a shame she's not awake; she's been asking

about you. But maybe she'll know you're here, somehow.'

I watched her walk away; her colourful patterned smock seeming painfully at odds with the strained look on her face. Then I went and sat next to Sandra's bed, and listened to her quiet, chesty breathing.

At least I could envy her this rest. I'd slept in fits and starts last night – coming finally awake with such suddenness that I must surely have been dreaming a moment before. But if I had, I couldn't remember it – which I found even more unsettling than some of my actual nightmares, making me wonder what visions I might have missed. What warnings . . .

I wondered if I still looked as forlorn as I felt. I'd been as pale as a ghost when I got up, and not much had happened to put the colour back into my cheeks since then. I'd not had the chance to tie my hair back yet, either; it was still hanging loose around my collar. I felt half-ready, out of step – like a waif off the street, with no enthusiasm at all for the shift ahead.

Sandra slept on.

Oh God, keep her safe, I thought: from all this death around her.

I waited as long as I could, but she didn't stir. At last, with some reluctance, I rose and slipped away.

In the corridor outside I hesitated briefly; trying – almost despite myself – to pick up traces of what I'd sensed that time before. But there was nothing. No echo. Just another empty corridor.

With a glance at my watch, I hitched up my bag and hurried down it.

As if I wasn't depressed enough, I learned at Report that we'd probably have two deaths before the end of the shift.

The first patient – a man in his twenties – was to all intents and purposes dead already. Only our machinery was keeping his heart and lungs going. A courier, he'd been with us for the three days since his bike had gone under a bus. The second set of brain-stem tests had been carried out this morning – with no one in much doubt about what the results would be.

The other patient had come in yesterday, while I'd been off. He'd been mugged or something: brutally beaten up, his skull smashed so badly that, after last night's emergency operation, no one had been able to piece the jigsaw together again. I found out they'd packed his brain with cotton wool.

'The relatives all know?' I asked, resignedly.

'Yep.' Jez scratched his nose. 'Ben's family are down-stairs in the chapel. Murdoch said he'll talk to them as soon as they come back.'

'Tests were negative?'

He nodded, once.

Ben was the cyclist. I could hear the hiss of his ventilator from here. I hoped they hadn't been praying for a miracle down there; they sure as hell weren't going to get one.

'Tony Campbell's parents are up in Scotland; the police have only just been able to contact them. Someone'll have to ring them when the time comes . . .'

Well, what a shitty day this was turning out to be.

'Ben's wife was telling me he had a donor card,' said Sue, looking thoughtful. 'Said that, if the worst happened, at least there'd be some good to come out of it for someone . . .'

'They're agreeable, then?'

'As much as anyone can be, I suppose. Murdoch knows; he'll raise it.'

'Good . . .' I broke off as the alarms started up around Tony's bed.

'Hello, he's off already,' Jez murmured, with a sort of fatalistic calm.

'We're not resuscitating, are we?' I asked, getting up anyway and walking quickly over. Johann joined me at the bedside, and shook his head. Lucy, who'd been changing an infusion at the time, helped me switch everything off. And that was it.

We screened off the bed while Johann formally certified death. Then he went to phone the Coroner's office, while Lucy and I got on with laying our patient out.

I made the last entry in Tony's nursing notes: a cross in the margin, and RIP beside it. The nurse's final gesture of respect.

Phoning his mum and dad had fallen to me, of course. I'd almost ended up in tears myself, listening to their incredulity collapsing into grief. The worst part was the distance between us; the blind, crackly ether. I knew I was just a voice on the end of the line, a name without a face. Not a person they could relate to in their struggle to cope with my news. I'd finally hung up with a guilty feeling of relief.

'All right?' Lucy asked quietly.

I glanced up from the notes. We'd had quite a conversation while we'd worked; it had lightened the air between us somewhat. I leaned back in my chair with a rueful smile.

'Yeah. They took it badly, as you'd expect, but . . . Well, it's done.'

'Ben's family are back. In the relis' room. Murdoch asked if you could sit in.'

I slumped, and pulled a face. 'God, it's one damn thing after another in this place . . .'

'Well, you're good at it, Rachel. *I* know that as well as anybody, remember?'

Good with the grieving: the ones left behind. Fair comment, I supposed.

I'd been down that road before them, after all.

Slipping into the relatives' room, I sat and listened while Murdoch explained about brain death, and us being unable to do anything more. Ben's wife – she looked about twenty, and rather obviously pregnant – kept nodding vigorously, even as the tears ran down her cheeks. Her voice was still steady as she asked about donation. Murdoch confirmed that everything would be straightforward.

'I'm glad,' she said, fixing a smile to her wet face. 'I'm so glad his life won't all be wasted.'

'Would you like some time alone now?' Murdoch asked – and she glanced at Ben's parents for approval before managing one more nod.

We left them to it. Half-way through the interview she'd groped blindly for my hand; I squeezed it now, and gently slid mine clear.

'I'll see you before you go,' I whispered, and followed Murdoch out. As I quietly closed the door behind me, Sue caught my attention and came over.

'There's a police officer come about Tony Campbell – for the Coroner. He needs to go through the notes for his paperwork. I've put him in your office.'

'Fine . . .' I acknowledged Murdoch's smile of thanks as he went towards his own office, doubtless to tie things up with the transplant team; then walked back with Sue to the station. Tony's casenotes were all signed up and waiting. I took them in to the policeman.

He was standing with his gloved hands behind him, his cap in one of them; studying my overcrowded pinboard without expression. Still wearing his yellow over jacket, like he'd come straight from traffic duty. A sergeant's chevrons glinted on its black epaulettes.

'Here we are,' I began, walking past him to my desk. 'If you want to make a start, I'll let the doctor who certified know you're here . . .' I put the folder down, and turned back towards the door.

To find him blocking my way.

I pulled up, startled – still expecting him to shift. He didn't. No word of explanation; his face remained blank. Its pale, stolid planes made me suddenly think of a piece of bled meat.

Oh God, I've been found out.

Someone must have spotted some clue – or seen me

talking with a suspect. And now I was going to get arrested in my own department: led away with the whole world watching. Murdoch would know, and Sue and Jez and Lucy. And *Jesus*, what would Nick say . . . ?

'Please sit down, Miss,' the Sergeant said – his tone as neutral as his features. He might have been giving directions in the street; except for his eyes.

His bloodhound eyes. They let me know – at last – who I was dealing with.

Oh Christ, I thought: and felt my scalp start crawling.

I did as he'd advised me: very carefully. Sinking down into my chair, as though dragged by the weight inside my stomach. Wide-eyed I watched him draw up another, across the desk from me, and settle himself comfortably.

His gaze held me nailed for a moment longer; then he looked down at the casenotes. Leaning forward, he opened the file, and smoothed its pages flat. It was only then that I noticed the finger missing from one of his gloves, exposing the callused flesh. The right forefinger.

The trigger finger.

'The Coroner will need to know who was present at death,' he told me formally, raising his eyes again.

I stared at him, mouth open. After a pause – and with the grimmest suspicion of a smile – he returned his attention to the notes.

Someone walked casually past outside.

'I see a Dr . . . Meier has signed the entry recording death,' the Sergeant went on, frowning. 'What is his first name, please?'

'Um . . .' I swallowed drily. '. . . Johann.'

He had his pocketbook out. 'Would you spell that, please?'

My mind had gone quite blank: I couldn't remember. It took maybe half a minute of mental hunt-and-peck to piece it back together.

'Now, Miss . . .' he said, still writing. 'You've got yourself into something way too deep. Right over your pretty little head.' The eyes came up once more. 'You've got one chance to get out of it now.'

I was almost squirming against my chairback: trying to put as many feet of space between us as I could.

'Who else was present at death?' he asked, without visible change of gear.

'I ... I was. And Staff Nurse Clarke. Staff Nurse Collins ...'

All the names were going down into his little black book. I wanted to stop myself, but I couldn't.

'And death occurred at 13:37pm?'

'Uh. Yes.' I craned reluctantly forward to check. 'Nearly twenty to two ...'

He nodded with satisfaction.

I waited, heart pounding.

'And where is the body now?'

'Downstairs ...'

He nodded again; then leaned towards me. Close enough for me to study his shaving cuts.

'Make no mistake, Miss: we always get our men. *Always*. That's why they *pay us*.'

I believed him, too: the gloating confidence of the statement brooked no argument. And how could even Razoxane hold her own against killers who'd hijacked the power of the *state*?

He eased back, his thin smile fading; jowls settling back into place like putty.

'I think that's all I need. Thank you, Miss.'

He got unhurriedly to his feet and put his hat on, drawing it down over his receding hairline. Settling the peak above his stare.

'You will shortly have another unnatural death to report?' he said; scarcely bothering to phrase it as a question.

I nodded, numbly. 'He's ... confirmed brain-dead. They'll switch off life-support as soon as his organs have been taken for donation ...'

'That won't happen,' he cut in, quite matter-of-factly.

'No' – God, why was I *arguing?* – 'it's all right, Dr Murdoch's going to ring the Coroner's office . . .'

'The Coroner will refuse his permission.'

I thought of Ben's wife; of her brave little smile, like sunlight through the showers. *So glad his life won't all be wasted . . .*

'Oh God, what for?' I demanded shakily.

'I have advised against it,' the Sergeant said.

Sheer disbelief left me speechless. He had already turned away, towards the door, before I managed to untie my tongue.

'*Why?* I mean . . . what the hell does it matter to *you?*'

'Why not?' He glanced impassively back at me. 'We're not in the blessing business, Miss. We do no one any favours.'

I couldn't help myself; I clambered up and crossed the room towards him. 'No, listen. *Please.* He's nothing to do with . . .' And that was as far as I got before his hand shot out to clamp my jaw shut like a vice. All I could do was snort for breath as he forced me back against the wall.

'Listen to me . . . *Miss.*' His leather fingers closed still tighter as he said it; I thought my jaw was going to come unhinged. Effort – or enjoyment – bared his teeth. 'That man will be *wasted* as a *warning*. Do you understand me?'

I made a small, squeaky sound. Even that was almost more than I could manage.

'But you can become a donor in his place,' he added: hissing the words against my cheek. 'We'll arrange it with pleasure. Remember that, before you speak to your Consultant.' His free hand settled on my breast. 'I'm sure there are many who'd like to receive your sweet little heart.'

I'd squinted my eyes against his closeness; now I felt them bulge.

Still holding me effortlessly upright with one hand, he reached under his jacket and unhooked the radio handset from his belt. His eyes never left mine as he raised it to his lips.

'Whisky Alpha from Whisky Indigo One . . .'

As we both listened to the crackling pause that followed, the worst thought yet occurred to my cowering brain. The very worst.

Whisky Indigo.

Wiking.

'. . . *Whisky Alpha receiving . . .*' his radio said, conveying the speaker's voice in all its coldness. Another vanload of them out there in the gathering night. And suddenly I almost squealed, as two and two came inexorably together.

Wampir.

'Just leaving premises now,' the Sergeant said. 'All clear?'

'. . . *Affirmative. No problems . . .*'

The Sergeant signed off, and re-hung his handset before finally releasing my face. I gasped and sagged back against the wall: aware of a prickling numbness round my mouth as the blood tried seeping back. The cheek he gently patted felt like latex.

'Remember. And forget.'

Expressionless, he went out.

I just stayed where I was: both hands pressed tight to my aching mouth. My skin felt like cold turkey – even under my clothes.

Wiking.

My mind was crimson with gouged-out eyeballs and torn-out tongues. I knew he'd do as much to me, and more – without a moment's thought. Sudden tears stung like splashed vinegar; the feeling brought things home more horribly still.

Reminding me I still had eyes to show my grief.

Chapter 15

An awful burden had been lifted. In a way I felt relieved.

Razoxane would have to lay off now: lay off, and let me go. Her enemies knew all about me. I could follow her no further. Getting me killed would profit her nothing.

I told myself so all the way home.

I also dwelt on what the Sergeant said: that this was my final warning. Last chance. Which surely meant they'd let me take it. No need for me to worry that a police transit might screech to a stop alongside me as I walked the last leg from the bus-stop. No need to fear being snatched and driven northward, out of London and into the dark. No need.

I lost count of the times I looked behind me.

At length – against all odds – I made it home. The house was well-lit and welcoming; Nick, on a day off, had resisted the temptation to spend the evening in the pub. Perhaps some of my nagging was getting through.

I told him we'd had two deaths to deal with – which doubtless explained my monosyllabic glumness to his satisfaction. It was something we'd both got used to, after all: giving each other time and space to get over what we'd seen at work. After the carnage at Kentish Town, he'd had one or two nightmares of his own.

When I came downstairs from changing, he was making the drinks in the kitchen. The smell of my Horlicks being mixed came drifting to meet me, so warm and familiar it was almost poignant. I went through and hugged him gently from behind, resting my head against his back.

'Listen, Raitch . . .' He said, still stirring. 'Say if you don't think this is a good idea . . .'

Sounds ominous I thought wryly. 'Try me,' I asked aloud.

'Well . . . I've got this really good mate at the station. Been on the job much longer than I have; he's looked out for me a lot this past year. I was wondering . . . if I could ask him round for a meal.'

'Chinese or Indian?' I asked innocently, nuzzling his neck.

'*Well*. I was, actually, wondering if we could maybe enjoy some of your delicious cooking . . .'

'Oho. Flattery will get you *nowhere*, mate.' I gave him a little squeeze; already feeling a bit better. It's amazing how resilient people can be sometimes.

'No, it's true,' he protested cheerfully. 'Seriously, Raitch . . . It would be great if you could.'

'Course I will,' I murmured. 'We can compare rosters, and then you invite him as soon as we're all free. What's his name?'

'Colin. Colin Taylor.'

I nodded; I'd heard his name before. Pulling back, I let Nick turn and hand me my drink. I was just taking my first sip when the phone rang.

'You can get that,' he grinned. 'I've already taken two calls from double-glazing firms this evening . . .'

I gave an exaggerated sigh, and went back into the hall to answer it. Leaned my head into the receiver. 'Hello . . . ?'

'Still don't want to accept our special introductory offer, eh?' Razoxane said.

Somehow I managed to hang onto both the receiver and my mug.

'Still there?' she asked after a moment.

'What do you want now?' I croaked.

'To tell you what happens next.'

'Listen . . .' I paused while Nick walked past, stroking me casually across the shoulders. Waited until he was back

in the lounge. Then swallowed, and began again. 'Listen
. . . One of them came to see me at work. A Sergeant. He
said . . . I had one chance to get out of this now.'

'And you believed him?'

'Well . . . what else am I supposed to do?'

I could almost sense her shaking her head. As slow and
sombre as a metronome. 'Don't let them fool you, Rachel:
there's no easy way out. They're just playing you along.
Once you've been separated from me, they'll wait until
you're beginning to bask in sunny relief . . . then snatch
you off the street – and start cutting.'

'*Stop it*,' I hissed.

'It's the truth: why not face up to it? You've seen what
they are behind their masks. They'll let no one get away
with that.'

I wanted to scream down the phone at her; to try and
reach her – wherever she was – with the hate I felt inside
me. The hate that was fuelled by fear.

'When's your next day off?' she asked remorselessly.

'Day after tomorrow . . .' I mumbled.

'Go to Moorgate at lunchtime: Finsbury Square. You'll
be met.'

'Razoxane. They'll *know*.'

'Not if we're careful. They're only human, after all;
more's the pity . . .'

'But if they've got the City staked out . . .'

'Morris knows he's pushing his luck already,' her quiet
voice insisted. 'Really pushing it. They're an extermination
unit; usually they hit and run. Every hour longer they stay
on the streets, they risk their cover being blown. So they
have to keep moving, before suspicion sets in: shifting their
roadblocks and switching their patrols. Keep your eyes
open, and you'll slip through the net.'

I listened, unconvinced. Only human, she said; but I
already had the finely-honed instincts of a fugitive, and
could imagine their eyes everywhere: watching me from
every corner. Only human; but their radio-net gave them

an almost supernatural advantage. Voices from out of the air. The speakers unseen, but somewhere close . . .

'Didn't I tell you that a little learning was a dangerous thing, Rachel? You can't just walk away now.'

Could I ever?, I thought back bitterly; and felt something trickle down my cheek.

'I'll see you,' she said, and hung up. I almost moaned despite myself. It was like a door closing; a light going out. Whatever I felt about her, she was still my guide through all of this. I was just a blind girl groping in her wake. And for the next day and more, I'd be feeling my way forward on my own.

Shakily I replaced the receiver. Sniffed, and wiped my eyes. Then went back in to Nick.

He'd seemed to appreciate the feel of my breasts against his back, with nothing beneath my sweatshirt to contain them. I hoped he was feeling randy tonight.

Right now I could really do with being screwed silly.

Next day, in the midst of routine paperwork, I let myself start doodling.

Bank, I wrote on a sheet of scrap. Then *Liverpool Street* below it. And *Moorgate*. And *St Paul's*.

Four stations in the City.

What the hell was this about?

I put the thought on hold while I answered the phone; scribbling some path. results down beside those names. The thing rang again before my hand was off the receiver. Somebody's relative: we talked for a good ten minutes. When I finally hung up, the little list was waiting to reclaim my attention once again.

I knew what there was at Bank, of course: that *thing*. Ankerite. Down in the tunnels. The word that crawled to mind was *nesting*. Not like a bird, but like an insect – or a rat. Razoxane had picked up its trace at Moorgate and tracked it there. Then given the nest a good old poke.

The memory made me flinch.

How many more of them were there? She'd said *Ankerites*, hadn't she? Plural. I thought of Liverpool Street; St Paul's. Had the bombings there been something to do with setting other demons free – turning them loose into the tunnels?

And might there be still others that she hadn't bothered to mention?

I studied the list. There was no line common to all four, I knew that much. No way could I work out which other stations might have *monsters* lurking just beyond their lights.

Bank. Liverpool Street. Moorgate. St Paul's.

'. . . Mornington Crescent?' asked Jez, leaning over my shoulder.

I glanced round, guiltily. 'Hi. Just, er . . . doodling.'

'Trying to predict where the next bomb's going to be, then?' he asked drily.

I smiled, and shrugged it off.

'Murdoch was in a strop this morning, wasn't he?' Jez went on, changing the subject without another thought.

He had been, too: we'd heard his end of the telephone conversation clearly through his office door. Words with the Coroner's office about last night's cock-up.

That's how everyone saw it; how I'd heard it explained. It seemed the wrong police officer had got the call – one unfamiliar with procedures. He'd advised the Coroner to refuse any request for removal of organs, pending further enquiries; then gone off without even completing the necessary paperwork. And while the Coroner's harried secretary had tried to straighten things out, Ben Phillips had breathed his last.

A cock-up of the first order; and now backs were busily being covered. Everyone at the local cop-shop was claiming someone else picked up the assignment; nobody quite knew who. Murdoch, in his zeal, had even called me in and asked if I could remember the man's number. No, I'd said, I couldn't.

So there he was, breathing cold fire and demanding disciplinaries; and all I could do was walk back to the desk thinking how they must be laughing up their sleeves. The bastards.

I hadn't been able to face Ben's wife when I went off last night; I'd practically sneaked off the unit. And that had been before the final insult to her injury. I couldn't bear to think what she must be going through today.

Bastards.

This time I felt strongly enough to really mean it.

Fright and fury: each was feeding off the other. Each threatening at any moment to gain the upper hand. All I could do was hope that Razoxane really was the lesser of two evils. And pray she knew her black business well enough to shield this city from whatever it was she planned to summon up.

On the way home, walking down into the tube, my eye was caught by the scrawled headline on a news-vendor's stand. A typical piece of *Standard* journalese.

TERROR POLICE SEAL CITY

Terror police.

Biting my lip, I kept on walking.

Chapter 16

Finsbury Square at lunchtime was cold and crowded. I kept my head down, and tried to think myself invisible.

There were no uniforms in sight, but that didn't mean much. My paranoia was working overtime anyway. I started by sitting on a bench, with my back to the main flow of traffic on City Road — but soon got too restless and twitchy to stay there. For all I knew they had men on the roofs, all ready to snipe at a sitting target. Keeping on the move felt marginally safer. So reluctantly I set to trudging round the square: glancing around me with growing nervousness.

I was beginning my second circuit when I came across the street preacher. He was standing with a Bible or prayer-book in one hand — haranguing the passing office workers. Few gave him a first glance, let alone a second; I found I couldn't blame them. The words 'Sodom and Gomorrah' reached my ears, which didn't augur well.

I really hoped he wouldn't catch my eye. Sometimes it was easy to scoff; I enjoyed playing devil's advocate whenever the Jehovah's Witnesses turned up on the doorstep (Nick normally left us to it). But sometimes I'd have mixed feelings, too, particularly when challenged in the street; self-righteousness fused with a vague, uneasy guilt.

When did you last stand up for something you believe in?

'The Lord told Abraham he would sweep away those cities — because of their wickedness . . .' the young man was saying earnestly. A covert glance as I closed the distance showed me the scruffiness of his clothes; his boots looked worn-out with walking. Patched jeans and an old blue coat. I guessed he probably lived with the poor and homeless – rather than just pontificate about them. But spouting on about the wrath of God wasn't going to win him many converts.

The preacher paused to watch the pinstripes sweeping past him; then continued in a louder, bolder tone. 'But Abraham turned round and said this: "Far be it from thee to do this – to kill good and bad together! For then the good will suffer with the bad. *Far be it from thee!* Shall not the Judge of all the earth do what is just?"'

Hardly the usual evangelist's angle, I thought wryly: someone talking back to God. Pleading for a place like Sodom. A couple of people had stopped to listen now. I slowed my pace as well – intrigued.

The man smiled at his impromptu congregation.

'So, the Lord said, "Very well. If I find fifty good men in the city, I will spare the whole place for their sake." And Abraham said: "But what if there are only forty-five . . . ?"'

An off-white biker's scarf was knotted at his throat: a poor man's dog-collar, I supposed. His hair was fairish and short, his beard scrubby. I paused at a safe distance, and listened while he continued his account.

It was a story I'd heard before, and rather liked. Abraham humbly but tenaciously haggling with God in an effort to save his fellow men. Wrath met with reason: an appeal to justice, and to mercy . . .

'. . . and the Lord said: "All right, then – thirty." To which Abraham replied: "Forgive my presumption, Lord . . . but there *may* be only twenty . . ."'

And at the end, the preacher made his point. Every city could be saved. Including this one. His audience duly drifted off, and I was about to do likewise when his face came round towards me. Quickly I dropped my gaze.

'If you could spare just a moment longer, sister . . .' he said amiably, '. . . I'd like to introduce you to a friend of mine. A good friend . . .'

His tone was more reasonable than most, at least; rather quiet and good-humoured. He'd spoken Abraham's words with feeling. I did him the courtesy of pausing to fish my crucifix out.

'You're preaching to the converted here . . .'

'That's good to know.' He gestured with his Bible, opening it at the place he'd been saving with his thumb. 'Can I just share some lines with you . . . ?'

I shrugged. Why not?

'"I saw the tears of the oppressed,"' he read, his voice and face becoming grim, '"and there was no one to comfort them. Strength was on the side of their oppressors, and there was no one to avenge them. I counted the dead – happy because they were dead. Happier than the living . . ."' He looked up at me again: unsmiling. '*Ecclesiastes*. Sobering stuff, isn't it? By the way – McCain would like a word.'

Oh *God*.

I could only stare as he closed the dog-eared book, and tucked it away in his frayed coat pocket. Still not smiling; but I caught a glint of bleak amusement in his blue-grey eyes.

'Don't be afraid, Rachel,' he said softly after a moment. 'Only believe. Come on . . .'

He didn't sound Irish, this one; but that was hardly a reassurance. It seemed that Razoxane's cohorts were everywhere – crawling out from under every stone. Maybe street-corner evangelism was just as good a cover as begging. Most people studiously ignored you either way.

So was he carrying a gun as well as a Bible? Ready to strike terror into the people he'd just smiled at? I felt a sick sense of betrayal in my stomach as he beckoned me on towards the nearest bus-stop.

'You don't look too happy,' he observed as I caught up.

I made a non-committal noise.

'You're scared of her, aren't you? McCain, I mean.' His

fleeting smile held genuine sympathy. 'That's good. I won't need to warn you how truly dangerous she is.'

This time he read my sullen look correctly. 'Ah . . . You think I'm one of her familiars. Am I right?' He shook his head without offence. 'It isn't true, Rachel. I serve God, and no one else. McCain still follows her darker way. But I would not spurn her just for that.'

A bus pulled in at that point, wheels sliding up against the kerb. He checked the number, nodded to me and we climbed aboard. He paid in small change; I flashed my travelcard. Still no wiser as to our destination, I followed him up onto the top deck and a seat in the front.

'You . . . know about her then?' I ventured cautiously, while we waited to move off.

He braced one booted foot against the window bar: staring forward through the glass.

'I know she's a murderer,' he said evenly. 'I know she's a witch. But I also know she's trying to find her way home. And if God will still welcome her, how can I not?'

I wondered if that was still her motivation, then; just like the last time. The fallen angel's dream of paradise regained. Whatever the cost.

But how could raising demons ever lead to her redemption? It made no sense. And nor was I sure this personable preacher really knew the worst about her.

Necromancy. Terrorism. *Madness*.

The bus pulled smoothly out, and turned northwards into City Road.

'My name's Gary, by the way,' he said as we edged through the traffic. 'I preach the Good News to the rich; they bloody need it. And you're a nurse, right?'

I nodded.

'So how did you get mixed up with McCain?' There was frank curiosity in his tone.

'Long story.'

'I imagine it is,' he murmured after a pause. I sensed him

163

studying me, but kept my eyes on the road. Watching for policemen . . .

'Sort of a love–hate relationship, isn't it?' Gary went on drily. 'I know the feeling . . .'

I snorted. 'I wouldn't say love-hate, no. Not even hate–hate. More like hate–*loathe*, really . . .'

He laughed.

We were out of the City now, the rampant dragon that marked its northern boundary well behind us; through Old Street's intersection too, and still travelling north. If I stayed on this bus long enough, it would almost get me home.

How close to home would Razoxane be waiting?

The thought sank like a stone to the pit of my stomach; but at least it was a relief to put the City behind us. Everything seemed to be focused in on the Square Mile: the ancient acre under all those modern buildings. Maybe (I mused hopefully) the dragons that guarded its approaches were really part of some invisible barrier: there to keep something inside from getting out.

Just so long as they succeeded . . .

I glanced at Gary. 'I quite liked the sermon back there. Not a side of the story you usually get to hear . . .'

He gave a small shrug. 'People don't want to hear about fire and brimstone; why should they? What good's that to them . . . ?' He fell silent as we crossed Regent's Canal; then touched my sleeve. 'All right: next stop.'

We got off near a newsagent's. I hovered uneasily, hands in pockets, while he looked around us. The road was fairly busy, but there was a gone-to-seed stillness in the air – flooding back in whenever a car was safely past. Patches of waste ground opened out the landscape. On the far side of the canal, a derelict warehouse or factory rose grimly against the sky. Its bleakness seemed to sum up the whole area round this crossroads.

'Okay,' said Gary softly. 'Back across the bridge.'

Right away, I knew where we were headed.

The factory loomed up as we approached it – seeming larger and more forbidding with every step. The brick walls of the nearer building were begrimed with soot; but some glass still survived in the highest windows, and glinted in the sunlight. The place just sat there brooding, on the edge of the stagnant waterway; a desolate barbican to hold the bridgehead. Gary waited until an oncoming car was past, then led the way down the side-road to its main gates.

They were locked and chained; a notice on the fence warned of security guards on the prowl. I caught a whiff of woodsmoke nonetheless. A hint of habitation.

Gary moved down the fence to where a sheet of corrugated iron seemed to be plugging some gap. He lifted it aside, and I saw the wire behind it was all unknitted, and we could both squeeze through. Which, carefully, we did. Waiting for him to drag the rusty sheet back into place again, I glanced around.

There were several people watching.

I gave a little start; then took a breath, and forced a smile. No one smiled back.

The factory's two main buildings were separated by a concrete courtyard, almost choked by withered clumps of nettles. From this angle – this close – the four-storey shells seemed to tower like cliffs, blocking off the sunlight and most of the sky. The reception committee were sitting or squatting round a small, almost smokeless fire in the shadow of one of them. The several scruffy layers of clothing worn by each was enough to tell me that this was the closest thing to home they had.

'It's all right,' Gary said behind me. 'This is Rachel. She's a friend of McCain's.'

That won some flickers of interest. I walked over with him, picking my way between nettles and bits of brick; they all watched me come.

The far side of the yard was open to the canal; I could see right across to where we'd been standing a few minutes before. The sunny side. It seemed a very long way off.

There were six or seven of them, of varying ages. Two were women; one little more than a girl. I looked from face to face, trying to find something of the character in each, behind the masks of beard or dirt or windburn. A couple were well drunk (there were beer cans strewn around like spent cartridges), their eyes as blank as fogged windows. Another, apparently still sober, gazed up at me with an eerie kind of awe. Something in his stare suggested he wasn't on quite the same wavelength as the rest of us.

He was the one who said: 'Have you come to hear your fate as well?'

I swallowed, and raised my eyes to break the contact. Beyond him, where the sediment of premature dusk was at its thickest, some crude lean-to bashes of cardboard, blankets and bits of wood had been built against the wall. Ground floor windows peered out from between them like eyeless sockets. And someone else was sitting there: wrapped up in black, head bowed. Only this close did I notice her. And only then did the ashy brim of her hat come up, to show me her ashen smile.

'Rachel,' said Razoxane drily. 'Afternoon.'

She was sitting on a wooden crate, and hunched forward over a second; playing patience with herself, or so it seemed. Some cards were already laid out before her, and she was idly fingering the pack as she contemplated the spread.

I took a wary step closer; despite my distaste, I leaned forward to look for myself. The pictures on the cards were faded – but they'd clearly been colourful once, and the designs were like none I'd seen before. Tarot cards, I guessed after a moment.

She set down another; then raised her head once more. 'Quite impressive, aren't they? Sixteenth century Italian. Just think of it, Rachel: how many fingers have touched them, these past four hundred years; how many fates they've foretold . . .'

They looked old enough, I reckoned grimly: all dog-eared and worn. I didn't bother to ask who she'd got these off. Whatever the reply, it was unlikely to be encouraging.

A *master grave-digger* . . .

'So what do you want?' I muttered, straightening.

She riffle-shuffled the remaining cards with a pasteboard whirr, and pensively reshaped the pack. Then smiled thinly up at me. 'Maybe to tell your fortune.'

'I don't believe in those things,' I said flatly.

Her smile widened. 'You sure? They can tell you so much; mean whatever you want them to mean. See . . .' she turned the topmost card between two fingers, and showed me it '. . . The Moon. Reminds me of Stevie there, who men call mad because his mind works differently to theirs.'

The youth with the hungry gaze had already turned to watch her lay her cards. Now he glanced at me, and nodded.

'I was in hospital,' he confirmed seriously. 'But then they let me out. I wanted to tell them what I'd dreamed, but no one listened. No one but Gary here. And McCain . . .'

I nodded back, uncomfortably. Aware that I was very much part of the society that had cut him off (I still found him a bit unnerving) – and of the health service that had abandoned him in the wilderness of London. At the mercy of *wolves*.

'And this . . .' Razoxane continued, a fresh card in her glove and grubby fingers '. . . is the King of Cups. Like Jim, who's not been sober since I've known him . . .'

'Away with ye, woman,' one of the drunks growled; yet something in his tone – and in Razoxane's grin – suggested that this was a scene they'd played before; and were pleased at its revival.

Still smiling, she set down the card among the others, and turned the next.

'Ah'm no pissed,' the man called Jim grumbled in the background. '*Youse* lot're pissed . . .'

'The Fool,' said Razoxane breezily, ignoring him;

displaying the next baroque image. 'For Gary, because he's a Christian.'

'Well, thank *you*,' I murmured sourly. But she shook her head.

'It's not an insult, Rachel; you should know that. Refuse to comply with the rules of a rational world, and you'll always be dismissed as a simpleton: a clown. But some of us know other worlds. And older wisdom.'

She had a point, I supposed: so sharp it actually made me feel a little guilty. But even if Paradise was really her goal, I knew the worlds and wisdom she had in mind were very different from those Gary and I might aspire to. Different, and infinitely darker.

The people by the fire were passing fags around. They weren't in a packet; probably they'd been begged for, one by one. A fistful of smokes, to stave off the nerviness and hunger pangs and cold.

'Want one?' a fair-haired bloke asked me.

I shook my head. 'Er . . . no, thanks: I've given up.' A quite inadequate response, but I was too thrown to express it any better. The gesture had really touched me.

'I'll leave you with the Witch of Endor, shall I?' Gary asked, sardonically.

'Going to suffer me to live, then?' Razoxane grinned up at him.

'Just this once, perhaps.' His expression, still amiable, grew earnest. 'I'll bring you home, McCain. One day.'

'Maybe I'll beat you there,' she said lightly.

'Not on the road you're taking. Believe me. But it's never too late, sister. And someone's always waiting – until the last of us gets back safe.'

Razoxane only smiled.

'I'll see you around,' Gary said to me. 'God bless.'

I watched him join the gathering round the fire, setting off a cheerful exchange of banter; then looked back at Razoxane.

'Got a card for me?' I asked after a moment.

She drew one in answer, and held it out on her palm. A shrouded skeleton, wielding a scythe. It had no name — nor needed one.

I don't believe in this, I thought; *it's just her little game.* But my stomach turned over anyway.

'Don't worry,' she said drily. 'It doesn't mean death as such. Not always. More often, a change of direction; an upheaval. Something that makes you see the world through different eyes.' She laid the card down with the others. 'And that's what I've got to offer you this afternoon. Revelations. If you come with me, and share them, your life won't be the same again.'

As if it wasn't falling down already. As if I had a choice. I had an almost bilious urge to spit out something to that effect — but I was in this up to my nose already; why open my big mouth? I just gave a sullen little nod.

'So how many of these are terrorists too?' I asked after a pause. Keeping my voice low just in case.

'None of them. God, no.' She seemed grimly amused at the suggestion. 'Jim there used to be a sergeant-major in the Scots Guards; he'd go *berserk* if he knew what I was up to.'

'So . . . nobody knows?'

'Not about them, no. We stay separate: scattered. To these good people I'm just a fortune-teller; someone with the Sight. They respect that. Gary knows more than most — but still not nearly enough.'

I kicked morosely at a piece of brick, sending it skittering away. Glanced at the circle of smokers again; then back at her.

'So how long before Morris finds this place too?'

She shrugged. 'Who knows?'

'For God's sake, Razoxane. Don't you care?'

'This business will be settled soon,' she came back evenly. 'And then we'll have other wars to fight, on other fields, and this city can rest in peace. So come with me, Rachel. And let me show you what we have to do.'

* * *

As the afternoon wore on, we crossed London; walking back down to Old Street, and catching a northbound tube. The wait on the platform was daunting enough – only one stop up the line from Moorgate. The breeze from the tunnel's mouth felt like the eerie respiration of something lurking to the south; the train that finally came crashing into view had already passed through that station, and Bank, and all the black lengths of tunnel in between. Seeing those faces sliding by and slowing to a stop, I couldn't help thinking of what might already have watched them from the darkness – maybe close enough to breathe against the windows.

I'd needed a moment to marshal my strength before stepping aboard.

Razoxane gestured me up and out at Camden Town. We were well clear of the City now: it added to the relief of our ascent into daylight. I let her lead me through the mainstream rush of the High Street into quieter backwaters; tree-lined streets. But the leaves were dead and gone, and only brittle twigs reached up towards the sky.

'Been here before?' Razoxane asked, as we came to Primrose Hill.

I shook my head – and felt a little sorry that I hadn't. It rose before us, broad and green, like an island in the sombre urban sea; a quite unexpected refuge.

We started up the path towards the top. Not hurrying; the incline soon grew steep enough to make me dig in my heels. Not speaking, either – though the silence between us was oddly comfortable in its way. Razoxane had hung her hat behind her neck again, and seemed almost to be savouring the quiet.

There were benches at the highest point, but no one much was using them – it was too chilly for sitting around. The sun had gone in a while ago; the day was slowly greying out. I turned, and saw London spread before me: toytown-small, yet seeming almost close enough to touch.

Nick and I went up to Hampstead Heath sometimes, to walk and enjoy the view across the city; but this was much nearer to the centre – a last piece of land cut off by the tide. Beyond the foliage of London Zoo, a forest of towers and spires rose up through the faint, frosty haze. The Post Office Tower was still imposing; but the dome of St Paul's looked as fragile as an egg. I studied the panorama almost hungrily – lapping up the detail. It was a sight I wanted to remember.

'"And the devil took him to an high place . . ."' said Razoxane behind me, a smile in her voice '". . . and showed him all the kingdoms of the earth . . ."'

I glanced round irritably. 'Look, pack it in, will you?'

Maybe those shades hid a glint of mischief in her eyes; I wouldn't have been surprised. But then she shrugged, and redirected her blank gaze towards the city.

'Quite a sight, isn't it?' she murmured after a minute.

I nodded – suddenly a little wary. Remembering what she'd promised me this afternoon. I guessed it was coming now.

'Imagine . . .' she said slowly '. . . if you'd been standing here an age ago. Nineteen hundred *years*. When almost all of this was fields and forest . . .'

Like with Moorgate before, it was a struggle: thinking a city away, foundations and all. I looked at her again.

'Before Lundenwic, they called this place Londinium. The first London. Nineteen centuries ago it was just a shanty-town – something you'd scarcely see from here. Close to where the City stands now. See . . .'

I followed her pointing finger back towards St Paul's, and the monolith of the Nat West Tower beyond it.

'The Romans built it – and Boudicca burned it down. Boadicea, you sometimes call her. They still dig up the ashes she left behind. There was a firestorm here; a massacre. And worse . . .'

Still watching the City, I waited grimly for the worse. It all seemed like a history lesson, impossibly distant – but

I'd already learned another lesson well enough. How the past could reach up through its grave-soil to touch – and twist – the unsuspecting present . . .

'Some citizens were taken alive,' Razoxane went on. 'But only to be butchered. Sacrificed. Ritually slaughtered. The land was still under the shadow of the druids, and now they demanded their due. Some prisoners were dedicated to the river-gods, body and soul. Their heads were hacked off – and thrown into the Walbrook.'

'The what?' I asked.

'A stream; long hidden now. Built upon. Buried. But some said that it was haunted by the souls of the people who'd died there. That their spirits had somehow been bound by the rites of their sacrifice.'

'And . . . it flowed where the City is now?'

She nodded. 'Right through it. By medieval times it was an open sewer – before they covered it in. There were culverts in London Wall, taking it down into the bowels of the Old City. They must have seemed like gateways to the underworld itself: all noise, and blackness, and bars to block the way. Yet the old tales of river-ghosts were gradually forgotten. And down in the blackness, things began to brew.

'What you might call the incubation period, took centuries to pass. The spirits of the dead congealed beneath the City; becoming stronger. Feeding on night-soil. Mutating into *demons*.' She glanced at me sidelong; smiled at my grimace. 'Well, what else would you call that thing we saw the other night?'

I didn't bother to dispute it. Demon was the word.

'The earliest manifestations I've turned up were in the 1500s: haunted cellars around Lothbury and Cannon Street. A certain Renaissance scholar wrote of *Ankerites* – dwelling deep in their hidden cells. Offering up their canticles of hate. Because that's all that they can compass now: a rage against all things living. All things free. All things which are not cursed as they are . . .'

I nodded dumbly. Rage and hate were what had followed us up the lift-shaft at Bank, that much was certain. I could still feel it: the cold, corrosive breath of something *evil*. I wondered if I'd ever have the nerve to take the Underground alone again.

Razoxane kept talking.

'The stronger they got, the further they could crawl. Some followed the course of the stream to Moor Gate, and the place you now call Liverpool Street. There were Roman burial grounds under both those sites, which seem to have drawn them. Possibly they can leech off the energies that still linger in such places; or maybe they just gravitate towards misery and death.'

In the pause that followed, the distant rush and murmur of traffic carried clearly up to me: the sounds of a city alive. But it was the silence behind those sounds that really registered. The stillness of the voids beneath the streets.

A term I'd recently seen in someone's casenotes crept into my head. *Occult sepsis . . .*

Without warning, Razoxane walked over to the nearest bench and sprang casually up onto it – turning to stare down at the cityscape from a higher point still. There was an almost avid look on her face now.

'You know the speed of light?' she asked me.

The non-sequitur threw me for a moment; and so did the relish in her voice. She was enjoying herself, I could tell – which was always a bad sign.

'Hundred and eighty-six thousand miles a second,' I said cautiously. Physics was never my strong point at school, but some things stuck.

She nodded. 'Now, how about the speed of darkness?'

I thought of that black shape racing towards us: coming so fast. I swallowed, and had no answer.

Razoxane stood looking down at me, her smile indulgent now. Sort of. A breeze stirred her frayed coat tails round the ragged cuffs of her jeans.

'Hatred is an elemental force,' she said mildly. 'An

173

essence you just can't grasp with mere words. You have to draw cosmic comparisons, even to begin to understand how powerful it is. Look to the stars. You know what a black hole is?'

'Vaguely.'

'It's a good parallel. Appropriate. If one of those sucked you in, it would crush you to nothing in twenty *millionths* of a second. Think of it. If you can begin to grasp that – that sort of absolute destruction – you'll have some idea of what we're up against.'

I looked back towards London. Maybe half-expecting it to start subsiding as I stared: collapsing into the depths beneath. 'And . . . you think it's a good idea to turn these spirits loose, then, do you?' I tried to make it sound sarcastic, but the quaver in my voice belied me.

Razoxane was still studying the view. Something told me it was our height advantage – looking down upon a *city* – that really held her rapt.

'I told you,' she said after a moment: 'I'm going to set them free. Free of this earth altogether. For nearly two thousand years they've been condemned to linger: no wonder the focus of their evil's so intense. But they hate because they can't hope. And hope is something I can offer them now.'

The notion of Razoxane giving hope to anyone was enough to make my jaw drop. When I managed to get it working again, I said: 'Well the one under Bank didn't seem too interested, did it?'

She shrugged. 'There's work involved, to bring them round. Hard and dangerous work. Because even they were people once. And people prefer the devil they know, Rachel. Even when it *is* the devil.'

The temperature was falling as the afternoon waned. The cold was getting more discomfiting by the minute. But the chill I felt now came mostly from within.

Razoxane dropped lightly to the ground, and straightened. Smiling still.

'Come on,' she said, with that old, cold irony of hers. 'We've seen enough from Primrose Hill. It's time to go back down into the everlasting bonfire.'

'Why?' I asked, as we descended slowly. 'Why are you doing this?'

'I've got my reasons.'

I remembered what Gary had told me – about her wanting to find her way home. The prodigal daughter in search of her redemption. 'Think you're on a mission, do you?' I muttered.

I didn't really think she'd rise to it. Her quiet laugh surprised me.

'Why not? Setting the prisoners free is the will of God, isn't it?'

'You reckoned you were doing the will of God last time – and look what bloody happened.'

'All right. So I thought destroying that cabal would be enough. It wasn't. This time will be different, Rachel. Freeing trapped souls, and letting them fly. On wings as eagles. And I'll follow.'

In order to commit the greatest evil, you must first believe you're doing a great good. Who'd said that? Which wise man? I glanced at her, and wondered if I should just let it go. But in the end I found I couldn't.

'Razoxane, listen . . . Whatever you're after, you won't find it by killing innocent people. Blowing them up. You *can't.*'

'I haven't the choice,' she came back flatly. 'It might take *hours* of communion to bring one to the brink – but there has to be some act of destruction to push it over. Some elemental *shock*. It's like snapping someone out of a trance – except that the trance is a state of being . . .'

Shock was the word that really registered – again with a clinical weight. Like toxic shock: the sort that ruins your system. Kills you. I let out a small, despairing sigh, my hand in my hair.

'I'm not expecting you to like it,' Razoxane said calmly. 'But you need to understand. You're good at that, after all: trying to comprehend instead of just condemning.'

It was the first time I'd felt guilty about that aspiration.

We walked in silence as far as the railway bridge, then stopped again. I could just about see over the sidewall and onto the tracks, flowing south towards Euston or wherever. Turning away, I rested my back against the iron, and gave Razoxane a sulky look.

'So how many have you already *liberated*, then?'

'Two; at St Paul's and Liverpool Street. Which leaves the one under Bank; and probably one at Moorgate.'

'How do you know, though?' I asked.

'About the Ankerites? It's been a while since I learned of their existence.' She looked past me, down the empty lines. 'There's a night route across London for those who know it; one of many old tracks. I was following it on my way up country when I fell in with a fellow pilgrim. We shared our tales — and his whetted my appetite for more. A tale of demons that dreamed beneath the City. So, I started to search. And at length I turned up some writings by that scholar I mentioned earlier. An occultist. He claimed to have identified — and even communicated with — things he called Ankerites, which lurked under medieval London. This was before the Fire, of course; but I managed to place his references. He'd worked it out, about the Walbrook. The next step was to go divining . . .'

I watched her fish her spinner out, and turn it thoughtfully between her fingers.

'By the time the sewers and tubes were dug, it seems some of them had grown strong enough to leave the course of the stream altogether; like the one I tracked down at St Paul's. A source from the last century reckons there was one under Aldgate, too, at one time; but I've been down there again and again, and found no trace. There was only a faint echo at Moorgate — as if that one's withdrawn deep into the dark. But the Bank Ankerite is the strongest I've encountered; like a cancer at the heart of the City. It's going to be the hardest to excise.'

A train passed below us then: an endless Inter-City job, snaking down towards its terminus. I waited for the rattle and clank to fade before asking the inevitable.

'And afterwards . . . you're going to blow the bloody station up?'

'Not the whole station, no.'

Oh, well, that's all right then.

'. . . But whichever platform it manifests on will need to be gutted.'

'What if your *terrorists* have other ideas?' I challenged her, still wincing.

She gave a soft snort of amusement, still watching the receding train. 'Who, they?'

'They're not stupid, Razoxane. What if they won't play ball?'

'I think they will, Rachel. I'm having to exert some . . . influence on them; but not much. They're already consumed with their vendetta against your country. I just have to propose, and they quite happily dispose.'

She closed her grimy hand around her spinner. *A fistful of spades*, I thought.

'I was fortunate to find them,' she went on drily. 'It's quite difficult to set a tube station on fire; and ritual slaughter tends to draw attention. This way you get an instant of chaos – of *flux*; it just breaks their grip, and flushes them away.

'They were so naive, you know: brother Frank and his comrades. His *active service unit* . . .' She pronounced that last with an ironic Irish twang. 'They thought hiding among the homeless would be such a good idea. They never dreamed that there'd be someone in the midst already – just waiting for people like them.'

'God help us, you'll use anybody, won't you?' I murmured, with something approaching awe.

After a moment I added: 'Including *me*.'

'At least I've told you my tale,' was her reasonable reply. 'You know it all now. That's your advantage.'

I made for an unconvinced shrug – and felt an image flash across my mind. A glimpse of Razoxane shovelling slime. As if gouging out a grave; or robbing one . . .

My head was still crammed with her explanations – details it might take hours to digest – but I was suddenly sure that she hadn't told me everything. That she was keeping something back.

I almost pursued it; then lost my nerve. I knew enough already. Let it lie. Pushing myself back upright, I continued on across the bridge, with Razoxane trudging at my side.

'So what about Morris?' I asked wearily, as we walked back towards Camden Town. 'Where does he fit in?'

'Where indeed? Think of him and his men as carrion birds . . . here to feast on this whole decaying carcass.'

'So what does that make you, then?'

She smiled. 'The scarecrow.'

She was certainly dressed for the part, I thought. But she still put me more in mind of those glowing-eyed hyenas in the car-crime ads. A scavenger herself.

'Most people would say that Morris is mad,' she continued drily. 'A psychopathic sadist. But he's not. It's just that most people can't cope with a world in which men like him are sane.'

I wasn't sure I could, either.

'Let me try and explain things to you this way,' she continued calmly. 'Think about your Second War. The Japanese. A demented, evil enemy – yes?'

I opened my mouth – and hesitated.

Razoxane gave an approving little nod. 'You're right: there aren't such easy answers. A medieval culture given twentieth century weapons, and they waged their war accordingly. They behaved the same way your people behaved in about 1400. And your people couldn't cope with that – so they simply called them evil.

'It's similar with Morris and his mercenaries. Except that

they haven't been retarded; they've regressed. Back to a thought-world of absolute brutality.'

I shrugged up inside my coat in a sort of slow-motion shiver. Medieval. Just the word made me think of dirt and blood and rusty black iron. People with hacked-off hands, hung up in cages. Nick had dragged me round the London Dungeon once. I hadn't enjoyed it.

'Remember it, Rachel,' she was saying. 'They're twentieth century born and bred; they act and talk like all the boys you grew up with. But their attitude's out of the *Dark Ages*.'

Still hunched up, I asked: 'So . . . what happened to them, then?'

'Simple. They were trained to kill – and found they had a taste for it.'

'Soldiers?' I ventured.

'Mostly. Not your ordinary foot-sloggers, though. The specials. The shock-troops. The ones your society's most scared of. Why else do you think they're venerated?' She gave me a small, ironic smile. 'Superhuman: less than human. Because they lost part of their souls along the way. The quality of *pity*.'

And when have you shown pity, you hypocritical cow? I didn't say that out loud, of course; just waited for the rest.

'Morris recruited the most pitiless he could find for his private army. The ones who'd be wandering from war to war for the rest of their days, because killing was the only life they knew.

'He tempered them in Eastern Europe. They were a paramilitary unit, hiring themselves out to the highest bidder . . . for the dirtiest jobs. Then, sometime last year, they came back. But they didn't stop.

'You recall those news stories last autumn? That family of Travellers who'd broken down . . . and when someone from their convoy went back to help, they found them burned in their bus. And then those vagrants who got herded into a derelict church which was set on fire. All Morris's work. Evil for evil's sake.'

'But *why*?'

'Who knows?' was her casual response. But not quite casual enough, and I realized then that she *didn't* – and was perceptively unhappy with the fact.

It didn't cheer me up much, either. I listened anxiously as she continued.

'Morris has his own private war going on. It's crossed Europe and lasted years. The enemy is anyone alive.' She shook her head then, as if in awe at her own words. 'You know what he told me once? That God had already done all the good, so the evil was up to him. "I *improvise*," he said . . .'

'So . . . he's protecting the Ankerites purely because they're evil?'

'Presumably.'

Oh, Razoxane, I thought. I heard that heartbeat's pause. I'm getting to know you too well, my nasty little sister.

There's something you're not telling me.

Whatever, I didn't pick up on it. I still didn't have the nerve.

Had she walked to Yugoslavia in those dusty boots? Had her pilgrimage taken her that far? I could picture Morris and his men in autumn-coloured camouflage, peddling their loot for tarot readings . . .

Medieval warlord meets Dark Age Traveller.

By the time we'd passed back through the bustle of Camden to the bus-stop by Sainsbury's, I was beginning to wonder when we'd finally part. I had weirdly mixed feelings: wanting on the one hand to be free of her, and able to breathe again; reluctant, on the other, to lose sight of my protector.

My angel of death.

So I made no protest when she halted with me: jamming her hat back on again, and leaning against the old church wall to await the oncoming traffic. Nick was on the last of his Lates tonight; if she wanted to come all the way home, she could.

'Think I'm a hypocrite, don't you?' she said under her breath; flicking ash from her sleeve in a mockingly fastidious gesture. Watching it fall.

'When did I say that?' I came back, too quickly – and felt the warmth fade from my cheeks as she turned her head.

'You didn't; but you thought it. Your face is full of it. And you're right: I've forgotten what pity feels like, too. But that's something I'll find again, when this is done.' She looked back towards the road; and when she spoke again, I barely heard her. 'Whatever else, I've never killed a man just on someone else's say so, Rachel. Nor simply because I've been paid.'

From the high crossroads at Manor House we walked slowly back down towards Stoke Newington, through a grey and frosty dusk.

It had been a long, long day.

The clouds had thinned enough to clear the moon: its ghostly disc hung over the park, and I felt it patiently pace us all the way – growing gradually brighter as it crept into its own. I glanced at it again as we crossed the street. From this angle it seemed to float just above the great church spire – as if to mock that high, proud building.

I let us in. 'I won't stay long . . .' Razoxane said as she wandered on into the lounge. It made me remember being walked home after my first date, back when I was still in school. The thought brought the briefest smile – which died as the implications caught up.

Maybe that's just what she'd done. Seen me home safe – because the streets were safe no longer. Not for me.

Swallowing what felt like a bubble of phlegm in the back of my throat, I went through after her. The room was dim with dusk now, and she'd chosen the chair in the dimmest corner to curl comfortably up, like a cat.

Black cat. Witch's cat.

I didn't sit myself; although my feet were practically numb, I was too uneasy to stay still. Stepping up cautiously to the window, I peered out through the nets. The street was empty; the park at its end deserted.

'All right,' I said at length, turning back. 'I'm not an innocent bystander anymore. So what happens now?'

'Maybe anything, Rachel. After all, I'm improvising too.'

'Good, well, that's a help . . .' I couldn't conceal the hurt behind my sarcasm: the helpless, achy feel of being used. 'Listen, you've already walked in and screwed my life up. *Again.* What more do you want?'

'You,' came her calm reply. 'I want you. We're like sisters, you and me. Two faces of the moon: the bright and the dark. We need both to win this war. I told you before – we've walked apart too long.'

That was debatable, to say the least.

'Morris wages war on medieval terms,' she elaborated drily; 'so we need a medieval set-up of our own.'

'How do you mean?' I asked faintly.

'Someone to kill, and someone to pray.'

I just stared at her. Sitting there in the dimness, wrapped up in her coat, she seemed not quite real; a shadow herself. Soaking up the dusk like a sponge.

'Lost for words?' I just glimpsed her smile through the gloom. 'Start with St Francis. Didn't he thank God for Sister Moon – and Sister Death?'

I looked away.

'Got a light?' she asked after a while.

I looked back again, surprised. Then shook my head. 'I gave up, remember?' I told her piously.

'You'll have matches in the kitchen, though.'

I hesitated for a moment – then relented, and went to fetch the small packet of BryMays from the cupboard above the cooker. Coming back in, I tossed it across; she caught it deftly. Then lowered her head again, and I watched her half-gloved fingers go through the motions:

that old, familiar sequence that ended with the rasp and flare of yellow. But even the match-flame couldn't quite pierce the faceless dark beneath her hat brim.

In silence, she let it burn.

The tiny tongue of flame stretched upward, glowing gold. As it began to spread down the blackening stick, she turned it slowly in her fingers – trying to preserve it; but in vain. Hot bright yellow quickly cooled to luminous blue, quivering like a ghost as it died. And then it was out, with just a wisp of pale smoke to mark its passing.

A pause. Then she let out a shaky breath.

'You see that? Light and life. A shred of Heaven – that's why it always reaches upward. But it goes, and I can't follow. Can't even bear to look, without these glasses . . .'

It struck me then that Razoxane was an addict; and her fix came in twenty pence boxes. Not pyromania at all, but something even stranger – and far more poignant.

'This life's like a night with no stars,' she went on grimly. 'There's nothing to guide me. I've even tried praying, but no one answers. And I've had enough now, Rachel. I want to go *home*.'

There was raw frustration in her voice – and something more. A vulnerability I'd never dreamed to hear. An echo of a lost little girl.

Climbing back to Heaven up a mountain of dead.

Later, when she'd gone, I went tiredly upstairs; still without switching on a light. The door to the spare room stood open, and on an impulse I walked in. The wide, uncurtained window seemed to draw me, and I found myself gazing out across benighted back gardens, away from the streetlamps and the moon. And up above, the clouds were passing, glowing orange from the lights of London.

It was ages before I could tear myself away; watching in haunted fascination as they drifted, shapes of angels, across the vast night sky.

Chapter 17

Weaving my way down the busy aisles of Sainsbury's, I found myself still hoping I could lose myself among them – as if the bright lights and bustle would somehow overwhelm my fears. This was reality, after all. This was the everyday. Doing the house shopping on a rainy winter's afternoon.

Nick, who knew his place, was pushing the trolley; I was in charge of the list. It wasn't often we could do this together, and the novelty made even this routine chore seem rather fun. Usually.

Today it was beginning to drag.

Still, I tried my best to keep smiling: for his sake as much as anything. My moodiness had begun to rub off, these past few days, and things had been a bit tense at times. I'd made mention of deaths on the unit getting me down – which sounded a little selfish, considering he'd just spent a couple of cold shifts knocking on doors, following the abduction and murder of a little boy.

The worst of it was, he seemed to think it was something he'd done. Upset or annoyed me somehow. Walking back to him now with my latest selection, I managed a grin – and saw how gratefully he lapped it up. It made me want to kiss him then and there.

Instead I consulted the list again.

'Right, then . . . On to the meats.' I tugged at his sleeve. 'C'mon, we're nearly done.'

I didn't let go as he steered the trolley back into the main aisle; just slipped my arm through his, and snuggled briefly up against him. 'Listen, I know I've been a bit of a pain recently. Sorry.'

'Shhh. Don't worry.' He reached for my hand, and squeezed it. 'My fault too. We all get our off-days in jobs like these.'

So we wended our unhurried way on through the clumps and clusters of fellow shoppers. I watched a harried-looking mother trying to reason with her offspring; a silver-haired old lady choosing cat food. Yuppie-types who'd maybe got off early from the office. And students who made me feel almost old. None of them looked like people living in a war zone.

But only because they didn't know it yet.

Shrugging off that most unwelcome thought, I gently disengaged myself from Nick to choose some mince for the freezer. His mate was coming round next week, and I'd decided that one of my chillis might be a nice idea. I picked the extra-lean for a change; we could afford to splash out this once.

Nick leaned comfortably forward over the trolley's push-bar. 'What we do now, Kemo Sabe?'

'Pay, unfortunately.' I gave the list a last once-over, then raised my eyebrows. 'Your card or mine?'

'Reckon I can handle this one.'

As we made our way back towards the checkout, I leaned over to study the trolley's contents. 'Nick, if we can get this lot into three bags, could I hop off at the library? I've got some books to go back.'

'No problem.' He gave me a sidelong smile. 'Can't have you getting fined again, now, can we?'

I smiled sweetly back at him. 'No, that's right: we can't.'

The bus made slow progress through the grey, wet streets, but we got there in the end. I glanced back at Nick from where I waited by the exit doors; he grinned encouragingly. Three stuffed bags of shopping huddled round his feet like orphans – but it was only a short walk home from the next stop along.

Then the doors unfolded, and with a little wave I ducked out into the drizzle.

The library was a welcome refuge: warm and comfortably quiet after the slosh and hiss of the road outside. After unloading my paperbacks on the returns counter – and lingering just long enough to ensure they'd been checked back in – I made my way over to the History shelves.

There were a couple of books on Roman Britain; another on the Dark Ages; and one on the history of London. I took them all to a table and settled down. With trepidation, I began to turn the pages.

The index notes for Queen Boudicca led me to the first great fire of London.

That had been in AD 60; her rebels had burned it to the ground. And just as Razoxane had said, the conflagration had been accompanied by carnage. I studied the quoted accounts with faintly nauseous fascination. Women had had their breasts cut off and stitched to their mouths. They'd been impaled on stakes. People had been gutted, hanged, burned, crucified.

Skulls had been found in the bed of the Walbrook stream.

And as if all that wasn't upsetting enough, some of the background detail made my fine hairs rise as well. A sense of awful, impending doom had apparently overtaken the Roman colonists, before the first blow fell. A man called Tacitus had written of shapes like corpses washed up by the tide; moans – and shrieks – in empty buildings; a phantom town in ruins. Reading, I got an eerie impression of their plight – these settlers in a land they thought they'd tamed. Suddenly the roles had been reversed, and they'd found themselves trapped, cut off; surrounded by vast, bleak, hostile countryside – and hearing the stirrings in its forests. The sounds of something crazed and hungry, coming for its revenge.

Perhaps, in those final days, they'd begun to believe in older gods than theirs. Older, and darker too.

Nineteen centuries on, the city I lived in was just as complacent, even though it rested on the ashes, soot and bones of its ancient forebear. But there were malevolent *survivals* of that first massacre, and now they'd been woken. I wondered sickly if history might yet repeat itself . . . then slammed the last book closed, as if to trap that thought within it. But in vain. A moment later, I felt its buzzing begin afresh, inside my aching head.

That night, I dreamed again.

The first one was mercifully short, which made it no less scary. Without warning I was in a church, filled with shadows and foggy incense; a few votive candles staining the gloom. I raised startled eyes from my prayers, to find a black shape waiting before the altar – a form with no face.

Razoxane.

I knew her at once, though her head was bowed, her hat brim hiding her features. Her body was as still as an inked silhouette, so that only the hands seemed alive – her pale, protruding fingers standing out as she shaped and shuffled a pack of cards. I watched it split apart and blur back together in her grasp – like a master magician's sleight of hand. And then she took the topmost card, and held it up.

The face of a goat. It leered at me.

Il Diavolo.

I gasped in fright and flinched away; she raised her head. No face was there beneath the hat, just bottomless dark, and two blobs of orange light like glowing coals.

I woke with a start. Straight up to the surface. If I'd been a diver, I'd have died of the bends.

A thick silence filled the bedroom – so dense that I had the sudden, panicky thought that Nick had stopped breathing. But after a moment I felt the gentle stirring of his back, and relaxed against him with a sigh.

I was curled up close already; but if I'd clutched at him

while I was under, or whimpered in his ear, he hadn't woken. Not so surprising, really: he'd a lot of lost sleep to catch up on.

I shifted uncomfortably. The shock of my dream had settled inside me like a pint of cold sick. I couldn't get that horrid card out of my head. The grinning goat. It took a long time to convince myself that the room temperature hadn't fallen; that those weren't stealthy footsteps I'd heard on the stairs. That it had all just been a product of my spooked subconscious. Nothing more.

My mouth felt furred-up and dry – but I wasn't about to leave the safety of bed to get myself a drink, nor even risk my head above the duvet. For all I knew she could be there in the darkness – waiting patiently for me to stir.

I lay listening to the silence for many minutes, but nothing moved in it. We were alone. The house was empty and secure. After a dreary while, I began to doze again.

As my mind slipped its moorings, a faint noise reached me through the gloom. A distant rasping. Not a part of the real world, I realized with a strange detachment; my ears were already deaf to that. This was something inside my head. There'd be no escaping it.

All I could do was drift into the dark, and follow the scraping spade.

At first I just floated: face down in black water, like a nude, drowned swimmer – limp and weightless, at the mercy of ghostly currents. The sounds of digging came and went. My stomach seemed to swell with acrid gas.

Abruptly I was ashore and floundering. Not on dry land, though, not terra firma: mud sucked and bubbled beneath me as I clambered to my feet. I found that I was dressed again, my long raincoat trailing in the mire. Rain beat down against my heavy head.

I lifted it, ploughed the hair back from my eyes – and saw the building site around me. The battle-zone. And not ten yards from where I stood, Razoxane was up to her waist in the hole that she'd dug.

Her back was to me; but as she turned to slop a spadeful of wet earth aside, I saw her tense – then slowly move her head, as though trying to catch me from the corner of her eye. Even as I waited in rigid apprehension, hugging my wet clothes round me, it struck me that in this dream condition she had a blind spot – and I was in it. Sensed, but – somehow – not seen.

After a skin-crawling pause, she resumed her digging.

I watched another soggy lump come up; heard the blade go squelching down into the mud again. Scrape . . . slop. Scrape . . . slop. *Shit-shoveller*, I thought numbly.

A part of me had stayed detached throughout; and now that part began to reason. My sleeping mind was showing me symbols, it insisted – just like the time before. Picturing Razoxane's quest to liberate things from their underground prisons.

To raise the dead.

The blade of the shovel struck wood.

The shock almost broke my grip on the scene. Even as I groped for a purchase, I heard her draw the iron down the length of what I instinctively knew was the lid of a coffin. It squealed like chalk down a blackboard – and symbolism or no, I was suddenly and mortally afraid.

Razoxane straightened, and pushed up the brim of her hat; it dripped and overflowed. Then she turned again, and looked right at me – as if she'd known where I'd been standing all along.

I lost my grip completely: let go, and fell back into the darkness; back into my bed. Even as I landed, I remembered what had happened when I'd dreamed this sequence last time.

Oh God, Nick, wake me up. Please wake me up.

But nothing happened. No shouts from overhead; no crushing CPR. Just silence. *Normal sleep*, I thought hopefully. Despite the knot in my belly, I tried to make myself relax.

'. . . *waste, though,*' someone murmured after a minute. ''*specially when they're as young as her.*'

I didn't open my eyes; they were open already. Sight seeped back into them, along with a dismal daylight.

I was on my back and staring at a plain white ceiling.

This wasn't right. Not right at all. I could even smell a tang of disinfectant. And then a nurse leaned into view above me, and drew aside my sheet. She was wearing a dour expression – along with a disposable plastic pinny and latex gloves.

I wasn't wearing anything; the atmosphere chilled the already cooling perspiration on my skin. And once again I couldn't move a muscle – not an eyelash – as she looked across my frozen stare to talk to someone else.

'*She must have been really desperate, you know. How many did she take?*'

'*Couple of hundred, according to A&E . . .*'

Brisk, business-like tones – but not without compassion. And behind my blank face, I'd already started sobbing with fear. It was all so horribly detailed: as vivid as a vision. A vision of the future.

Last offices. They were going to lay me out.

Gently they began to wash me: soaping the sweat of my death-throes off my body. Talking casually as they worked. The feel of their shiny latex fingers made me want to squirm, but I was utterly powerless. With professional calm they cleaned my breasts and belly; my flanks and thighs. My left arm flopped loose as they turned me to do my back.

Oh God let me wake up.

I knew what was coming next; I'd done this job myself, too often. I even hoped the knowledge would be a handle, something I could haul myself back into wakefulness with. But it wasn't.

The quieter nurse stooped to sponge me clean between

the thighs. Then she took some cotton wool wadding, and began to stuff it in.

'You okay?' Nick asked muzzily as I came back from the bathroom.

'Um . . . yeah. I've been a bit sick.' I climbed into bed and settled carefully down again. He murmured his concern, and I let him fold loose arms around me; but still felt too delicate to be cuddled. And even after a cold glass of water, my breath still reeked of bile.

'Reckon it's something you ate?'

'Dunno. Could be . . . a bug going round or something . . .'

'Don't go in tomorrow,' he advised me softly. 'Take a day sick.'

I just nodded miserably, and tucked my chin into his shoulder. After a minute or two, he was off again, and I was left behind – feeling very alone, despite the warmth of his flesh beside me. Very aware that, while his mind was elsewhere, and dreaming brighter places, there'd only be me to listen to this silence, as a parliament of shadows reconvened around our bed.

It was still dark when he left for his early turn. I just turned over, and tried hopelessly to doze. But my mind was still too restless; my limbs itched and tingled. In the end I found myself counting the minutes to the start of *Today* (half-past six, for God's sake), when I could switch on the radio and let in the outside world.

After the news had come round twice, I grudgingly got up and phoned work. My stomach still felt sore enough for me to report sick with a clear conscience; Jez sounded quite concerned. The Late was covered, he assured me. No need to worry. Go back to bed.

As if I could.

I was glumly studying the paper when the doorbell rang. Probably the postman with a package. Or the milkman for his money. I hesitated, not really wanting anyone to see me in this state: my hair was a mess, my complexion pasty. Then again, it could be something important.

Something to do with Nick.

That sort of fear had always been there, in the depths of my mind; but recent events had brought it much closer to the surface. I had a sudden image of a wretched-looking copper on the doorstep, breaking the news with his eyes before he'd even opened his mouth.

'*Miss Young. . . ?*'

I tried to smother the thought, but still got quickly to my feet. Tightening the belt of my dressing gown, I walked through into the hall; had nearly reached the door when it occurred to me that the person on the other side might be wearing a sergeant's uniform.

'*We warned you. Stupid bitch.*'

. . . and a stiff-armed shove in the chest would send me stumbling back as the black anoraks came crashing in. Police raid. *Wiking* strike. The neighbours might look on in interest, and never hear the screams . . .

I stopped and swallowed. My hand was already extended towards the latch. 'Who's there, please?' I asked in a weak voice.

No answer.

Perhaps they hadn't heard. We'd had a good thick door fitted. But thick enough?

The bell shrilled again. This close, it made me jump.

Just the postie – surely. And getting colder by the moment, if the frost on the windows was anything to go by. Shaking off my paranoia, I opened up.

It wasn't the postman.

It wasn't the Sergeant, either.

Leaning up against the doorpost, the girl called Jackie turned to greet me with a faint and chilly smile.

Chapter 18

I found I hadn't the strength to do anything but let her in. My tongue felt too thick to shape a protest; still less were my arms up to slamming the door in her face. So I just stepped aside — trying not to let her brush against me — and stared helplessly after her as she went on into the breakfast room.

She was carrying an old sports bag. It pulled her arm down straight.

Closing the door again with nervous haste, I followed her through. She'd placed the bag on the table, and slumped down onto the nearest chair. I watched from the doorway as she tugged off her moth-eaten mittens and started massaging her fingers. After a moment she glanced at me again.

'I'll have a coffee thanks.'

With a sort of sneer — it was all my self-respect could summon up — I went over to the cafetiere and poured the dregs into a mug; slopped in some milk and practically banged it down on the table top before her. Unruffled, she took it in both hands and started sipping. I retreated to the wall: put my back against it, feeling under-dressed and vulnerable in just my dressing gown and socks. She, by contrast, was muffled in several layers of old clothing: protection from the bitter winter night. I didn't doubt there'd be a gun under all that, somewhere.

And what was in the bag? Not just blankets, that was for sure.

'What the hell do you want?' I asked at length.

'Well now Rachel: what sort of way is that to greet a friend?' She almost drawled the words, her smile mocking;

but the irony had a sharp, hard edge. I saw it glinting in her eyes.

'Look . . .' I swallowed again. 'I don't know what R . . . what McCain's told you – but I want nothing to do with any of this, all right? Just bloody let me be.'

'Well, I see we can count on your support in our hour of need . . .' she murmured. The irony had cooled to sarcasm already; her expression was all distaste.

'Tough. I didn't ask to get involved.'

'No, of course you didn't.' There was contempt in her tone now. 'Fucking fence-sitter, that's all you are, isn't it? All the same. Big with the words, but when it comes down to helping out, you don't want to know . . .'

It was hardly the best of situations to lose your rag in, but suddenly I didn't care. Rage came in a stinging rush.

'Listen, you little cow, I work in ITU, right, and I saw what your bloody bombs did to someone with a wife and kids. You burned his *face* off. So what did he ever do to you? Don't give me that fence-sitting crap; you make me *sick*.'

I ran out of breath at that point, and just glowered at her while I got it back. My eyes were wet, but more from anger than anything else. Outrage both at her and at my own situation – trapped here in Razoxane's war, like a character in someone else's nightmare.

Jackie had gone white – whether from shock or fury I couldn't tell. Thought of the latter made my stomach stir uneasily; now that the first flush of ire was past, I remembered I was sharing my house with a cold-blooded killer. Folding my forearms across my stomach, I rubbed my elbows inside my dressing-gown sleeves and waited nervously for her response.

It seemed ages until she could trust herself to give one. Her voice came out squeezed tight with anger; but there were darker undertones I couldn't quite catch. Right then I hadn't time to try.

'So *I* make you sick, do I? Remember Tom Brandon?

The guy we came to rescue? You were there, for Chrissake. You saw what the bastards did to him . . .' She shook her head, as if even the memory went beyond belief; I saw its ghost in the depths of her stare. Then her focus sharpened once again. 'Far as I'm concerned, the rule book's out the fucking window now.'

'Yeah, but . . .' I hesitated: getting my balance on this high-wire. 'That wasn't the police, was it? Couldn't have been. They wouldn't kill their own blokes too . . .'

'You'd be surprised,' she murmured, with infinite cynicism: the sort you just can't meet with reason.

After a pause, I tried a different tack; more quietly this time.

'All right, then. Say there's bad on both sides. Say you've got reasons. They all turn to shit if you murder innocent people. Don't you *see* that?'

Jackie gave a mocking little snort. 'Oh, sure. If the warning gets ignored and somebody dies, we're murderers. *Fine.* And if you lot are bombing Baghdad, and wipe out a few women and wee ones while you're at it, then that's just "collateral damage", isn't it. Not the same thing at all . . .'

'There haven't *been* any warnings,' I muttered.

Another pause. Then she made for a dismissive gesture. 'Frank says we're done with pussy-footing around. This is a war . . .' She said it firmly; but that undertone was there again. This time I thought I recognized discomfort. And maybe doubt.

'Is that what you think?' I tried to keep my voice in neutral; like my face.

She stared back at me for a moment – then shrugged.

'Okay. So I'd prefer to give fair warning. But Frank's in command. And . . .' She hesitated, as if sensing she was about to put a foot wrong.

'And McCain?' I prompted softly.

'McCain says we mustn't give warnings,' was her slightly wary answer. 'Not this time. There's a new Brit reprisal unit on the streets, y'see. They're the ones killed Tom. She said something like that could happen . . .'

Yes, I thought. *I bet she did.*

'But you still don't think it's right . . . ?' I persisted hopefully. There was a chink in their iron armour here, I knew it. If I could just exploit it somehow . . . get them to give some kind of warning . . . then at least I could be saving someone's life — or limbs.

I could always try phoning in myself, of course: but where would it get me? *A caller with a Midlands accent warned of a bomb in Bank station, sometime this week. Or maybe next . . .*

Big help.

Jackie was watching me, her stare suspicious. 'Don't you go putting words in my mouth,' she said flatly.

'I'm not. But it's a nasty business, isn't it?'

She flicked her gaze away; then back at me.

'Wars are always nasty. I learned that one at my mother's knee. My grandfather's too. And if you're a woman volunteer, it's just the same as any other field: you've got to be twice as ruthless to be thought half as brave.'

There was a tang of resentment in the words — perhaps at what her war had done to her; but acceptance along with it. Something told me I'd win no more admissions of doubt from her this morning.

'So . . . how did you get involved with McCain?' I asked cautiously; just as Gary had asked me.

Jackie leaned back in her chair. I saw the faintest trace of bemusement on her face as she shaped her answer; maybe so faint that she herself hadn't realized it was there.

'We met her on the street. God knows how she guessed who we were; but she was a sympathizer right enough. Listening to her talk . . . It gave us a buzz we really needed. Made it all seem clear . . .'

I nodded, unsurprised. She had a way with words, did Razoxane. 'But . . . she's not Irish though, is she,' I pointed out.

'So what? Our aim's the same: to make this country bleed. She's an anarchist or something, isn't she? Like they say: my enemy's enemy must be my friend . . .'

A reflex spasmed inside me: too bitter and twisted to be a giggle. It almost made it to my throat before I choked it.

They'd be safer making friends with a *jackal*.

My gaze came back round to the bag. I nodded. 'What's in that?'

She gave it an almost casual glance. 'Semtex; can of paraffin . . . and a load of nine-inch nails.'

My mouth opened in an O.

'Peelers were getting close,' she went on drily. 'Breathing down our necks. McCain said to move our stuff here. There's more explosive following. Plus some guns and ammo . . .'

'Get it out,' I whispered.

'I don't want to argue with you, Rachel . . .' It sounded like a plea.

'Good. Get it *out*.'

'Listen . . .'

I turned away, my lips pinched tight; afraid of what might come if I kept talking. Part of my mind was clamouring to tell her – to confess that I was living with a copper, just to see how she reacted. The rest of me shied away in panic from the prospect. God, there was a copy of *Police Review* lying on the sofa in the lounge . . .

I heard her get up, and come quietly towards me. Almost shivering, I waited for the tug on my sleeve, the voice in my ear.

I wasn't prepared for the fist in my hair.

A squeaky gasp of pain was all I could manage as she yanked my head back – dragging me out of the room like a recalcitrant child. Before I could marshal strength enough to struggle, she'd wrenched me round in the hall and shoved me forward. The doorway to the lounge loomed up; I bounced bruisingly off the jamb. Then I was being propelled towards the sofa – Nick's paper in plain sight –

and flung down onto it. Panting, I tried to turn my head; it came up against her gun as she leaned forward.

Now the voice in my ear.

'I don't like to do it this way, Rachel. You think like a nurse, and I can understand that; two of my sisters are nurses, after all. But you're in up to your snotty little nose now, and if you don't co-operate I'll fucking kill you. All right?'

I managed a sob of sorts. She took it as a yes.

'There's a good girl . . .' She withdrew her knee from the small of my back, and let the air flow free into my lungs. I gulped it down. Close beside my cowering head, her pistol clicked as she disarmed it; and then she'd straightened, pushing it back beneath her filthy coat. A dustbin smell had thickened in the room.

'Twice as ruthless, Rachel. I *mean* that.' She waited until I'd sat shakily up before returning to the breakfast room.

I followed on unsteady legs, my hair still in my eyes, to find her downing the last of her coffee. She smiled thinly as I appeared in the doorway.

'Mind you get this well hidden, now. Before your boyfriend comes home.' She tilted her head to one side. 'Works in your hospital too, does he?'

I nodded with cartoon urgency.

'And of course, you wouldn't dream of telling him . . .'

'*No,*' I almost snapped.

She dipped her head approvingly, and set her mug down. 'Good. The stuff's quite safe, by the way. Harmless, without a detonator. It's not going to blow you up or anything.'

Under the circumstances, that wasn't much of a relief.

'I'll be seeing you, then,' she told me calmly, and came on out. I avoided looking at her as she passed; my attention was in any case absorbed by the bag on the table. There was an evil, crouching stillness to its crumpled shape.

The front door opened with a creak; she slammed it closed. And suddenly I was alone again.

Alone with a bomb.

It took me quite a while to summon up the nerve, but at length I lifted it gingerly by its handles and carried it upstairs. Practically on tiptoe. She could say what she liked about detonators; I still expected to trip and start it ticking.

We'd amassed quite a bit of junk in the spare room by now. I pushed the bag to the back of a cupboard, and covered it with clothes. Out of sight was hardly out of mind, but at least it was a start. Then I went dolefully back into the bedroom, and curled up on our unmade bed.

Right away I felt the difference. Our house was haunted now; a ghost had taken up residence under our roof. Whatever I did here from now on – be it making supper or making love – I knew I'd feel its presence, like some malevolent squatter in that unoccupied room.

That afternoon I scribbled Nick a note about wanting to get some fresh air and clear my head, and ventured out into the chilly daylight.

My head needed clearing right enough. My mind felt like a video stuck on cue-review: endlessly re-hashing the mess I was in. Skipping the boring bits to freeze-frame gory details.

I had to talk to, or with, or even *at* someone; but even as I got onto the bus at Green Lanes, I didn't know who. Sitting up front, I saw the grim towers of the City drawing closer, and changed my mind as often as the stops. Should I really try to track down Razoxane? Or look for Gary? Stop off at Regent's Canal – or push on into the centre?

I thought about the death-squad on patrol; remembered the word that Jackie had used for the police.

Peelers.

Just an anachronism, used as slang; an echo of old scores still unsettled. But the literal meaning filled my head with raw, revolting pictures.

I got off at Regent's Canal.

From across the bridge, the factory seemed deserted. No sign of any movement; but I thought I glimpsed a shimmer of heat above the yard. Perhaps a home fire burning. Heart in my throat, I crossed.

Round in the side-road, I was still struggling with the makeshift entrance when someone came to help from the inside. I saw it was the girl who'd been here last time: the one who looked about fifteen. Her over-large clothes compounded the impression – a child dressing up from the jumble sale drawer. I'd done as much myself when I was little; but the homeliness of that memory felt light years away from the here and now. This girl's clothes were soiled, her pale face pinched and grubby. I guessed she hadn't had much of a childhood, however old she was.

Pulling her sleeves back down over her hands like makeshift gloves, she hugged herself and watched me clamber through. Her eyes were serious.

'You're McCain's friend, aren't you? Rachel.'

I nodded. 'And you're . . . ?'

'Lisa.' She seemed surprised that I would want to know.

'Is she around?' I asked, peering past her. A couple of the others were drinking by the remnants of the fire.

Lisa shook her head. And again when I asked about Gary. Seeing a dead end looming up ahead, my final try was, when might they be back?

She shrugged. 'You can wait if you like.'

I followed her nervously back towards the fire, half-expecting to find Frank or even Jackie there. But there was only a youngish bloke in specs, and . . . Jim, wasn't it? The King of Cups. Well into them already.

Lisa squatted down on her heels. I did likewise, concealing my discomfort; ignoring King Jim's bleared, unblinking stare.

'How well do you know her?' I ventured after a pause. 'McCain, I mean.'

'Not very,' Lisa muttered, leaning forward to poke at the embers. 'If you want to know the truth, she gives me the creeps; the way she comes and goes. And always so cold. Even her smiles are cold . . .' She glanced at me. 'You know her any better?'

I gestured vaguely. Yes and no.

'She's in trouble with the cops, isn't she?'

'I . . . think she might be,' I conceded.

'There's word coming up from the street,' the bloke with glasses put in grimly. He was draped in an army surplus greatcoat; his combat boots were open, tongues protruding. But the specs still gave him an oddly studious look.

I turned my head and kept my tone flat. 'Is there?'

'That they want her dead. There's a special unit from out of town. Vermin exterminators.' He spoke without blinking; assessing my reactions. I kept them in check.

'I was talking with a friend,' he went on softly. 'Bloke who lives on the road. Usually keeps well clear of this shit heap, but he was down for a gig or something. Told me about something he saw up Stevenage way . . .'

He paused to draw on his half-inch stub of cigarette; I looked at Lisa. From her set face, she'd heard this already – and was waiting to see its effect on me.

'His van was stopped on the hard shoulder, right,' the man with specs resumed. 'And someone says, watch out, the cops are here. Three police vehicles, travelling south. But they just cruised past in the fast lane. Two transit vans, black ambulance glass – and a landrover with wired-in windows. All travelling with lights, though it wasn't dusk yet.

'He sometimes watches for warhead convoys, my mate does. Protesting and all that. He told me he got the same feeling from watching those three vehicles pass as he would from seeing a convoy of nuke transporters on the road. The same feeling.'

I felt a sick little tingle in my stomach; knew just what his mate meant. They'd been on their way then. Wiking and Wampir and . . .

'"Wotan" ring any bells with you?' he added, deceptively casual; still watching.

Whisky Oscar. Morris's own call-sign. But in itself it

meant nothing — beyond the make of the strip lights in ITU. The bloke from Works brought replacements round in boxes . . .

'Pagan German,' he said as I shook my head. 'Their god of death and battles . . .' His lips formed a humourless smile. 'Don't look so surprised. Just because I sleep rough, it doesn't mean I'm thick.'

'Sorry . . .' But it wasn't surprise that had warped my expression. The word re-awoke images of gathering, gloomy forests — and ancient evil.

'That's the whisper I heard. Wotan's on the streets. And those three vans coming south . . .' He lowered his voice, like a conspirator. 'The A1's an essential military route into London, you know that? STAG, they call it. Whoever those bastards are, they're specials.' He nodded to himself; then looked back at me. 'I'd steer well clear of her, if I were you.'

Would that I could, I thought.

Specs went back to smoking his cigarette. An unfriendly silence settled. I didn't much fancy hanging around; I got the feeling I was here on sufferance as it was. Perhaps I should just go home, then.

Or venture deeper into the City, and see if I could find her there.

God knew, I didn't want to. I'd already crossed one bridge to get here; a few hundred yards further south and I'd be right over the line. And for all its cars and futuristic buildings, this was still a citadel of sorts: one with torturers on the loose through its upper levels; and demons in the dungeons.

But Razoxane knew all its twists and turns. Her quest was the key to everything. I had to see her. So after a brief delay, I thanked Lisa and her friend, and took my leave. Outside, on the main road, I hesitated for a few minutes more despite the cold; then started walking south, towards Old Street station, and the tombstone towers beyond.

*   *   *

I lingered again – for ages – at the swirling junction of Old Street and City Road; torn between catching a train, or continuing on foot and on the surface. The thought of actually riding the underground route to Moorgate and Bank tied my stomach up in knots: it felt like a dishcloth being wrung. But to walk it in the open would leave me horribly exposed, with watchers all around me: hence my wretched hesitation – caught between the devil and the deep, dark tube.

At least the trains would be busier this afternoon – and perhaps the Ankerites withdrew and slept while they were running. Perhaps they were nocturnal creatures.

Then again, the night never ends down there.

At last I went down into the station and took the first train south; sitting up in the front coach, so that as we pulled in to the platform at Moorgate, I could see every person waiting. Razoxane wasn't one of them. With fear now lodging like a bone in my throat, I got off.

She wasn't on the northbound platform either.

I checked my watch: it was gone four o'clock. Nick would be home, and wondering where I'd got to. But having come this far, I couldn't give up now. I heard the next southbound train come banging in, and went back down the passageway to join it.

Bank was a much worse proposition. I wasn't sure I could face the Central Line platforms again, even with people round me. Following the straggle of passengers towards the exits off the Northern, I raised nervous eyes to look for directions.

'Rachel. You shouldn't be here.'

God, I wished she'd stop doing that.

She was lounging in one of the link corridors: sat on her heels with her back to the wall, out of sight of the platform cameras. Her hat brim and coat were powdered with fine, white ash, as if she'd just taken refuge from a nuclear fallout – the remnants of some rite to renew her strength, I guessed. And as I stared down at her, an eerie little thought stole into my mind. Desert people speak of dust-devils; perhaps she was the grim equivalent for cities.

Ash Angel.

Razoxane raised her head. No ash on her face, at least – but it was the colour of ashes nonetheless.

'What do you think you're doing?' she asked coldly.

I swallowed, but the bone stayed stuck. 'Listen, I had to see you. Jackie's been round to my place; said you'd told them to dump their stuff there . . .'

'That's right. We need a safe house. Where safer than yours?'

Half a dozen outraged responses sprang to mind; but I knew they'd be a waste of breath. All I could manage – in a small, despairing voice – was: 'What if Nick finds out?'

'Hide it well and he'll never know.'

'*I* will, though.'

'You know a lot of unpleasant facts that others don't, Rachel,' she pointed out drily. 'What's one more?'

I just slumped against the wall beside her. The latest twist of this whole nightmare was making me feel almost physically sick. Poor Nick hadn't a clue how I'd betrayed him: letting the home we shared be turned into a terrorist arms dump. With cheerful resignation he was studying for exams while his whole career was hanging in the balance. Not to mention his life. How do you hide that from the person you love?

He'll see it in my eyes. He'll know.

'You need to get home,' she murmured, toying with her spinner. 'I've made my preparations. It's time to begin.'

'What . . . what're you going to do?' I asked.

'Bring it back to the surface. More slowly,' she added, seeing my face freeze with horror. 'A far more intricate ritual, this time. I'll be here all night, and probably most of tomorrow. Communing. Convincing it to trust me . . .'

The idea of her haunting the empty station through the

small hours of the morning turned me cold. Some of it was empathy as well. I could imagine her all alone down here, behind locked gates – and once more discovering she couldn't bind the beast.

And if she got killed, where the hell did that leave me?

'Come on.' She got to her feet, and jerked her head towards the northbound platform. I followed her onto it, and down to the end. There were only a handful of people along its length; to me, their bored expressions seemed almost blissful.

Razoxane looked back towards the far tunnel mouth; then dipped into her pocket. As I watched, she brought out a crumbling handful of dust and extended it before her.

No, not dust, I realized; ashes.

'Don't come near this station for a day,' she told me softly. 'Don't come *near*.'

And even as I nodded, the ash began to stir.

The stuff was so fine that the first breath from the tunnel set motes of it drifting – before I'd even felt the breeze myself. The cool touch on my cheek made me glance round quickly; but of course it was only an incoming train. As the glow of headlamps grew out of the depths, so the ash went smoking from Razoxane's palm, carried off into the tunnel by the rising wind.

She murmured something guttural under her breath; then spread her hand completely, and let the last of the plume trail off. As the train emerged into the light down the far end of the platform, she looked at me again.

'It's started. Now get out of here. And *pray*.'

I didn't need telling once, never mind twice. Boarding the train, I flopped down into a seat that faced the platform. The last I saw of Razoxane as it pulled out into the dark was a look like apprehension on her colourless face; and her fingers toying with the gothic cross inside her turned-up greatcoat collar.

*　　*　　*

'I was beginning to get worried,' Nick murmured; I could see the relief behind his smile. 'Nice walk?'

I gave a non-committal sort of nod.

'Well it's put some colour back into your cheeks, at least,' he told me.

Only because it was cold out there; I'd probably still be looking like a slept-on sheet otherwise. As an afternoon out, it had cleared some of the cobwebs – but not the spiders that had spun them. My mind was still crawling with those.

Had he sensed it yet: the ghost in the upstairs room? There was practically a cold spot on the landing . . .

'Fancy coming down the pub after supper?' he asked casually, setting the table. I made an unenthusiastic face.

'Um. I'd rather not . . .'

'No problem.' He went back into the kitchen to get the bread.

'No, but it's your darts night, isn't it? Look, don't let me keep you in.' I followed him through. 'Off you go, enjoy yourself. I'll be all right.'

'You sure?'

'Course I am.' I managed to grin. 'Give us that.'

He passed me the half-loaf of wholemeal. Fresh from the breadbin, it still smelt faintly of pine.

Home. It was details like that which made it real.

And tonight, while he was out of it, I knew *they'd* come – bringing guns and bullets to add to their fire-and-nail bomb: defiling it more thoroughly than any burglar. And by the time they were gone, our home would have been turned back into just a house again. A soulless shell.

Haunted.

I didn't doubt they'd be keeping watch: and so it proved. Less than fifteen minutes after Nick had left, the doorbell rang.

I went through to answer it, as slowly as someone following a coffin. Maybe the wait had made them edgy, because they were all inside before the door was fully open. All three of them.

I hadn't seen Frank for a while; his close-up, flinty stare came as quite a jolt. Brendan, with his serious face and beard, still reminded me absurdly of a renegade social worker. Jackie just gave me a look, as if defying me to voice any more objections.

They dumped their bags on the table where Nick and I had eaten supper. Metal clinked. Frank stepped back, and raised his eyes to mine.

'Four carbines; ammunition and grenades. All right, then?'

I nodded heavily.

'Jackie tells me you're none too keen,' he added, smiling: the expression entirely without humour. I glanced away, found Jackie watching. Her own face held no comfort.

I swallowed. Shrugged. Said nothing.

Brendan had wandered on into the kitchen; I heard the fridge door sucking open. In the circumstances I could hardly voice objections. I'd no choice but to listen, with a kind of fatalistic chill, to the crack and hiss of one of Nick's beer cans. I hoped to hell he hadn't counted them.

My stomach didn't really sink until Frank and Jackie sat down at the table and began making themselves comfortable.

'Um . . .' I moistened my lips. 'Listen, my boyfriend's going to be back soon, you'd better go . . .'

'Will he, by God?' Frank paused to swing his dirty boots up onto the freshly-cleaned tabletop. 'And there were we thinking he'd gone down the pub.'

Brendan came back through, swigging from the can. He sat down as well.

'No need to stand on our account,' Frank said drily, enjoying my helpless discomfort. I just stared back at the three of them: looked from face to scornful face. It was like coming home after a break-in to find the intruders have taken over your house and claimed it as their own.

'Are you going to tell her or shall I?' Jackie asked; talking to Frank but watching me.

'You can if you like.' He seemed amused.

I waited, my chest aching; keeping my eyes on Jackie's. Despite her treatment of me this morning, I was still searching for a way in. Some affinity somewhere. Her flicker of doubt was the only hope I had.

'We're going to carry out our next attack tomorrow night,' she told me. No trace of doubt in her tone at all now; just cold confidence. 'We're going to plant a bomb. And you're coming with us.'

A joke. I waited for the punchline.

It didn't come.

'Oh God no,' I said at length; it came out so quiet it sounded almost conversational.

'Oh *yes*, Rachel,' Frank said. 'Time to get off your backside and put your bloody money where your mouth is.'

My gaze switched back to Jackie. She'd tilted her head back to rub her chin; it made her expressionless stare disdainful.

'Was this your idea?' I almost spat.

She didn't bother to reply; but I guessed it had been. Maybe I really had got to her this morning, and this was her way of getting back. Or maybe they simply wanted me as involved as possible – pre-empting any idea of going to the police.

Brendan gulped beer, and belched.

'You're a Lilywhite, Rachel,' Frank went on, as if I hadn't spoken. 'No one knows you from Eve. So you can go on ahead, and check the coast's clear. With that fucking reprisal unit on the loose, I'm taking no chances.'

The enormity of the prospect left me numbed. 'Wh . . . Where are you attacking?' I whispered; already knowing.

'Bank Underground.'

All part of Razoxane's plan, of course. The seal on her ritual. Presumably she'd told them when the bomb had to blow; made sure they didn't interrupt her incantations.

Don't come near . . .

'We'll hit it between nine and ten o'clock,' Jackie said. 'So . . .'

'We'll do it in the *rush-hour*,' Frank cut in across her. 'That'll give their papers something to scream about.'

Jackie blinked; hesitated a moment. 'McCain said . . .'

'Is she fucking running this group or am I?'

The way he snapped told me far too much. His role had been usurped, and he'd realized it. Realized that an outsider – and a woman at that – had started to dictate their list of targets. Whatever flatteries she'd fed him with, they weren't enough; whatever bewitchments, his will was breaking free.

The way Jackie's pale face fell told me something too. No warnings, they'd agreed that; but the later the bomb went off, the fewer casualties there'd be. Maybe that was the deal that she'd made with her conscience. But Liverpool Street had been bombed in the early evening; and this one would be earlier still.

The thought of a blast in such a confined and crowded space turned my skin damp and cold all over. But not as cold as the thought that grew spines inside me. If they (and I) went in earlier than Razoxane had instructed, her work might not be finished . . .

'One more word from you,' Frank rasped as I opened my mouth, 'and we'll shoot your boyfriend's kneecaps off. And maybe his balls. If you run out on us tomorrow, we'll pour petrol through your letterbox and set it on *fire*. Am I getting through to you, Rachel?'

Oh, he was; and what could I say? That he was being used in ways he hadn't dreamed of? That if Razoxane's rites were disrupted, a demon could be unleashed into the tube? Something that could start by devouring us all – and maybe not ever be stopped?

No way out. God help me. None at all. In desperation I looked at Jackie.

She looked away.

Chapter 19

A dull *bong* echoed down the platform, announcing an expectant crackle of live air over the PA.

'This . . .' murmured Jackie mechanically '. . . is . . . Northern Line . . . formation service . . . Control room . . . Euston.' Still reading the advert across from us, she paused, then added: 'For your discomfort and inconvenience, we have turned off all the escalators.'

I gave her a rather startled sidelong glance – she was smiling thinly to herself – then returned my attention to the drinks ad too.

You can't have a sense of humour: you're a bloody terrorist.

Perhaps it was her way of dealing with the tensions of what she did. We nurses make macabre jokes to help us cope; and so do coppers. Why not terrorists as well?

And she was tense, all right: I could almost feel the aura round her. It prickled like static. I guessed from her voice that her mouth was dry, her lungs slightly short of breath. Her hands were doubtless sticky with sweat inside her gloves. All of which went twice for me.

Just gone seven, according to my watch. The King's Cross platform was still fairly crowded; but the rush-hour flow was thinning with each southbound train that passed. It was the only crumb of comfort left for my hollow stomach.

A compromise had been reached last night: a meeting on the middle ground between Frank's ferocious self-assertion and Jackie's commitments to her conscience. It hadn't been easy; he'd clearly felt that any backwards step would be an admission of defeat – and maybe a denial of his manhood too. Giving in to Jackie's weakness, as he called it; or to Razoxane's strength.

In the end it had been Brendan's doubts that had forced him round. Even Brendan wasn't sure about killing quite so many people without warning. And even as they'd hammered their conclusion out, I'd sat there, counting seconds: just waiting for Nick's key to rattle in the door.

They'd been gone when he got back, of course. But not by long.

I was on a day off today. I'd had the whole of it to brood on what was coming. One thing I kept coming back to was the way Jackie had argued her case last night: putting the argument that wholesale slaughter might damage their support. It had cut more ice with Frank than an appeal to his conscience. She'd been clever.

Or maybe that was really how she thought.

I glanced at her again: wondered if the doubts that I'd sensed had been purely pragmatic – toning things down for the good of the cause. The very idea left me feeling horribly alone: even sitting here, sandwiched between her and some bloke with his nose in the *Standard*.

The bomb was in a duffel bag between her shins: quite innocuous to look at. I lowered my gaze reluctantly to where her restless fingers were fiddling with the drawstring. It was so hard to imagine the light and heat and crushing force compressed in there; but the prospect of its release sent perspiration trickling coldly down my spine.

The man beside me didn't sense a thing. Nor did the young couple standing hand in hand in front of us, or the tired-looking exec with his briefcase, or anyone else on this platform. Three stations bombed in the last few weeks, but people were still trying to take it in their stride. The Spirit of the Blitz, according to some of the papers; but I reckoned the belief that it'll never happen to you played just as big a role.

Four minutes to the next train.

Just the two of us were here together – though I had the

itchy suspicion that Brendan might be shadowing us, in case I tried screwing things up. When I'd met Jackie under the departure board upstairs, and seen the bag hanging from her shoulder, I'd known she was the one who'd be planting the bomb. It was a salient reminder that she was into this as deeply as anyone. Whatever her misgivings, she was still a murderer.

And I'd be her accomplice, unless I could think of something. Which I couldn't.

Running both hands back through my hair – a despondent, helpless gesture – I raised my eyes to the indicator once more. The first train was three minutes out now: less than a mile.

'You catch this one,' Jackie murmured beside me. 'Take it to Bank, get off and sniff around; look out for anyone loitering. Make sure you're back to meet the third train.'

The arrival time of that one came up as I watched: thirteen minutes. All the time I'd have to check the station.

What if Razoxane was there?

What if she *wasn't*?

'You remember the code?' Jackie asked, and I nodded jerkily. *Stand if there's danger; sit down if it's safe.* She'd be in the front coach, watching. If I was standing, she wouldn't get off. 'And don't get it into your head to stand up anyway,' she'd hissed on our way down here. 'Because I'll be leaving this thing somewhere, even if it's Leicester bloody Square . . .'

Two minutes. I tried to swallow: tried to lubricate a dryness like a throatful of talc.

I thought of Nick. Self-defence classes was tonight's excuse; run especially for nurses in the hospital's Physio gym. He'd been trying to get me to go on something like that for a while, and was pleased. It had been all I could manage to keep my face straight, my smile in place, as he'd stroked my shoulder.

'That's good, Rachel. You won't regret it.'

Won't I? I'd thought.

A thin, metallic whispering started up along the tracks. I heard the rumble behind it; felt the breeze.

'All right, then . . .' Jackie said.

I slowly stood, and looked northward for the lights. They glared from the dark like oncoming eyes. Then the coaches were out of the tunnel and sweeping past me: grey and gleaming, brightly-lit. Some of the people inside were even smiling.

For me it was a ghost-train nonetheless. Stepping aboard, I felt like I'd stepped back through time – to find myself riding that doomed train to Moorgate, all those years ago. Riding it, and realizing: even as it sucked me down into the grave.

With a sort of numb fatalism, I watched the stations come and go. Angel. Old Street. Moorgate itself. We waited for maybe a minute in the tunnel outside Bank; I was practically squirming by the time the train lurched into motion once again, and brought us in to the platform.

I got out, and looked both ways: peered between passing bodies as the doors thumped closed behind me. A hiss – and then the train began to move. I watched it gather speed: the guard leaning out of his door until he'd passed me, then ducking in as it slid shut. A moment later the tunnel took them; the glow of lights receded round the corner. The clunk of points and sleepers died away.

I felt like I'd been left in the lurch.

There was no sign of her. As people with places to go brushed past me, I lingered on in gluey indecision. Razoxane had begun her conjurations on these Northern Line platforms; presumably the Ankerite could move at will through the warren of tunnels – and manifest on either level. But after the station had closed for the night, she might have wandered: perhaps as far as the Central Line. I could imagine the workmen who passed through here during the small hours catching glimpses; hearing footfalls.

Finding no one. A legend or two more about the haunted Underground could have been born last night.

But where had she finished up? Where would the ritual be consummated? Wherever, she'd have told Jackie to leave the bomb there. I glanced up at the indicator; her train had closed the distance somewhat. Only nine minutes behind me now.

Taking what remained of my courage between my teeth, I hurried after the last of my fellow-passengers, and on through the link to the Central Line. My heart was punching in my chest, sending adrenaline burning round my system; but I still had an ice-cold flush as I stepped onto the eastbound platform. For a brief and horrid moment, I thought the temperature had dropped again.

Still no sign of Razoxane – nor of anyone else for that matter. The platform was still, and draughty. Distant thunder rumbled from the depths. The westbound line was empty too. Swallowing, I went back down to Northern.

The train in between must have come and gone; the ghost of a breeze still stirred the air. No-one seemed to have got off this one. I found I had the platform to myself.

Wearily I sat down on a bench halfway along. Perhaps Razoxane's business was already finished then: the Anker-ite placated, and ready to be purged. All it needed now was for Jackie to plant her bomb, and we could both get the hell out. I glanced down towards the airless tunnel; then back at the exit. There was still no one else in sight.

My watch said seven-twenty.

I felt an uneasy little twinge in my stomach. Not quite sure why, but . . . there should be *somebody* around. Quite a crowd had got off my train and drained into the exits; but no one had replaced them. The Central Line platforms had been equally deserted. Mid-evening at a busy City junction, but it felt much later – like waiting for the last train south. I realized then that something was . . . not right.

On an impulse, I got up and went down the link corridor to the parallel platform. That was empty too. The eerie hush made my skin tingle. I was just beginning to get really nervous when I heard the gathering rumble from the north.

Relief. I raced back to the southbound platform, saw lights approaching, and just managed to plant my bum on a seat before the train emerged from the tunnel.

And steamed straight on through.

I watched in growing disbelief as the coaches clanked past. For a moment I saw Jackie staring out at me from the first one, her face almost comically perplexed. And then she was gone, carried off into the dark with all the rest, and I was alone again: the train's spooky wail still lingering in its wake as it sped on towards London Bridge.

Oh shit, I thought helplessly. Oh *shit*.

The bloody trains weren't stopping. People were being prevented from coming down. Security alert or something; maybe even a fire. The station had been closed – and I was stranded. Down here. Underground.

Someone stepped out from the passageway right beside me.

The rustle of clothing made me jump – to my feet, almost. I just managed to stifle a squeal of fright. And the ragged man flinched back from me, looking almost as startled himself.

I smelt the alcohol that stained his coat; when he opened his mouth a moment later, I smelt it on his breath as well, and heard it in his broken, bleary mumble.

' 'Scuse me, miss. 'Scuse me . . .'

Oh piss off, I thought desperately. He must have been lurking down here somewhere, out of the cold, and I could tell at once that he was no more than what he seemed. Iron-grey hair, and a face like old, red rust. The blue of his eyes seemed smeared into the whites.

'Could you spare us some change please, miss . . .'

My heart was still vibrating from the shock of his appearance, but I still found his cowed courtesy oddly touching. Biting back a more irritable retort, I shook my head. 'I've got none, I'm afraid . . .'

He came round to stand before me, walking carefully.

'Just ten pence for a cuppa,' he cajoled, as if I hadn't spoken. I reckoned it was human contact he was after as much as money; maybe more. But tonight I really wasn't in a state to give it.

The drunk reached down and took my hands where they rested on my lap. I swallowed, but didn't resist; didn't even change my dispirited expression as he gently squeezed them through their mittens.

'Please, lovey. Just ten pence . . .' *Or only a smile.*

'This bloke giving you trouble, Miss?' a new voice asked me briskly.

My head swung round – and though my body stayed sitting, my heart and guts leaped up inside it, and seemed to clog my throat.

The Sergeant didn't wait for a reply. He took hold of the drunk and hauled him back upright. I felt his fingers slip through mine with a sense of hopeless horror; the beggar himself was too befuddled to react. The Sergeant wrenched him round, seizing the man's lapels in his black-gloved fists.

I saw the others round us then: closing in down the platform from left and right. Aiming their ugly carbines right towards me. While the Sergeant still wore his yellow jacket, these three were muffled in sombre anoraks. Between their turned-up collars and the peaks of their caps, I glimpsed eyes that showed less pity than the muzzles of their guns.

Peelers. It was the only, awful word my mind could grasp.

'Please, sir . . .' the beggar faltered. 'I didn't mean no trouble . . .'

The Sergeant smiled genially. 'Of course you didn't. But we can't have you bothering your betters, now can we?' He looked to the gunman on my left. 'Evans.'

The Peeler lowered his carbine slightly, and smiled over its sights. He looked very young. 'Yes, Sarge?'

'What's the law like on begging, Evans?'

The other's smile became a grin. 'Firm but fair, Sarge.'

'Exactly. Firm, but fair.' And without further ado, the Sergeant lifted the drunk off his feet and flung him bodily down onto the rails.

There was a crackle and hum; a gagging sound. And then a bitter, cooked-meat smell was in my nostrils. I just sat there, saucer-eyed. A wail of revulsion started up from my stomach, but by the time it reached my lips it was only a whimper.

Then I squealed aloud as the Sergeant grasped a fistful of hair and yanked me to my feet.

'Come on, bitch. The Boss would like a word.'

It felt like my hair was coming out at the roots. The pain was paralysing: I couldn't even *squirm*. He hoisted me up until I was teetering on tiptoe; then turned casually towards the Peeler on our right.

'You *did* fix the cameras, didn't you?'

'Yes, Sarge.'

'Good. Now then, Miss . . .' He dragged me on over to the platform's edge: I glimpsed a tattered, shapeless bundle on the line. There was the faintest haze in the air – like in the kitchen, after you've been frying. I screwed my eyes shut; then opened them in panic as he forced my blind head forward.

'You see?' his voice continued, as I began to shake. 'He's lucky. You'll envy him.' He pulled me upright again, and then I was being marched towards the exit. His Peelers followed; one waiting until the rest of us were past, his pale eyes scanning the platform, before falling into step behind us.

My thoughts fled ahead, trying to gather themselves before the racket of footfalls could stamp them out completely. If I was being taken up top, there would surely be people waiting in the station – a crowd kept back at the ticket barriers. Somehow I'd have to get it through to them that these weren't policemen. Somehow, as I was frog-marched past their staring faces, I would have to make them intervene and save me.

Easy thing to think, of course. In reality, I knew, I could scream myself hoarse and nobody would lift a finger. All they'd see was a terrorist suspect under arrest. Some of them might even try putting the boot in . . .

The Sergeant relinquished his grip as we reached the exit, and shoved me towards the nearest man; the Peeler caught me by the collar while I was still struggling for balance.

'Get her back to the carrier. I'll take another sniff round Central.' He was unslinging his own gun as he spoke; the one that had hung muzzle-down behind his shoulder. A pump-action shotgun with pistol grip. I flinched as he worked the action.

He was hunting Razoxane. He knew she'd been down here. I thought of her being cornered, like a rat: would all her evil magic be proof against a blast from that?

Vermin exterminators, the bloke at the bash had said . . .

Then he was striding ahead and up the steps; we heard his boot heels echoing down the empty passageway beyond. My escorts followed at a more casual pace. The bloke with a grip on my coat was chewing gum.

I found my eyes caught by the carbine he hefted in his free hand; the outsize trigger-guard giving it the look of a kid's toy gun. A backup magazine had been bound to the first with masking tape. We paused halfway up, and I caught a closer glimpse of the other man's weapon. This one was bigger, heavier-looking, with a wooden butt that had something taped to it. With dull surprise I realized it was a postcard icon; some sort of Orthodox design . . .

'Where's Dave got to?' my Peeler muttered irritably.

The other man – Evans – turned to look. Presumably Dave was the one who'd been covering our rear. He still hadn't reached the bottom of the stairs.

A moment passed. Then Evans drew a radio handset

from under his anorak and thumbed it on. 'Whisky Indigo Three . . .' In the pause that followed, he saw me staring at his carbine and smiled unkindly. 'Nasty piece of work, innit? *Sturmgewehr* 44. Souvenir from Sarajevo . . .'

His radio crackled faintly.

'C'mon Dave, pull your fucking finger out.'

I felt the cold then: creeping up towards us.

It rose like a sluggish tide up harbour steps – the very breath of winter. The first touch snapped my nerve and I tried to pull away; but my horrified gasp had given the Peeler an instant's warning, and he hauled me viciously back round. I opened my mouth to protest, to plead . . . and found nothing I could possibly say.

Then Evans's handset went haywire: spewing an ugly babble of whines and whispers, the kind of ghost-gibberish you get when tuning your radio – only much more ominous. Startled, he switched it off.

Silence from the platform we'd just left.

Evans glanced up at the two of us, and jerked his head at me. I was still groping for his meaning when the bloke beside me took his carbine in both hands, and rammed its heavy butt into my belly.

For a moment I thought he'd split my stomach.

The agony was blinding: I fell like a sack, doubling over to slither down the next two steps. Tears spilled from my eyes, but I hadn't breath enough left to sob, let alone scream. All I could feel was the freezing stone against my wet cheek – and a bolus of molten lead on its way up from the furnace of my guts.

Oh God I'll choke on it.

They both ignored me. A few steps further up, the one who'd hit me stood still where he was: I sensed him taking aim across me, towards the right-hand corner. And Evans began side-stepping downwards, his back to the opposite wall; his own gun braced and ready.

A thin gruel of bile was in my mouth. Something lumpier had almost reached my throat. And all the time the chill was thickening. The Ankerite was coming. I couldn't bloody move.

Something scraped stone, just round the corner. The moment that followed seemed to elongate like gum, drawn taut and stringy. And then the man called Dave stepped backwards into view.

Evans let out his breath in an audible gasp. '*Jesus*, mate. Don't do that to me, all right?' He shifted his gun off target as he spoke.

But Dave seemed not to notice. A preoccupied glance up at his companions, and then he was peering back onto the platform; his finger still teasing his own carbine's trigger.

'What's up?' the bloke above me asked.

'Dunno. I . . . just get this feeling we're being followed.'

A weird, gargling noise came in response. It sounded awful – and much too close. I forced my head round.

Razoxane was right behind the Peeler who'd hit me, cutting his throat.

He reared back in her embrace, hands scrabbling to stop her; losing his grip on his gun, which clattered to the steps beside me. Blood slopped down his front like ketchup as the blade – a kitchen meat-knife – slid under his jaw. Razoxane's face leered over his shoulder, teeth bared in a rictus-grin.

A shout from the bottom of the steps – and then she'd pushed her pistol out from under his left armpit and started to shoot. In this narrow space the blasts were deafening. Cowering down, I glimpsed Dave thrown back against the Line maps, his mouth opening wide in a technicolor yawn. Evans got off one racketing shot before her bullets caught him too, and split his skull like a dropped egg. Both Peelers hit the spattered, scummy floor together.

Razoxane kept their colleague standing around a moment longer – then jerked the cutting edge clear of his throat. Knees buckling, he toppled: pitched forward past me. His thick, dark blood went spilling down the steps ahead of him.

I moaned.

Razoxane just stood there, looking down; that big, bloody knife in one hand and the pistol dangling from her other. I saw it was the same ugly, steel spudgun she'd carried last time. Seventy years old, or so she'd claimed . . .

Then she started down towards the corpses, pushing the gun back into whatever hiding-place it had beneath her coat. 'Okay?' she murmured as she passed; and I found I could manage a nod.

Kicking the first Peeler over onto his back, she hunkered down and – quite calmly and methodically – began to mutilate the body.

My throbbing stomach spasmed again. My nausea, cooled by shock, was suddenly redoubled. I clapped my hand to my mouth, and waited for the worst.

'Just grit your teeth and hold back the big bits,' said Razoxane helpfully. Withdrawing her glistening knife, she proceeded to the next sprawled heap. Began to cut again.

With a supreme effort, I managed to keep the contents of my stomach in check. '. . . Ankerite . . .' I whispered.

She nodded, still dissecting: with such precision that her scruffy gloves were barely stained. 'I know. It's waiting.' Finished with Evans, she turned her ghastly attentions to Dave's surprised-looking carcass.

'Oh God . . .' I had to swallow again before continuing. 'What're you doing . . . ?'

She wiped the blade on the Peeler's anorak and held it up. Even under the remaining patina of gore, it gleamed. More than a knife; less than a sword. The shaped wooden haft might have been moulded to fit her grasp.

'This is the Scramasax,' she said softly. 'Remember me telling you? Morris knew I wanted it, so he used it as bait – and I came and got it. That was two nights ago; he lost three men. No one's found them yet, so he must have buried or burned the bodies . . .'

I tried sitting up, and felt my gorge rise. Bone-aching

cold still filled the stairwell. The stink was almost more than I could bear.

'It's a blade of power,' Razoxane went on. 'If I commit these three to the Ankerite with it . . . we may not need the bomb.'

Hauling myself to my feet, I paused until the slime inside had settled. Watched her finish cleaning the blade. Straightening, she slid it into her belt.

'It'll take them now,' she said, with grim satisfaction. 'There'll be nothing left by the time anyone gets down here. Come on.'

Turning my face away from what she'd done, I let her lead me stumbling up the steps. For a moment I thought I felt the cold back there increasing; then it was fading away behind us.

'What about the Sergeant?' I asked faintly as we went on down the corridor. The idea of being stalked through this deserted labyrinth suddenly robbed me of all the breath I'd won back.

'Oh, he might still be down here,' said Razoxane drily. 'But more likely he'll have gone back up to the surface. Fast. Too many real policemen around by now. The death-squad intercepted the alert, and got here first – but they knew they wouldn't have long . . .'

'What alert? I mean . . . how did they *know*?'

'I was wondering that myself,' was her cryptic response. The way she said it put me instantly on the defensive.

'Well *I* didn't tell them,' I muttered needlessly; then clammed up as another thought occurred.

Had Jackie decided enough was enough? Phoned in some vaguely-worded warning so that the mission would have to be aborted? God, no wonder she'd sent me on ahead . . .

'We just need to wait until your police give the all-clear,' Razoxane was saying. 'It shouldn't be long. Then we can get the hell out of here . . .'

Hell was the word, all right. Underground turned to

Underworld. Blood, and ice, and something creeping out of the deepest dark to feed . . .

Hysteria hit me like a clinical stroke. A bolt from the black. It turned my limbs to jelly so that I staggered into the wall and almost slithered down it. My face twisted out of control. All I could do was clutch at the tiling as hoarse, retching sobs began to rack my body.

'Rachel . . .' She took hold of my shoulder, pulled me round to face her. 'Come on. You've come too far for this now . . .'

I panted helplessly back at her, my eyes overflowing. And then she slapped my chilly face. Hard. The stinging impact left me gawping.

'Going to live to tell the tale?' she hissed. '*Are you?*'

After a pause, I meekly nodded. Eyes still wide and wet.

'Good.' She grasped my coat and tugged. I faltered after her.

'The ritual worked,' she continued, glancing back. 'It was . . . exhausting. But it worked. The butchery back there might be enough to seal it. The Ankerite will glut itself . . . and maybe wake from this dream of its own accord. This nightmare that's lasted nineteen hundred years . . .' Her voice trailed off; but once more I heard the wistfulness in her words.

We were following the signs towards Monument: the escalator link with the Circle Line. They'd presumably re-open that station first. We could weave ourselves into the returning crowds, and escape from beneath the City of Crows.

Escape. The word soared in my head like a dove – and flew straight into a window.

'God, Razoxane. They'll come for me at work now. They'll bloody kill me . . .' And my imagination, ever help-ful, pictured the Sergeant returning to my unit with his shotgun, striding in with a smile on his face. I've yet to go on a Control & Restraint course that deals with shotguns.

'Listen, Rachel . . .'

(*'Don't listen, do you, Miss?'* he'd say – and turn his gun on the nearest bed. The nearest helpless patient . . .)

I turned my frightened gaze towards her: it bounced back from the impassive blankness of her shades.

'They won't come to your hospital again. Or follow you home. I promise you that. Angel's honour . . .' She said it with straight-faced certainty – which wasn't much comfort.

Promise of protection or no, it made me shudder.

By the time we reached Monument, there were already a few people waiting on the platform, and more filtering in by the moment. I stopped, and looked hopefully for the waiting time – then jumped as Razoxane drew me onward. Towards the exit.

'Hang on,' I mumbled as we approached the escalators. 'What if they're still around up there?'

'What indeed? I want to see if Morris came to gloat . . .'

I didn't. But nor did I want to be left on my own. So I just let the grinding escalator carry me up towards the darkness, gripping the handrail tighter as that gruesome thought of retribution repeated on me again: the Sergeant's shotgun blast spraying blood and drugs and plasma in a soaking shower . . .

Looking up the road as we emerged into the sharp night air, I saw that Bank junction was still sealed off and pulsing with police lights. They'd cast their net at last – but much too late: we'd all slipped through it. If it had been Jackie who'd tipped them off, she'd probably phoned a newspaper or something from King's Cross, and not named the target directly – hence the delay in closing stations. But the Peelers, listening in, had worked things out much quicker.

Oh Christ, it had been close.

Razoxane was already strolling off towards the barriers, and I trailed wretchedly in her wake. There was quite a crowd gathered, and we slipped into it. Beyond the tapes that spanned the street, a number of City of London coppers stood keeping an eye on us. Vans and patrol cars had been hastily parked; a stationary motorcycle's strobe beacon was flashing in our faces.

A senior officer in a long, dark coat came walking across the junction, speaking into his handset as he moved. Silver pips on his shoulders; short fair hair beneath his cap. With a chill of fundamental dread, I realized it was Morris.

No one gave him a second glance. Not one real policeman sensed the wolf in uniform passing through their midst like a ghost. He crossed very close to me, his face expressionless in the spectral blue pulse of the strobe; pausing to listen to a reply over his radio. I watched, transfixed: unable even to blink as he passed a casual word with one of the coppers on the cordon. Then he was striding back towards Mansion House; and after a moment another man, whom I hadn't even noticed, detached himself from the shadows of the nearest Underground entrance and followed, his carbine held close across his chest.

One of the City policemen gave him an incurious glance, then returned his stolid gaze to us.

Razoxane pulled at my sleeve; I had to stifle a gasp. 'I think the show's over for tonight,' she murmured in my ear. 'Let's go.'

As we trudged back towards Monument – I looked behind me more than once – she smiled to herself, and said: 'He's not going to be too happy after this. He really isn't.'

It was the almost cheerful way she said it that really turned me cold.

Next morning, on the early news, there was an item about three youths who'd disappeared last night on their way home from the pub: They'd been found alive: someone had dumped them in the Docklands. After cutting off their hands, ears and noses.

I pushed away my untouched bowl of cereal, and just sat there, very still, in the dimly-lit kitchen: struggling not to think of their screams.

Chapter 20

Work, when I got in, was almost a relief. Apart from any-thing, it was pouring with rain, the torrents sluicing bitterly down from the darkness above, so the sense of refuge was warm and welcome. One last dash from the tube station and I was out of the storm and into the dry, bright light.

All I could do was pray that the riders on that storm – they were out there somewhere – would sheer off, and keep their distance. Razoxane had promised as much, hadn't she? The word of my guardian angel: it was all I had to cling to.

I could still imagine them gathering round the building, though: like bedraggled carrion birds taking up their perches. An unkindness of ravens. A *murder* of crows . . .

Upstairs in the unit, there had been some changes since I'd last been on. One patient had died; a couple more had gone back to the wards. Others had come in to take their place. Jean, handing over from the night shift, gave me all the gritty details.

One of the newcomers had been admitted to the Med. Unit during the night with some sort of fever – but he'd started fitting, developed breathing difficulties, and been sent on up to us; query neurological involvement. He was in one of the side rooms; I glanced across, and saw a dim blurr through the fluted glass partition as someone attended to him in there.

'As for Past History . . . he was attacked by some dogs a couple of weeks ago . . .' Jean was saying, briskly business-like as ever. 'Hospitalized for several days at UCH. They're sending his notes over this morning . . .'

'You reckon it's tetanus?' Lucy asked, scribbling.

'Could well be, Lucinda,' Jean said sagely. 'We shall see what Dr Murdoch says on the round this morning. Now, then: Rosemary Jameson . . .'

Clinical tetanus. Bloody lockjaw. If it was, he'd be on the ventilator for several days while the paralysis worked its way out of his system. Something else for us to plan around. With a mental shrug, I started a new entry in my notebook for the next patient down the list.

Only we early risers got to see the real rain. By the time people with more civilized hours of work were coming onto the streets, the pre-dawn downpour had slackened to a drizzle. By afternoon, the day was beginning to brighten up.

I wished my mood would follow suit; but the closer we got to knocking-off time, the more uneasy I became.

I'd got here in one piece, despite the darkness – but now I had to make it home again. Maybe they hadn't been ready for me this morning. Maybe they were waiting for me now.

Storm-crows, I thought helplessly; watching from their perches on high, dripping eaves. Did Razoxane really think she could scare all of them off?

Whatever she *thought*, in another two hours I was going to find out for myself.

Nick's mate Colin was coming round tonight; we were supposed to be having a fun evening. I wasn't sure whether I should be fixing my thoughts on it in the hope of being distracted from the here and now – or dreading the prospect of having to play the cheerful hostess when I felt like curling up and crying. But Nick had been looking forward to this all week, and I couldn't disappoint him.

I thought of bedtime last night: him gently touching the livid bruise on my tummy, left by the Peeler's gunbutt, and raising awed eyes to meet mine. 'Christ, they play rough at those self-defence classes of yours . . .'

And I, who'd seen four people horribly killed that evening alone, had actually managed to smile.

* * *

I made my way home with my heart in my throat: trying to blend with the afternoon crowds. The wan, chilly sunshine made the streets seem marginally less threatening – but I still couldn't shake off a creepy feeling of being followed. The wail and whoop-whoop-whoop of a siren from somewhere nearby brought me out in a cold, sticky sweat.

I thought I glimpsed blue lights flickering in the distance, but saw nothing more. Could have been an ambulance coming in, of course. Could have been.

I stayed close to other people all the way: squeezing into the fullest coach of the northbound tube; the claustrophobic lower deck of the bus from King's Cross. Surely no one was following me now, but the feeling of unease still lingered. My skin kept tingling; my stomach turned. It was as if I was being literally *shadowed*: my every move matched by someone – or something – I couldn't see.

But I was the only one to get off the bus at the bottom of our road; the cars behind it cruised on past without anyone giving me a glance. And as I plodded the last few yards towards home, so that jittery feeling faded, and I suddenly found myself appreciating the afternoon light, quite golden now; and the freshness of the rain-scrubbed air.

With a last glance around at the gate – the street was quiet and empty – I went inside.

Nick was home already. I found him drinking coffee in the kitchen, listening to the radio. He couldn't disguise his relief when I came in. 'Am I glad you're back,' he murmured.

I raised my eyebrows. 'Something up?'

He nodded towards the radio. 'Report on the news about a shooting in the City this afternoon. There were casualties, but they couldn't confirm how many. One was a police officer, according to first reports . . .'

'What . . . was it terrorists again?'

He just shrugged; and I caught a glimpse of his own

dejection behind the relief he felt for me. *Another policeman injured – or worse – in the line of duty*: it said too much about the way society was going. And besides, it could have been him . . .

I walked back out to hang my coat up, and hoped that the hot flush of guilt on my cheeks wasn't as visible as it felt. I had a horrible feeling that Frank might be behind this: escalating things another step after last night's aborted mission. He'd be furious at the reversal, I knew that much. But Jackie could tell him that it had been no fault of mine . . .

Unless, having tipped off the police in the first place, she was content to keep quiet, and let Frank draw his own conclusions.

Standing there in the hall, I looked slowly round at the letterbox. Then down at the doormat. Worst case scenarios sprang irresistibly to mind. Would the sound of splashing liquid be enough to wake us – or would we sleep on through it, and the *whump* that followed, and the crackle as the flames began to feed . . . ?

With a dry swallow, I looked away. Razoxane would protect me from them as well as from the Peelers: I believed it because I had to.

After a pause, I returned to the kitchen and put my arms around him. Held him close.

'Don't let things spoil tonight,' I murmured after a moment. 'Let's have a really nice evening. I reckon we both need it.'

PC Colin Taylor turned out to be black. I spent the first five minutes kicking myself for feeling surprised.

He was a little older than Nick, with a calm, engaging manner and a mischievous smile. And he liked my cooking too, which didn't hurt.

'Now that . . .' he murmured, reaching for his glass again '. . . is what I call a *real* chilli. Like you get in *proper* Mexican restaurants.' He took a long drink, and grinned at me. 'Sort of place where the waiters all wear bandoliers, and have sweat-stains down their backs, and slam your food down saying, "here is your dinner, peeg..."' He delivered the last in a guttural growl that almost made me giggle.

I caught Nick's eye; he gave me a grateful little wink. I'd done us proud tonight – but the actual meal was the least of it really. Even though we'd probably all been a little reserved to start with, the ice had melted quickly, and now we were getting on like ... like ...

A house on fire.

Losing my smile for just a moment, I took a swallow of wine, and forced the thought down with it. The other two didn't notice.

The discomfort didn't last. It felt so good to be able to relax for a while: at ease, enjoying conversation. We tossed topics back and forth; talked across each other with enthusiasm when they grew contentious. Colin's rich West Indian accent merged with Nick's ebullient Watford and my quiet Coventry. It livened the place up no end; made it feel like a home again.

Nick's hand sought out mine where it rested on the table-top, and squeezed it. I squeezed back, and felt a little guilty. Sometimes I almost wished I was being more conventionally unfaithful to him; it would be so much easier to cope with ...

'Anyone want some more wine?' I asked at length, and went through to get the second bottle from the fridge. Managed to open it without destroying the cork. Coming back, I found the blokes deep in fresh discussion.

'... miserable gits, though,' Nick was saying, more seriously. 'Won't even pass the time of day. Anyway, I thought MDP were limited to the Establishments and places ...'

'No, we've had serials on secondment before,' Colin said, nodding yes to me as I leaned towards his wineglass. 'Probably got nothing better to do these days. But I know what you mean ...'

'Now, boys, no talking shop please . . .' I moved round the table to top Nick up.

'Their Inspector's okay, though,' he persisted as I started pouring. 'Had a long chat with him. And he was interested, you know? He *listened* . . .'

'What's his name again?'

'Morris,' said Nick. Then: 'Jesus, Raitch . . .' as I spilled wine all over his lap.

'Sorry.' I swallowed. 'Slipped.'

He took it in good part, clambering ruefully up to sponge it off in the kitchen. I just stood where I was, heart punching; my hand pressed to my mouth. Colin, smiling, had to urge me not to worry.

I smiled weakly back, but my heart wasn't in it. My mind was skating out of control. What the hell had they been doing up in this neck of the woods? Had they found out where I lived?

And did Morris know Nick was my boyfriend?

The thought of the two of them so close made me feel faint. I had to sit down, waving Colin's concern aside as politely as I could. Because something – some sick suspicion – told me that he knew all right; and had used Nick to send me a message.

Rachel. We're getting closer.

By the time Nick came back, I more or less had a grip – but still felt like I'd had all the stuffing knocked out of me; so it came as a relief when Colin glanced at his watch shortly afterwards, and said that he'd best be making tracks.

After he'd left, I came back through and set about clearing up the plates. Nick was obviously pleased with the way things had gone, which gave me some comfort – but not enough to fill the hollow ache inside me.

A rattle from the hall as Nick dead-locked the door. I knocked back the last of my wine, and stood there for a moment while my brain soaked it up; then took the piled plates on into the kitchen.

'He's a really nice bloke, isn't he?' I said to Nick as he wandered through after me.

'He is. I'm glad you liked him.'

I dumped everything in the sink, and squirted gooey green Fairy liquid over it; then paused to give Nick a sidelong glance. It was something I couldn't help asking. 'Does he ever get . . . trouble because he's black?'

Thinking about it thinned his smile. 'Sometimes. Yeah. We've got racist blokes in the Met, same as anywhere else. But I think it's getting better. I hope it is . . .' He pondered that ruefully for a moment; then nodded towards the sink. 'You want to wash or dry?'

I kept the tap turned on until the sink was full, the contours of the crockery all but submerged. Then looked back at him, and shook my head. 'Let's leave it.'

'I'm on early turn tomorrow, remember,' he pointed out, a little uncertainly. 'It's all going to be waiting for you when you get up. C'mon, let's . . .'

'I'll manage,' I assured him, wiping my hands. Then I went over and took firm hold of his shirt front. 'Now come on.'

'Rachel . . .' he murmured: a last, half-hearted protest. But he was already starting to grin. Me, I was past that stage by now; my face was serious. Tonight I wasn't even in the mood for foreplay. There was just a single-minded urge to burn away the shadows; and a healthy glow of natural lust.

I drew him towards the stairs.

'Listen . . .'

'You're wasting breath, Nicky boy.' I paused to swallow some of it; then drew back, my stare almost solemn. 'Now come with me . . . up the wooden hill . . . to *Bedfordshire*.'

Yet even in the dark with Nick I didn't feel safe. Even screwing him, I could feel the fear surge up again to fill my belly.

And he was the cause, for all he didn't know it. We'd

reached a plateau of unearthly calm, with me sitting there astride him: my top half cool and naked in the night. And he'd reached dreamily up to stroke me, running his finger down my tingling sternum, between my breasts. His voice was a murmur: almost awed.

'. . . oh Rachel, my angel . . . My bright, bright angel . . .'

A compliment indeed – but right now I could have done without it: knowing that whatever tarnished brightness I could boast of cast a long, dark shadow behind it. One that licked up all my love and pity with its bitterness and grief.

I could imagine Razoxane's mocking gaze against my back. The very thought set my bare skin tingling.

We finished fiercely, with no more words. And after he'd drifted off, I was left lying there against him, watching the ceiling. Too cold for him to warm me – inside or out.

Perhaps an hour passed before I slipped away as well; and then not for long. Something woke me as sharply and completely as a nightmare, though I could remember nothing. And when I finally raised wary eyes above the duvet, it was to find pale moonlight staining the ceiling – and Razoxane staring patiently in between the curtains.

She must have been standing on the old shed roof. Only her face was visible, tinged blue by the moon. No shades tonight. I saw her wink once.

Nick shifted sluggishly against me; slurred something, and was silent.

Razoxane nodded downwards.

Fuck off, I mouthed at her. Unruffled, she sank from view.

Which left me no option, really. (Oh, I could stay here nice and snug, of course – and wait for her to come up and bloody get me.) I sat carefully up, slid my legs from the bed and stood. The mattress settled with a gentle creak; Nick didn't stir.

Quickly I shrugged into my dressing gown and stole

noiselessly out. The landing outside was dim; the stairs descended into blackness. No sound drifted up from below. Hugging myself, I went on down into the pit: tiptoeing from stair to creaking stair.

The hush at the bottom was thick and hissing. I waited, motionless; straining my ears. Then something stirred in the black hole of the breakfast room. With tight-mouthed trepidation I followed the sound, back into the lingering smells of supper: chilli, wine and garlic all greasily congealed . . .

The room that had been so bright and warm a few hours ago felt like a walk-in fridge now. I hesitated on the threshold; then groped for the light switch – and Razoxane's voice came out of the dark.

'Leave it.'

I jumped, despite myself. But my eyesight was growing accustomed to the gloom now, and I began to make out an unfamiliar shape at the table: it materialized slowly as I watched.

'I'd rather we did without the light,' her voice continued drily. 'It bothers my eyes.'

She was slouched in one of the chairs: resting both booted feet on the tabletop, and shrouded in her coat, as ever – head pensively bowed.

'*Now* what do you want?' I whispered hoarsely.

'A word.'

I glanced instinctively towards the ceiling.

'Don't worry, we'll not disturb him. Sit down . . .'

I had the impression of her unseen face coming round to watch me as I crept across the room, giving her as wide a berth as I could. I settled in the easy chair in the corner, and drew my legs nervously up.

'Hear the news this evening?' she asked.

'Yeah . . .' I guessed which item she meant, as well: though it had changed by the time we'd tuned in to the six o'clock bulletin. Two people shot dead in the City – but now no mention of policemen. The first report must have proved unfounded. I'd heard Nick breathe a quiet sigh of relief.

'Two of Morris's men were waiting for you this afternoon,' Razoxane went on casually. 'They'd have killed you, too; if I hadn't killed them first.'

I swallowed hard.

'And did you get the feeling you'd been followed? All the way home?'

'Er . . . yeah.'

'I've given you a second shadow, Rachel. Sort of a familiar spirit. Something to be my eyes and ears . . .'

For a moment, nothing registered. Then a wave of fear and disgust broke over me. I huddled up in the chair, my skin creeping.

'Don't worry,' her voice insisted, 'it's not going to hurt you. It's got no thoughts of its own. But it keeps watch on you and your house – just like I promised.'

Still cringing, I hastily crossed myself. 'Jesus, I don't want it. Get it *off* me.' I blurted it as if I meant some giant spider clinging to my shoulder; right now I felt as if there was.

Razoxane sighed patiently. 'Rachel. You already keep it at arm's length just by being the sort of person you are. It can't even cross your threshold, because you had this place blessed one time . . . didn't you?'

I nodded. That had been soon after we'd moved in. Nick had thought it a great joke, but it had meant a lot to me: a simple little ceremony that made the place alive. *God bless this house, and all who enter it . . .*

'Can I . . . get a candle?' I ventured faintly. She didn't object, so I found my way to the kitchen drawer and lit one up: silently cursing my shaking hands. Its dim, dancing light smeared the room as I came back in and set it on the corner table, behind her back. Then I walked slowly round to face her.

Razoxane raised her head. Her pale, naked eyes looked metallic in the candle glow. I decided I preferred her wearing shades.

'So what happens next?'

'I was coming to that.'

I waited, fingering my crucifix inside my dressing gown.

'What time will your boyfriend be leaving?' she enquired.

'Half five-ish,' I said cautiously.

'As soon as he's gone . . . you need to go too. Meet me at the bottom of the road.'

'Oh, God, now what?' I murmured.

'Work to be done, Rachel. In the dark before dawn. Something you need to see.'

There was a creak of floorboards from overhead.

Razoxane swung her scuffed boots from the tabletop and rose to her feet as smoothly as a ghost. 'I'll see you at half-past five,' she told me, as I heard our bedroom door click open. With adrenaline stinging my stomach, I walked over to the candle and blew it out. Her cold smile vanished in the dark.

A minute or so later, I heard Nick's footsteps on the stairs. But by the time he'd tracked me to the kitchen, the striplights were fully on, and I was leaning rather sheepishly against the worktop with a glass of fizzing water in my hand.

'Oh, hi . . . I've got a bit of indigestion. I came down for some tablets . . .' I took a sip to prove it.

He grinned sleepily; combined with his mussed-up hair, it made him look more boyish than ever. 'I wondered where you were . . .'

I gave him a wan smile, and drank again before it could congeal.

Save it for a few hours' time, I thought bleakly. *I'm wondering where I'll be then as well.*

Chapter 21

It seemed I'd scarcely closed my eyes before the creak of the emptying bed told me the evil moment was here already.

I lay face-down and listened, as though trying to drown myself in the pillow, as Nick came back from the bathroom and quietly dressed. I heard him go creaking downstairs. The sound of the distant kettle swelled and faded; his cereal spoon scraped the bowl. After a minute's silence, the front door opened, and closed again. His footsteps clicked away along the lamplit pavement.

Dry-mouthed but wide awake now, I got up and quickly pulled my clothes on. Jeans, thick socks, warm blouse and a sweater; the central heating hadn't kicked in yet, and I could feel the frost out there. Downstairs, in the dimness, I sought out my coat and mittens; scarf and woolly hat. He'd had nearly ten minutes' start now – surely beyond the point where he might double back for something. With a last, nervous swallow, I ventured out into the night.

The street was quite deserted; the sound of my footfalls seemed loud enough to wake each unlit house. But Razox-ane, as promised, was waiting at the end of the road.

She was hugging herself, her fingers pushed into her arm-pits; the gesture made her look more like a tramp than ever. So did the way she'd wrapped her scarf round her head and face beneath her hat, leaving only the eyes visible to watch me come. It seemed the flat orange glow of the streetlamps was at a level she could stand.

She loosened the scarf as I reached her; let it slip clear of her smile. The way it framed her face made me think of a monk's shabby hood.

'Gone cold, hasn't it?'

I nodded brusquely. The chill was already beginning to chew.

A single car passed on the main road, heading south. She glanced after it, then looked back at me.

'Come on. This isn't the weather to be standing round in.'

We set off in the wake of those dwindling tail-lights; but then they vanished round a distant bend, and we were alone again. The silence of these empty streets was deep and unsettling, as if the houses we passed were full of people who'd died in their beds. But here and there a light was on, and more cars passed from time to time. Even in its sleep, the city stirred.

'Where are we going then?' I muttered, head down.

'Just a couple of miles,' she answered obliquely. 'An old meeting place.'

I recalled something she'd said way back on Chalk Farm Bridge — about *night routes* across London. It made me wonder if we were walking one tonight: following the ghost of some ancient track that once linked separate villages. We were heading down towards Canonbury and Essex Road: the same route I took to work. I'd seen it after dark before, of course; but at this forsaken hour it all seemed different. Older, somehow. Grimmer too.

Another car passed — and seemed to slow. I glanced up, and realized it was a police car. For a heart-crushing moment I thought they were going to stop ... but then it picked up speed once more, and was quickly lost to sight. I let out my breath in a luminous sigh, and kept on walking.

We came to a crossroads. No traffic in sight now, but Razoxane paused like some wary night animal: checking in all directions before proceeding through it. The dark bulk of a church lay just beyond, its spire rising like an iron spike against the gloomy orange sky. She backed towards it, surveying the way we'd come once more; then turned and made straight for the door.

It wasn't until we got there that I realized the place was

238

derelict: its windows boarded up. A dim sign proclaimed it was under the protection of some security firm or other (until it got turned into a bingo hall or something, I thought sourly). The doors were recessed behind a spiky iron gate. Both would be locked fast, of course.

They opened at her touch.

The gate squealed like a rat as she pushed it open. We slipped through into the shadow of the porch. The double doors looked even more imposing – but she simply flexed her hand above the rusted ring, then gripped and twisted it. It gave with a muted creak. All I could do was stare as she eased the near door inwards. A death-rattle creak stretched ahead of us into the dark, and faded away. Peering past her, I felt the fine hairs rise all over me: even the chill out here seemed suddenly preferable to that bottomless black interior.

'Come on,' she murmured, grasped my coat and drew me into the darkness after her.

This may have been a house of God once, but it didn't feel like one now. The blind, unbreathing murk engulfed us like mud. I found myself groping for Razoxane's sleeve and gripping it in turn: in search of comfort – however cold.

A dry rasp in the dark – and then a match-flame grew from her upraised hand; I saw her squinting against the glow. The flickering light pushed the shadows back a pace or two, and showed a bare floor under our feet. The place had been emptied of pews; stripped of all its fixtures. Giant shapes still lurked around the edges of our halo; but as my eyes grew more accustomed, I saw that they were just shadows, snagged on the building's inner contours.

Some stark iron fittings had been left against one wall. One was a votive candelabrum, tall and skeletal. A dozen thin white candles had been embedded on its upturned bed of spikes, and now Razoxane passed her dying flame from wick to wick, kindling a constellation there. The grainy gloom withdrew a little further. But not by much.

The place was just a shell, I could see that now. But where the featureless dark had been hideous and frightening, this candle-stained bleakness was merely mournful. We were standing in an empty carcass: all its guts were gone. Without quite knowing why, I went through the inbred motions, genuflecting towards the non-existent altar, before turning back to Razoxane again.

She'd removed her hat and scarf and was rubbing her fingers idly through her hacked-down hair. Scratching at lice, I shouldn't wonder. But her bleached eyes stayed on me.

'So, now what?' I asked, trying to ignore the cold.

'We wait for the sermon,' she answered drily.

I grimaced, and glanced around – half-expecting to see a ghostly congregation gathering with the same intent. But the church stayed still and empty. When I turned back to Razoxane, she'd lowered her gaze. Something round and smooth and silver was glinting in her gloves.

It looked like an old pocket watch, still trailing its snapped-off chain; the impression confirmed as she flipped it open to study the face. For a moment her expression stayed blank; and then a slow smile came. A look of chilling satisfaction. It made my skin creep just to see it.

Gently she eased down the lid again, and slipped the strange thing under her coat.

My own watch said half-past six now; there were more cars swishing past on the road outside. I was just opening my mouth to say something else when the door's dry hinges creaked.

Scared, I spun on my heel – and saw it was Jackie. She eased in through the door and closed it carefully. By the time she'd crossed the floor to join us, the bounding of my heart had steadied to a jog. I swallowed a throatful of something bitter.

'All right?' Razoxane asked, and she nodded tersely – then looked at me. Her expression seemed to doubt I could be trusted; which, coming from her, was pretty rich.

'She needs to be here,' Razoxane pre-empted her. 'She needs to see.'

Jackie shrugged. I just hugged my elbows and wondered grimly what sights were on the menu. Whatever, I was unlikely to enjoy them.

A restless minute passed. Then the door scraped again, and this time two people came stumbling in — one of them supporting the other. Just past the doorway they wobbled and veered; then came forward again. A stale reek of alcohol reached my nostrils. With a start, I realized a couple of drunks had wandered in on us.

But then the bloke who was doing the holding raised his grimy face, and I saw that it was Brendan. Despite the stains of spilt booze on his clothing, I knew at once that he was sober; could see it in his fierce, fixed expression. And though the other man's coat had been likewise splashed, I was suddenly aware that he wasn't drunk either. He'd been beaten to a stupor. Half of his face was black with blood and bruising.

Brendan dumped him in the middle of the floor and straightened up. He was panting softly. From where I stood, transfixed, I could still see the other's sagging features. It was nobody I'd seen before.

I looked back at Jackie. At Razoxane. And at the sight of their faces — so entirely without pity — it felt like my stomach had curled up and died inside me.

Silence. A pregnant pause that must end in miscarriage — or abortion. Then the last of tonight's unholy congregation slipped in under the preacher's watchful eye. I recognised Frank without surprise; wrapped up in his hospital blanket like someone commemorating hunger strikers at a St Patrick's Day parade.

He closed the door and came forward slowly; acknowledged Razoxane with a curt, unsmiling nod. Whatever his previous protestations, I guessed who'd be running this particular show.

Five of us, standing round the man on the floor. Like

the others, the bloke was dressed for the streets; holes in his shoes as well as his gloves. He was still conscious – but with scarcely strength enough to grovel. All he could do was gurgle when Frank stepped forward and kicked him viciously in the side.

I turned helplessly to Razoxane; but she was donning her hat, like a judge about to pass the sentence of death. Jackie glanced across, and shook her head.

'Don't waste your breath; he's a bastard Peeler. It was McCain found him out . . .'

Oh God, I thought. Oh God.

An undercover copper. For all I knew, a drinking pal of Nick's. And now they were going to kill him in cold blood: before my very eyes . . .

'He touted on us last night, then?' asked Brendan.

'Let's find out,' said Razoxane lightly.

'For God's sake . . .' the man on the stone floor mumbled. He had a Glasgow accent, doubtless genuine; there was too much pain and fear in his voice for fakery. 'I dunno . . . what ye're bloody *on* about . . .'

'Do you not?' Frank sneered, and stepped back to aim another kick. But Razoxane's raised hand stopped him.

'That's enough,' she said softly. 'No need to cause unnecessary suffering.' The twinge of irony in her tone left plenty of room for the other sort.

Nausea swelled inside me at the prospect. I wanted to break away and run, but found I couldn't budge: like I was frozen to the floor. But something else kept me rooted here as well. The knowledge that I couldn't leave the poor sod to die alone . . .

'There are two roads to every truth,' Razoxane told the battered man, as though casting a pearl of wisdom at a pigsty. 'The easy and the hard. The hard way means using powers you don't want to *dream* of. Sharpening my mind to a spade that'll dig out your brain . . .' She smiled faintly down at him. 'But I'm a reasonable woman, as my friend here will tell you – so I'll try the easy way first.'

She nodded to Frank and Brendan, who closed in, grasped his arms, and hauled the helpless copper to his feet. Razoxane stepped forward, her switchknife snapped open – and suddenly the bloke was gagging on the blade.

'Still got your tonsils?' she asked conversationally.

Her victim gawped back at her, his eyes frantic: fighting the reflex action that might at any moment jerk his head back and lose him his tongue.

'How long have you walked behind us?' Razoxane wondered. Her tone was almost musing; the question surely rhetorical. He was hardly in a position to answer it.

I pressed my hands sickly against my mouth.

Razoxane delved deeper, like some demented oral surgeon. The copper's pinioned body thrashed convulsively.

'Don't struggle so,' she crooned. 'Death is *sweet* from the soldier of God . . .'

Even Jackie was looking a little green around the gills. Frank, face set, renewed his purchase on the copper's coat. Razoxane drew back, withdrawing her still unbloodied blade, and coldly smiled again.

'Ready to talk, betrayer?'

A wordless, gasping wail escaped from the man's mouth.

'Good,' she murmured. 'That makes it easier on us all. So tell me, brother Frank: why did you sell us out?'

There was a moment's stunned silence: no one quite believed they'd heard correctly. Then Razoxane looked directly at Frank – and Frank went stumbling back as if she'd punched him in the chest.

Razoxane didn't follow, except with her eyes. Their blue seemed unnaturally bright: almost glowing in the gloom. Frank gave a sudden snarl of pain.

Jackie and Brendan looked as shocked as I felt; the copper, unsupported, had slithered back to his knees, with Brendan still absently clutching his sleeve. Neither terrorist made a move to intervene as Razoxane stepped forward.

Frank was fumbling under his blanket: my heart rate shot up as I realized he was reaching for his gun. Razoxane just kept staring – and then Frank's pistol fell and clattered to the floor, leaving him clutching his head in both his hands. I saw blood oozing from his ears in streams as dark as treacle: as if some hideous noise had burst his eardrums, and was bearing down on him still. A noise that none of the rest of us could hear . . .

Razoxane's hands clenched to fists at her sides. There was a baleful, wintry light in her eyes now. Frank tried to look away, and failed. A moment later he'd suffered an epistaxis, the violent haemorrhage flooding out his mouth and nose. Spitting and snivelling blood, he dropped to his knees.

Razoxane resumed her casual advance.

'Lost your faith, didn't you?' she told him, as he tried to retreat. 'Couldn't cope with my vision. You'd prefer to sell out your comrades, and see them killed, than follow my lead . . .'

I couldn't drag my gaze off his twisted face, but I heard Jackie's indrawn breath beside me. The sound of someone punched – or stabbed – in the stomach. Her doubts had had nothing to do with last night's disaster; it was Frank who'd sent us in and shopped us.

Blood was coming out of his *eyes* now: black tears coursing down in the candlelight. But he raised them to Razoxane, and finally forced out the question he'd probably been nursing all along.

'Who . . . the fuck . . . *are* you?'

'I am the sexton who tolls the bell,' she answered softly. 'The mourner who walks behind you at your funeral. The one who plants the flowers on your *grave* . . .'

He choked then. The whites of his eyes rolled up into the red. He collapsed.

An awful, frozen silence filled the church.

After a moment, I risked a look at Jackie. Then at Brendan. The faces of both were blank with awe. No glimmer of compassion for their comrade-in-arms. I was forcibly reminded of those crazed religious cults, and the people under their sway. People who'll turn their backs on the things they hold most dear, and follow the calling of their leader without question . . .

She'd said fanatics were the easiest of all to use. I had an inkling why, now.

Razoxane thoughtfully turned, and walked over to where the copper crouched. He shrank away; my own heart turned over on his behalf. But then she jerked her head towards the door.

'You'd best be on your way. Forget everything and everyone you've seen tonight. Because if you even whisper it, I'll know. And I'll come looking.'

For a moment he seemed unable to believe she was letting him go. White-faced, he struggled to his feet as Brendan unhanded him; his eyes still fixed on Razoxane.

Razoxane smiled.

That snapped his nerve. He lunged away and staggered over to the door, fought his way out through it – and was gone. With numb surprise, I saw she'd kept her word.

'You're . . . sure he won't talk?' Jackie ventured.

Razoxane nodded, but didn't need to. We'd all seen the look in his eyes. He wouldn't breathe a bloody word.

'Dirty work,' she continued, following Brendan's gaze back towards Frank's body. 'But it needed doing. Now let's get moving. Go to ground again: I'll find you.'

'I'd . . . never have thought it,' Jackie came back, still hesitant. 'Not Frank . . .' I guessed she was trying to assimilate it somehow: forcing facts where they didn't want to go. Perhaps, deep down, a subconscious voice was telling her she should be screaming.

Whatever the inner struggle, I sensed her win it. Or force a draw. Glancing at Brendan, she made for the door. He followed quickly, as if afraid of being left alone with *her*. Which left just me in that unenviable position.

Razoxane came back over, pacing slowly through the fading candlelight; a couple of the flames had died already, and more were sickening. Reaching me, she dropped her gaze a moment, like a bashful little girl; then raised her grinning face to mine.

'You're *horrible*,' I managed, out of breath.

'Aren't I just? But I let the policeman live, at least. As for brother Frank...' she glanced casually behind her '...he'd finally guessed that what I was up to had nothing to do with his Godforsaken cause. He panicked: tried to terminate the group. So I had to deal with him.'

Her knife clicked closed; the noise woke an echo in the empty church. She pushed the bony handle back into her pocket, and regarded me thoughtfully. In this dying light, her eyes seemed clear and colourless.

If looks could kill ...

'We're nearly there now, Rachel. Just one more to do.'

I swallowed stiffly. 'Moorgate ... right?'

She nodded. 'Right.' After a pause, she added: 'There's sort of a problem.'

After a rather longer pause, I said: 'Like what?'

'I think the Moorgate Ankerite can manifest above ground.'

I tried swallowing again, and found the muscles of my throat had seized up.

Razoxane stepped past me; then round behind my back. I turned nervously as she began to circle me where I stood: too closely for my comfort.

'I've been tracking the City's ghosts,' she went on, quite matter-of-factly. 'Its night nomads. Just mindless spirits, for the most part – but one of them is different. I've picked up the same trace at Snow Hill in the west and Aldgate to the east. And this one's got a mind, all right – I've sensed it. Full of malice. Like black ice.'

The idea was unthinkable; I thought it anyway. One of those *things* crawling up from the tunnels and walking abroad – deep in the night, through the lifeless City. Still radiating hatred ...

Razoxane kept walking; her face going through its

phases in the candle glow like a ghostly moon. We were into the last quarter already.

'So what we have to do,' she continued, ignoring my open mouth, 'is lure it. Have it focus itself, so we can bind it – and let it go free.'

'What do you mean, "we"?' I asked faintly.

She came to a halt between me and the candelabrum, so that her face was all in shadow. New moon.

'I mean the two of us together,' was her soft reply. '*Sisters*.'

Helpless to gainsay it, I looked away.

'Come on,' she said after a minute. 'It's time you were getting home.' She turned towards the doors; then stopped. 'Oh, yes. Just one more thing . . .'

For no clear reason, my stomach clenched. But her smile as her face came round was amiable enough.

'Jackie. You've been trying to get through to her, haven't you? Trying to give her doubts.'

I felt my own face betray me: draining of warmth and colour in an instant.

Still smiling, Razoxane leaned forward. 'Don't do that, Rachel. All right?'

Her voice was calm and friendly; it chilled me like an ice-cube down the back of my neck. She turned away without bothering to wait for a reply.

I stared shakily after her for a moment; then followed.

Frank groaned.

I recoiled from his huddled body, biting on my hand to block a scream. Even as I fought for balance, I saw him spasm.

Razoxane had paused, quite unconcerned. 'Come on, then.'

I let my frantic gesture say the obvious; I couldn't trust my voice.

'No need to be afraid,' she told me calmly. 'I didn't kill him. That would have been too easy. For both of us.'

I looked fearfully back at Frank. He'd raised his head

now, and was drooling stupidly at me through the gathering dark. His eyes – half sealed with blood – were blank and glassy. A sound of unspeakable distress came keening from his throat.

I almost gagged. Horror and helpless pity conspired to choke me. The face he wore now was one I'd seen too many times – on people whose minds had not survived the streets. The ones whose brains had been addled by drink, dementia, or sheer despair . . .

'His mind's gone,' she confirmed, with clinical detachment. 'All his memories mashed. He'll wander the streets for the rest of his life – however long that is. Worse than a sentence of death, Rachel. A sentence to *Hell* . . .'

Frank's gawping gaze was still fixed on me. Slowly I backed away. Then, as he began to heave himself up, the last of the candles died – and I finally fled from the all-consuming darkness.

Outside, the street was busier; the stream of traffic quickening. A double-decker rumbled past, its brightly-lit interior full of faces. I turned my own away in fear and shame.

'Safe home, Rachel,' said Razoxane drily. 'I mean that.'

'And then . . . ?' I asked, head down; my voice still dull with nausea.

She smiled. 'I'll let you know.'

And so we went our separate ways. She turned south, towards the City; I headed wearily northwards again, in the direction of home. Perhaps it was a glimmer of daybreak that I glimpsed, up there beyond the streetlamps. But more likely it was only an illusion.

False dawn.

After a minute or two, that spine-tingling sense of something following in my footsteps began again.

Chapter 22

And after all that, I still had work that afternoon – a late shift to get through somehow. Travelling in on the lunchtime bus, I wondered how I was ever going to make it.

Five hours later: it felt like a different day – a different city, too, in the overcast daylight. The horrors of the small hours might as well have been a nightmare; but the chill in my stomach was reminder enough that everything I'd seen was real.

And the skin on my back kept itching.

That insidious sensation vied with one more unsettling still as I crossed the road towards the hospital: the conviction that someone was tracking my progress through a telescopic sight. The sudden blare of a horn almost made me break into a run. But I made it up the steps and in through the doors without incident.

It felt as if someone had just slipped through as they closed behind me. I almost shivered, but didn't turn. I knew there'd be no one to see.

Sod you, Razoxane. I suppose you think it's funny.

All the way to the unit, I could sense the spectre at my shoulder; but just before I got there, its presence seemed to fall behind, and fade. By the time I crossed the threshold, I really was alone. But I didn't doubt that whatever-it-was still lingered out beyond the doors – like something standing guard. It made me feel more prisoner than protected.

The unit was bright and looking busy. Taking a breath, I plunged on in. Lucy glanced up from adjusting a bedside syringe pump and smiled hello, as if this was just another day (which for her, of course, it was). With a numb sense of unreality, I stopped off in my office to lock away my bag.

A moment's stillness when I'd dumped it in my bottom drawer; then I glanced over my shoulder. From outside came all the overlapping sounds of a working ward, but the doorway was empty. No one there to see me dig out the rosary I'd brought, and push it down into my left breast pocket. The clustered beads could make their presence felt there: pressed close to my skin.

By the time we'd gathered for Report, I reckoned I was ready to slip back into the groove: there was more than enough to keep me occupied. The unit was full, with two patients critical – one of them the bloke with query tetanus, who'd deteriorated overnight. The first batch of microbiol tests had been inconclusive; Murdoch had ordered more. Something was bothering him about this one, according to Jean. He'd been in and out of that room all morning.

I could understand why when I went in there myself, accompanying the Physician he'd been admitted under. The patient, pale and sweaty, watched miserably as the consultant discussed him with his juniors. I hovered at the bedside, trying to look reassuring – which wasn't easy, since the medics themselves were at a loss, and looked it. Tetanus was still prime suspect, but septicaemia was tossed back and forth across the sickbed too. I wished they'd go somewhere else for their deliberations: there's something really scary about a doctor admitting he doesn't know what's wrong with you.

I was updating the patient's casenotes back at the station when something clicked inside my head. Clicked, like a snapping bone. Feeling suddenly hollow, I leafed back to the front sheet; and yes, the man's home address was Kentish Town. He'd come to us the other night because his GP couldn't get him into a closer hospital.

Kentish Town. Dog attack. Several days in hospital. Delerium. I crept cautiously forward through the other unit's notes – until I found the written confirmation:

recorded in black and white by some tired but dutiful medic. The half-heard word the patient kept repeating.

Wiking.

I braced myself against a growing shudder.

Razoxane had mentioned dogs. Nick had guessed at Dobermans. I thought of the ugly, healing wounds I'd redressed yesterday, and could almost hear the snarls. The poor man's body was still a mess of scars. Claw marks. Jaw marks. And he'd just been an innocent bystander.

What if those dogs were deliberately put on someone's scent?

The fine hair prickled and rose along my arms. It felt like two cold spiders scurrying up into my sleeves, to meet and mate behind my neck. The sensation was enough to make me flinch.

Murdoch emerged from his office then, and came briskly down the unit towards me. I thought I'd never seen him looking so grim.

'Rachel. A word.'

I rose and followed him a few steps on past the station – away from where Johann was talking to a GP on the phone; out of earshot of a family clustered round the nearest bed. A tightness in my chest told me this was going to be trouble, before he even opened his mouth.

'Mr Wells.' He gave a superfluous nod towards the side-room. 'From now on he's to have full barrier nursing – gowns, gloves, masks, the works. And minimal contact: no one's to go in there without my say-so . . .'

I just stood there with my mouth open for a moment; then, trying to sound professional: 'It's something contagious, then . . . ?'

'I'll say it is. I've just had Palmer from Control of Infection on. He's ninety-nine percent sure it's hydrophobia. God knows how . . .' He registered the blankness of my face then; not that I didn't recognise the word – I just couldn't accept it. He hesitated, almost abashed: as if unwilling to believe what he himself had said. In the pause that followed, I could hear the nearest ventilator hiss and suck – an eerie parody of breathing.

'Don't mention *anything* outside the unit,' said Murdoch tersely. 'There are other tests, and we need to try them all. But I think he's right, Rachel. I think the poor sod's got rabies.'

'You want to go first with the bad news?' Nick asked, reading my expression correctly.

He wouldn't know, of course. Not yet. Not even the police grapevine worked that fast. I decided it might be better if he found things out at his own pace.

'Oh . . . just another of ours on the way out. Bit close to home. Don't worry.' I settled myself next to him on the sofa. 'Want to tell me yours, then?'

His sidelong glance was sombre. 'I'm not sure if I should.'

I felt that slow, chesty upsurge of unease again. Fighting it, I reached out to touch his head; began idly fingering his hair. He would sometimes pull away when I started that. But not tonight.

He'd turned back to the TV screen: but just his profile was enough to show his indecision. I saw his skin tighten; his lips grow pursed. Finally he said: 'Listen . . . don't talk about this to anyone, right? Really, Raitch.' His eyes came round again, imploring now. 'I'll get in a hell of a lot of trouble if it gets out . . .'

I nodded quickly – still curling a lock of his hair around my finger. Drawing it tight.

Nick raised the remote and zapped whatever programme he'd been watching. Silence settled. Then he took a breath.

'You remember on the news . . . those kids who had their hands cut off and things? Well they're beginning to talk, now. And they're saying it was coppers who did it to them. They're screaming it.'

I tried to look shocked. 'God, no . . .'

'And it's getting round, of course it's getting round. We

had bloody rent-a-mob holding a demo outside the station today – raving on about police *barbarity* . . .' He shook his head, clearly appalled that such could even be suspected.

'Yeah, but . . . no one's going to really believe that, are they? Not ordinary people . . .'

'Oh, people will believe whatever the hell they want,' he muttered darkly. 'But this time it's worse than they think. Much worse.'

And this would be the bit that hadn't come out yet. What I was sworn to silence on. Well, I already had a case of clinical hydrophobia to keep under my cap – not to mention a gang of murderers with mad dogs. One more secret couldn't pose too many problems.

'There's someone going around pretending to be police,' Nick told me, his face as bleak as his voice.

I looked dutifully surprised. 'And . . . you reckon they did this, then?'

He nodded. 'There's something nasty going on, Raitch. Something very nasty. Those shootings in the City . . . the first report we heard was almost right. Two blokes in police uniform shot dead. Then they find they're not real coppers at all. Cast-off uniforms and dead men's numbers. *That's* why the subsequent reports made no bloody mention . . .'

The two Peelers who'd been waiting for me. I didn't need to fake a shaken look as I snuggled closer.

He slipped an arm around me. 'So, we've got someone impersonating police officers out there. And with so many coppers on the ground at the moment . . . drafted in from all over . . . we haven't a clue how many more there are.'

'You . . . think it's something organised?' I prompted: anxious to know how clear a picture they had now. It had taken his monolithic Met a while to wake up, but it surely wasn't too late. Maybe Morris's loan – his borrowed time – was about to be called in . . .

Yes. Oh please.

Nick shrugged. 'That's our guess. Gangland. Contract killers or whatever. But nothing's to be said.'

I frowned. 'Why not?'

'That comes from the top. They say it'll damage public confidence in the police. Especially in the current climate . . . with so many armed response units around.'

I could see their point, I supposed. Damaged public confidence wouldn't be the half of it. Panic was one word that came to mind.

In view of the Peelers' record to date, it might be justified, as well.

Rabid dogs, I thought. God help us. Rabid *dogs*.

'Besides,' Nick went on cynically, 'people might not even believe it. Say it was something we'd made up to cover ourselves. So: we have to track the bastards down without going public. Those are the orders.'

The hunt was on, then. The clock was ticking. But the closer they got to Morris, the closer he and his vicious cohorts would doubtless get to Razoxane – and me.

Full circle, Nick. If only you knew.

'Another thing . . .' he said; then wavered. Gave me an apologetic glance. 'I really shouldn't be saying this . . . but . . . there was some weird sort of . . . ritual thing about those shootings, apparently. They found these Roman coins on the bodies – on their eyes and in their mouths. Genuine ones, too, so I heard.' He spread his hands. 'Who knows, it might be a clue. We're checking museums, coin-collectors, fences . . .'

But not the observers of ancient customs, I thought dully. Not those who paid – however mockingly – the dues of the phantom Ferryman.

And how many men had Morris lost to her now? Was it eight? *All part of the game of cats and mice*, she'd told me; but now I guessed the game was almost up. After eight lives lost even cats lose their patience; stop toying with the mouse and move in for the kill.

I had a horrid feeling that things were picking up speed: racing through the dark towards a climax. A destination as final as that dim, solid wall at the end of the Moorgate line.

'But let's leave it, eh?' Nick muttered. 'You've got enough on your plate without my troubles.' A pause; then he squeezed my shoulders. 'Fancy an early night?'

'Thought you'd never ask,' I said.

Chapter 23

Down in the tube the following evening, moodily waiting for the next train west, I became aware of a commotion at the end of the platform – and realised I wasn't clear of work yet.

Someone seemed to have collapsed: there were people gathering – probably more in curiosity than concern. My heart sank even as I turned my head to look. My uniform was already drawing hopeful glances. No chance of me looking the other way.

After a fraught, fragmented shift, this was all I needed. Not bothering to hide my irritation, I trudged down to see what I could do.

'Excuse me, please . . .' But they were already making room, glad to step back and stare while someone else took charge. All except one, still down on one knee beside the supine body. He glanced up as I craned forward, and I found that it was Gary.

'Rachel . . .' He tried, and failed, to smile; I reckoned he looked as tired as I felt.

I squatted down beside him, my sinking heart already in my stomach. The bloke on the floor was quite obviously dead. His eyes were glazed, half-open; a bubble of spit had caught between his lips. Like Gary, he was gutter-scruffy, his open coat revealing layers of jerseys.

Instinctively I felt for a pulse in his scrawny throat, and found nothing. I was just working up the nerve to try some token mouth-to-mouth when Gary touched my shoulder and drew me upwards and away.

'Leave him; let him rest.' His voice was quiet, but now he raised it. 'Someone called for an ambulance?'

'There's a hospital just down the road,' said someone, and went on up the stairs — so nonchalantly that I wasn't sure if he was actually on his way or not. Gary returned his gaze to the body.

'He's not the first this month. He'll not be the last, either. You know what this city is, Rachel? Just a cemetery without crosses.' He rubbed a grubby hand across his forehead, then turned to me. 'I need some air; you coming?'

I wasn't sure if I should; but there was nothing either of us could do for the poor bloke now. So I broke away from the small, unravelling group and followed him back upstairs towards the street. No one seemed interested enough to ask where we were going.

Out in the cold again, he dug his hands deep into the pockets of his threadbare coat, jumping briefly on the spot to get warm. I waited, restless, hugging my own coat round me. It was windy tonight, and the breeze came from the City. Which hardly augured well.

'I'm doing the rounds tonight,' he murmured. 'My parish visits, you could call them.' He smiled briefly, as if at some bitter joke; then looked at me in earnest.

'You're coping? With McCain?'

I nodded.

'Has she been on to you again?'

'Yes,' I said — summing up my disgust in the syllable.

'You have to be so careful, Rachel. A *legion* of dead men have been this way before her.'

'Which way?' I asked uneasily.

Beckoning me with a jerk of his head, he started to walk. Reluctant as I was, I followed. With the intermittent wind in our faces, we headed deeper into the City.

'I don't know the whole of it,' he admitted. 'But I hear whispers. The prayers of the dying. Whatever she's really up to, you need to keep well clear.'

Easy enough to say, mate. Especially when leading me right back towards her hunting ground — and Morris's too. I began to drag my feet.

'Listen . . . I really should be getting home . . .'

We were close to St Paul's already; the roads lay wide and empty in the fuzzy street-glow. A set of traffic lights stayed resolutely red, as if holding up the passage of ghosts. Our own pace dwindled to a stop beside them.

He was about to say more when his gaze, already restive, slid past my head – and locked. I turned at once.

Razoxane was watching us from over the road: beside the chunk of ruined church that marked the corner.

My fingers knotted to a fist around the strap of my bag as she slowly advanced to join us. Her shades had melted into the shadow of her hat brim, leaving her whole upper face in darkness; but her mouth was a thin, unsmiling line. Then, as she passed close to the traffic light, its scarlet glow tinged the whole of her bleak expression.

A car sped past as she reached the pavement, heading west; and the City was still again.

'Talking about me?' she said after a pause.

We neither of us answered.

That antique silver watch was in her hand. She slid her thumb across the lid in a curious, circling gesture – then extended the thing, still closed, towards Gary like someone brandishing a weapon. A glance at Gary's face found apprehension there – which boosted my own. But he stood his ground.

'Want to see?' she asked him, her voice still dangerously soft.

'I'm not afraid of it, McCain,' he came back flatly.

I looked back at Razoxane: saw the thin, ironic smile reclaim her features. 'No,' she agreed after another edgy moment; 'I don't believe you are.'

She closed her fingers round the watch – or whatever it was – and dropped it back into her pocket.

'Shouldn't you be about God's business?' she suggested pointedly.

Gary hesitated; looked at me. 'Will you be okay?'

I nodded heavily. 'I'll be okay.'

'All right, then . . .' He returned his gaze to Razoxane. 'I'll see you, sister.' Then smiled at me. 'Take care.' We both watched him walk away, until his shape was lost amid bright lights and deeper shadows.

Razoxane paced around to stand beside me. 'Fancy a walk?'

'*Razoxane*. I'm knackered.' *And cold, and very nervous.*

'It won't be long . . . Nothing like a spot of *vampire*-dodging to concentrate the mind.'

I quickly looked behind myself.

'We're all right at the moment,' she purred. 'There were a couple of Whisky-Alphas prowling round here earlier, but they've moved east again now.' She glanced about us. 'I've been trying to get a fix on the last Ankerite. Something's been this way again. But all you pick up is the trail . . . like what a slug leaves behind in a cellar.'

I shivered, not entirely from the cold. 'Well, would you prefer to run right into it?'

'I'll have to, won't I? In the end; in my good time. Meanwhile . . .' She turned again, pensively; scanning the deserted junction. 'I've come back down the course of the Walbrook, looking for clues. This part of London's full of echoes. Let's see what we can find.'

Without further ado, she set off briskly northwards: away from the bone-white bulk of the Cathedral; heading up towards the Barbican. I scuttled after her – drawing closer as we crossed that side-street where Morris's transit had been lurking last time. But tonight the length of its kerb was empty.

I wasn't reassured. There was a sense of desolation to the City at night: like a place abandoned to its phantoms. Even the intermittent traffic from London Wall was only passing through – with silence waiting, poised, to fill the gaps.

Razoxane went lightly up some steps onto the highwalk. Perhaps she was seeking height advantage; I just felt uncomfortably exposed. As she paused to survey the streets around us, leaning forward against the railing, I turned my shoulder to the wind, and shook.

'Scared?' she enquired.

'Of course I'm bloody *scared*.'

'Don't worry. I doubt if it's abroad tonight.'

The chill wind changed direction, as if disputing the fact.

I moved uneasily up beside her, peering down. There was the faintest haze of frost beneath the streetlamps. 'Is it, like, physically underground somewhere?'

She shrugged. 'There might be some remains. A cavity of bones and rubbish in the Red Layer; a hidden cell. But that's just its chrysalis now. You saw how the one at Bank could materialise at will – and I thought it was the strongest. But this one can project itself as far as the surface; it's stronger still.'

And even angrier? I was still gnawing on the thought when she straightened up and went on towards the footbridge.

I hurried to catch up. 'Does Morris understand what he's doing? Taking sides with something like that?'

'He understands. Oh yes. He, of all people, understands.' She glanced behind us, briefly. 'Plain human butchery wasn't enough; he's come in search of elemental evil. I don't suppose he's told his men, though; and I don't suppose they care. Just so long as they've the chance to keep on killing . . .'

'But they have to have a reason,' I complained, as we crossed above London Wall. 'People can't just kill for *nothing*. Surely . . .'

'Rachel: listen. It's *what they do*. The army was their home – it psyched them up to be berserkers; then left them to find their own way. For Morris they were ideal material. Drifting; damaged. He sucked them out of your society, and forged his own hermetic unit – loyal only to each other and to him. You've heard of group dynamics? They apply to death-squads most of all.'

I lapsed into unhappy silence.

From the bridge, we followed the walkway eastwards. The contrasts in this area were almost surreal: crumbling ramparts hemmed in by ultra-modern buildings. Construction sites lay here and there as well – like acres of no-man's land between the future and the past. And everything bathed in the same weird orange light. It felt like a city in limbo.

Razoxane turned left, down a flight of steps; I trudged miserably in her wake. We were into the Barbican now – and not too far from Moorgate. The thought just emphasized my jitters.

She paused as we reached ground level, and produced her spinner: turned it thoughtfully on its axis; then led the way out into an open space.

There was an old church tucked away here: bizarrely out of place in this modern setting. It was clearly undergoing renovation – enclosed in a skeleton of scaffolding and festooned with draped tarpaulins. It looked like the shrouded carcass of a dinosaur.

Beyond it, a small oblong lake gleamed under floodlights, like a latter-day moat. We walked across the paving stones towards it.

'Why do you have to keep dragging me around, anyway?' I grumbled. Meaning: I want to go *home*.

Razoxane smiled. 'For every dark angel, a bright one.'

'I'm no angel,' I muttered. 'As you very well know.'

'Lost your innocence at last?'

I actually managed a cynical little laugh. 'Shall I tell you something? I wanted to be a Nursing Sister from when I was little, and you know why? Because they always wore blue dresses like the Virgin Mary's. *That's* how bloody innocent I was.'

The long tarpaulins rustled in a twist of wind, and sagged into stillness again.

'Good to know you've grown up a bit since then,' said Razoxane drily. 'But I still need your light, Rachel: your faith, and hope, and charity. Especially when dealing with shadows like these.'

I shuddered; turned on the spot. 'This Ankerite. What does it *want*?'

'Well . . . by any definition, these creatures are insane – so it's hard to tell. You'll remember they're drawn by suffering and death. The smell of old ghosts in ancient earth. That's why burial grounds attract them; and other places that smell of the sick and the dead . . .'

I walked moodily over to the railing and leaned against it, peering down into the water. Razoxane's slow footsteps passed behind me.

'The Ankerite under St Paul's will have been drawn by such remains,' she continued. 'There's the site of a Roman cemetery just to the north . . .'

'Gary reckons this whole city's a cemetery without crosses,' I murmured.

'Not quite,' said Razoxane calmly. 'Variation on a theme. Look . . .'

I turned to do so – and recoiled against the railing. 'Je*sus*!'

In point of fact, it wasn't; but the man who loomed above us had been crucified as well.

He hung there, motionless: staring down. His body spreadeagled on a St Andrew's cross of planks. The ugly X had been lashed to the scaffolding like a part of its framework: overshadowed by loose billows of tarpaulin and the church itself. The people who lived across the floodlit moat might not even notice him until daybreak.

Another down-and-out; I could smell the meths from here. Perhaps they'd used nailguns on his wrists and shins, to make a quicker job of it. He might still have been alive when that had happened. But he clearly wasn't now.

My hand was at my mouth. 'Oh God, *why* . . . ?'

Razoxane regarded him critically; then glanced at me – and grinned.

'I imagine Morris thought he wanted putting up for the night.'

I just turned back to the lake, and waited for my nausea to subside.

'Sorry,' she murmured amiably. 'Couldn't resist that.'

But my thoughts were wallowing in mud already. Hadn't some of Boudicca's victims been crucified as well? Or burned, or hanged, or butchered. And as for the women . . .

Instinctively I crossed my arms over my breasts, and hugged them.

'This is what I think it wants,' said Razoxane: 'revenge.'

I glanced at her sidelong as she stepped up to the rail beside me; but her own gaze was directed downwards, into the glowing depths. She didn't raise it as she spoke again.

'After all that time they've spent rotting in the earth, they're *inimical* to human life. This one's reached the surface with two thousand years of suffering to repay; and here's Morris, doing things like this. Doing evil to define his very self. You don't need much imagination to see how they can use each other . . .

'Now, we'd best be getting on.'

I gave the crucified corpse a final glance, and quickly crossed myself. With a mental apology for leaving him in that horrible position, I went scooting off after Razoxane.

She stopped again at the top of the next flight of steps: paused to peer around the corner, then beckoned me up beside her. I craned out cautiously to look – and caught my breath.

There was a single, dark figure on the footbridge we'd crossed a few minutes back. Standing motionless; watching the cars that passed below him.

We slipped away east, and reached Moorgate a few minutes later: safely north of the station's bleak façade. Razoxane came with me to the bus-stop, where a well-lit double-decker was ticking over. One that could take me out of the ring of steel, and home.

'Did you pick anything up, then?' I asked her at the doors.

She shook her head. 'All quiet again tonight. I'll move further east . . . see if anything's been stirring.'

We parted without goodbyes. I boarded the bus, went upstairs for a wider view, and settled grimly down to wait. The streets were quiet. After a minute, I saw Razoxane drift across them like a piece of windblown litter, and vanish in the shadows.

Off on the next circuit: pursuing her relentless search across the City. But as I waited for the bus to move off, a fresh unease began to throb within me. Freed of her presence, my mind kept coming back to Gary's warning; the suspicion he'd so ominously voiced. *A legion of dead men have been this way before her.*

I still wasn't sure if he'd meant before or after they had died.

Chapter 24

London, from the north, looked as bleak and brooding as the sky above it – like Highgate Cemetery writ large.

Sitting dejectedly back against the bench, I let my gaze drift. I'd known that Primrose Hill would draw me back, and here I was. Perhaps I'd come hoping to get things into perspective; but even this height advantage didn't help. The breadth of the horror was still more than I could grasp.

And I was in too deep, and drowning. Try as I might, I couldn't *comprehend*. I'd even tried to put myself in Morris's place: to understand him, somehow. He'd done appalling things – but why? Surely not just for the sake of it. If only I knew what was driving him onward, it might make sense of his savagery. Might make him easier to face.

If not to stop.

Something I'd received through the post this morning had brought a mocking new perspective of its own. A cheery, relentlessly upbeat circular from one of the girls I'd trained with: our sort of self-appointed Set Leader. As well as sharing bits of news about half-forgotten friends, she'd included advance notice of a tenth anniversary get-together. Other halves welcome. A creche for the kids. *It'll be great to catch up on everyone's news*.

I'd left it on the breakfast room table. The tear stains were probably still drying.

Someone's dog came bounding past – I almost cowered – and scampered around on the nearby grass. Further downslope, towards the trees, two boys were playing with a Frisbee. All part of a peaceful winter afternoon. All right for some.

'Hello there, Rachel. Enjoying the view?'

My head turned quickly – and it was Jim Stanley, coming up with his hands in his anorak pockets and a grin on his face. My first reaction was something like guilt: I gave an automatic smile back, and tried not to think how long it had been since I'd last helped with a soup run. Or how many excuses I'd made up . . .

Not that he'd hold it against me: he wasn't the type. Stopping beside the bench, he watched the dog chase its own tail for a moment; then lifted his gaze towards the city.

'You live round here, then?' I asked, before the pause could set into a silence.

'Camden Town. I come up here a lot. Even when Max there doesn't want to stretch his legs . . .' He took an appreciative breath of air, then glanced at me. 'How've you been keeping then? I've not seen you for a while.'

'Oh . . . I'm surviving.'

'Working you hard, are they?'

I gave a rueful sort of grin. 'As ever.'

'Listen . . . come back for some tea, if you like. You've met Judy, haven't you? She'd be glad to see you.'

I hesitated for a moment: not really looking for an excuse, just instinctively reticent. But a hot cup of tea was a tempting prospect on an afternoon as dull as this one. And right now I could do with the company.

'That'd be nice,' I nodded gratefully. 'Thanks.'

We both watched the dog for a while; but my gaze kept straying beyond it. Back across the outlines of London. Despite another spell of reluctant research work, I still couldn't picture the ancient settlement buried beneath it. Not a stone had been left standing; what was once the countryside around had been engulfed. A rumoured battle-field at the ford of a stream was now the stark reality of King's Cross. Legend had even located Boudicca's unmarked grave beneath the station. All of it forgotten now. People passed by in their thousands, and never knew.

I wished I was as ignorant as they were.

Jim's dog came padding towards me, and sniffed hopefully at my knees. Its muzzle was wet and sticky with saliva. I cringed back, and kept my hands well clear.

'Don't worry,' Jim said cheerfully, 'he's just being friendly.'

I'd heard that from dog-owners before. Usually just before the friendly bugger sank its teeth into the nearest available limb.

What if the virus was beginning to get around?

'Don't like dogs much, eh?'

I managed a sickly smile.

'Here, Max. Good boy . . .' Jim stooped in welcome and fitted a leash; fondling the animal's head before straightening up. 'All right, then?' he asked me.

'Fine. Just lead the way.' Getting to my feet, I turned my back on the slaty city, and felt it slip away behind me as I followed him down off the hill.

We strolled back through Chalk Farm and into Camden: the same route Razoxane and I had walked that time before, though I preferred not to think about that. His house was in a quiet side-street, away from the crowds and the traffic. A nice, roomy place, I reckoned, staring up while he fished out his keys. Three solid-looking storeys. Years of British weather had taken their toll; but maybe a home *should* look lived-in. They'd given it character, as well as cracked paint.

A delicious smell of cooking beckoned us on in as soon as the door was open. The dog went bounding ahead, barking enthusiastically. 'Jim, keep that animal out of my kitchen,' came Judy's warning voice.

I couldn't help smiling. The hall was warm and cosy: the front door closed tight on the frosty afternoon. Jim redirected the dog into the lounge and shut it in, then motioned me to follow him through. 'I've brought Rachel Young back for a cup of tea,' he called ahead. 'Met her up on the Hill . . .'

'Hi, Rachel,' Judy said as I reached the kitchen. 'Haven't seen you since before Christmas . . .' There was a great vat of stew on the cooker, and she paused to give it a stir. I had pretty much an invalid's appetite at the moment, but the aroma was almost enough to give me hunger pangs.

'Cooking for an army, are you?' I wondered.

'Who knows? We've got open house tonight. It's as well to be prepared . . .'

I nodded, still admiring the kitchen (pine, but unpretentious). Jim had mentioned this initiative of theirs before. Now that their kids had left home, they'd started opening their doors to people off the streets. And not as a glorified soup-kitchen, either; rather, a table shared. *We were afraid it might seem patronizing, at first,* he'd told me. *Crumbs from the rich man's table, that sort of thing. But it's working out well. We've even got our regulars, now . . .*

Judy tasted a spoonful of stew, and seemed satisfied. Like Jim, she wasn't far into her forties; brisk and agreeable, with blue eyes and sandy, sensibly-cut hair. From the first time we'd met she'd been friendly, forthcoming: coaxing me out of my natural quiet. Her unforced generosity and Jim's sometimes put me to shame – though I knew they'd hate for that to happen. And they were neither of them religious. Not at all. I found that quite a salutary reminder, too.

The kettle boiled a minute later, and Jim made the tea. 'Will Paul want a cup, do you think?' he asked. Judy glanced ceilingward, and shrugged.

'Our son's back from university for his reading week,' Jim explained, leading the way back towards the living room. 'There's tea if you want it, Paul,' he called as we passed the staircase. '. . . He's not quite sure how to take the altruism of his aged parents,' he confided drily, as we settled down in armchairs.

I glanced around. The room, which seemed to double as a study, was full of casual clutter. Books everywhere. Leaning back, I studied some of the spines. Politics, environment, serious fiction; but stuff like crime and sci-fi too. And not a little humour.

'Nice place,' I murmured.

He smiled. 'Bit big for us now, with just the two of us. That's what gave us the idea of having open house here.'

'I wish I had your dedication, you know.'

'Don't, Rachel. There's no need. We're lucky to be in a position to share what we have. Christ, it's *your* dedication I envy – being a nurse and all. I couldn't do that.'

I shrugged modestly, and sipped my tea.

'Keeping you busy, you said . . .'

My mind flitted back to the restrained, sedated figure in the darkened side-room. The convulsions had begun, now. They came quite suddenly. They were awful to watch.

I tipped my weary head against the chairback. 'Oh, it gets you down, sometimes. You can't help it. And not just work . . .' I hesitated, then pushed on. 'It's just, like, everything's so depressing at the moment, you know? People doing dreadful things to each other . . .'

I had to unburden myself on someone, even if they never got to know the worst of it. Jim nodded gravely. 'Terrible, isn't it? Those bombings . . .'

'And those lads who got . . . attacked.' I paused. 'You don't think that was really the police, do you?'

He shook his head. I felt a tiny trickle of relief.

'You're right about it all just getting you down, though. All this violence, this killing. So *mindless* . . .'

'They reckon they've got reasons, though,' I ventured (devil's advocate: drawing him on). 'The terrorists, I mean . . .'

'Depends how you look at it. Subjectively, yes they have: they've got a deep sense of injustice, they feel they've been dispossessed and wronged – certainly. But take a step back, and you see how pointless it still is. Objectively, the killing gets them nowhere. Wasted lives. Just banging someone else's head against a brick wall.'

He had a point. I mulled it round with another mouthful

of tea. But I knew I wouldn't be able to let it lie. It was the sense of *anarchy* out there that really scared me: death and destruction run out of control. I needed, for sanity's sake, to find an order in it somewhere. Some reason why terrorists could blow up a tubeful of people; why mercenaries could mutilate in cold blood.

Why, nineteen centuries ago, men had skewered and disfigured the women of Roman London . . .

Someone — presumably Paul — put his head round the door at that point: giving me a slightly wary glance before looking to Jim. 'Okay for me to borrow the car tonight, Dad?'

'I should think so, yes. This is Rachel, by the way; she helps with the soup run sometimes. She's a nurse.'

Paul's guarded expression lightened somewhat: he turned to me again. 'Yeah? Which hospital do you work in?'

I told him; saw his interest. It turned out he had hopes of becoming a medical lab technician. I reckoned he was also a little intrigued to meet a nurse in mufti: dressed in jeans and baggy jumper like anyone else. His first assumption had probably been that I was one of these disreputables his parents had started inviting in.

'He's a good lad,' Jim murmured after he'd gone; I smiled at the tinge of pride in his voice.

A cold dusk was coming down outside. The nearest streetlamp was on already. I looked at my watch.

'Time I was getting on, I think. I'd like to be home before dark . . .' I looked in on Judy to say goodbye, and the two of them saw me to the door.

'You're welcome to stay for supper, you know,' Judy said; but as I pointed out, poor Nick would be wondering where I'd got to. 'Come over soon, though,' she told me firmly. 'Both of you. It'll make a nice change, cooking for just four.'

I set off for the tube station feeling warm and comfortable inside: rather better than I had all day. Not really concentrating on the oncoming pedestrians in Camden High Street, I came up short when someone in my path said: 'Rachel . . .'

I raised my eyes – to find Gary smiling back at me, young Lisa beside him. He had an arm draped round her shoulders.

'Er . . . hi.'

'We're eating with some friends tonight,' said Gary amiably. 'A couple of good people who don't mind who they share their meals with.' He gave Lisa a little squeeze; she'd rested her head against his shoulder, her face expressionless and calm.

I just nodded: not offering any connection of my own. 'How are you?' I asked, a little lamely.

'Oh, we're managing. You want to come along?'

'I'm just on my way home . . . I'd be glad to, otherwise. Really.' I meant it, as well. Jim and Judy hadn't let filthy clothes and street-smells put them off, and I was learning too.

'Dunno how many are coming,' Gary went on. 'The word just gets round. But there'll be enough responsible folk there to make sure no one takes advantage.'

'Like you,' Lisa murmured.

'Nah. I'm just going for a good time . . .' He grinned at her, cracking laugh lines round his eyes; then looked back at me. 'It's just like the Book says, Rachel: many will come from the east and the west, and sit down for supper in the Kingdom of God. The outcasts'll eat before the Chosen. And the reward will go to the ones who least expect it.'

Again I nodded. I knew what he meant.

His look became more serious. 'You were okay, the other night?'

'Yeah . . . We make out, me and her. Unfortunately. But thanks.' I found a wry smile of my own. 'Hope you have a really good time.'

I watched as they continued on towards the Stanleys'; then turned again towards Camden Town tube. Despite the grime of the place, its glowing entrance and luminous sign stood out like a welcome in the gathering gloom.

After we'd eaten that evening, I wandered upstairs to get something to read – and found myself drawn to the Julian of Norwich book. Something she'd written was stirring in my head like an unborn thought. I flicked my way through, and found it.

You shall not be overcome.

Being a wise woman, she'd qualified that of course: a warning to those who expected an easy ride. *He did not say, 'You shall not be tempest-tossed, or wearied, or diseased.' But He said, 'You shall not be overcome.'*

The people I'd met today had unwittingly conspired to brighten my mood; but the underlying cause of my depression was still down there. Everything was coming to a head, I was sure of that now. In my mind's eye I could almost see the red lights burning in the tunnel's dead end. And Razoxane claimed to be in control, but was she? Or were we both of us stuck on a runaway train? Getting closer by the second.

And faster all the time.

PART 3

Death is Sweet from the Soldier of God

Chapter 25

'You're really tense tonight,' Nick murmured in the dimness; gently stroking. 'What's on your mind?' A mild enquiry; but I could sense the concern behind it.

'Just tired,' I insisted. 'That's all . . .'

He explored a little further. 'Bloody hell, Raitch, your hairs are standing on end. Come here . . .' He gathered me to him tight, and we lay in silence for a while. The feel of his flesh was warm and comforting; but the fine hairs on my body stayed erect for many minutes, before softening into down.

'It's that patient of yours, isn't it?'

The fact that someone in our hospital was dying of rabies had been made public now; the media had shouted about it good and loud. Michelle had sworn she'd seen *Twenty Things You Didn't Know About Rabies* in her boyfriend's copy of the *Sun*.

'Yeah, well . . .' I swallowed. 'It's a bit stressful for us all, at the moment.'

Whatever grisly details had been printed in the papers, they couldn't convey the harrowing reality of nursing a hydrophobic patient. For me, the worst of it wasn't the fits or the fearful hallucinations, but the lucid moments, the pockets of calm, when Richard – as we knew him now – was able to contemplate exactly what was happening to him.

'Help me, Sister,' he'd whispered today, lying exhausted on his sweat-stained sheets. '*Please* help me . . .' But there was no help to be had. No hope.

He might last another three days.

Tonight, as I'd brushed my teeth, the froth of toothpaste

oozing from my mouth had brought it all back to me afresh. I'd frozen up: just staring at myself in the mirror while the contents of my mouth congealed. Then spat and spat into the washbasin, until the last of it was gone.

Nick slowly stroked my hair. The effect was soothing: soporific. Eventually I let myself go limp. The pictures in my head clouded over. Down I slid, into the darkness.

Where Razoxane the grave digger was working.

I heard her before I saw her: heard her muddy shovel grate on coffin-wood. The familiar clammy wetness crept over me, making me shiver in my sleep. Then vision followed, filling out the landscape like a spectral dawn.

Razoxane was yards away: head down over her labours. The hole she'd dug was wider now, and deeper. It made me think of a cavity wound – glistening and raw.

Some irresistible compulsion began drawing me towards the edge.

I struggled to resist – to turn and run – and found I couldn't. My own mind held me prisoner. My subconscious had something to show me. And whatever, it wouldn't be denied.

So I picked my way forward, step by sucking step: as cautiously as someone passing a sleeping dog. But if Razoxane was dreaming this scene from her side too, and sensed my presence once again, she didn't show it. Her face, when I glimpsed it, was set and sombre.

The edge of the pit was already sagging; I came as close as I dared, and peered downwards.

The coffin was uncovered now, apart from a coating of slime. As soon as I saw it, I felt dread convulse inside me, like icy indigestion.

Something awful lay under that lid. I could feel the chill of it from here – far colder than the rain. Something monstrous, compressed into that narrow space.

It was like coming to a tower in the midst of a wasteland, and finding the first atomic bomb about to blow.

How far can you run in thirty seconds? Far enough?

Staring helplessly down at the coffin, I realized the digging sounds had stopped. There was just the hiss of rain, like the end of an old record. I looked up sharply.

Razoxane was leaning on her spade, watching me.

Smiling.

Even as I recoiled, I felt the mud beneath my feet begin to move. With a gush of fright I realized my side of the pit was caving in. I tried to backtrack: groped for balance. Too late. A great chunk of slimy clay collapsed inwards and took me with it. Before my mind could summon up a scream, I was dropping straight towards the coffin lid.

The impact never came. Instead I was delivered back into the darkness of deep sleep: free-fall. My stomach shrank as I began to plummet. I tried with all my mind to think myself awake before I hit whatever must come next.

Terminal velocity: I remembered that from physics, too. After what seemed a five mile drop I must have reached it. But I still landed in my bed in one piece.

Stillness then. Silence. Darkness. I lay unbreathing. The mattress felt hard and cold, as if I was resting on its naked springs. After a wary while, I tried to move.

I found I couldn't.

Before I could try again, a flare of light filled my eyes like a falling sun. Unable even to squint, I lay there, blinded: seeing only the fierce and featureless white. But gradually, as my scalded sight became accustomed, I realized it was the glare of an operating lamp. A theatre light, slung low.

A thick, distinctive smell had clogged my nostrils by then. Formalin. Which they use in mortuaries . . .

A man leaned into view above me, blocking out the blaze. Green coveralls and bin liner apron; pale yellow surgical gloves. As he glanced aside, I registered the scalpel gripped in one of them.

'Ready when you are, Dr Ryan,' he told someone out of my sight-line; his Geordie accent amiably brisk. Absurdly,

277

it was that liveliness which clinched it — along with the absence of a mask to cover his bearded smile. Suddenly I knew who this must be.

Anatomical pathology technician.

Mortuary Man.

For a moment longer he stared down at me, his expression detached and impersonal. Then I felt him cut me across the chest: like a finger pressing firmly, leaving a line of numbness that grew swiftly into pain. With barely a pause, his blade was between my breasts, and drawing coldly downwards. I had the horrid impression of being unzipped like an old coat. I wanted to shriek, and couldn't even sob, nor bat an eyelash.

People were talking around me: their words muffled as if by water. Shiny green ghosts at the edge of the aching light. A distant voice murmured something about the soccer; someone closer, overhead, laughed shortly. Then I felt latex fingers grasp the lapels of my flesh, and spread them wide. The weight of my breasts slid off to left and right. The pain was hideous. But the clearness of my head was far, far worse.

I heard as well as felt my ribcage opened: the crunch of cartilage and bone. I even caught a glimpse of my whole glistening chest plate — sternum and stumps — as he lifted it out and laid it casually aside. And surely I was dead now: dead and gone. *So why was I still here?*

In all my agony, I wished only that I could cry; that the tears in my eyes would alert them to the horror of what they were doing. Someone would see, and shout *STOP* . . .

But they were all too busy gassing even to notice. Just a routine job, to them: maybe one of half a dozen today. And now the technician was in among my organs. Delving, cutting; tugging clear.

I felt myself being emptied: pulled apart. Just stale, sterile air where my stomach had been; a greasy hollowness for guts. At one point he prised my mouth open and dug inside to cut my larynx loose, setting off a burning gag reflex even though the vomit had nowhere left to come from. Then heart and lungs came out of me together, dripping. But still my wretched soul remained.

I could even picture myself: a limp, pale husk, laid out on the cold metal table. Slack-mouthed and sleepy-eyed, my hair pasted to my clammy forehead – like a waif dredged up out of the river. Wide open to the world now: gaping and red. As naked as a girl could ever get – even my bones were bare, my spine exposed – with all those blokes standing round and staring; talking as if I wasn't even there . . .

'. . . *analysis of the stomach contents. This afternoon, probably . . .*'

'. . . Do that. I'll have one of my lads come over and pick it up . . .'

Someone standing beside me: in shirt sleeves beneath a green polythene apron.

'. . . *buy you lunch afterwards, Inspector . . . ?*'

'I'll look forward to it, Doctor,' Morris said pleasantly. He leaned forward to look me in the face – and something in his lingering smile told me he *knew*. Knew I was still here, and suffering. Then he drew back, as the mortuary technician moved round behind me.

'. . . *just the brain, and we'll be done . . .*'

I tried to find him with my frozen gaze. Even Morris. Tried to force my thoughts through to him, and beg him to make them stop.

The technician laid a gentle hand on my brow, and smoothed my damp hair back.

Please *please* PLEASE . . .

But no one heard – except Morris himself, perhaps. And Morris never said a word as the technician dug his scalpel in behind my ear, and slowly began scalping me alive.

And with that final pain I woke, rose back into reality – and came up screaming all the way.

* * *

'You sure you're all right now?' Nick asked again, his voice still slightly hoarse. Leaning forward to look me in the eyes.

I sniffed, and nodded. His hands stayed tight on my shoulders; by the glow of the bedside light, he looked almost haggard – face bleached and hair in spikes. I had to sympathize. He must have had one hell of a fright.

'I can't sleep again tonight,' I whispered. 'I really can't . . .'

'Shh. That's okay . . .'

'Oh God, I need a bath . . .' I could still feel those probing rubber fingers on my skin – and under it.

'Have a shower.' He saw my hesitation, and gently touched his forehead to mine. 'C'mon. I'll come with you . . .' A glance over at the alarm clock, and he managed to piece together a sleepy smile. 'All right, so it's . . . half-past four in the morning. But what the hell. It's been long enough since we've shared a shower . . .'

I wiped my wet cheek with the back of my hand. 'Nicky, there's no need . . .'

'Now shush,' he said again. 'Serious now, Raitch. I'm here, and I'm with you. You don't have to be alone tonight. You don't have to be alone.'

'Sod off,' I hissed at the empty corridor. 'Just leave me be, all right?'

I'd got so used to the ghost at my shoulder that I sometimes almost forgot it was there. But then some creepy reflex would set me shuddering – as if I'd felt it breathe against my neck.

I backed away, glowering. I could scarcely sense the thing; but I knew it was there. Crouched between me and the door I'd just come in by. Once more it had shadowed me to work. And this morning I'd really had enough.

'Leave me.' I brandished my fist warningly at the empty air; my rosary was clenched inside it.

A pause. Then the presence seemed to draw back.

Perhaps it was biding its time. I waited for a few moments more, then turned reluctantly away.

A cleaner was coming up from the opposite direction, pushing her trolley; watching me with undisguised interest. People behaving oddly are a staple sight of inner city hospitals, of course; but they're not usually the ones in uniform.

I gave her a challenging look, though my cheeks felt about to singe. She breezed on past, and turned off towards the laundry. Breathing a small sigh, I looked back down the bleakly-lit corridor.

Go away, right? I mouthed. *Fuck off. Just. Fuck. Off.* And with that I resumed my walk towards the lifts.

I felt quite satisfied after that. By the time I reached the unit, I was probably looking much less depressed than Sue did as she greeted me.

'Hard night?' I asked. She was fully gowned up over her uniform, with a mask hanging loosely round her neck.

She gestured. 'Richard.'

'Oh. He's . . . gone has he?' I asked, hopefully.

Sue shook her head. 'No. Poor sod's still hanging on. He's been hallucinating for the past hour, though . . .' Grimacing, she went on towards the Sluice.

That took some of the wind out of my sails too. I cast a glum glance towards the dimly-lit sideroom – all seemed quiet in there now – then went on into my office.

There was a shadow in this unit: hanging over us all. Even in here I could feel it. A shadow of madness. A shadow of death. We deal with death every week. It hadn't prepared us for something like this.

But the work went on. A few minutes later, the rest of the team had joined me for Report. Someone had boiled the kettle, and a smell of scalded coffee came with them. The bright, cheerful light in here and at the desk contrasted with the dimness of the bed area. Diodes and readouts glowed green and scarlet in the gloom. Outside it was still full dark.

Johann emerged from Richard's room as I was about to begin, draped in a wrinkled green gown that reached to his ankles. He tugged his mask off as he came over; glancing up, I saw how tired he looked.

'Good morning, Rachel . . .' He gave me a weary, stubbled smile. 'Do you know what is the worst thing about being on call? That moment when you realize there is no point in going back to bed . . .'

'Tell me about it . . .' Theresa murmured, searching for a request form at the station. Stethoscope dangling; hair hanging loose.

'How's he doing?'

'Not well, Rachel. Not well.' He reached for the notes.

'Any chance of a coffee . . . ?' Theresa asked.

'Sure, help yourself. You too, Johann.' I settled back in my chair, pen poised. Fixing my attention on the nurse in charge. 'Right then, Lynn. Who's first?'

Today we were quite heavy: I didn't have much time to myself until mid-morning. Only then, as I made a start on some procrastinated paperwork in the office, did I really begin to wonder what my dreams were trying to tell me.

Take the coffin. As grim and gothic as something from a Hammer film – but I knew there'd be no vampire asleep in there. Nothing so mundane. Like any dream of fleeing or falling, this was just my mind using ready-made images to put across some deeper truth. The question, of course, was: what?

I remembered the dread I'd felt, just looking. That awful sense of pent-up *power*. There'd been a heavy metal cross bolted to the mud-stained lid, as if to seal it. And what had Razoxane said, back on Primrose Hill? Something about black holes. Fallen stars. Impossibly condensed – and unbelievably destructive . . .

Razoxane. Digging something up. Disclosing it.

The knock at the door made me jump; but it was a welcome distraction. Someone's relatives wanted a word.

We chatted for a while; I somehow managed to reassure them. When I came back in, the thread I'd cut loose was there waiting to be picked up.

So: maybe it was just a nightmare about Ankerites then. That seemed to explain things neatly enough. And the bits that always followed . . . dragging me ever deeper into the experience of death . . . were no more than expressions of my darkest fears.

That had to be the answer – but it failed to neutralize the acids in my stomach: because on that level I was sure there was more to this than just the Ankerites. Beyond the bounds of mere mistrust, my instincts still insisted that Razoxane and Morris were playing their ghastly game by quite another set of rules.

When I finally got home that afternoon, my angel of death was there to greet me. Waiting with a smile to tell me the worst.

Chapter 26

This time she really was playing patience with her Tarot pack: laying out its sinister suits on our breakfast-room table. She scarcely glanced up as I came in from the hall.

'About time. I was beginning to get bored.'

It took me a moment to unfreeze; the first glimpse of that black shape through the doorway had made my limbs seize up with fright.

The room was dull with the light of a fading afternoon; but it was Razoxane's presence that really leached the life from it. Every homely detail seemed suddenly fake and fanciful. It was like coming home to a soap opera set.

'Your boyfriend's out and about,' she observed thoughtfully, turning a fresh card in her fingers; still studying the spread. With her back to the window, she'd once more dispensed with her shades – but all the rest of her clothing was in place, ash-dusted hat and all. If I'd lingered just a little longer over hanging up my coat, I'd have picked up the smell which filled my nostrils now.

'He's working overtime tonight,' I muttered; but of course she'd known that. She must have. She wouldn't have just turned up on spec, ready to murder anyone she found in the way.

Would she?

Razoxane set down her card. The next in the suit of Swords.

Reluctantly I walked over and took the seat facing her. Slumped sullenly back in my chair. Everything was focused here between us, now. The house seemed like an empty shell. The street outside was another world.

Razoxane raised her pallid face; her probing eyes. Her smile.

'Four suits, see . . . One for each Element. The Ankerites had their baptism in fire, and earth, and water . . .' She indicated Staves and Coins and Cups in turn; then laid her finger on the Swords. 'And now the last one's coming up for air.'

It was hard to remember that Ankerites had been people once. I thought of the only glimpse I'd had; that maimed and screaming mouth. Had it been a man's or a woman's? No way of telling even that.

'So how are we supposed to *lure* it, then?' I muttered.

'Not easily. But there's a way.' She paused over placing another card. 'What we need is an enclosure. Somewhere it can be trapped.'

'Back in the Underground?' I suggested timidly.

She shook her head. 'Not now it's reached the surface: back in the most volatile element. It won't turn back now.'

I let my gaze stray up towards the mantelpiece Madonna. Today it looked like what it was: a lump of plastic. Dispirited, I turned to Razoxane again.

'Can it leave the City, then?'

She nodded. 'Once it's strong enough . . . or so the theory goes. Carried on the wind, like a contagion. It might even, ultimately, take on material form; some occultists have predicted that. So now's the time we have to stop it.

'At the moment it's still ringed by your skyline. After its cell, and the catacombs of your Underground, the world has suddenly opened out. It will be wary. But there are shadow-strongholds all around it – and they can promise shelter from the sky.'

Staring back at her, I thought of St Paul's at night: floodlit like a luminous skull. White on the outside, but full of darkness within. And all the other old churches that lay brooding within the City. Hallowed ground. Where better a place to catch a lost soul?

Razoxane read my pensive look. Her smile should have

warned me then and there. But I tried to keep on hoping – and felt myself grow colder by degrees as she inexorably spelled it out.

'It's drawn by places of despair, remember: by cemeteries and such. Morbid remnants it can scavenge. And there are places on the surface where people have gathered in pain – and fear – for centuries. Where death visits every day.'

My mouth dropped open.

'You needn't gawp at me like that, either; it's the obvious choice. I remember this town two centuries back, when I was learning my medical lore – even then the hospitals were like places apart. Half-church, half-charnel-house. Think how many thousands have sweated their misery into those sites since then. And how many ghosts they've left behind them.'

But my thoughts could get no further than an image of that underground wind, howling down a hospital corridor at night: bringing its hate and its eyeless head . . .

'Which hospital?' I whispered, without much hope.

'Yours is closest.'

'Oh, *God* . . .'

'It's already out there, Rachel,' was her grim rejoinder. 'Crouching in the dark. Ankerites can't see light like we can . . . but they perceive wavelengths of the darkness. From its viewpoint, your whole building's just a citadel of suffering: an outpost of Middle Hell. It'll breach it sooner or later; whatever we do.'

I swallowed – and saw my hospital at night. Like St Paul's in reverse: bright-lit wards on the inside, but the exterior was a black, forbidding rampart. In chilled silence, I glanced down at her cards.

Swords and Staves and Coins and Cups. Medieval images that jarred with my modern world; but the barbarity and witchcraft she'd brought with her were all too real. As were the demon visionaries.

I overbit my lip. 'It won't be after living people, though . . . ?'

'No: the shadows in your hospital will be the bait.' She

286

allowed herself a smirk. 'Think of them as my Judas ghosts. And yes, it has a loathing for living souls — but it won't get the chance to start on them.'

'So . . . how would you stop it? I mean . . .' The dread that simmered inside me began to bubble up. 'Not a *bomb*. Surely to God . . .'

'Rachel.' She smiled in mocking admonition. 'What kind of girl do you think I am?'

'One with no soul,' I hissed.

Razoxane's smile became a grin.

'Perhaps. But there are less drastic means to extirpate a spirit — even when it's grown this strong. With your help, I'm prepared to risk using them. And afterwards, my work here will be done.'

Oh it will, will it? I thought acidly.

'You don't think so?' she enquired.

'What about Morris, then?' was my hasty retort.

'We've stayed one step ahead of him so far. All we have to do is keep the distance for a few nights longer. Once the last Ankerite is wiped away, he'll move on. There'll be nothing left to keep him here.'

I nodded hopefully; but my mind had unearthed that slimy coffin lid again. The sudden urge to ask if she'd shared my vision rose inside me like an undigested meal. For a moment I wavered, and almost let it all come spewing up. But in the end, as she sensed my enquiry and paused in expectation, all I could manage was: 'What . . . do their names mean? Wiking and things?'

Something in her eyes — like dark amusement — made me wonder if she'd sensed my loss of nerve; but her answer was mild enough. 'Those are just Morris's little jests. *Wampir* . . . the old, East European form . . . for his night-duty section. *Wiking* — an SS Regiment in your Second War — for the day-squad. And *Wotan*, the pagan god of battles — for his own.'

I supposed they'd been pronounced with Vs originally. But anglicized, they had a weirder, esoteric sound.

Unnerving.

The air in the room was growing grey now; dimness gathering like dust. I glanced towards the light switch — then thought better of it.

Razoxane laid her hat aside, and gave her head the briefest shake, as if to clear it. I caught a rare glimpse of fatigue in the gesture. Combined with her undernourished look, it made her face seem very young beneath its grime and grubbiness.

The contrast with her cold and *ancient* mind was quite unsettling; but I still found myself trying to picture what she'd looked like at the start. Still in her present incarnation, as she saw it — but before she became a witch. Perhaps her wintry eyes had been winsome once. Perhaps her fine-boned face had been attractive.

Razoxane's gaze, so fleetingly unfocused, came back to me again.

'I could do with a drink,' she told me quietly. 'Something hot.'

This despite the central heating, which had been warming the rooms since three. Despite her jersey, coat and gloves, as well. She was like someone with one of those diseases of the circulation, at risk of gangrene from the slightest drop in temperature.

Dutifully I filled the kettle, then trudged upstairs to change. I was really tempted to stay up there, as well, and hope if I waited long enough she'd go away. But I knew there wouldn't really be much point.

By the time I came back down, she'd collected her cards — and laid her pistol on the tabletop beside them. Giving the gun an uneasy glance, I went through to make coffee for us both. 'You have it black, don't you?' I called, as if she was just a visiting friend.

'Well remembered.'

'Lucky guess,' I gritted to myself.

When I brought the mugs in, she was studying something — turning it pensively before her eyes. A snub-nosed bullet,

I realized: the size of my little finger. She waited for me to take my seat before looking up from it.

'A blunt instrument – that's all this is. A piece of brute force. It takes more than one blow to finish a man. Sometimes a lot more . . .' She closed her hand around it, and rested her fist against her chin. Then continued in the same, musing tone. 'That's all that guns are really about, Rachel. Nothing special; no mystique. Just a means of chopping and bludgeoning someone to death with a few little twitches of your finger . . .'

I looked down at the pistol. The metal was dull with age. I could make out the word *Astra*, emblazoned on its worn rubber grips.

A car chugged past outside. Apart from that, the street was silent.

The gloom had grown thicker. Razoxane picked up her cards again, and began idly sorting through them.

'Want to see the future, then?' she asked.

I pulled a face. 'I told you: I don't believe in those things.'

'Why not?'

'They're just cards, that's why.'

'True. But the message comes from how they fall, Rachel. And that depends on how they're shuffled.'

As I watched morosely, she sent the full pack slewing in an overlapping row across the tabletop – then turned the end card to flip the whole lot over. Despite myself, I blinked.

Razoxane grinned faintly through the dusk, and gathered them up; let them sideslip from one hand to the other, and back again. A moment later they'd been formed into fans, opening out in each hand. Then back they came together in a blur.

My gaze flicked up to her amicable face. 'Razoxane . . .'

She paused. 'What?'

'Stop bloody showing off.'

She gave an unperturbed shrug, and finished with a slow shuffle of the pack. Then started laying the old cards out, face down. I waited, my chin in my hands. For no obvious reason, my heartbeat had grown louder.

Razoxane set down the seventh card and leaned back. 'Go ahead,' she invited softly. 'Pick one.'

I shook my head.

'What's the problem? If . . . as you say . . . they're only cards, you've nothing to be scared of. Have you?'

She was right, of course. But still I hesitated. In the end it was probably pride that made me reach for the middle card, and turn it over.

'*La Forza,*' Razoxane said, nodding: as if she'd expected it.

I peered at the faded picture. It showed a woman, strong and stylised. 'What's that supposed to mean, then?'

'Depends on the context. Strength, fortitude . . . female intuition. The Enchantress, she's called sometimes.'

'Meaning you, presumably.'

She smiled and shook her head. 'Actually, I think it could mean you.'

'Sod off,' I said, slapping it down. 'I'm not a bloody witch.'

'I *know* you're not.' She gave a mock-exasperated sigh. 'God, a Christian, of all people, should recognise *symbolism* when she sees it. This is your potential, Rachel. The strength you have inside you. It's already brought you this far, hasn't it?'

I forced an indifferent sort of shrug.

Still smiling, Razoxane inclined her head towards the cards. 'Next one.'

I glowered at her for a moment; then turned another. The designs were less distinct now – the room in twilight. But I saw it was another female figure, cold and stern-looking. Queen of the suit of Swords, to judge by the blades in evidence.

'*La Regina delle Spade,*' Razoxane said. 'A strong and solitary woman. Your modern deck would call her Queen of Spades.'

'Definitely you,' I muttered.

She did not deny it. Staring back at her, I thought of that sinister spinner she carried in her pocket. I didn't need telling that Swords – like their later counterparts – were a sign of bad fortune.

'Notice how your instinct chose them,' she purred insidiously. 'One after the other. Like two sisters.'

'Crap,' I countered. Half-heartedly.

'What about the next one, then?' she invited.

Still trying to put a sceptical face on it, I turned the next card. And the next. Seven of Cups. Knight of Swords. Then an image of a tower, struck by lightning.

'That's interesting,' she murmured. 'See how it followed the Knight . . . could mean the overthrow of some violent enterprise . . .'

'You're just making this up as you go along, aren't you?' I accused.

'Shush. The tale's nearly told.' She waited for me to turn the last card – as carelessly as I could manage – before leaning forward to study the spread.

'Could mean bloody anything . . .' I pointed out, defensively.

'Perhaps. But I think there's a definite message here, Rachel.' She paused again, her fingers steepled against her lips; then raised her eyes once more.

'Let me read it to you this way. The two of us – together. Violent men. A journey, perhaps across water. A crisis . . .' She sat back, her expression unreadable: apart from anything else, it was getting too dark for me to see it clearly. The sound of a passing car slid through the stillness, and faded into it.

'What I think the cards are saying is this. Someone from over the water is coming. Someone with hate and violence on their minds. To me that means colleagues of brother Frank and his team. Come to wipe them out before they do any more damage to the Cause . . .' She seemed to hesitate for a moment; her tone, when she continued, was almost apologetic. 'The way the message spelled itself out for you . . . so clearly . . . might be some kind of warning. They might have traced elements of the unit back here. They could even be coming here tonight.'

There was a long pause. Then, with an effort, I cleared my dried-out throat. 'And . . . you can tell all that just from the cards, can you?' Unnerved though I was, I couldn't keep a hint of awe out of my voice.

'Well . . . not exactly.' I heard the undertone of humour then: the sardonic smile beneath her words. 'It's just that they've already driven past here twice.'

I gaped at her.

'Checking the place out,' she continued calmly. 'No lights on: nobody home. Give them a few minutes and I expect they'll start breaking in round the back. They had to find the place sooner or later.'

'You mean you knew?' I managed. 'You *knew*?'

'I had a sort of idea,' she admitted modestly.

'Oh God . . .' I whispered, and started to my feet.

'Rachel, listen, just . . .'

'. . . we've got to . . .'

'Sit *down*,' she rasped – and down I sat, as stunned as if she'd slapped me. The dark amusement was gone from her voice now: like flesh stripped away from a bleak and pointed bone. She spoke with *authority*. While my mind was still whirling, my instincts just obeyed.

'Want to let them know you're in?' she asked remorselessly. 'Want them to come in shooting?'

I found my scared, small voice. 'But we'll be *trapped* here.'

'Will we, now?' Her pale eyes had caught the last of the light – standing out in her shadowed face as balefully as a cat's. 'Let's just wait, and see.'

I twisted round, peering helplessly into the darkened kitchen. Through the one visible window, I could just glimpse our pokey back garden, overgrown with gloom. A narrow footpath ran beyond the wall; most of its lamps had been smashed and not replaced. If we ever get burgled, Nick had predicted – with professional grimness – then that's the way they'll come . . .

I looked back at Razoxane. At least she was facing the right way, and ready – which left me feeling horribly vulnerable, presenting an intruder with my unprotected spine. But I didn't dare move again. All I could do was sit frozen, sickened with fear: listening to the pummelling of my heart – and the high-pressure hiss of the blood inside my ears.

It seemed we waited ages: so long that a tiny spark of hope began to glimmer. Then I heard a stealthy thud, and something rustling in the bushes. It wasn't the wind. The crack of a stepped-on twig confirmed that.

Another long pause. Then one of the kitchen windows started creaking.

I pressed my hand against my mouth, for fear my breathing might betray me.

Someone was trying to jemmy open the window over the sink.

Razoxane's gaze slid down to the pistol at her elbow; then back to me.

I heard the window-catch give with a dull scrape. Silence again. No human sounds: no whispered consultations. It was like listening to a haunting. The thought made the hairs on my nape – already rising – stand up straight.

Then the window was pulled open, on quietly protesting hinges.

Razoxane's hand dipped under her coat, and came out with her spinner: casually rolling it between forefinger and thumb.

The sound of someone climbing in. Terse breathing. Boots on woodwork. My hand was still in place, but now it felt like I was holding in a scream.

Still she made no move to pick up her gun. Instead she set the point of the spinner against the tabletop between us . . .

– the Queen of Spades, I thought numbly –

. . . and flicked her wrist to set it spinning.

I felt the change of atmosphere at once. Currents of air began to stir in the shadows around us – as if this tiny thing was somehow whipping them into cold, cyclonic spirals. Then Razoxane craned forward, murmuring incoherently as she watched the spinner's motion, and I was filled with a smothering sense of dread.

Back in the kitchen, someone shrieked.

I'd never heard a man make a noise like that; the shock brought a physical spasm that slammed my knee against the table-leg and killed it dead. Even as I grimaced in pain – and Razoxane grinned – the man screamed again. And then the shooting started.

The blasts were deafening – like fingers jabbing deep into my ears. They shook the house; I could sense glass and fixtures shattering beneath them. With a little cry I half-fell from my chair, and hit the floor with force enough to leave me winded. Lightning flickered in the dimness; the frantic staccato of gunshots went on and on. Something invisible zipped through the room to smash the window like a brick. Razoxane never even flinched.

A moment later, the firing stopped – abruptly. I lay still where I was, my head full of throbbing echoes. A burnt, smoky stink was drifting through the house. Someone a million miles away was moaning softly.

Razoxane climbed unhurriedly to her feet; and now, at last, she lifted her pistol from the tabletop.

'It's finished,' she told me drily, staring down. 'Come and see.'

Almost on autopilot, I struggled up and let her lead me to the kitchen doorway. The thick, metallic smell of blood was there to greet me, blotting out the reek of gunfire. In the slaty light, the whole room looked to have been splashed with glistening black paint.

I could just about discern the bodies, three of them: one hanging halfway in through the window, his head in the sink. Their shapes were enough. I was really glad I couldn't see the detail.

Then Razoxane flicked the light on – all the brighter with its shade ripped away – and I got an eyeful of the worst. All blood and bulging organs. Like Theatre on a bad day, back when I was doing my training.

I turned my face aside, my cheeks chilled with shock. Our comfortable little kitchen was a ruin – drenched in crimson. One of the cupboards had been wrenched from the wall. The fridge hung open. The walls were so pitted with ugly holes they seemed to be decaying.

'Jesus, what did you do?' I breathed.

'Just used the thoughts they brought along themselves,' was her matter-of-fact retort. She'd slipped her shades back on against the light, which made her pale face all the more impassive. 'Their minds were full of hate; I simply gave it substance.'

And what demons of the mind those must have been. Enough to panic them so much they'd shot at everything that moved. Instant psychosis. Total wipeout.

One of them moaned.

I drew back with a gasp – and Razoxane turned her eyeless stare to see.

The man slumped in the far corner twitched and tried to speak; a bubbly sound of blood was all he managed. I glanced at Razoxane, and saw her gun was dangling from her left hand now; and the spinner of Spades was back in her right. As I watched, she brought it to her lips – the gesture almost thoughtful.

'The purpose of terrorism . . .' she informed her victim drily '. . . is to *terrorize*. Isn't it?'

The stricken man tried to cringe, and couldn't.

'Oh, don't hurt him,' I muttered. The words sounded all but meaningless in my own ears – spoken more in despair than in hope. But Razoxane looked at me, and shrugged.

'Whatever you say, Rachel. It's your house.'

She raised her pistol and fired at his head. The bullet

crunched his cranium like an axe-blow, spattering blood and pulp up the wall behind. The man flopped aside, blank-faced.

Razoxane turned back to me, and smiled at my open-mouthed horror.

'There you are. He won't have felt a thing.'

I should have seen that coming. I really should have.

Then she turned off the light, and flooded us with shadows.

'All right, now,' she said, as my wide eyes strained to cope, 'there'll be people here to check on you in no time. So get upstairs, up to your bedroom . . . pretend you were having a sleep when all this broke loose.'

My mind was a blank; a blackboard wiped clean. I didn't resist as she towed me back through the breakfast room and shoved me towards the stairs. I set my foot on the first step – and looked back at her.

'But there'll be police all over the place . . . and all those guns and bombs upstairs . . .'

'Don't worry: they'll not find those. Believe me.'

I swallowed, unwilling to drag my frightened gaze from her face.

'Go *on*,' she insisted. 'I'll find you when I'm ready.'

And up I went; fleeing from the horror she'd brought into my house. Even though I knew I could never outrun it.

Chapter 27

'Can I get you another coffee, Rachel?' the WPC asked gently.

The dregs of the first cupful were still cooling between my palms. I looked up from the muddy depths, and shook my head.

She nodded, and drew back a little way; I returned my miserable attention to my drink. All the noises of the Friday night shift were coming in through the open door behind her – echoing footsteps and loud, heedless voices. The custody area was just along the corridor; I'd been sat out there myself before they'd found me somewhere quieter. Doubtless one of their interview rooms, to judge by its bleakness.

I was still wearing my coat, but to little avail: the chill of shock had already set in. I felt on the verge of shivering.

Someone else came in, a burly plain-clothes man with greying hair. He took a seat across the table from me, and tried a reassuring smile. It didn't sit easy on his hardened features, but I was grateful for the effort.

'Hello, Rachel. My name's Mike Reeve, I'm a Detective Chief Inspector.' With the intro out of the way, his singsong tone became more measured; he had a Northern accent, not unpleasant. 'First of all, I can let you know we've raised your boyfriend, and called him back in. He'll be here presently.'

I gave a small nod. 'How much does he know?'

'Just that there's been a bit of a fracas round at your place. We've told him you're not hurt.'

I nodded again, and drew my coat up closer round me.

'Have you offered her another coffee?' he asked the

policewoman, who explained that she had. Outside, someone was stridently maintaining he'd been fucking fitted up. The WPC closed the door on his protestations, and shut us all in. It concentrated my mind wonderfully on this over-lit, unlovely room.

'Were they ... terrorists, then?' I ventured: hoping I struck the right note of disbelief.

DCI Reeve grunted. 'We reckon they were ...' I could feel the scrutiny of his eyes. The smile hadn't touched them.

'So what the hell were they *doing*?' I pressed on quickly.

'We were hoping you could shed some light on that, Rachel ...'

He said it casually enough; but it still felt like the contents of my stomach had suddenly frozen over. Staring back at him, I fought to keep my face straight.

'Oh God, I've no idea,' I murmured quietly.

'One possibility, you see, is that you've come into contact with them ... quite innocently ... and they were afraid you'd somehow blow their cover.'

I could only shrug.

'Can you think of any instances you've seen ... people acting suspiciously? Anyone Irish you've had dealings with lately ...?'

I made a show of giving it some thought. 'Not that I can think of, no ...'

'You're a nurse, I believe ...? What area do you work in?'

'Intensive Care.'

'Not Casualty or anything like that ... people just passing through?'

I shook my head. My mouth was now too dry to risk any other answer.

'Any interests outside work ...?'

'Well ...' I croaked, and swallowed. Twice. He waited. 'I help with soup runs sometimes. For the homeless.'

He nodded, looking thoughtful.

Someone knocked on the door.

'Come in,' Reeve called – and Nick cautiously did so; still in his anorak, cap in hand. Our eyes met at once, and held. It took him an effort to turn his attention to the DCI.

'PC Mitchell, sir . . .'

'How much has the sergeant told you, lad?'

'Only that . . . there'd been an incident in the vicinity of our house, sir. And that my . . . partner had been brought here for her own safety . . .'

Partner? I felt a giggle welling up; or it might have been a sob. Poor Nick, playing safe before a superior officer. He probably looked like this while giving evidence in court: words and expression carefully neutral. But the way his gaze kept flicking back to me rather gave him away.

'I'm okay, Nick,' I said – or meant to say. What came out was a damp little whisper. And Nick threw formality to the winds, crossed the room and pulled me up into a hug.

As I stood there, with my face pressed to his shoulder, I heard Reeve clear his throat. 'We'll give you a few minutes together, then . . .' He and the woman quietly withdrew, and left us to it.

'Oh Nicky, I'm sorry. I'm so sorry . . .' They were the first and only words that came to mind. My sinuses were raw with trapped tears, like a snort of salt water.

'Sshhh, now.' He stroked my back; my hair. 'No way was it anything you did.'

'The house is wrecked . . . everything . . .'

'Never mind the bloody house, what about you?' He eased me back at arm's length to study my face. 'Were you hurt? At all?'

I shook my head. The motion flicked a fat tear onto my collar.

'Jesus, Raitch. What *happened*?'

'I don't *know*. I was upstairs having a sleep and suddenly it's like World War Three downstairs. I just waited for the coppers to bring me down. They said . . . three people were dead in the kitchen. Terrorists . . .'

His face, already bleached, grew tighter; I had an idea what he was thinking. Doubtless Reeve had thought of it too, and would be interviewing him in turn. Nick was the policeman, after all. Mightn't it have been him they were after . . . ?

'Maybe they thought *you* were home . . .' I ventured: making sure. Taking the attention off myself and dumping it on him. The flicker of fear in his eyes made me feel sick.

'Oh Lord, no . . . I mean . . . I've not been involved in any anti-terrorist operations, even . . .'

'Yeah, but . . . you might have stopped one of them, without knowing,' I suggested, ruthlessly.

He shook his head; but it didn't dislodge the hurt and helpless look from his face. The very *possibility* . . . I watched his hand plough back through his short hair, leaving it springing up in tufts.

A peremptory tap on the door, and Reeve came back in. Nick turned, and stiffened instinctively. I just hugged my elbows.

'All right?' We both nodded woodenly, and he gave a satisfied grunt. 'Any ideas about why it happened, then?'

Nick gestured. 'Maybe they were . . . trying to get me.' I got the impression he'd said that just to hear what it sounded like. Pretty unpleasant, to judge by the way his expression faltered.

Reeves didn't bat an eyelid. 'Any run-ins with Irish people lately?'

'None that I remember. I'll have to check . . .'

'Do that. Anything at all that might be useful. There's another angle we should look at, too . . .' He turned to me. 'You said you did some work with the homeless. I've had information that tells me an active service unit has infiltrated that community. It's possible they were trying to use you somehow, and you let slip that your boyfriend was a copper. So they panic, and try killing you both. It's something we need to consider . . .'

I shrugged.

300

'Ring any bells?' he persisted.

'She's . . . had an awful shock this evening, sir,' Nick murmured in the background. That must have taken nerve, I thought.

Reeve glanced at him; then relented. 'I know, lad. Just don't want the trail to get cold. Don't worry, we'll get you both sorted. They're making arrangements to get you into an empty police flat somewhere, tonight.'

'You think there's . . . more of them out there?' I asked.

'Witnesses saw a car being driven away at speed, so there's at least one more. Maybe they'll try again, for whatever reason. So you'll not be pounding a beat for the next couple of weeks, Mitchell. And as for you, Rachel, I'd suggest you stay off work for a while . . . until we've a better idea how the land lies. They might even know where you work.'

I swallowed. 'And there's no clue as to what . . . actually happened tonight?'

'Not yet. Far as I can make out, they come in with all guns blazing and end up shooting each other.' Reeve cracked a bitter smile. 'But what do you expect from Irishmen?'

Under the circumstances, I didn't find that particularly funny.

Chapter 28

'Well, Rachel,' Murdoch murmured. 'I don't quite know what to say.'

That could have been the precursor to anything, of course; I shifted uncomfortably in my chair. Even though I knew him well enough by now. Even though I could see his concern written clearly on his face.

The desktop between us was a wide expanse of stacked papers and old casenotes, all splashed with wintry sunlight from the window. Elsewhere, the shelves crammed with books and journals made the office seem darker; almost oppressive. Beyond the closed door, I could dimly hear the unit ticking over.

I ventured gingerly out into the silence. 'I'm sure it needn't be for long ... perhaps a week. Just to be safe.'

His hands had been steepled beneath his chin; he raised one now. 'Rachel. D'you think I'd expect you to come to work when it means risking your *safety*? By all means, take as long off as the police advise.' He leaned forward, frowning with genuine anxiety. 'How are you coping? It must have been dreadful for you ...'

I gave an offhand shrug. 'Well, they've moved us into police accommodation ... just a flat, you know, but ... we're managing. Still a bit jumpy. But we're managing. Thanks.'

It was a pretty bleak place they'd found for us, actually. Minimally furnished; all plain brown carpet and blank white walls. The staleness of the air had filled my nostrils the first time I walked in; some suspicious sniffing had picked up a musty foretaste of damp. No one else had lived here for a while. And when we'd unpacked our hastily-stuffed suitcases, the place seemed no less lifeless.

It was on a quiet street, at least.

'If there's anything we can do to help,' Murdoch was saying, 'just let me know. Ring me at home if you need to. I mean that, Rachel.'

'Thanks,' I murmured again: feeling a bit embarrassed, but grateful with it. 'Like I said, I'll be back as soon as I can . . .' As it was, I knew there'd be some problems plugging the gaps; that our Bank and Agency budget had already gone overspent on winter sickness. I couldn't help but feel a twinge of guilt as well.

When I emerged, it was to find Jez and Lucy waiting: they beckoned me over to the station, anxious to hear the truth behind the rumours. Their concern, like Murdoch's, was real enough; but I was just as keen to know how things were faring in my absence. Business this lunchtime seemed fairly quiet; a covert glance towards the side-room prompted Lucy to explain that Richard Wells had finally succumbed during the night. She sounded relieved. I didn't blame her.

No trace of him left now. The bed would have been stripped and scrubbed – the linen stuffed into a crimson laundry sack. Disinfectant and daylight had cleansed the room of its shadows. Whenever we lost a patient, there was always another to take his place, and we'd adjust accordingly; but I guessed that Richard had been erased from the record with particular thoroughness. He'd be downstairs now, encased in one of the leak-proof cadaver bags we kept for infected bodies; tagged with Biohazard stickers.

Hadn't Razoxane once threatened me with a similar fate?

The phone rang on that gruesome thought, and Jez scooped it up to speak; Lucy smiled and slipped away to attend to the nearest patient. Suddenly I was standing around like a spare part. Not their fault – but it gave me the dispiriting feeling of being an outsider in my own unit: watching the uniformed professionals getting on with the job. With a lame goodbye – Jez gave me a wave, still talking – I took the hint, and left.

By the time I'd reached the lift area I was dragging my feet – not quite sure where I wanted to go next. The prospect of coming in at all had been quite scary at first, but I'd wanted to talk to Murdoch face to face: I owed him that much. Getting this far had boosted my confidence a bit. But now I had the long run home to think of.

The day outside was cold and bright. So where, I wondered, did *Wampir* go when the sun was up? Probably some lock-up garage. Kids might be playing soccer now outside its blank metal door, never dreaming of what lurked inside. And its crew of Peelers: did they sleep? Or were they still in their seats, sitting patiently in darkness? Awaiting the dusk . . .

Whatever; Wotan and Wiking were doubtless out on the prowl. I just hoped it was Razoxane they were tracking.

On an impulse, I turned my steps south, towards the Children's Unit. Playing for a little more time, of course; but I wanted to see Sandra again too. And if they'd finally let her go home . . . well that would be a relief in itself, after what Razoxane had told me. About luring an Ankerite inside these walls.

But Sandra was still in: sitting up in bed, as if expecting my visit. She gave me an earnest little smile, like somebody who'd aged beyond her years.

'Oh, Rachel: I'm glad to see you.'

She sounded it, too. There wasn't just the usual bright welcome in her voice; I heard relief as well. It suggested how fragile her brave face really was.

'Same here,' I said, smiling back: as casually as I could. 'Sorry I've not been in for a bit. How are you today, then?'

She shrugged. 'All right, I s'ppose.'

The giant bear was slumped in her bedside chair. I gave it a glance. 'And how's . . . Ted?'

'George,' she corrected, putting on a mock disdainful look as befitted my ignorance. 'His name's George.'

I nodded. 'Hi, George.'

'George is very well, thank you.'

But you're not, are you? I thought, drawing up another chair. Still, the introductions had taken her mind off whatever was bothering her, if only for a moment. Perhaps now I could start to coax it out.

'Have they told you when you're going home yet?' I wondered; first things first.

'Mummy talked to the doctors yesterday, and they said Friday.'

'That's great,' I told her; fervently hoping she'd not be disappointed. Not again. 'I bet you're really looking forward to it. I know your mum will be.'

'Rachel, I want to go home *now*.' She almost sobbed as she said it, brave face melting as I watched.

'Shhh,' I whispered. 'You've been such a brave girl, and it's just a few days more . . .'

'I don't like it here,' she whimpered back. 'I have bad dreams. Something horrid comes to the door at night and tries to get in. I can feel it. And when I wake up and start crying, the night nurses get cross.'

I felt a wave of gooseflesh creep under my clothes. It took an effort to keep my tone steady, my expression only mildly concerned. 'What sort of thing is it, then?'

'I don't know. But it's terribly cold.' She sniffled wetly. 'In the dream . . . oh, Rachel . . . it starts breaking through the doors, and everyone else is asleep and they can't hear it, and I press my buzzer but nobody ever comes . . .'

'*San*dra . . .' Forcing another smile, I leaned forward to stroke her forehead. 'You're quite safe here – you know that, don't you? There's always someone near at night: the nurses will always hear you. And they're not *really* cross . . .'

Her crumpled little face seemed unconvinced.

'I know how you feel, though,' I added softly. 'I get bad dreams sometimes, too.'

'What, like . . . that one?'

I nodded. 'Just like that one.' *And worse, as well.*

There was a sucked-in feeling where my stomach should be. The effort of keeping my smile in place was almost painful. I remembered that unexplained chill I'd felt outside – right back when all this was just beginning. That eerie sense of something sneaking up. Just the shadow of a long-lost patient, or so I'd thought. One of Razoxane's Judas-ghosts. But what if it had been something else entirely?

Sandra was eyeing me seriously. 'Rachel . . . are there ghosts in the hospital?'

'Of course not, no,' I said, with the sort of glibness that kids can spot a mile off.

'Oh. Because one of the nurses said . . . I heard her . . . about how creepy the place was after dark. She thought someone was following her through the corridors when she came up to work, but when she looked, there was nobody there.'

'Perhaps it was just her imagination playing tricks on her,' I suggested doggedly. But my instincts were itching now, like painful pins and needles: goading me to get moving. Razoxane had to know this. While she talked of trapping the Ankerite, it might already have crept into the building of its own accord. And if – as she'd predicted – it was seeking revenge for all it had suffered, maybe instinct had led it to this most vulnerable of wards: the place where, once fully-focused, it could really do its worst.

Perhaps tonight would be the night it flowed in through those doors, like a flash-flood down a sewer: foul and black and choking . . .

'Don't you believe in ghosts, then?' Sandra asked.

I hesitated; but she was too bright a girl to keep it from. 'I do, actually. But I'm not sure exactly what they are.'

'Do we turn into ghosts when we die?'

God, this was getting a bit deep. 'No, I don't think we do. We just go to a different place, and carry on there . . .'

'Is that Heaven, then?'

'That's what some people call it, yes.'

'Is Gail in Heaven?'

'Who's Gail?' I asked, after a slightly wary pause.

'One of the nurses. She was in a car crash. Everyone was really upset. They didn't want to tell *us*; but I could hear Mandy crying, so I listened really hard . . .'

You can't hide much from children: not if they want to know. 'So . . . when was this?' I murmured.

'Yesterday, I think. I didn't believe it for ages, though. I *saw* her on Saturday . . .' A tear oozed, glistening, down her cheek. 'And . . . and nurse Janet was killed in an accident too. She was my friend, and she wasn't even able to say goodbye. It's not *fair*, Rachel. Why do people have to die?'

No easy answer to that one at the best of times; but I could only stare at her now. My heart-rate seemed to have gone from 0 to 60 in the last few seconds.

Too many nurses dying.

This latest girl could have crashed of her own free will for all I knew; but what if it had been a hit and run? Then there'd been that nice Janet Nicholls, asphyxiated in her flat. And . . . (my mind seemed to spin, like a floppy disk being searched for files) . . . and Lucy's best friend Anna, burned to death in her car. Three, in the last three weeks.

Too many.

Not that I thought the Ankerite could have killed them. To fake an accident took guile and reason – and from what I'd seen of them, the things were about as reasoning as bubonic plague. But this one now had human agents to be its eyes and bloody hands: led by someone who'd burn down this whole hospital (with everyone inside it) for no apparent reason other than that to do so would be *evil*.

Perhaps they'd already done a recce on the place: murmuring to their radios in the dimness; probing empty corridors with their torches. A couple of nurses might have glimpsed them — and been hunted down and murdered for that transgression.

So . . . what if Morris was planning the worst atrocity of all?

No longer just protecting his demon. Paving its way.

A nurse came round with some medication; I jumped at the chance to say goodbye. Loath as I was to leave Sandra, I knew I had to get moving on this one. Drying her eyes with my hankie, I kissed her forehead and let her hug me — then drew gently back.

'I . . . might not be able to come in for a couple of days. But we'll still be thinking of you: your mum and all your friends and me. Even in the middle of the night. So you'll never be alone.'

She sniffed. 'Thoughts aren't *real* though, are they?'

'Yes they are. Real as angels — and just as close. So come on, give us a smile . . .' She managed one after a moment; it cheered me up as well. 'God bless, Sandra. I'll see you soon.'

'Don't forget George,' she chided.

I straightened, smiling. ''Bye, George.'

But glancing back at that bear brought a grisly piece of memory to mind: the sort that can lurk for years in silent depths before floating to the surface. Back when I was a staff nurse, a young woman on the ward had died of cancer, and I'd had to pack her property up. Her comforts had included cuddly toys brought in by her husband: friendly-eyed bears and fluffy rabbits. I'd just crammed them in with the toiletries and clothing: stuffed everything together into a bulging plastic bag. And when I'd finished, they were still peeping forlornly out at me.

Maybe seven years on, the memory still stung my eyes. As I walked off the ward, my smile felt like a mask nailed to my face.

* * *

Regent's Canal was the place to start looking; I caught a bus north from the City, as I had that time before. As it swung through the traffic, I sat up top and waited, my heart pumping faster with every moment we wasted at a bus-stop or break in traffic.

The old factory came in sight at length, and I got off at the nearest stop – letting the bus get well clear before crossing the road. The place loomed overhead, as sombre as a medieval fortress, despite the sunlight. My stomach felt hollow with apprehension as I picked my way along the fence; but my chest was tight with a different kind of dread.

What if she *wasn't* here? Where would I go then?

I pushed nervously at the corrugated iron entrance: feeling bound to announce my arrival somehow – like knocking on someone's door. Its rusty scraping set my teeth on edge. I began to squeeze my way past, wondering if Lisa or someone would come to help me in this time.

They didn't. Instead someone tried to smash my skull in.

The only warning was a single, crunching footfall. I turned my head – and the figure lunged to meet me, arm upraised. I cowered, slipped, and awkwardly collapsed, still only halfway through. The swipe aimed at my head merely ruffled my hair; as I hit the ground he moved in on me again. Peering up, numb with shock, I registered the house brick in his hand.

His face above me. Fierce, frightened, furious face. I squealed, I couldn't help it: covering my own with my arm.

'Andy!' someone shouted. 'Pack it in! Lay off her!'

The pause that followed was thick with the slogging of my heartbeat. Then Andy – or whoever it was – let his tautened upper body loosen up. His breath hissed out. The brick dropped from his mittened hand, and *cracked* against the concrete.

He didn't bother to help me up; just turned and stomped away. I lay where I was for a moment longer; then swallowed a metallic mouthful of saliva, and began to struggle up.

It was Gary who'd called him off, of course – he was coming over now, his own expression set and serious. 'Rachel, what do you want? You shouldn't be here . . .'

I was getting tired of people telling me that: as if I had a choice. Getting to my feet, I slapped ineffectually at the dust on my coat – then thought of his filthy parka, and gave up. I couldn't help glowering as he came to a halt before me. 'What kind of welcome do you call that, then?'

Gary met my stare full-on. His face was drawn, his sandy hair awry; the scarf at his throat hung limp and loose. I could see a handful of others in the yard behind him, standing round the remnants of the fire. They all looked restless and edgy.

'What's going on?' I asked, a bit more diffidently.

'We're clearing out,' he came back grimly. 'Soon as we've got all our stuff together. You mustn't stay, Rachel.'

Well, getting their stuff together wasn't going to take them long; they were wearing most of it. Frowning, I glanced back towards the others. Big Jim, the King of Cups, was there, still sitting: probably too sloshed to find his feet. The rest looked like they'd just finished scavenging through their own bash, cramming shopping bags and refuse sacks with anything worth carrying. The bloke with specs who'd warned me of *Wotan* was staring bleakly back at me. Fair-haired Andy was watching too, without apology. He could have dashed my brains out. And once upon a time he'd offered me his last cigarette . . .

'What's happened?' I asked Gary – almost whispering now.

The preacher pulled an ugly face. 'There's been a crackdown on the likes of us. It's been going on all day. People have been beaten to death, Rachel. There are rumours that some have been *shot* . . .'

Morris, I knew at once.

'. . . I was down by Waterloo when the riot cops went through Cardboard City. They had dogs, they just turned them loose . . .'

I put my hand to my horrified mouth.

'And they'll find their way up here soon enough,' Gary went on steadily. 'Our only chance is to shift, and then scatter . . .'

It was happening — now, today, of all days. The game of cat and mouse was over. The Peelers had broken cover.

'Fucking bastards,' Andy growled behind him. Recalling the mix of fear and fury I'd seen on his face, I guessed he'd probably expected me to be a Peeler too.

Gary shook his head wearily: even he seemed dispirited. Drained.

'It's insane. Like they've just passed a law making begging a crime against the *state*. I heard folk were just thrown into a police van and driven off: no one knows where. One old man had his skull cracked by a rifle-butt. A couple of us had to take him to Casualty . . . otherwise I'd have got back here sooner.'

Andy: 'Can't they leave us alone? Can't they fucking well leave us alone?' Maybe it was the fear, or maybe the fury, but I got the chilly impression he was no longer in control. Not quite.

'So we haven't much time,' Gary finished: 'and you should forget you ever knew us, Rachel. I mean that. Don't look so shocked: something like this has been in the wind for a long time, the way things were going. The way people talk. The ones who care will have to start all over again.'

He turned to look at Andy, motioned for him to get a move on with the others; then brought his gaze back round to me. And lowered his voice.

'It's McCain they're after, isn't it?'

I tried to look startled. 'Is it?'

'Oh *Rachel*. Don't insult me. You know much more about her than you've said.'

'Sorry,' I muttered, shamefaced.

Gary's face stayed sombre. 'The closest anyone heard to an explanation was that the cops were after terrorists. Is she mixed up with them?'

I gave a small, reluctant nod.

'God help us,' he said after a moment: sounding genuinely grieved.

'It's worse than you think,' I told him quickly – feeling suddenly spurred to share my burden, the awful cross I had to bear. 'She's just using them. She uses everybody. This is about witchcraft, and raising the bloody dead. And those weren't police this morning; they're mercenaries, out to stop her.'

He just stared at me.

'You can't save her now, Gary,' I murmured, shaking my head. 'Only yourself.'

'And you, Rachel?' he came back quietly. 'Can I save you?'

I didn't answer.

A distant, eerie sound crept into the silence between us, before being sucked away by a change in the wind. A sound like something wailing in the wilderness. Police sirens, somewhere in the City.

My stomach turned a somersault.

The wind changed again. The whooping, banshee sound came with it. Already closer.

'Oh, shit,' I whispered. The word seemed almost comically inadequate.

It could have been a real police vehicle, of course: on its way to answer a call, quite heedless of us. But I couldn't make myself believe it. And nor, I saw, could Gary.

'Too late,' he breathed, turning his face towards the fence. 'They got some poor sod to talk. Too bloody late, Lord . . .' Then his hand shot out to grasp my shoulder. 'Come on, Rachel. We've got to get you hidden.'

I let him lead me across the yard towards the main building: its black and gaping doorway. 'Wh . . . what about you?' I protested weakly, fighting the quaver in my voice.

'We'll manage.'

Against Morris? 'No, listen . . . you've got to lose yourself in here, quick. They'll . . .'

'. . . fire-bomb the place to flush us out,' he finished harshly. 'Won't they?'

I couldn't deny it. Not after Kentish Town.

'So some of us will have to try speaking with them,' Gary said. 'It'll give the rest a chance, if nothing else. Now get inside.'

There was the scuff of running boots across the yard. I turned, saw Lisa racing over. 'The fucking cops are coming!'

'Get in there with Rachel,' Gary snapped back; there was more than just brotherly concern in his voice now.

'. . . they've blocked the road, down past the junction . . .'

'I know, come *on*.' He snagged her threadbare sweater and shoved her after me. 'And keep your bloody heads down.'

Even on the threshold I paused; and not just because the dank and stinking interior felt as stifling as a tomb. Lisa had stopped too, still short of the doorway. 'Gary . . .' she began.

'I'll be okay. I'll put the fear of God into them.' He gave an unconvincing smile; it faded fast. 'Just, whatever happens, *stay hidden*. Please.' He glanced at me. 'I think McCain went north; she said something about Camden. I'll try to send them south or somewhere . . .'

Another burst of siren, sounding very close now. I thought I heard the roar of an engine under it.

We ducked inside, Lisa and I, and drew back from the light of the doorway. But neither of us was willing to lose sight of the blokes outside. Through the nearest window, its screen of broken chipboard knocked askew, I watched Gary gesture his mates down into a small, protective huddle round the fire. 'We all act dumb, all right?' I heard him saying. 'It's the only way we're going to make it through . . .'

The ex-psychie patient (oh, God, I'd forgotten his name) looked quite lost. So did Jim, though that was probably the drink. The rest showed a bitter mix of apprehension and defiance as they peered towards the fence.

Gary had fished up a hand-rolled cigarette from one of his pockets. His hands, as he lit it, were not quite steady. I watched his match-flame set the end alight; then the fire was sucked in upon itself as he drew sharply on the smoke.

And the big police transit came crashing through the gates.

It hit them at an angle, slewing in from the side-road, and wrenched them wide open. A length of chain snapped like cotton; fencing sagged. The driver kept his foot down and drove on into the yard. The riot shield was down across his windscreen, making the van seem like some maddened, blinded beast. The siren was dead, but the blue lights kept on flashing.

The doors were opening before he'd scrunched fully to a stop. Side and rear: the Peelers came tumbling out of it like paras. Within seconds they'd deployed across the yard, aiming their guns at the little group from three directions. Sub-machine-guns. Shotguns. The faces behind wiped clean of all emotion.

Peeping fearfully out from our shelter, I saw the land-rover that followed. Wire mesh encased its windows. Even before I heard the muffled barking from within, I knew this was the dog truck.

Wiking.

The Sergeant climbed out from behind the wheel; the bastard was actually *beaming*. As ever, he was wearing his luminous jacket, unzipped over his uniform. The man who jumped down from the opposite side wore plain black fireproof overalls, and a heavy leather belt around his waist.

I jerked my frightened gaze towards the transit.

Inspector Morris was standing there beside it.

Apart from his five-o'clock shadow and loosened tie, he might have come straight off parade. His cap sat squarely;

the knee-length coat was pure, unblemished black. He was regarding Gary and the others with an amicable smile; idly crumpling his leather gloves between his fingers.

He'd brought perhaps ten men; I was too petrified to count them. Some of the disguises were wearing thin now: anoraks scuffed and greatcoats shabby. Fingerless gloves, and doubled magazines. A couple had even come without their caps.

Morris jerked his head. Even from here, I could see his blue eyes twinkling.

One of the Peelers walked slowly over to the men around the fire. I watched, and winced inside with every step. Fear clogged my throat like phlegm.

The man with specs was the one he came to first. Without a word, he slammed his carbine into the poor bloke's wary face. Specs went over backwards, groaning; the others cowered back. But before King Jim could react, the Peeler had snatched a bottle of booze from his unresisting hand and up-ended it all over his victim. Then, quite casually, he tossed aside the bottle, produced a lighter, and set the man on fire.

I almost screamed; but my throat was too thick to let more than a whimper out.

Yells of horror from the dossers; they tried to scramble clear – and came up against a burst of hideous snarling. Two big, demented dogs were out of the landrover now, and straining at their handler's leash. The man with the leather belt looked like he had them just about in check. A rictus of effort – and relish – twisted his face.

The man on fire screamed and writhed, engulfed in burning bluish-yellow. The dogs barked in frenzy, rearing up. I saw the spittle flying from their jaws.

Then Morris gave another nod. Two more men moved in to join the first. I had my hands pressed to my face now – but not to my eyes. I couldn't stop watching as, between them, they *stamped out* the flames.

When they'd finished, the man whose name I'd never

learned was a blackened, battered ruin. His killers backed away: widening the space around the stunned survivors. Even the dogs, in all their madness, had lapsed into watchful stillness.

'And that,' said Morris affably, 'was just to let you know we've no time to piss about.'

I could see Gary's face in profile; he'd gone as white as a ghost. Behind me, further back in the dimness, I could hear Lisa's teeth chattering with shock.

Still smiling, Morris pulled his gloves on tight. Then pushed up the peak of his cap.

'I was reading one of your fine newspapers the other week,' he continued, conversationally. '"*Hang the bastards now*," its headline said. An admirable sentiment, I thought. We have here a noose for every one of you.'

He glanced aside; I followed his gaze. And nooses were being produced, all right – but they were rigid, and kept their ugly shapes. It took me a moment to realize they'd been fashioned from wire.

'Because it's terrorists we're hunting,' Morris went on, remorseless. 'And most of all, we want the one who calls herself McCain. You've got thirty seconds to tell me where she is.'

No one said anything for a moment. Then Gary swallowed, audibly. 'We . . . don't know anyone called that.'

'Five seconds deducted for every wrong answer,' Morris said drily. 'Try again.'

'I . . . all right . . . *someone* called that was here,' Gary faltered. 'But that was weeks ago . . .'

Morris made a show of tugging back his sleeve. And suddenly, absurdly, I heard my dad's words in my head: the ones he'd gleefully exclaim when we were watching soccer, back when I was small. *The referee looks at his watch* . . .

The dying seconds. *Injury* time.

'For Christ's sake, friend. *We don't know where she is.*'

316

Morris simply gestured. One of the men with nooses ambled forward.

'Oh Holy Mother of Mercy . . .' murmured Jim. He sounded stone cold sober.

'This is not a merciful occasion, old man.'

'Leave him,' Gary shouted. 'I'm the one you want.'

I heard Lisa's sob of indrawn breath in the silence that followed.

The man with the noose hesitated; looked back at his leader. But everyone else's eyes were fixed on Gary – mine included. The preacher sat waiting, his face still the colour of cold ashes; but I sensed an eerie air of calm about him now. Like a condemned man who knows he's past the point of no return.

'You know where she is?' asked Morris.

A slow nod.

'Where?'

Gary took a moment to extract his crimped cigarette. No trace of a tremble now. His voice, when he spoke, was quiet and steady.

'I can't tell you that.'

'Oh Jesus . . .' Lisa murmured.

I sensed her moving forward, towards the doorway. Instinctively – fearfully – I caught hold of her sleeve as she passed, and jerked her back.

'For God's sake don't,' I hissed.

For a moment I thought she'd try to struggle clear. Then Morris spoke again, and froze us both.

'You're very stupid,' he observed pleasantly.

'. . . I'm thinking of *you*,' Gary told him, the aftermath of a swallow in his words. 'You and all your men . . .'

A tingling pause. Morris regarded him quizzically.

'Meaning what, exactly?'

Gary shrugged. 'Meaning . . . once you know where she is, you'll already have one foot in the grave.'

'That so?'

'Word of the Holy Ghost,' said Gary softly.

I had my arm round Lisa now, holding on — and she was holding me. The smell of her clothes and body scarcely registered.

Morris gave a mirthless little chuckle. 'I think we'll take our chances. Thanks all the same.' And now, at last, his false smile faded: cooling to a stone-cold stare. 'Where is she?'

'Suit yourself. When I saw her this morning, she said she was heading south. Clerkenwell. I don't know where exactly.'

Morris considered that for a moment; studying Gary's face with narrowed eyes. Weighing the words against it. I waited, my heart pounding. Then Morris nodded, half to himself.

'We're obliged.'

And on that courteous note, he hauled a revolver out from under his coat and shot Gary in the head.

Lisa's wail was muffled by my shoulder.

The vicious crack of the gunshot went echoing round the yard. Gary's head, snapped back in a whiplash motion, rolled loosely sideways on his neck. His lifeless body slowly toppled. He lay still.

Morris lowered the revolver, and looked round at his men.

It was signal enough: he didn't even have to smile. The watching Peelers began to shoot at once, methodical as machines. No wild spray of bullets; just brief, surgical bursts at each helpless target. Emptying stomachs. Opening skulls.

Within seconds there was no one left alive.

Morris had already holstered his gun, turned back towards the transit. Even with my ears still aching, I heard him speak into his handset.

'Seven and Five . . . we still secure?'

'. . . *affirmative* . . .'

'Disengaging now; get ready for pickup . . .'

'Newman!' someone shouted. 'Check the building.'

Adrenaline slugged through me like a fist. For a second or so longer we stayed clinging together, unable to move, or even think; then struggled apart, and fled for deeper shadow. I fetched up in a crouch against a corner, down among whispery cobwebs and the ancient stink of urine. I'd scarcely stopped moving when the Peeler stepped in through the doorway. The end of his gun lit up.

A wide-angle torch, mounted just below the muzzle. The beam swung close overhead, almost solid with drifting dust. I buried my face in my sleeve, my heart so loud he would surely hear it. But the bleak light passed me by; and as the dimness thickened again around me, I could only listen, breathless, to the measured, gritty crunch of his boots across the floor.

A rustle of movement came from across the open room. The light was on it in an instant. And Lisa was cowering there, staring back into the beam like a petrified rabbit. Tears had left trails down her grubby cheeks. She whimpered faintly.

The moment held, like a tableau in ice. I waited for the blast I knew was coming. And then the Peeler jerked his gun, in a simple, urgent gesture of dismissal.

Lisa, sobbing, gazed back at him in disbelief; then ducked and ran, fleeing deeper into the derelict building. The Peeler just stared after her, waiting until her stumbling footfalls had faded in the darkness; then turned on his heel and went back out into the daylight.

The engines of landrover and transit were already revving. I heard shouts, and boots, and slamming doors – and then they were moving off, turning out of the yard and heading fast for the main road. Silence fell behind them like a pall.

All I could do was huddle up in that grimy corner: sucked dry with shock. So drained, I couldn't even cry.

But I was safe now. Safe where I was. Just so long as I didn't move, or breathe, or even blink . . .

It took physical effort to struggle clear of that cold, cocooning numbness – but I summoned the strength from somewhere. Knowing that if I didn't move *now*, I never would: I'd still be here shivering when the real cops arrived. Clambering up – just managing to keep my breakfast in its place – I ventured timidly out into the daylight.

The yard looked like a Chinese restaurant's rubbish tip. After the cats had been through it.

With that thought in my head, my breakfast *rose*. No stopping it. I just braced one hand against the brickwork, and let it come.

Probably . . . *bleuurghh* . . . the shock, as much as the revulsion. After all . . . I'd seen worse sights since becoming a nurse. Burns, and . . . RTAs, and . . .

Bodies were strewn about like refuse sacks. Blown open. Bleeding. A shape wearing Andy's jacket had been hit in the head, so hard that the skull had burst apart along the sutures. A bloody sludge of brains was glistening in the nettles.

I spat, and mopped my mouth, and looked round at Gary. He was lying there on his back, his blank face bloodless; its dirt and stubble seeming all the darker. With both eyes closed, he had the wasted look of someone sleeping off a sickness. Blood was pooling under his head, like an unclean halo.

'Oh God, I'm sorry . . .' I whispered through my fingers. 'I'm sorry.' It was all I could think of to say.

If he somehow heard me, I knew he'd forgive my leaving it at that and making for the gates. No sense in lingering; a sensible soul like his would want no eulogies. And besides – as he'd have doubtless told me – there's a time to pray, and a time to *shift*.

I looked back once, but there was no sign of Lisa. She'd be curled up deep in the darkest shadows of the factory by now, alone with her grief and horror. I came to an undecided halt by the shattered gates: loath to leave her behind in that lightless building. But after a moment I steeled my stomach and kept on going. The poor kid was safer where she was.

Razoxane. I had to find her. Morris and his men were on the rampage. I had to find her *now*.

Chapter 29

On the jittery journey northwards, strap-hanging on the tube (my stomach was too screwed up for me to sit), I found myself reviewing the moment when that Peeler had had Lisa in his sights . . . and let her live. I tried to draw some reassurance from it, however faint.

But there was little to be had.

Coming up from the depths at Camden was almost as unnerving as emerging from cover back at the factory. Maybe they'd second-guessed me somehow, and were waiting at the top of the escalator, just out of sight. With my heart pumping heavily, I forced myself forwards, into the crowd beyond the kiosks: looking nervously for uniforms. There were none to be seen. Keeping my head down, I wended my way out onto the pavement – and slipped into the broader picture: the breezy weekend bustle of Camden Town.

There were fewer people on the streets I took towards Primrose Hill; but my heartbeat had steadied to a thrum by the time I got there. Even if Morris hadn't taken Gary at his word, there was just too much of London for two vehicles to cover: they couldn't be everywhere at once. And this was surely their last fling now; the masks were off, as well as the gloves. So long as we could keep ahead of them for just a few hours more, they'd have had their chance – and lost it.

I spent half an hour on the hill. She didn't show. Perhaps she'd already come and gone, of course; perhaps I was walking in her fresh, cold footsteps. And the longer I waited, losing confidence by the minute, the more vulnerable I felt up here: exposed to the eyes in the city below me.

After a while I came off the crest; but the suburbs around seemed just as watchful. I had a growing sense of isolation: of being stealthily cut off.

Encircled.

The waning sun let shadows come creeping into the foliage round the park.

A few stirrings of breeze through the gloomier corners, and that was me finished. I followed what was becoming a familiar route, down into Chalk Farm and across the railway tracks to Camden. Now that my hasty search had come to nothing, I felt my spirits ebbing; reaction gurgled in to fill the gap.

It was like the onset of food poisoning. Nausea, stomach cramps and a cold, clammy flush. I had to lean on a wall to get my balance, as well as my breath. The prospect of the long haul back to our safe-house was too dispiriting for words.

Jim and Judy's place was only a street or so away. Surely I'd be welcomed there, beckoned in from the cold. Allowed to rest, no questions asked, while I got myself together.

I glanced at my watch: it was nearly four o'clock. Perhaps they'd be out – be it doing the shopping or walking the dog – and there'd be only gloomy silence to swallow the chimes of the doorbell; but I had to try. So after a momentary pause, I pushed myself off like a swimmer, and headed in the direction of their house.

There was no sign of occupation when I got there. The unlit windows looked positively mournful. But maybe there'd be someone in the kitchen at the back. Or somewhere.

Please be in, I thought, and pressed the button. *Please.* I was about to ring again, for longer, when I heard footsteps in the hall, and glimpsed Judy through the frosted glass. 'I'll get it, Paul,' she called, and opened up.

She'd been in the kitchen, right enough: still wearing an apron over her jumper and jeans. There was a smudge of flour on her forehead.

'Hello, Rachel.' Her enquiring look gave way to pleased surprise. 'How nice to see you.'

I opened my mouth to say hello back – and burst into tears.

Poor Judy's smile collapsed into concern. Gathering me in, she led me through into the living room, her arm around my shoulders. I tried to close the floodgates but I couldn't; the sudden surge had caught me unprepared. I could only sob helplessly as she eased me down beside her on the sofa. Part of me felt desperately embarrassed: protested I was twenty-*nine*. But the relief was almost blissful – being able to let myself go at last. Flushing out the misery like bile.

'Rachel . . .' She drew my head against her shoulder, and touched my dripping cheek. 'What on earth's the matter?'

I shook my head, still crying quietly.

'Shhh . . .' She paused to examine the grime on my scuffed sleeve, then gently raised my face to meet her own. Her eyes were anxious. 'Rachel, what's *happened*? Have you been . . . attacked or something?'

I sniffed, and smeared my tears with the back of my hand. It stemmed the flow; but my voice, when I managed to speak, was still broken up by hiccups of distress. 'No . . . nothing like that. It's just . . . a friend of mine got killed today . . . an accident . . . and . . .' At which point, seeing the commiseration flood into her face, I reckoned I could leave it there. 'Sorry,' I finished, sheepishly.

'Oh, Rachel, you poor girl. How dreadful for you.' It might have sounded trite from someone else; she said it with genuine sincerity. After a while, when my breathing had eased, she added: 'Do you want to talk about it?'

I shook my head again. 'No . . . thanks. I'll be okay in a minute . . .' All I wanted was to rest here against her: to be comforted like I hadn't been since Mum died. The thought almost set me off again.

I sensed rather than heard the door being opened. Judy glanced across me, and mouthed something, giving her own head a little shake. Son Paul, I guessed, come to see what all the commotion was about. I didn't look round; and after a moment he quietly withdrew.

Judy produced a tissue from up her sleeve, and dried my eyes.

'Feel a bit better?'

I did, actually; as if the outpouring of grief had helped to purge me. I gave her a wan little smile.

Judy beamed. 'I'm so glad you came here. You really don't want to keep something like that bottled up inside you. Now . . . would you like a cup of tea or something?'

I remembered asking a distressed relative the same thing just the other day. One of nursing's less celebrated rituals. *Put the kettle on, there's bad news to be broken.* Being on the receiving end felt quite peculiar.

'Please.'

She patted my shoulder, and went on into the kitchen. I sat where I was for a minute: watching the clock on the video count the seconds. Then sniffed, and got to my feet, and went through after her.

The kettle was making preliminary seething sounds on the worktop; she had cleared a place for it among her cake-making things. The yellowish paste in the bowl smelt rich and sweet – fresh eggs in butter, flour and sugar. Judy had paused to study the mixture, as if debating whether to give it a quick stir.

'Don't let me interrupt,' I said. 'I'd hate to spoil it.'

She gave me a grateful grin, and reached for a spoon. It was warm in here, the oven on already; the windows misting up. I wandered over to where her cookery book was propped open on a stand. Dependable Delia Smith, I noticed.

'Do you cook much, Rachel?'

'When I've time.' Saving her place, I turned some pages. 'Sometimes . . . being on shifts and everything . . . it's just grab the first thing out of the freezer, you know? I haven't baked a cake for *ages*.'

Judy smiled to herself, still stirring.

I pulled out a hanky and blew my nose. My sinuses were still a bit raw, but some of the weight had gone from my chest – as if I really had cried buckets. The flow of my thoughts came fresher now: no longer clogged by miserable black mud.

I was glad of the respite, but knew I hadn't time to bask in it. All sorts of mayhem could be going on in the streets while I tarried in comfort here. I was going to have to get stuck in again before very much longer.

But first things first.

'Could I . . . use your bathroom?' The sting of need grew stronger even as I said it.

'Course you can. Upstairs, first door on the right.'

I took my time; sat still for a while when I was finished. This lovely house felt like a *home* – but the outside world was waiting all around it, as if it had been built in the middle of No Man's Land. As soon as I was out of the front door and into the greying daylight, I'd be on my own again.

Apart from the angel of death – if I could find her.

I was just pulling up my briefs when the doorbell rang. The drawn-out double chime was almost languid. Someone stirred in the next room: Paul, of course. I rinsed my hands and turned the tap off. Looked round for a towel.

'Mrs Judith Stanley?' the voice from the doorstep asked. It was a woman. The slightly hesitant formality in her tone made me frown slightly.

Judy must have nodded.

'Are you the wife of Mr James Stanley?'

I felt a ghostly hand begin to squeeze my stomach.

'Yes. But . . .'

'I'm WPC Miller, Mrs Stanley. May we . . . come in please?'

'Has something happened to Jim?' Being Judy, her voice came out calmly enough; but it was dry with shock already. She knew. You always know.

'If we could just go inside . . .'

The landing creaked outside my door. 'Mum, what is it?' Paul called down.

'Who is this, please?' the policewoman said, already inside the hall.

'This is my son,' said Judy, voice still firm. 'Paul, would you come down here . . . please . . .'

Oh *Christ* I thought, my fist against my mouth.

There were no two ways about it: Jim was dead. He had to be. RTA, perhaps – or heart attack. Even while Judy had been trying to cheer me up, the staff at some mortuary had been going through her husband's wallet in search of an address.

What the hell should I do?

Oh *Judy*.

'We're really very sorry, Madam.' A man's voice, slightly muted: they were in the living room now. 'I'm afraid we have bad news.'

'Please,' said Judy bravely. 'What's happened to my husband?'

Inching open the door, I crept out onto the landing. Ashamed of myself for wanting to hear.

'Mrs Stanley . . .' the WPC began.

'Is he . . . hurt?'

'He's in good hands,' the policeman told her gently. 'I was able to speak to him before we left. I gave him an assurance.'

In the pause that followed, I could picture the hope rise to brighten her dulled eyes. Hope she scarcely dared to feel. I knew, because I shared it. Let him be injured, just so long as he's *alive* . . .

'I'm so sorry, officer,' Judy murmured: trying doggedly to keep herself in check. 'I don't even know your name . . .'

'Inspector Morris, Madam,' was his serpent-smooth reply. 'Ministry of Defence Police. I told him we'd call on his widow on our way home.'

*　　*　　*

They must have left the front door slightly open: even as I scurried back into the bathroom like a frightened rabbit, at least two more Peelers came in from the street. This time they closed it properly. I heard the deadlock turn. A moment later, one of them was on his way upstairs.

Squeezed into the gap behind the open bathroom door, I sensed him pause on the threshold: peering in. I held my breath. Literally. Both hands against my mouth.

The horrid moment passed, and so did he: moving on to check the other rooms. I could hear his handset crackling, spitting out bits of other people's conversations. Finished, he came back and trudged downstairs.

'Oh God,' came Judy's plaintive voice. 'Who are you? What do you want?' She sounded like someone who'd been slapped in the face by a stranger.

'We understand,' said Morris amiably. 'That you and your . . . late husband shared your meals with homeless people. Got to know them. Perhaps you can tell us where someone can be found.'

She started to falter a reply – and Paul's voice cut across her, pitched high with fright and anger. 'Get the hell out of our house, we know our rights . . .'

The words were squashed abruptly to an agonised groan. I guessed he'd been punched in the solar plexus. Very hard.

Morris clicked his tongue. 'Young people these days. No respect for authority. Bring him along.'

I listened to them moving to the kitchen: wanting to stop my ears now, not my mouth. Paul retched dryly. Judy sobbed. There were muffled sounds of struggling.

'Get him onto the table,' Morris said flatly. I heard its legs creak as they did so. A frantic, smothered, gagging sound came next. I had the awful impression – I prayed it was wrong – of a tea towel being stuffed into Paul's mouth.

'. . . why . . . ?' was Judy's whimper.

'Please don't waste our time, Madam, we've had a long day. There's a beggar in black who calls herself McCain. We want to know where she is.'

Only horrified silence answered him.

'I do believe you're withholding evidence from us, Mrs Stanley. That's a serious offence, you must know that. Hughes . . .'

'Yessir?'

'What's the law like on the withholding of evidence?'

'Firm but fair, Sir.'

'Indeed it is,' said Morris. 'Firm . . . but fair.'

Oh no, I thought. Oh *no*.

The rattle of opening drawers came next. He was sorting through their contents: I knew it as surely as if I could see his black-gloved fingers. 'A rolling pin,' he observed brightly, a moment later.

'Oh God . . .' breathed Judy: still audibly struggling to fight back tears. 'Oh, please . . .'

'A sharp knife . . .' continued Morris, as pleasantly as someone doing the voice-over for a gameshow conveyer belt. 'And a corkscrew.'

A choked sound from Paul.

'A freshly-boiled kettle . . .'

'We've never even *heard* of a McCain,' Judy burst out. There was an edge of panic in her voice, but not on her own behalf. 'I *swear* to you . . .'

'And Rachel Young?' he countered, like a mousetrap. 'You've heard of her?'

Poor Judy: caught completely unawares. Her startled silence said it all.

'McCain's accomplice,' Morris purred. 'She's dropped out of sight as well. Perhaps you could tell us where *she's* hiding?'

The hand of fear was working my stomach like an air-bag at a cardiac arrest.

'I . . . haven't seen Rachel for weeks,' Judy blustered; but her courage lacked conviction. Not even I would have believed her. And venturing back out to the head of the stairs, I felt a sick sense of collapse inside me – as if my stomach itself had sprung a leak.

But it was worse than fear now: I was facing fate. The knowledge that I could hide from this no longer. I simply couldn't.

I heard Morris slap the rolling pin against his palm.

'Please don't hurt my son,' said Judy, almost calmly. 'Hurt me, if you don't believe me.'

'You're a loving mother, Mrs Stanley,' was his reasonable response. 'Love will sacrifice itself – but never another. So . . .'

I hovered in horror on the brink of the staircase: knowing I was dead if I went down there.

Knowing I was *damned* if I didn't.

'Hold his hand out . . .' Morris ordered. Then: 'Watch yourselves.'

With my heart in my throat, I started to descend.

The rolling pin came down with a shattering bang. I heard a sound like five Christmas nuts being cracked together. Paul's stifled scream was a one-note wail. Judy's muffled outcry was just as anguished.

'You must understand us, Madam,' said Morris, insistently polite. 'It's our daily bread.'

I gritted my teeth and kept going. Step by trembling step.

'After I've broken his other hand . . .' the smiling torturer continued, talking across her tears, 'I'll cut his ears off. Then see what we can do with scalding water. Unless . . .'

I reached the bottom step.

'. . . there's anything you'd like to tell us?'

I felt as if I was sleep-walking towards the front door. My heart was still thudding like a drum machine, but my mind was millpond-calm. Time became toffee: it seemed I had all day to turn the key. Then, with my hand on the latch, I turned my head towards the kitchen.

Love will sacrifice itself . . .

'Morris, I'm here, you bastard!'

My voice cracked as I yelled it, letting panic leak coldly out. And I was back in real time again as I wrenched open the door, stumbled out onto the pavement and ran like bloody hell.

I knew they were behind me as I pelted down the road: I didn't dare look back and see how close. But maybe, in their haste, they'd quit the house together – leaving Judy alone with her maimed son and the memories of her husband. I hadn't time to hope for more than that.

I rounded a corner, swerving between pedestrians like a soccer star – and the whole morass of Camden market was there ahead of me, packed with people enough to drown in. Panting, I put on a spurt, my coat tails flying: thanking Christ I'd chosen to wear trainers. With the heavy-duty boots of my pursuers pounding in my ears, I wove my way into the thickening crowds – then dodged across the road without looking. A car horn brayed in my ear. I plunged on into the teeming railway yards.

This must have been a thriving depot once. Fallen into disuse, its narrow passageways and high, grey buildings had an oppressive, gloomy air, like something out of Dickens. But the market had spread on through it, and now it thrived again: a warren of hole-in-the-wall boutiques and robbers's caves. It had once been my favourite haunt on frosty Saturday afternoons. Today it felt as claustrophobic as a rat-run.

Veering left, I ducked into a doorway; a bright bazaar that reeked of incense. It made the outside world seem all the colder. With one wide eye I watched the first Peeler slow to a halt and glance around him: perhaps a dozen yards away. At least he wasn't carrying a carbine, but I knew there'd be a pistol under that anorak. People streamed past him without much interest. Probably thought he'd come after a shoplifter or something.

'Can I help you, love?' a woman asked.

I looked back at her and swallowed; tried to smile. 'I'm all right, thanks. Just . . . er . . . browsing.'

She drew pointedly on her cigarette. I glanced out again,

and saw the Peeler speak into his handset, head inclined.

How many were they? Just the four – or was he calling up reinforcements? One of the others joined him while he was still talking: hatless and kneading his gloved hands aggressively together. A quick consultation; then the second man walked over to a furniture boutique and disappeared inside. His companion proceeded into the archway ahead, past stalls lit up against the settling dusk. The whirr of generators carried crisply on the air.

Still short of breath, I slipped out of the doorway and on down the side passage, using racks of old coats as cover. They'd doubtless left someone to guard the entrance I'd come in by – and sent someone else to watch the only other exit from the warren, down the far end of the yards. So did that leave just two of them to search? Or had Morris brought the whole of Wotan with him?

With aching apprehension, I crept and scuttled through the maze. The whole garish casbah felt like a warren, all right: one that had been blocked off in readiness for gassing. I half-expected the people browsing round me to sense the dreadful danger. But they didn't, and looked right through me.

I almost walked right into the first Peeler by the snack stands: he missed me by a whisker, eyes elsewhere. Feeling sick with shock, I kept sidling furtively on towards the entrance at the Camden end. To find, as I'd feared, another of the bastards waiting.

He was standing there, arms firmly folded: looking cold but confident. Peering out from behind the hanging rug I was pretending to inspect, I watched him turn his face to study each group of people leaving the yard. No way would I get past him. No way.

I glanced behind me. Another black-clad figure was working his way down the stalls on my side.

Fear snatched at my windpipe: pinched it closed. I looked helplessly back towards the entrance – and saw the sentinel had been accosted.

It was a middle-aged man, red-faced and obviously incensed. Perhaps he'd had his pocket picked. He was confronting the Peeler now with the air of someone demanding action.

I moved without thinking. If I'd thought, I'd not have dared. Latching onto a knot of cheerful passers-by, I put my head down and strode towards the gap.

The argument came clearer the closer we got: the red-faced man becoming angrier, the Peeler losing patience. The chill in the latter's clipped, unfriendly tone might well have dissuaded a person less irate; but this gentleman was having none of it. And the Peeler, despite himself, was beginning to get involved: taking his eyes off the entrance to meet his challenger full on.

'. . . on anti-terrorist duties. *Sir*. Now I must ask you to . . .'

'. . . are you a bloody policeman or aren't you? A crime has been committed . . .'

At which point I hurried past, skin crawling; nodding my bowed head as if following the group's conversation.

'Look, just piss off, you old fart,' I heard the Peeler rasp behind me, even as I slipped through the net. Reaction left me weak at the knees, but I forced myself onwards: keeping up with one shoal of people, then another. It was surely downstream all the way now – following the flow towards the station. I came to the bridge over the canal, and fell into step along its narrow walkway.

Halfway across, I glimpsed the transit lurking on the other side.

It was parked with its nose and vacant gaze towards me, waiting there on my side of the road. I slowed to a stop, letting people around me go jostling past; then backed up against the current, not taking my eyes off the vehicle until it was out of sight again. I was so mesmerized with dread, I scarcely noticed shoves and mutters; and only belatedly remembered the Peelers on foot I'd left behind me.

I twisted quickly round to stare. The faces that stared

back were growing indistinct as the daylight waned, but none of the people at my heels looked like pursuers. Swallowing, I watched for a gap in the traffic, and quickly crossed the road, then started southwards once again. Too near to even think of giving up now. Just two hundred yards to go . . .

I kept my head well down as I passed the transit: watching from the corner of my eye. The shades of ambulance glass were gone, I noticed – the men who sat inside looked very bored. All of them were capless. A couple were even playing cards.

The pressure left my chest like a vice being released. A genuine police van – crewed by real coppers. Once more I wavered: wondering if I could possibly go to them for help. Maybe even try to get myself arrested . . .

But no. Even in a cell, I wouldn't be safe. Too many uniforms coming and going. Dragging my gaze away, I kept moving.

The sound of a vehicle chugging up behind me: coming slowly, against the one-way traffic. I risked a fast, frightened glance over my shoulder.

The Wotan transit was crossing the bridge.

Even as my heart leaped, it flicked its headlights at the other van in casual acknowledgement, and cruised on past it. I saw that the nearside door was slid wide open onto blackness, like a hole in a polished skull. Morris was up in the cab beside the driver, resting an elbow on his wound-down window: watching the carefree crowds.

I'd reached the crossroads at the bottom of the rise by now, and scooted hastily across it with the last stragglers; the lights had changed already, the cars to left and right were revving up. I didn't want to look back again, but I couldn't help it: I had to keep track of the thing. It was still coming at a crawl, but getting closer. A couple of irritable whoops on the siren stopped the traffic for it, and it slid across the crossroads in my wake.

Morris, looking. My glimpses showed a face as calm as

a bus passenger's, watching the world slip by. But I could feel the ice in his eyes.

With the real coppers' view now effectively blocked, one of the Peelers dropped out of the van and started pacing the pavement alongside it. His bulky yellow overjacket hung open; he cradled his carbine in both hands. People gave him curious glances – and kept on walking: which showed how common a sight it was these days.

Towards the stalls, the crowd was getting thicker. I wormed my way into it. ''Scuse me, please,' I bleated, with frantic politeness. '. . . 'Scuse . . .'

I glanced back again. The Peeler on foot was adjusting his earphone. Then the van we'd left behind us at the bridge just blew apart.

I saw the fireball first – a gout of lurid orange in the dusk, as though a sun had come down in Camden Lock. The sound caught up a second later, and numbed my ears. People around me ducked and cowered: screamed or swore. I just stood there, swaying, my eyes on the inferno at the crest of the rise: the hulk of the gutted van engulfed in flames.

The Peeler on foot had instinctively flinched when it went up, but didn't even bother to turn round. That told me everything, of course – or near enough. The matey flash of headlights might have dulled suspicions, but not for long. With all manner of reports about maniac cops beginning to filter in, an unrecognized transit patrolling their ground would have got them onto their radio in the end.

But not now.

The crowd was milling like sheep. 'Bloody IRA *bastards . . .*' shouted someone. And then the rest of the Peelers came baling out.

They all carried carbines now, deploying across the road like the assault-troops they still were. 'Armed police!' yelled one, quite unnecessarily. Bystanders drew back from them with awe. And all the time their heads were moving, scanning the restless herd. One's piercing gaze slid past me.

And came straight back.

'There!' he snapped, but I was running already – racing on towards the station: fighting my way through the stupefied press of bodies. I knew someone would get their act together in another moment, and try to drag me down: pin me to the pavement for the crowd to kick my ribs in. A terrorist atrocity, and somebody running from it. It's her. She's one of *them* . . .

I made it, just. A couple of blokes tried to block me, but I dodged past them, and skidded in through the station entrance. The ticket hall was bulging, a cushion of bodies – people straining to see what was happening. I sank into them, kicking and elbowing: all the things you dream of doing in the rush-hour. A moment's stifling resistance – then breakthrough. I ran past the unmanned kiosk, and went pelting full-tilt down the escalator beyond.

Most people were standing dutifully on the right. Those who weren't heard me clattering down behind them, and quickly shifted. I was leaping two steps at a time, so fast that only my momentum was keeping me balanced: I'd fall headlong if I faltered. Down and down and down I raced, my palm rubbing raw along the handrail, and from the top I heard a fresh commotion, and boots on the steel steps.

I hit the bottom without breaking stride, my gaze leaping towards the platform indicators. *Here* was the magic word beside one of the trains, and I swerved left, went flying down the concrete stairs to southbound, and saw the open doors ahead of me. Gasping for air, I fairly flung myself into the carriage, and found a seat to slump down in – waiting for the doors to hiss and close behind me.

They didn't.

All right, I'm here, you can bloody go now. I tasted blood in my mouth. Sitting helplessly back, I realized I'd developed a sickening stitch.

The train whirred busily to itself, and then fell silent.

Oh Jesus, I prayed. Come *on*.

They must have reached the bottom now – their carbines cocked and ready. Even if we began to move this instant, it might well be too late. If we were still pulling out when they arrived on the platform, they'd probably fill the coach with bullets to get at me.

That police van could have been destroyed by a grenade. Perhaps they had grenades . . .

People sat motionless around me, as if resigned to their fate.

The doors gave a sigh of blessed release, and rattled closed.

I almost sobbed as the train lurched into motion. The platform outside slid by, and then away, and we were engulfed in blackness, the coach lights just holding it at bay. Craning forward, I glimpsed a yellow jacket emerging in our wake. But too late to stop us now. Too late.

I felt like I'd just run a marathon. My throat was parched, my lungs heaving. I peered up at the line map, then looked at the man across from me.

'Bank?' I panted. 'This a . . . Bank train?'

'You what, love?'

I hadn't the breath to repeat it, but he cottoned on. 'Yeah. Morden via Bank. Nearly missed it, eh?'

I sagged wearily back, and shut my eyes.

The City branch gave a straight run down to Euston before veering east. As we sped on through the dark, I could picture the scene back on the surface. The Peelers who'd missed our train would have radioed back up, and Morris's transit would have taken off at once – wailing its way through the traffic and into the side road that ran parallel to Camden High Street. I could almost feel it pacing us, the driver's foot to the floor. A hard right at the end, and Eversholt Street would be stretching out before them – straight as an arrow, with Euston Station waiting at its point. Perhaps the speeding van was right above us now, its sirens blaring, scattering people out of its way. A desperate race. But surely the tube was faster.

Coming up to Euston now . . . and the train began to slow. Began to stop, still here in the tunnel. My heart beat painfully faster in proportion. But after a gut-knotting pause we were picking up speed again, and pulled into the platform a moment later.

I sat where I was, breathing rapidly through my mouth, while people around got off. I could follow their lead, of course, and try losing myself in the labyrinth; or maybe catch a Victoria Line train, and get well clear. But what if the Peelers really had kept pace, and were already on their way down here? Perhaps I'd run right into them.

And perhaps they'd reach this platform before the train pulled out again.

The City branch ran deep here: they'd have two levels to descend. With my stomach squeezed tight, I sat waiting. Being immobilized scared me stiff; but the prospect of venturing out was now equally unnerving.

I could almost see them, coming down. Make way, please. Armed police.

The doors slid smoothly closed again, and we were off.

Reaction was building up inside me. It left me weak and giddy, but I fought against it. Next stop was King's Cross, and I knew I'd be getting out there. Any further south would be too close to Moorgate.

King's Cross — St Pancras. I hauled myself up, and peered warily out onto the platform before getting off. The coast was clear.

They'd lost me now — at least for the moment. And now I'd half a dozen lines to choose from. But my first and overriding instinct was to breathe fresh air again. The atmosphere down here was as oppressive as a crypt's.

I knew it was a risk, but I felt too stifled not to take it. There seemed to be only one vanload of the bastards, and some of those had been left at Camden Town. Morris and the rest must be ready to cut their losses. And besides . . .

Razoxane might be round here, somewhere in the waning daylight. Haunting King's Cross, as she had in my dreams. I could think of nowhere else to resume my search. That was what decided me, in the end.

I came up slowly, in stages – like a deep-sea diver. The corridors and escalators were busy, and I stuck with the crowds, my chin sunk firmly onto my chest. At one point I passed a busker playing something lively on a penny whistle, which cheered me up a bit. I was fleetingly sorry I hadn't the change to show it.

By the time I reached the surface, the dusk was thickening above the streetlamps. I was tempted to hang around the station; but Razoxane – if she was here – would doubtless have crept into a darker corner. Down among the drunks and the litter. Perhaps she was watching me now.

Stepping out onto the forecourt – the cold came seeping in through the gaps in my coat – I went wandering cautiously past the bus queues, in the direction of the old Scala cinema and Pentonville Road. A lot of the homeless tended to congregate down here on the border zone. I didn't feel up to venturing among them; but maybe Razoxane would break cover and come to meet me.

She didn't. I got begged from a couple of times, but that was all. I went as far as the darkened bulk of the Scala, shabby and forlorn now. I remembered it from when I was a student: going to all those weird and wonderful films with my girlfriends, before sharing a cab back down Euston Road to the UCH nurses' home . . .

Happier times. The memories hung in the air like ghosts around a haunted house. I glumly turned away and started back. Walking briskly: trying to look assertive.

I really didn't want to venture any deeper into the district; but I couldn't just cut and run. I turned up York Way, following the blind side of the station. If she was somewhere around, she must surely be aware that I was here.

I didn't see the shadow in the doorway until it reached out to grasp my collar. I was still fighting for balance when he swung me round to face him. I glimpsed lean, mean features and deepset eyes, but the rest was darkness: zipped-up anorak, and pulled-down cap. Even the hands that held me were shiny black. Before I could so much as squeak, he'd slammed me *hard* against the wall. The impact emptied my lungs completely. When he let go, I could only slither downwards, coming to rest against a smelly heap of rubbish sacks.

People were passing, I realized dimly. Craning their heads to see – and walking on. Just some druggie being arrested. Guns involved. No sense in hanging round.

The Peeler raised his carbine one-handed, aiming down at my face – and flicked the built-in torch on. I squinted helplessly into the glare.

'Got you, you stupid cow.'

The light winked out, and he bent forward to grasp my coat and haul me upright. Back I went against the bricks, and sagged there, gasping. His head inclined towards his pickup.

'Whisky Oscar, from Whisky Alpha Six . . .'

'Escuse me, sorr . . .' a slurred voice interrupted. 'Would ye be interested in buyin' a copy of *The Big Issue* . . . ?'

The Peeler's head snapped round. A particularly dissolute-looking vendor was bearing down on us, proffering his sheaf of magazines. He wobbled as we watched; regained his equilibrium. Kept on coming.

'Only fifty pee, sorr . . .' he persisted hopefully.

'Piss off,' the Peeler snarled, and began to turn his gun.

Brendan shot him at point-blank range, the impact throwing the Peeler back into the rubbish bags: they sagged and split beneath him. The terrorist stepped forward and kept on firing, hammering him flat. The down-turned pistol cracked and kicked, wreathing its target in fading smoke. The Peeler's body slumped like one of the sacks; then ruptured – as shockingly as a pint-bag of blood bursting open under pressure. One full unit: the outermost spattering flecked my shoes.

I was still staring, pop-eyed, at the mess when Brendan grasped hold of my coat and hauled me after him: wrenching me round so hard I almost slipped. 'Come *on*, girl; don't stand there bloody gawping . . .'

He set the pace; I stumbled to keep up. We headed northwards at a brisk walk, without looking back. My gut instinct ached to break away and run – but my mind, shocked cold, was clear enough to know I mustn't. It's running people who draw attention – and tip suspicions into certainties. No one was close enough to have seen what happened; the crack of the pistol would have left people puzzled, but reluctant to assume the worst. A string of backfires, somewhere close; and two pedestrians, walking. A black heap of rubbish bags in the dusk. No need to get involved . . .

He was gripping my arm now: fingers tightening as he steered me on across the road. His free hand, still wrapped around the gun, was nestling beneath his coat.

A car slid past as we reached the opposite pavement, cruising down towards Pentonville Road. More traffic was coming from the south. Someone would have to realize soon. Perhaps in seconds. I strained my ears for the first wail of police sirens.

We kept going; in my state, still winded, the pace was punishing. He glanced back once, but I didn't have the nerve to. We reached the Goodsway intersection, and crossed it. Then the bridge over Regent's Canal. From somewhere further ahead, I heard the sound I'd been dreading: the lament of lost souls.

Brendan checked our backs one final time. 'This way, now,' he muttered, and yanked me onto a flight of steps beside the pavement. We went on downwards, into deeper gloom, and fetched up on the twilit towpath. The glacial surface of the canal still carried a faint sheen from the sky.

His arm slid round my shoulders, and drew me close.

'Leave it,' he hissed, as I instinctively resisted. 'We're just out for a quiet evenin' stroll, *okay*? Nice and slow . . .' He gave me a warning squeeze: I almost shuddered. There was nothing romantic about the smell of his mangy coat, either.

We started along the canal towards Camden. Strolling slowly, as he'd said – but my heart was still going at a sprinter's rate. We both of us looked back as the cop cars crossed the bridge.

There was little to see: just a glimpse of the lights, like blue electric sparks above the parapet. The howl of sirens peaked and plunged within the instant. These would be Armed Response Vehicles, if someone had been quick enough off the mark. I felt my stomach turn over.

Ahead, the towpath was deserted and unlit. We continued down it. Brendan's sweaty proximity made my skin crawl; I was suddenly convinced he'd set the seal on this fiction by forcing me into a snog.

But he didn't.

'The Peeler: how'd he spot you?'

'Dunno,' I mumbled.

'You're bloody lucky I was there,' he went on. 'If McCain hadn't brought me along . . .'

I glanced round sharply. 'McCain . . . where's *she*?'

He shrugged. 'She searched me out this morning . . . said she'd some business round here, and needed backup. Something to do with drugs, for all I know, but . . . you don't say no to her, do you?'

We were passing that gutted warehouse now. It towered above us, grim and gloomy: its scaffolding poked into the purpling sky. Whether it was Razoxane's lair or not, I felt a lot easier when we'd left it behind.

Again I tried to disengage myself; and this time he relented.

'Where is she now, though?' I asked.

'God knows. She said she'd find me when she was ready,

but ... I've not seen hide nor hair of her for hours now ...'

It occurred to me – perhaps from the almost plaintive way he said it – that she'd brought him here to set him up: as bait for something. Testing the waters around King's Cross, to see where the Peelers had laid their traps. Maybe Wampir had been waiting in ambush for her – and I was the one who'd waded blindly in.

But she'd said nothing about an Ankerite this far out – so what was the connection?

'You'd best be getting home,' Brendan was saying: no doubt unaware of what his comrades-in-arms had done to the place. What they'd have done to him too, come to that – if he'd been there.

I nodded, and glanced nervously back once more. But nobody had followed. There was just the calm canal, worming eastwards through the city like a CVP line. Right to the heart of King's Cross ...

'Where'd you get the *Big Issue* stuff?' I asked curiously after a minute.

'What, this?' He patted the bag still slung against his hip. 'Some bloke. I just tapped him on the head and borrowed them.'

I stopped short. 'You *bastard*.'

'You can stop coming on all holier-than-thou,' he told me drily. 'There's worse things been done. By both sides.' He kept on walking.

Unable to dispute that, I just glowered after him for a moment; then hurried to catch him up.

By the time I reached the corner of the street where we'd been housed, it was nearly eight o'clock. I'd told Nick I was just popping into work this lunchtime, to tie things up with Murdoch. He'd been unhappy with the idea to start with. Eight hours later, he'd be out of his mind with worry.

And I still hadn't thought of a remotely plausible excuse.

All through the tube ride, and the walk from the station, my thoughts had gone around in circles, and come up with nothing much. I could always say I'd been to visit a friend and the time had just flown; yes, of course I should have rung; I'm sorry, darling. Grovel, grovel. But I didn't really feel up to sustaining the pretence under the furious questioning that was bound to ensue. I kept getting flashbacks that put my mind right off the rails for moments at a time. Judy's face, and Gary's. Burning bodies. Blood and *bits*.

Judy. Whenever I thought of her, I heard Razoxane's words. *They leave nobody behind to tell the tale* . . .

I could just try telling him the truth, of course: the real depths I'd got myself dragged into. The prospect was so tempting. Before we went another step, his arms would be around me; I'd have his shoulder to cry on – and share the weight of my cross.

But then he'd be in this with me, past the point of no return. He'd demand to know more; try calling up his colleagues. And that, I was convinced, would be the death of us both. The poison in the system would start working its way towards us as soon as he plugged back into it.

So I'd no choice but to swallow my medicine. Not that I could blame him for blowing his lid. The evening news must have been like a foretaste of Armageddon, and he knew I'd been out there somewhere. He'd probably had his mates out, looking. There might even be dire threats of wasting police time.

Whatever, I could put it off no longer. Taking a deep breath, I continued down the road.

I was coming up to the flats when I became aware of someone crossing the road towards me. Even as my heartbeat quickened, a woman said: 'Rachel, is that you?'

I faltered, turned. It was a WPC, muffled in her anorak and scarf, and looking cold.

'Jesus, where have you *been*?' she continued, joining me under the streetlamp. 'We've had half the Met out looking for you . . .'

I swallowed. 'I'm really sorry,' I told her meekly. 'So many things came up . . .'

'Tell me about it.' She gave a mock shiver. 'Come on, let's get inside . . .'

I followed her round to the entrance; the hallway was in darkness, so no one had got round to replacing the striplight yet. She held the door for me, and I slipped in after her.

Light hit me full in the face: I swore and squinted. Torchbeam. Before I could think it any further through, I was seized from behind and held tight – my startled squeal muffled by a hand as cold and strong as a knight's iron gauntlet.

There was a dizzy, pounding pause, in which I remembered – crystal clear – the voice of the woman who'd come to Judy's house. *Mrs Stanley? May we come in please?* And then the torch ahead of me was lowered, and tilted up; and as I blinked, I saw it illuminate its holder's smiling face.

Morris.

His uniform looked as neat as ever. But lit from below like that, even his handsome grin became a Hallowe'en mask.

'Rachel,' he greeted me softly, as I squirmed and whimpered against my gag of flesh and bone. 'How nice to see you. We have been waiting patiently for your arrival.'

Chapter 30

'How's the prisoner?' Morris asked from up front.

'Comfortable, Sir,' said the Peeler with his boot on my throat. I wasn't, actually; but was hardly in a position to dispute it.

We'd pulled in on what sounded like a busy high street; a steady stream of traffic was purring past, and voices came and went along the pavement. The Wotan team were slouched in their seats around me, looking out through the one-way windows. I was lying flat on the floor, with my larynx half-crushed.

The outside world – so nearly within reach. I felt like someone drowning in shallow water, still able to feel the sunlight with her frantic, groping hands.

I'd lost track of our movements soon after they'd bundled me aboard. The van had speeded up and slowed; turned corners, stopped at lights. No one spoke. Nor, apart from some rough handling, had anyone hurt me. But that just made things even more unnerving: convinced me they were saving me for something worse.

My fear had swelled up like a bubble – then burst, to leave me lying cold and torpid: almost calm. I'd seen RTA victims react like that; your mind can only take so much. Even when I thought of Nick – hoping to God he'd stayed safe in the flat while the Peelers laid their trap for me downstairs – my feelings seemed vague and distant: hacked off from the here and now.

The air in the van was thick and fetid. Brut aftershave (like Nick used to wear, before I wore him down), mixed in with halitosis and stale sweat. But I caught stray whiffs of other stuff as well. Vomit. Old urine. Smells that told me I wasn't the first unwilling passenger to have travelled this way.

I felt my fear begin to grow again, like a new phase of the moon.

The van's side door slid open, clunking. I caught a snatch of conversation: kids walking home from the pub or pictures. Having fun.

The WPC climbed in, clutching a rustling paper sack. She'd left her hat in the van, and her straight blonde hair hung almost to her collar. I remembered how friendly that face had seemed, when I thought I was home and dry.

'Cheeseburger and fries,' she said.

One of the Peelers claimed them, and she went on through the orders, fishing them up out of the bag. Quarterpounder. Chicken bits. Big Mac with extra relish . . . I lay very still and tried hard not to think of being sick.

'Burger with large fries. Joe . . . ?'

'They're not *fries*,' the bloke with his foot down on my throat objected drily. 'They're *chips*, woman. Call yourself a Geordie . . . ?'

I could have shared a smile with people like this. My mind had to struggle to match them up with the things they had done. And the things they were going to do . . .

'Sure you're all right, Sir?'

'Quite all right, thank you, Miller,' Morris told her. 'Let's go on.'

And on we went. All I could do was watch the streetlamps sliding past above me – and listen to Peelers chewing overhead. The butt of my minder's sub-machine-gun rested on the floor beside my cheek. It was a different design from the standard carbines: short wooden body and a round magazine. Peering up, I could make out Cyrillic characters, carved deep into the stock. Another souvenir of past battles, I thought numbly.

We made a final left at length, and left the road: the orange glow of streetlamps seeped away. The transit crept on in first for a few more yards, then juddered to a halt. The engine cut away to silence.

The pause that followed lasted only a moment – but the rattle of opening doors was as jarring as if the silence had had hours to mature. Down in my belly, the cold bright moon of fear was full again.

The size eleven left my throat, and I was hauled, gasping, to my feet. The rear doors stood agape behind me. The Peeler pushed me out.

No steps. I dropped, hit tarmac and awkwardly collapsed.

'Any trouble, Hughes?' called Morris from the dimness.

'Prisoner fell out of the wagon, Sir.'

I heard him click his tongue. 'That was careless of her.'

I raised my head, and glanced fearfully around. We were in a yard of some sort; two of the Peelers were closing the iron gates we'd driven in through. The glow of the street lay on the other side of the wall. There were lamps on this side, too – but they were that cold, white type that seem to shed no real light. A building loomed behind us, all unlit.

A boot crunched down beside me: black on black. I was still trying to crane my head round when Morris grasped me by my collar and hair and yanked me bodily upright.

'Oww-ww . . .'

'Shh,' he chided softly – and began to frog-march me towards the dark front entrance. I hadn't the strength to struggle; nor the nerve. Some of his Peelers followed. The rest spread out, slipping into the darkness. Securing the site, I reckoned . . .

Securing the *school*.

I glimpsed the sign, and almost did a double-take. They'd brought me to a school. An inner-city one at that, to judge from its appearance.

In through the doors we went – they must have forced the locks – and on down the gloomy corridor: our footsteps echoing, re-echoing, bouncing around me. No light beyond the dregs from the neighbouring streetlamps, oozing in through the windows. It was like a nightmare march to an excecution. Out of some film, and into the real world.

We came to a foyer; Morris steered me towards some doors. I just made out the sign and logo on the one he elbowed open. The Girls' Toilets.

My lungs felt constricted: I couldn't breathe. He man-handled me through, into a narrow room bathed in bluish light from a lamp outside the window. The row of cubicles stood as silent as confessionals. The taps on the sinks gleamed dully. I groaned as he pitched me forward, down onto the cold dry tiles.

One of his men stepped over me and took up position by the washbasins.

'Where's McCain, then, Rachel?' Morris asked.

Such a casual enquiry. As if I could choose to keep silent. I swallowed helplessly, and said nothing.

He cocked his head to one side, smiling down at me through the dimness. 'Why protect her? A beggar, a mur-derer, an *outcast*. Why suffer on her behalf . . . ?'

I found my voice − or someone's. Mine didn't usually sound this thin, this reedy. 'I dunno where she is . . . Honestly . . .'

Morris considered that in silence; then turned to the man on the door. 'What's she look like to you, Hughes?'

'A stuck-up tart, Sir.'

'Mm. And what's the law like on prostitution?'

'Firm but fair, Sir.'

'Exactly so.' Morris glanced towards the man at my back. He nodded his head. I heard the plug fitted, the tap turned on. Water began to gurgle.

'Think it over for a moment,' he suggested.

'For God's sake . . .' I gave in to my rising dread, and glanced behind me. The stream of water looked like crystal in the ghostly light.

'It'll all be for nothing, you know,' his voice insisted mildly. 'We'll win in the end. We always win.'

I looked back round. Perhaps it was my terror that gave me the strength to sneer.

'Yeah? You've got a bloody high mortality rate, for winners.' It would have come out sounding better if my voice hadn't cracked halfway.

He shrugged. 'Acceptable losses. She's just one woman. Her time's run out already.'

'She's got advantages,' I muttered.

'What advantages?'

'She's insane.'

Morris studied me for a moment; then slowly shook his head. His shadowed smile showed something close to fondness.

'Oh, Rachel. I do believe you've been watching the wrong films.'

Behind me the tap was turned off.

'McCain,' he said, one final time.

I opened my mouth, but no words filled it.

One of the other Peelers stepped forward, took hold of my coat and dragged me up. My heart began to quiver like a punchball. From the corner of my eye I saw the nearest basin: almost full, the water still and shining.

Morris put his back to the wall and leaned against it.

'I would guess . . .' he told me drily '. . . that a good Catholic girl like yourself would have gone to a nice convent school. A bit like this one. And on somebody's birthday, I'm sure you and your friends enjoyed dragging them into the toilet and giving them a good ducking. Remember . . . ?'

Leather fingers slid into my hair, and knotted to a fist. The Peeler swung me round, and forced me forward. I had time to take one frantic gulp of air before my head was shoved into the water, hard – and held there.

It was freezing cold: like an iceberg freshly melted. Drawn from the mains at midnight. A convulsive shiver kicked through me. I clenched my aching teeth.

After a moment the blood began to thunder in my skull.

My lungs started smouldering. Thick, stale air, demanding to be let out. I wanted to scream, and knew I mustn't. Mustn't. *Mustn't . . .*

Then my dripping head was hauled back up, and I let both lungfuls go. The air burst out of me with such force that I dimly expected blood and bits of lung to come up with it. Still locked in the Peeler's grasp, I found myself faced with my open-mouthed reflection, wet hair strung across my gawping, frantic face.

'Drowning . . .' said Morris thoughtfully beside me '. . . is a traditional remedy for witchcraft. And you walk with a black witch, don't you, Rachel? Risking your sweet little soul. Perhaps you too are already contaminated.'

With a small, regretful sigh, he nodded – and before I could even wail, I was under again.

They kept me down for longer, this time: taking me right to the edge. I squirmed and struggled – helplessly wriggling my hips. It did no good. My head began to sing, then split. My lungs caught fire. I knew, with a fearful detachment, that they'd wait until the very last second before letting me up.

The very last second came – and went.

That's it now: give me air, I screamed inside. *I'll talk. I'll tell you anything.* But the iron weight on my back was unrelenting. I gave a final, desperate twist – and then reflex forced my mouth open.

Air bubbled out, and water gushed back in. It filled my nose and clogged my throat, before scalding down into my lungs. Even in my terror, I realized the truth. They'd tired of trying to make me talk. This time I was down for keeps.

I threshed and kicked in agony and horror – but already my thoughts were scumming over. The flames in my chest were going out, as though the cold had quenched them. The roaring in my ears became a murmur, faint and faraway. And then there was only the stillness of deep sea.

*   *   *

I came to, coughing: spitting diluted bile across the floor. I was lying full-length, the spattered tiling inches from my face. Back on dry land, I realized thickly — but my head was still swimming, and my lungs felt like they'd been pulled inside-out.

It took me a while to relocate myself. But Morris and his men were still standing there, like shadows all around me — waiting with pitiless patience for me to raise my bleary eyes.

I did so in the end. And Morris smiled.

'Well, Rachel . . . are you ready to sing yet?'

I hawked, and spat out something horrid. 'I . . . have *nothing* . . . to tell you.'

The gloating blue eyes didn't blink. He simply lifted his chin in a single nod — and the Peeler behind me pulled the basin's plug. With a giddy feeling of relief, I listened to the water go swirling down and out. The plughole sucked itself empty.

Then he put the plug back in again, and my stomach heaved afresh.

'Watch this,' said Morris calmly.

The Peeler had turned to face the sink, gripping its rim in both gloved hands. Staring down, as if in search of his reflection. For a dragging moment he didn't move. Then a shudder racked him and he craned forward, mouth yawning open. A gout of puke splashed down into the basin.

The smell stung my nose: made me grimace in puzzled disgust.

'Fast food these days,' murmured Morris. 'So difficult to keep down.'

Another gargling throatful joined the first — but with the plug in, it couldn't drain away. The basin would just . . . fill . . . up . . .

With a squeal, I tried to scramble to my feet — but the Peeler at my side was ready. Once more I was caught by hair and shoulder; forced back down onto my knees. Made to see, and hear, and smell it all as the vomiting continued.

'Sure you've got nothing to say?' enquired Morris.

'Oh Jesus, please . . .' I whimpered. The basin was half-full now. The stench was dreadful.

'. . . *Whisky Oscar One from Three* . . .'

Without taking his eyes off me, Morris unclipped his handset and raised it to his mouth. 'Whisky Oscar One.'

'*We have a possible intruder, over* . . .'

'Where?'

'*South wing* . . . *Heard footsteps at the end of the corridor* . . .'

'Check it out, then.' He lowered the handset, looking thoughtfully at the others.

A squirt of static; then the woman's voice. '*Whisky Oscar Five. I've got one on my side as well, Sir* . . . *Just seen him* . . .'

In the pause that followed, the Peeler at the door brought up his carbine. There was a quiet click. I didn't need to be a firearms expert to guess that was the safety catch.

'*Whisky Oscar Six* . . . *Something moving, round the back here* . . .'

'Shit.' Smiling no longer, Morris moved to the door; then glanced back at the Peeler who'd been puking, and gestured towards me. '*Watch* her.' Like I was a piece of his luggage or something.

He strode on out, the door-keeper making way, then following. The bloke who held me shoved me sideways, made a noisy show of priming his own carbine, and trotted after them. I heard another message come crackling over Morris's radio as their footsteps clicked away.

The remaining Peeler wiped his mouth, and grinned at me.

The door of the nearest cubicle burst open, and Razoxane lunged out.

Her boot had crashed into the Peeler's stomach before he could begin to react. The impact flung him back against the basins, arms helplessly outspread; his own gun caught behind him. Stunned, off-balance, he began to slither downwards – and Razoxane was on him like a she-wolf, pouncing to grasp his lapels and slam his head against the edge of the puke-filled basin. The porcelain cracked – or was it the bone? The Peeler spasmed, went limp, and crumpled to the floor.

Razoxane straightened up, and adjusted her hat – then flicked out her switchblade and bent over the body. The bleak flash of the blade was doused in black as she stabbed, and stabbed again. Finished, she rose and looked at me. In that eerie light, her grin was as pale as a skull's.

'Hello.'

I let a moan of nightmarish relief come seeping out.

She walked across, grabbed a fistful of coat and hauled me upright. 'Come on, we've got to get moving.'

I stumbled after her on jelly-legs – out of that awful torture chamber and into the foyer beyond. No echo of sound was there to greet us. Just a hissing hush.

Then a stutter of gunfire from somewhere outside.

'Perfect,' she breathed, and steered me off down a corridor in the opposite direction.

'What's going on . . . ?' I mumbled, glancing nervously back.

'They're shooting at shadows,' she explained, still pushing the pace; not bothering to follow my gaze. 'Things I summoned here. They'll find no trace of them, though – and now they've given themselves away . . .'

I stifled a cough: it scorched my throat. 'Were you in there all the bloody *time*?' I demanded hoarsely.

'Of course. All I had to do was wait. Now, quiet for a moment . . .' She led the way down to a fire door and pushed it open; listened. Then beckoned me on out into the night. Another staccato burst of shots cracked through the air as we edged around the playground, making me flinch; but it came from the far side of the building. I heard a distant shattering of glass.

The wall was the final barrier. We scrambled up and over it, like a couple of truants, and dropped into the alleyway beyond. I felt like collapsing there and then.

'Come *on*, Rachel,' she muttered, as I clung to the stonework. 'We need to be well clear before they realize.'

I stared numbly back at her for a moment; then swallowed and got going once again, trailing woodenly in her wake. My wet hair already congealing in the chill night air.

'So how the hell did you *know*?' I persisted.

Hours later; miles away. I felt the weight of both. I'd had a go at towelling my hair dry with my jersey, but it still hung damp and stringy. At the moment I was perched on somebody's front garden wall, a hedge digging into my back. Taking a shaky breather.

Razoxane had wandered a few yards down the pavement, staring over the rooftops at the brightening eastern sky. The foretaste of dawn. She turned as I spoke, and came walking slowly back.

'Part of it was Mindsight . . .' she said. 'But I also know Morris well enough. Know his little foibles. I don't know if you remember . . . A few months ago, that school on Merseyside. When the pupils came back one Monday morning to find some poor bitch drowned in an unflushed toilet. The inquest couldn't decide if it was murder or not – what with her being an addict and all; but that was Morris's lot. That's his taste. What turns him on.'

I pulled a face. 'And that's "proactive interdiction", is it?'

'Pretty much.'

My shoulders slumped. 'God, Razoxane . . . The things they did yesterday. Gary's dead, you know that? Everyone at that bash is dead. A police van got blown up in Camden. People tortured, murdered . . . everywhere. They've gone bloody berserk . . .'

'They're out of time now, though. Yesterday was a

gamble: all or nothing. And they lost us. Morris won't risk them on the streets again in daylight . . .'

'They've found out where I'm *living*,' I burst out.

'So they have: but I don't think they'll come back.'

'Oh, *don't* you?' I muttered.

'Lightning never strikes in the same place twice – and neither does he. That would make the game so much less interesting.'

I gaped up at her. 'You still think it's a *game*?'

Razoxane smiled. 'Indulge us.'

Shaking my head, I clambered to my feet. 'So what now?'

'Now we'd better get you home: you need to rest. And then I'll get in touch again – tonight.'

'You never let up, do you?'

'Just striking while the iron is good and hot.'

I rubbed a hand back through my sticky hair. 'If I get through this . . .'

'Big if, Rachel,' she grinned.

'*Stop it*. If I get through this . . . I think I'm going to join a bloody convent.'

Razoxane chuckled softly.

'I wish you luck,' she said.

Chapter 31

Nick, to coin a phrase, was fucking furious.

I couldn't really blame him. I'd walked out of the flat at lunchtime yesterday, saying I'd be a couple of hours – and he'd heard not a word from me since. It was seven in the morning now, and I couldn't even slip guiltily in: I didn't have a key.

I pressed the intercom buzzer once, and waited. My mouth felt as dry as dead leaves. On the other side of the glass, the hall where Morris had lain in wait looked bleak and dingy in the dull light. Quite empty, as far as I could see; but returning to the scene of my abduction made me even more keyed up.

I glanced over my shoulder. No sign of Razoxane; but I knew she was lingering somewhere near. In case.

The intercom came to life. '. . . Hello?'

Nick's terse, distorted voice. I swallowed. 'Nick, it's me . . .'

There was silence from the other end. Then the door buzzed. I pushed it open and hurried upstairs, my heart throbbing.

He was waiting at the top – still wearing yesterday's shirt and trousers. They looked like they'd been slept in, if he'd slept at all. He hadn't shaved; his face was doughy with fatigue. His eyes were burning.

'And where the *fuck* have you been?'

I winced. 'I'm really sorry . . . look, can we go inside . . . ?'

He drew back, glowering; I followed him in, and closed the door behind me. Then went through into the living room to face the music.

'Jesus *Christ*, Rachel,' he burst out as soon as I'd crossed the threshold — as if even those few seconds of silence had been more than he could bear. 'Where were you? I've been worried sick.'

The sheer force of his vitriol made my eyes sting. I had to bite my lip.

'I've been phoning the station all night. They've been combing the streets. Every available man . . .'

'Nicky . . .'

'All you had to do was bloody *ring* me . . .'

'. . . I've been attacked,' I whispered.

That put him off his stroke for a moment; his mouth stayed open after the words had stopped, like someone in a badly-dubbed film. My tangled hair and grimy coat seemed to register for the first time.

'Well, serves you bloody right,' he snapped.

I sucked air in disbelief. 'You *what*?'

'You heard.'

Just the anger talking. Got a momentum of its own now . . .

'For God's sake . . .'

'Come on, then. What happened?'

Did he interview rape victims like this? Even as my mind put forward special pleading, I felt my outrage rise like bile.

'Some bloke dragged me into an *alley* . . .'

'When?'

'Last night . . .'

'Which nick did you go to?'

It took my seething thoughts a moment to grasp his meaning; *how many Nicks do you think I know?* 'I didn't. I . . . just walked.'

'So how come your hair's been wet, then?' he demanded, closing in.

'Um . . . I went to see a friend of mine. She let me use her shower . . .'

'But not her phone.'

I stared into his pale face; too angry myself now to improvise convincingly. 'Oh, just piss off, will you?'

'Have you been cheating on me, Rachel?' he asked evenly.

I felt cold shock soak through me. 'Christ, no . . .'

He hit me, then. Open hand across the face. It *hurt*.

'I don't believe you,' he said.

I raised my hand to my seared cheek – as if to check the skin was still there. My eyes widened. A moment before there'd been wetness welling up in them. Now my tears dried stillborn, like snowflakes in Hell.

Without a word, I turned and strode towards the bedroom. By the time he caught me up, I was stuffing clothes into a suitcase.

'*Now* what are you doing?' he asked, unnecessarily.

'Now I really am going to see a friend,' I told him through my teeth. 'And I'm fucking staying, too.'

'Listen . . .' The doubts had caught him up, now: I could hear them in his voice. But they were far too late.

'No, *you* listen.' I finished fastening the lid as I continued. 'I'm not going to stay here . . . with someone who knocks me around. All right?'

'Raitch, I'm sorry . . . Look, you know I've never laid a finger on you before . . .'

'First time, last time. You shouldn't have done that, Nick. You really shouldn't.' I brushed past him, back towards the door.

'*Rachel.*'

I turned at the front door, still giddy with anger. 'Goodbye, Nick. I might give you a ring in a day or so. If I can remember the number.'

Slamming the door on his perplexed and pleading face, I went quickly down the steps. Keeping my sobs in check until I was out on the street.

*   *   *

I rang him that night, in fact: sitting at the bottom of the stairs in Jean's house. She'd been wonderful when I'd called her; of course I could stay for a few days, what were spare rooms for? She'd fussed and fed me when I got there; listened wisely to my tearful account of the morning's row. I was careful not to give too many details.

It was she who'd suggested I give him a call. Tonight, while she and her husband were out and I could have some privacy. I was a bit reluctant: it felt like giving in. But she managed to persuade me.

'"Don't let the sun go down on your anger." Isn't that the phrase?'

It was an awkward conversation, like small-talk between strangers. I was feeling well in myself now – freshly showered, and wrapped in a size-too-large bathrobe – but the thought of the morning still made my cheek sting. It wasn't so much the blow as the fact that he'd been capable of landing it that really left me shaken.

'When . . . will you be coming back?' he asked at length: still hesitant.

'I don't know. I need some time to myself now, Nick. I need to think.'

'I'm really sorry, Rachel. I . . .'

'I know you didn't mean it,' I murmured. 'But it's done, now. We're both going to have to live with that.' I paused; but he stayed silent. 'Listen . . . I'll call again in a couple of days. All right?'

He managed a subdued goodbye. I echoed it, and hung up as gently as I could. Then looked over my shoulder, at the gloomy figure sitting higher up the stairs – half-absorbed by the first floor's shadows.

'So what happens next?'

Razoxane slid two handfuls of cards together, and slowly raised her head.

'The settling of accounts,' she answered softly. 'For which we're going to need a little help.'

'Who from?'

A faint smile twitched her bloodless lips as she selected a card, and held it up for me to see.

An ugly goat grinned coldly down at me.

The Devil.

Chapter 32

'I was speaking *figuratively*, Rachel,' she insisted, for the umpteenth time, as we waited on the platform.

'I should sodding well hope so,' I muttered.

She looked away again, still smiling.

God knew where we were off to now. I'd given up asking things like that. 'I'll meet you there at ten,' was all she'd told me. 'Eastbound platform.' So after breakfast, I'd told Jean I was going into town to do some shopping.

'Good idea,' she'd said, approving. 'Take your mind off things for a bit.'

It would take a damn sight more than a wander round Liberty's to do that; but I'd nodded anyway.

Seeking help from the Devil. Figurative or not, the idea made my stomach churn: grinding my breakfast like a pair of millstones.

The next train came rumbling in, and we climbed aboard, taking seats that faced each other across the central aisle. Razoxane made herself comfortable – to the obvious discomfort of the people to left and right – and took her dusty hat off. As we travelled eastwards, through increasingly unfamiliar stations, I watched her fiddling with its dangling leather thong: idly tying it up into a miniature hangman's noose.

How reassuring.

We came up from under the city, and sped on through sunlight. A few stations on down the line, she nodded at me and got to her feet. Resignedly I followed. We disembarked into suburbia.

Clear of the station, she put her hat on, letting the noose

trail down against the nape of her neck; then dug out her
spinner, and turned it thoughtfully in her fingers.

'It's been a while . . .' she murmured – mainly to herself.
'But I know it's round here . . . somewhere . . .'

'What is?'

'What we're looking for.' She grinned at my exasperated
look. 'Something that was hidden a long time ago. A
resource for a pilgrim in need.'

Lowering her head, she gave the spinner a couple of slow
turns; then looked up again, and round, like some animal
sniffing the wind.

'This way,' she said after a moment: and off we set.

'Are we getting warm, then?' I asked an hour later. The
frosty morning was anything but, and my coat and gloves
weren't keeping much of it out.

Razoxane had extended one bare finger and set the
spinner going on its tip; only a gyroscope could have
stayed in place there. Its elliptical wobble was growing
more and more pronounced.

'I think we're almost there,' she said, unperturbed by
the jittery sarcasm in my tone. 'It doesn't have much of a
signature . . . but I've got a fix on something now.'

We'd ranged over a square mile or so of streets and open
spaces. Perhaps there'd been a pattern in our rambling
progress, but if so I hadn't noticed. For most of the time
we'd walked in silence: Razoxane absorbed in her divinations. Or whatever they were. Even in daylight, the sight
of that spinner made my stomach tense. With every nervous
glance I gave those black, rotating spades, I recalled the
demon-things she'd summoned up before.

The next left brought us into a desolate street, lined with
half-demolished houses. They'd clearly lain like that for
quite a while – there were thickets of weed and nettles
sprouting up among the heaps of rubble. Some of the ruins
had a cutaway look, like dolls' houses – I could look up
and see the rotting wallpaper in somebody's bedroom. The

363

overall effect was like a stark, three-dimensional maze: the sort of thing that children swarm to, but someone had thought of that. The open sites had been sealed off with rusty chain-link fencing; those buildings still more or less intact had been boarded up and blinded.

'This feels promising,' Razoxane said, and glanced at my apprehensive face. 'Relatively speaking,' she conceded drily.

I grimaced, and looked around. There was nobody in sight; no noise, apart from the distant swishing of traffic, and a lone dog barking. The buildings lay in dismal silence, like emptied mausoleums in a cemetery.

Razoxane tossed the spinner, caught it in her palm and stilled it.

We found a way into the warren through a kicked-down door that nobody had bothered to replace. The room beyond was dim and stinking, but a glimmer of light seeped out of the fireplace that gaped in the far wall. Walking over, we found the back of the flue had gone, and we could just climb through – into an open field of debris and broken bricks.

Razoxane began to pick her way across it, heading for the next building; part of it had collapsed to join this mess.

I heard that dog barking again. It sounded closer, now: maybe out in the street we'd just left. It sounded pretty fierce, as well.

Enraged.

I looked at Razoxane, as she looked at me. After a moment she mouthed a word. It looked a lot like *fuck*.

We broke into a run together – or what passed for one on that crumbled, shifting surface. I promptly slipped, and for a frantic moment thought I'd sprained my ankle; but it could still bear my weight, and I was up again an instant later, and scrambling in Razoxane's wake.

More barking from behind us, sounding muffled and echoey now, and I realized the dog was into the first house. I glanced fearfully back as I reached a doorway, and caught just the briefest glimpse of it emerging, coming up over a heap of masonry and tiles. Alsatian.

In panic I plunged onwards – and almost stepped straight into a pit. The building I'd just entered had been totally gutted, just the four bare walls remaining. Even the floor was missing, exposing the cellars: they opened up beneath me, deep and dank. Spoil from the clearance had been banked up around the edges, sloping down like the crumbling edges of a crater. Almost mewling with fear, I struggled down along the wall, as fast as I dared – then faster still. There were two dogs out there now, filling the air with the anguish of their madness.

Razoxane was waiting at the other end: she grasped my arm and pulled me across the corner. My heel caught a loose brick, and sent it spinning down to shatter in the dimness.

'Come *on*,' she hissed, as if I had it in mind to hang around or something. We ducked through another doorway, and found ourselves in a wreckage-clogged passageway, open to the sky. It looked so clean up there: so blue. The sound of the dogs was disembodied, now. They'd already be casting around through the maze of walls and rubble, trying to sniff us out.

'Not in *daylight*, you said . . .' I panted, blundering after her. My voice was quavering out of control; I could almost feel their breath against the backs of my legs.

'I told you, I know Morris,' she snapped back. 'But he knows me, as well. I should have guessed . . .'

I looked over my shoulder, just as one of the dogs slipped into view, the same way we'd just come: clearly agile enough to skirt the open cellars. It latched on to us without breaking stride, racing down the passage in a black-and-tan blur.

'*Razoxane*,' I yelped.

She dived sideways through the next doorway, with me at her heels. I had a fleeting impression of what had once been a back garden, high-walled and narrow, as we lunged across it and into the house. The interior was thick with undisturbed shadows; the smell of decay so strong, I half expected motes of mould to float into my face. We crashed through the former kitchen (all its fittings torn out) and fled on towards the hall. The front of the house had been battened down with chipboard, and the gloom grew thicker with every step. We reached the stairs, and Razoxane made way and shoved me up first, then hauled herself after me. The old wood creaked and threatened to collapse. Something fast came snarling down the passage from the kitchen.

Razoxane shrugged out of her greatcoat and spun to face it. As the rabid dog came springing up the stairs, she flung the heavy garment down against it. The dog became a struggling bundle of black; still fighting free as Razoxane's switchblade unsnapped in her hand and she pounced, plunging the knife into an exposed and heaving flank. Blood geysered up the filthy wall; the muffled snarls became a weird, despairing howl. The second dog howled as loudly in sheer frenzy, hurtling in through the house to join the mêlée. As I watched from a terrified crouch at the top of the stairs, Razoxane dragged her knife clear, kicking out at the other dog as it scrabbled towards her. The eighteen-holer boot connected with its jaw, and might have stunned it for a second; but before she could withdraw her leg, it had seized the toughened leather between its teeth and was hanging on like living death.

The first dog twitched and whimpered; Razoxane threshed. With all my nerves rebelling, I came scuttling down to help – but even as I reached her, she managed to force the animal's head backwards. It twisted and teetered, out of balance; unwilling to let go. And then Razoxane wrenched her foot free, rolled onto it, and ripped its spasming throat out.

The silence that followed seemed unnaturally loud. I could almost hear the echoes fading, like exorcised ghosts. The hall had filled up with a fresher stink – of blood and canine urine.

Razoxane wiped her oozing blade on the nearer dog's fur. I watched her rub spittle off her cheek with the back of her sleeve. Millions of teeming, evil microbes smeared away, as casually as raindrops. Then she turned her pale, tight face to me.

'Upstairs, now. Quick. Their masters' voice won't be too far behind them.'

I retreated up the rickety staircase, and she followed, leaving hat and coat behind where they had fallen; her sullied knife still gripped in one hand. At the top of the flight, she opened her other fist, and I saw the spinner resting on her palm. All through the fight, she hadn't let it go.

'It's in this house,' she murmured. 'So let's see where . . .'

She started along the landing to the nearest doorway. The room beyond was bare, right down to the boards, and overshadowed with damp. Stepping in towards the centre, she slowly turned on her heel, the spinner extended in one hand. Watching from the threshold – those boards looked decidedly dodgy – I had the eerie impression of someone scanning with a Geiger counter: checking for lethal dosage.

The spinner didn't crackle; but a moment later she went over to the fireplace. Even the mantelpiece had been removed, leaving just a raw hole in the wall. She glanced at me – and grinned.

Down on the staircase, something creaked.

We both froze, listening. The stairwell was just round an angle of the wall, beside me. I could almost feel the hush that filled it.

Razoxane eased carefully down into a crouch, and laid her knife aside. She slid her pistol out from under her jersey as she straightened up again – flexing her naked forefinger through the guard.

Was that someone's shallow breathing I could hear? Or just the blood that hissed inside my head?

Razoxane crept towards me, her shades like black fog-lamps in the gloom.

A skittering of rubble from somewhere outside. My stomach reacted as if to a phantom punch. We'd been trapped in here: surrounded. Then the creaking on the stairs resumed in earnest, ascending towards us.

Razoxane lunged past me, craned round the corner and fired down into the stairwell. Three high-pitched, stinging shots. I heard a choked-off yell, and the sounds of something heavy tumbling back. Wood splintered rottenly. Razoxane recoiled from the line of fire, her cold smile vulpine.

'One down.' She didn't wait to see if there were more; just strode back into the room and over to the fireplace. Dropping to her knees, she ducked her head in and peered upwards.

I edged away from the head of the stairs, waiting numbly for the next set of footsteps: as if I'd hear them through the slamming of my heart. As I passed the first doorway on my left – across the landing from the room where Razoxane was working – a spill of unfamiliar daylight caught my eye. Peering through, I found the whole back wall was missing, giving a panoramic view out over the ruins.

I bit my lip, and crept in a little further. If I could see how many of them there were, it would surely help. Warily, I ventured towards the edge. The site below me looked like one of those aerial photos of Dresden after World War Two. I glimpsed a patch of yellow.

The Peeler had already taken aim; he fired as I reacted. Something sifted my hair and tore deep into the ceiling, leaving a puffball cloud of mouldy plaster. I hit the floorboards, sobbing for breath.

A glimpse was all I'd had; but I'd recognized the Sergeant – with his shotgun.

Oh bloody hell, I thought.

'Rachel . . .' Razoxane hissed from across the landing.

I scurried through to her. 'It's the bloody *Sergeant* . . .'

'Shh,' she said. 'I've found it. Look at this.'

Still in a crouch, I looked. She was kneeling over a

smallish leather suitcase, fiddling with the lock. Presumably she'd got it from the chimney; perhaps it had been hidden there for years. Or even decades, to judge from its battered, stained appearance. This house was old, perhaps Victorian. But the shabby case looked older.

Even with our nemesis gathering outside, I felt a nameless menace in here with me.

Then the lock had given way, and she lifted the creaky lid and threw it back. I wrinkled my nose at the dusty smell; then felt my eyes grow wide.

A gun was lying inside – a sort of single-barrelled shot-gun. But the muzzle was huge, like a hoover nozzle; wider. She lifted it carefully out, almost caressing the worn wood. Then glanced across at me.

'And *this*,' she murmured, 'is what men used to call the Devil's Tinderbox.'

There was movement in the house below us.

Razoxane seemed unruffled. She delved back into the case, and brought out a drawstring pouch; emptied the contents into her palm. They looked like dull ball-bearings: beads of lead.

The Sergeant's voice came floating up the staircase then. Too full of grim good humour for my comfort.

'Going to tell my Tarot, witch?'

Razoxane smiled to herself, but didn't answer.

Watching her tip the cluster of heavy shot into the muzzle, I was absurdly reminded of something we used to play when I was small. A nervy three-dimensional board game, full of traps and pitfalls triggered by a dropped ball-bearing. *Haunted House* . . .

More movement from downstairs, as if on cue. Rumblings in the house's empty belly. I rose, and backed away, towards the wall.

Haunted House. Be careful on the Creaky Floorboard.

The old wood creaked – and a burst of bullets came ripping upwards through it. I squealed and cowered, slumping back against the skirting board as the spot where

369

I'd been standing went up in spouts of wood-shavings and sawdust.

The shooting stopped abruptly, like an unplugged drill. I kept very still, my numbed ears ringing faintly: staring at the string of ragged holes. It looked as if some monstrous worm had been at work, devouring the wood before my very eyes.

Nick had once assured me that police carbines couldn't fire on automatic. The Peelers clearly had no truck with that.

Razoxane had rolled to the doorway; she gathered her legs beneath her now, and rose. The shotgun-thing was hefted in her right hand; her pistol in her left. She jerked her head.

I stole along the wall to join her, almost choked by the throbbing in my throat.

Another stream of shots came chewing through the floor, this time on the far side of the room. Fountains of dust reached up to touch the ceiling. We darted across the landing under cover of the noise, into the room with the missing wall. The floor erupted almost at once.

Only Razoxane's arm across my stomach stopped me plunging on into the spray. We both lurched back against the wall as a whining, spitting dust-devil prowled blindly round the room. Then died away. I saw motes and splinters settling in the sunlight.

'Clever . . .' Razoxane breathed. She looked at me. 'Two carbines and a riot gun.' Her thumb found the hammer of her antique shotgun, and hooked it back.

'Still with us, ladies?' the Sergeant called.

There was a fireplace in this room, too – like a smashed, empty mouth. After a moment Razoxane started side-stepping towards it.

I rested my head against the wall and watched her go. The haunted house was still again. A caption from the board-game's box kept looping through my mind: so banal it was almost ominous.

Be very careful on the stair: the Whammy Ball can get you there.

Or anywhere else. The whole place was a death-trap, ready to spring. And here we were, caught, like two of the game's witch-sisters. Wanda the Wicked, and Glenda the Good . . .

Razoxane was down on her haunches now, staring into the fireplace. When she began to clamber through, I felt my stomach lurch – as if I expected it to swallow her like a throat.

Crouched awkwardly in the cavity beyond, she looked towards me again, and nodded downwards. I nodded back, still not quite comprehending – but maybe the old flue was our way out. If we could just climb down inside it . . .

Razoxane shifted – and abruptly disappeared. There was a rumble and clatter of displaced bricks. 'Oh, *shit* . . .' she yelled, the word sucked after her down the shaft.

Ghoulish Gertie drops it down the chimney, I thought insanely.

Sound exploded through the downstairs rooms – the roar of pistol, carbine and shotgun, triggered together in a single blast. But the carbine had the last word, hacking on through the echoes before spluttering into silence.

I stayed absolutely still, my mittened hands against my mouth. Then the trembling began. I could almost hear the Sergeant's mocking words; his climbing footsteps. *Rachel. Alone at last.*

Then Razoxane's voice came drifting up the flue.

'You want to stay up there all day?' I could tell, even from here, that she was grinning.

You *bitch*, I thought, with unspeakable relief, and went stumbling downstairs. My heart rose like a fist into my throat as I edged past the bodies of the dogs; but neither breathed. Just beyond, at the foot of the stairs, the first Peeler lay sprawled, his eyes wide open. The radio on his chest still picking up distant voices, as if the corpse was talking to itself.

I went down the hall to what might have been the breakfast room, and peered in. Most of the outer wall was missing here; the neighbouring house had been razed already. A stagnant pool of daylight stained the carpet of rubble. Three bodies were crumpled up amid the rubbish.

I swallowed, and ventured in. The nearest Peeler lay face-upwards, still clutching the carbine sloped across his chest. His features were unreadable; they looked like they'd been plastered with tomato puree.

A rustle of movement made me wheel – and Razoxane was crouched there in the fireplace, caked with dust. Still clutching both her guns.

'Bloody *hell*, Razoxane . . .' I breathed.

Her shades were still in place, but I saw her eyebrows flex in amiable acknowledgement. She squeezed out of her nest, and straightened stiffly up.

'I hadn't planned on outflanking them quite so dramatically . . .' she said. 'But still . . .' She paused to flex her arms, her knees – then nodded back towards the door. 'Fetch us my coat, could you?'

I went meekly out, and back to the staircase. Her coat was still draped over one of the dogs, like a scruffy shroud. I reached out gingerly for it, my head full of the meaty animal stink that clogged the stairwell.

There was a low, chilling growl in the dimness. I gave a little shriek and stumbled backwards.

Her pistol blasted, almost in my ear. The bullet spattered blood and bits of fur. The growl was stilled.

She smiled disarmingly. 'Sorry.' As I stood there, shuddering, she stowed the handgun away and went forward to retrieve her soiled coat. I watched her shrug into it, switching her shotgun from hand to hand; seemingly oblivious to the blood and piss that stained the garment. Then she stooped for her hat, and settled it in its place.

'Are we going now?' I asked in a small voice.

'In a minute. Just one more thing to do.' Turning,

she retraced her steps into the breakfast room. I caught up as she sauntered across to the Sergeant's supine corpse.

It looked like he'd caught her load of Whammy-Balls full in the chest. The yellow jacket had sunk in on itself, snagged up in his shattered ribcage. A thick, *passata* pulp was soaking through it. His slackened, putty face showed something like surprise.

Razoxane dug inside her coat, and came up with a single, tatty card. 'Your Tarot, Sergeant.'

I glanced at the design. Angels swooping down from a Heaven in flames. *La Giustizia*.

'Judgment,' she murmured, by way of explanation. Stepping forward, she rested one boot on the dead man's chest, and bent down to push the card between his teeth. Then straightened up. Still smiling.

'And *I* don't even charge,' she said.

We saw the waiting landrover as we emerged. It sat in silence at the roadside, its seats and dog compartment empty; an air of abandonment hanging over it already. Even so, I was reluctant to go near it – as if the lurking hulk still had a mind of its own.

Razoxane had no such qualms, of course, and strolled on past: the Devil's Tinderbox back in its case and tucked comfortably under her arm. I followed – and felt my hackles rise as something crackled awake inside the vehicle.

But it was only the radio, I realized after a moment. They'd left it switched on, still tuned to the Met's own network. A bored exchange of traffic reports receded behind us.

Abruptly my legs felt as weak as a newborn foal's. I stumbled sideways, caught hold of the wall and took a shaky breath.

Razoxane turned. 'You okay?' Her voice was quiet, now: almost concerned.

I stayed leaning there for a silent moment longer; then

swallowed, and straightened up under my own steam. 'Yeah . . .'

'You know what you're going to do, then?' she asked drily.

I met her sombre smile full on — and nodded.

'I'm gonna live to tell the tale,' I said.

Chapter 33

'Two hundred years ago,' said Razoxane slowly, 'there was a legend about this gun. People said it could fire for ever, never needing to be recharged.

'That wasn't strictly true, of course.'

I sat back, silent: watching her run a piece of rag along the lines of the Devil's Tinderbox. The weapon certainly looked old enough – its wood and metal dulled by age, its silver chasing tarnished. I guessed it must be a blunderbuss or something.

We were down in a basement flat, beneath an empty house. The place had the feel of a squat, abandoned in haste: some old, stained bedding and other belongings were still strewn across the concrete floor. But whoever had been here previously, this was Razoxane's foxhole now.

Perhaps she'd sent her ghosts ahead of her, to clear it.

On the street overhead it was still early afternoon; down here it felt much later, dusk already. She'd brought me back here by way of a dingy snack-bar, wolfing down a fistful of sandwich as we'd walked. Me, I doubted if I'd ever have an appetite again . . .

'It belonged to a witch-hunter once,' she continued, polishing. 'Until they hanged him for practising what he persecuted. You don't need a charge of gunpowder to fire it. Just ashes. It reconstitutes the energy that went into their burning: an alchemical reaction. Plus, you can fire all sorts of interesting things from it. Like nails.'

I wrinkled my nose. 'I thought a blunderbuss did that anyway.'

She shook her head. 'Not really. Wouldn't do an ordinary one much good. But this can swallow anything – and spew it out again. Bits of metal, broken glass, you name it. Which is just as well . . .' she thumbed back the hammer, '. . . since the grapeshot's a bugger to get hold of.'

I'd always pictured blunderbusses with big, flared muzzles, like ear trumpets; but this one's flare was little wider than a test-tube's. An anachronistic weapon: the eighteenth century version of a sawn-off shotgun – but I got a spooky impression of the still older power inside it.

Razoxane lifted it up against the side of her head, and squeezed the trigger. The hammer, carved like a snake, sprang forward. *Click.*

Satisfied, she laid the gun across her lap – and dug out that old pocket watch of hers. Her dusty hat brim dipped to cover her shades as she bent her head to study it, turning it unopened in the fingers of one hand. Then her gaze came up once more; and her solemn, thoughtful stare became a smile.

'Want to see?' she asked softly.

I remembered Gary's reaction to that question. Swallowing, I shook my head.

'It's all right,' she reassured me: guessing why. 'I haven't charmed it. Take a look.' And with that she tossed it to me.

Instinctively I caught it – and almost dropped it when the lid flew up.

It wasn't a watch.

The face was black, with concentric silver rings of symbols. Instead of two hands, there was a star shape sprawled across them: five major points, on an X of lesser fins. A pentagram – but not a perfect one. The lowermost point was largest.

As I watched, it trembled – and began to move.

I closed it with a snap, and stared down at the lid.

'I found it in a Spitalfields junk shop,' said Razoxane drily. 'Many years ago. It's a means of divination. Charm it before showing it to someone, and they can read their fate on its face: the pentagram inverted would show that death was soon and certain...' She grinned at my grimace. 'It can also act as a compass, for someone who needs to know the way; but not like one you've ever known. It shows a person the road to their destiny. Few have had the courage to use it.'

She reached across and took it back. Quickly I rubbed my emptied palm across my coat.

Back on the unit, the afternoon shift would be well underway. Jean, working a Late, would doubtless have things well in hand. I could picture IV stands against the windows, like skeletal silhouettes; their LED readouts glowing...

How's Rachel today, I wonder?

Razoxane was fingering through her Tarot pack again.

That pile of antiquarian books beside me was doubtless hers. God knew what those might have inside them. I raised my eyes again – to find her watching.

'Various writings I've collected,' she murmured. 'Clues to the existence of Ankerites. They won't mean much to you.'

The topmost book turned out to be in German, which didn't help. I skimmed through some yellowed pages anyway, and found them full of cribbings: marginal notes. 'How old's this?' I asked.

'Turn of the century.'

'So... there are European sources, then?'

'That was written by someone who studied ritual killings – in many cultures. He visited London in the 1890s. Trying to dig something up on the Whitechapel Murderer.'

I frowned uneasily. 'And that had something to do with ... this?'

'Perhaps. We can't be sure. You can take your pick of theories. Crowley reckoned the Ripper was conducting a black magic ritual, to raise a demon...' She noticed my blank look. 'Crowley. Aleister. No?'

I shook my head.

'Not a very nice man,' said Razoxane, and left it at that.

I wondered if the scribbled notes were hers. The ink looked as old as the paper, faded in. I found one reference ringed, for added emphasis. *Matt. 12: 43–44.*

That was presumably Biblical: I made a mental note to look it up.

'It's true there was a Roman cemetery at Aldgate,' she was saying. 'Outside the old city wall. Perhaps an Ankerite went to ground as far east as there. Maybe those murders were somebody's attempt to raise it. My guess is, it was already extinct. All a waste of breath and blood.

'Anyway . . . friend Morris will be licking his wounds, now. The way is clear.'

She drew a card and set it down before her. The Tower. 'Let that stand for your hospital, right . . . the citadel.'

The fact that the Tower was falling didn't exactly reassure me.

The Moon card came up next. 'In the darkest hour,' she murmured.

The third card was the Ace of Swords.

No comment for that one. She permitted herself a secretive smile, and looked back at me.

'You want to do it tonight?' I ventured.

'All things at the right time,' said Razoxane softly.

I thought of Sandra's sleeping face. 'Remember what I said . . . about the kids' ward.'

'No need to worry: I've got it all worked out.'

Oh, I'm sure you have. I gave in on that sour thought, and picked another book up. She'd marked her place in this one with a folded sheet of paper. I caught a glimpse of writing, and opened it out one-handed; anything to keep my mind distracted for a few minutes more.

There was a pause.

'. . . Razoxane . . .' I said.

'Mm?' She'd pocketed the rest of the pack, and returned her attention to the gun.

'You know I was telling you about . . . those nurses who've been killed . . . ?'

She nodded, head still bowed.

I swallowed, but it didn't help my voice. The words were still pinched thin and tight.

'How come you've got one of their addresses?'

Another pause. It became a silence even as I listened. Janet Nicholls's name seemed to swim before me, penned in an archaic hand. Razoxane still wrote her *s* like an *f*.

Her hat brim, when it finally came up, revealed an almost rueful smile.

'Damn it, Rachel. I'm getting careless.'

I gaped at her. '*Razoxane* . . .'

'Well what do you want me to say?' she asked reasonably. 'All right, so I blocked the flue of her bedroom heater: stuffed it with rags. She died quite peacefully, I'd expect . . .'

My mouth stayed open, but only breath came hissing out; as if one of my lungs had sprung a leak.

Razoxane leaned forward.

'I had to do it, Rachel. I ran into her while I was scouting round. Tried to pass myself off as just an opportunist down-and-out . . . but she was suspicious. I could tell. I couldn't take the chance. Can't you see that?'

Just like old times, I thought in horror. A lapse into her lethal paranoia. I became aware of her fingers flexing – perhaps unconsciously – round the stock of her gun.

'And . . . the others, too?' I ventured: avoiding eye contact – or what passed for it, with those staring shades.

I sensed her shake her head. 'That wasn't me. It probably wasn't Morris, either. Just this shitty little world we live in, Rachel. Or hadn't you noticed?'

Oh, I'd noticed all right. But even as I tried to absorb what she'd just told me, new images grew in my head like sudden fungus. A couple of nurses leaving the kids' ward, chatting . . . unaware of the shadow at the dark end of the corridor, turning its spinner slowly in its fingers. And when their footsteps had faded into echoes, that shadow moving up to the closed doors – and peering in.

'What were *you* doing up there, anyway?' I demanded hoarsely.

She picked up the Tower card, and tapped it pensively against her teeth. 'I've mapped out your whole building. All those miles of corridors. The Surgical cloisters. The Medical keep. I knew from the start that I might need it. If one of them got loose.'

I swallowed; the dregs of my breakfast stirred. But the words that rose suddenly to my mouth tasted far more bitter.

'It's you that Sandra dreams of, isn't it?' I blurted. 'Someone hateful, trying to get in. It's *you*.'

Razoxane didn't answer.

'And that thing I could feel in the corridor outside . . . was one of *your* ghosts. Your familiar spirits. *Wasn't it?*'

'*Listen* to me, Rachel,' she snapped back. 'This is an *Ankerite* we're dealing with. You've seen how powerful they are – and that's just its potential. These books contain all sorts of warnings, all manner of threats: possession, contamination, *incarnation* . . .' She paused on that crescendo, and shook her head. Then continued in a quieter, more conciliatory tone.

'The surviving Ankerite can definitely move above ground. I thought it had crawled away to die at first, the trace was so faint . . . but then I found its trail on the surface, right through the heart of the City. So what I told you before was true enough. I need to summon it somewhere: bind it. Then put it out of its misery – and ours.'

I kept making small, convulsive nods – as if in time to the jolts I felt with each new step of her argument. The flat seemed like a dungeon now: an underground prison into which I'd been locked, with only a killer for company. The full light of her ruthlessness was at last coming clear, like a cold moon through clouds: shining balefully down on my hospital, without pity for anyone inside it.

But it was that casual admission of murder that had

really left me numbed. An innocent girl. A *nurse*. That, more than anything else, made me sure I was on borrowed time myself now. Too deep into the red.

'You don't seem convinced,' Razoxane said mildly.

Stay calm, my mind advised me. *Play it cool.*

'You cold-blooded *bitch*,' I spat.

'Is that a compliment?'

Without quite thinking, I scrambled to my feet; then did think, and hesitated. She was still sitting with her back to the grimy window, her head tipped back to watch me; her face corpse-calm.

'You'd lure that thing into a *kids' ward* . . . ?' Now that I'd made my move, I felt exposed and shaky; her comfortable stillness seemed to give her the advantage. It crossed my mind to just bolt for the door – and how would she react to that? Come after me with her naked knife . . . or simply shoot from where she sat?

Suddenly I found I didn't care.

Razoxane smiled behind the toppling Tower.

'Consider how much it hates,' she came back coolly. 'How much it wants revenge. Where better? Where more tempting?'

I was shaking now: furious, despite my fear. 'Not even your terrorists . . .'

'Oh . . . I won't be needing them for this. Just the two of us, Rachel.' A wicked glint of irony lit her face. 'Ourselves alone.'

'Well you'll have to bloody *kill me* first.'

And with that I turned my back and made for the door. It was like an open invitation: the skin between my shoulder blades went as tight as a drum. But she didn't even stir. With my heart jamming up against my sternum, I strode out into the tiny hall, shoved the front door open and climbed the gritty steps towards the daylight.

The dungeon below stayed dim and silent.

I reached the pavement like someone coming up for air, and kept right on walking. The street was empty; even the breeze had stagnated in the cold. I could still feel the *depth* of the pit behind me: I didn't dare look back. Then I'd reached the corner, rounded it and was hurrying west – just mastering the urge to break into a run. I'd put several more streets between us before I let myself feel the first twinge of relief.

She'd let me go without a word.

Part of me knew it had been too easy; but perhaps she'd had no choice. No way was I going any further. I'd told her the truth when I said I'd rather die.

How close had she come to taking me up on that? For how many seconds had my life hung in the balance? I felt a moment's giddiness at the thought. It's not a prospect you can ever really be prepared for.

But the cold scales of her mind had found in my favour. Maybe for old times' sake. Or maybe because she saw me as a sister, the fair face of the moon – and to murder me would be to mutilate herself.

Even the damned in Hell must be amused . . .

Well maybe they were; but I'd been the fall girl long enough. If I depended on her to protect me, I'd be in her thrall for ever. I'd made the break, and fought my rear-guard action. Now I had to burn the bloody bridge.

After which . . . what? Across the road from the tube station now, I slowed to a halt. The hospital had to be warned, of course – but what the hell could I *say*? Even if I phoned in a bomb warning, they'd be stood down in the end. I could keep on trying until they traced me, or dismissed me as a hoax. And then the way would be clear for Razoxane and her Ankerite to settle their business. In a ward full of sleeping children.

Cars kept swishing past, disrupting my thoughts like boats through water. I had to find somewhere quieter, where I could sit down and think. Or maybe get onto my knees and *pray*.

Back to Jean's house? I knew I couldn't. Horror seemed

to follow at my heels. I imagined Jean, like Judy, opening up to find Death waiting on the doorstep.

Which just left the flat in Finsbury Park: the same refuge I'd stormed out of only yesterday. And all I had to cling to was what Razoxane had told me. That Morris didn't strike in the same place twice.

You'd better be right, you bitch.

I lingered for ages at the end of the street: peering down towards the flats. The shadows had lengthened in the past half hour, giving everything a sinister cast. Parked cars seemed to lurk along the roadside. The skip at the kerb made me think of a monster's jaw, still crammed with chewed-up wreckage.

With the sun screened off, the chill was taking on an edge. The resistance of my coat was breaking down. It made me realize that I myself was homeless now – just a borrowed bed or the open streets to choose from. My eyes were smarting with the cold already; but that thought made them sting.

Yet still I hesitated. Perhaps it was even pride. Despite everything I'd been through, some stubborn part of me still baulked at going back to Nick so soon.

A car cruised by on the busier main road. I gave it a nervous glance, but it didn't slow. A gap in the traffic stretched out behind it, filled with silence. There were no pedestrians close. Now seemed like as good a time as any.

Someone appeared behind the entrance doors as I approached them, and I felt my heart flip over; but it was just another resident, a middle-aged woman, coming out. She even held the door for me. I scuttled through with a jerky nod of thanks.

The hall was still without a light. I climbed the steps with leaden feet, and turned towards the door of the flat.

It was slightly ajar.

I stood there on the landing, staring. No light showed

through the crack; no breath of sound leaked out. It was my chance to turn and run.

I didn't take it. There was nowhere to go. If Nick was being held in there, I might as well join him. I didn't see much point in going on alone.

It was suddenly such a tempting prospect: to give up, and just go under. After all these weeks of struggling, a final peace. Tears welled in my tired eyes at the thought.

Submission; but my heart still rose towards my throat as I stepped forward and pushed the door. It opened smoothly inwards. Nerves tingling, stomach balled, I stepped in across the threshold.

The flat beyond was swamped in muddy light. As silent as a grave.

There was no one behind the door to grab me, so I swallowed and kept advancing. The atmosphere was stale and acrid; a smell in the air like beer boiled dry. The central heating was turned on full, making the place more stifling still. The ghost-breath of condensation fogged the windows.

I found him in the living room – laid out on the sagging sofa. His face was blank, his stubble one day thicker; but after a moment I heard his wheezy breathing. He was asleep.

Apart from him, the flat was empty.

Relief almost took my legs from under me. It was the second time today I'd resigned myself to dying – and survived. Bracing myself against the back of the sofa, I peered down at him. Judging by the smell and the cans on the coffee table, he'd been drowning his sorrows: perhaps ever since I'd walked out. At any other time I'd have blown my top, finding him pissed out of his head like this. But this afternoon I couldn't see past the vulnerability of his upturned face. He looked as helpless as a little kid.

I slowly shook my head. Oh *Nick*.

I was glad to see him, even in this state. I kept watch for a minute longer, like the loving nurse I was; but he didn't stir — so I straightened up, and wandered on into the bedroom. The sight of the rumpled, unmade bed was like a poke in the eye — which showed how deep my basic training ran. The realization brought a wry smile to my lips even as I went over and dragged the duvet back into its place.

Thank God for something *ordinary* to do. I was just smoothing down the pillows when the sound of sirens crept into my ears.

I froze as my heart leaped inside me. Two vehicles, at least — perhaps a dozen streets away. Maybe fire, or ambulance. Maybe not. I waited, not willing to move until they'd faded.

They didn't. The next outburst was definitely closer.

Perhaps they'd even pass this street — but only to answer their call. Surely to God . . .

Morris never strikes in the same place twice.

Unless some cold soul conducted him back. And showed him a lamb to be slaughtered.

I felt sweat break out all over me, like icy blisters. Perhaps I'd been right, and Razoxane couldn't kill me: couldn't murder her sister face to face. But there were others who'd do her dirty work for her — leaving her free to finish her nightmare mission.

She'd guessed where I'd gone, of course; and now she was the one setting fire to the bridge between us. The speeding sirens wailed again — and I knew she'd sold me out.

Rage and terror surged inside me — each as helpless as the other. And then I thought of Nick. Even if I slapped him awake, I couldn't drag him; would never get us clear of here in time. So either I just upped and left him . . . or tried to lead the murderers away.

Which left no choice: not really. Even if I ran for it, I wouldn't live — not with myself. I blundered back through into the living room, but Nick was dead to the world. If they shot me in the street outside, he'd probably sleep through it. Which was only for the best, I thought.

On the verge of tears, I touched his face; felt the warmth of his skin one final time. Then hastily crossed myself, turned — and let out a yelp of fright.

Razoxane was lounging in the doorway: grinning like a demon Cheshire Cat.

'Well, were you going to die alone?' she said.

Chapter 34

Even as I pulled myself together, the humour faded from her face – to leave a calculating stare. Straightening up, she stood there for a moment like a summoning spectre; I half expected her to beckon, and back off into the dimness. But all she did was jerk her head.

'Come on.'

And with a last, scared glance at Nick – he snored on, undisturbed – I followed.

Jackie was waiting on the unlit landing. She looked tired and tense, her face as pale as it had been on that first evening. Our eyes met briefly – and shared our doubts. But her right hand was deep inside her heavy jacket: her gun already gripped.

The screaming sirens were closing in outside. I thought of evil spirits racing over rooftops, riding the wind. No obstacles to stand in their way . . .

We went clattering downstairs – Jackie taking up the rear and glancing backwards. Her pistol came into view as she caught up, and clicked beneath the pressure of her thumb. I had an irresistible vision of some hapless person coming in from work, and running into us three on our way down. Some welcome home that would be.

Things were picking up momentum now: going downhill so fast I hadn't time to feel scared. The hall opened up before us; the front door seemed to swoop towards my face. Razoxane reached it first, rammed through it, and we burst on out into the remains of the day.

'Brendan!' Jackie shouted, veering off across the road. Razoxane shoved me sideways, down between two parked cars. The first Peeler transit came screeching round the corner and down the street towards us.

The first glimpse I got stayed locked in my head. The riot shield was down over its windscreen, giving the thing a mad, masked look. Its radiator strobes popped like flash bulbs. At that speed the driver must have fought the wheel right round to make the corner; as he straightened out, he clipped a car and sent it slewing sideways. The crunch of metal made me wince. The transit scarcely wavered.

I hit the pavement on my hands and knees. Every detail seemed magnified: each crack and stain stood out. Panting with panic, I scrabbled towards the nearest garden wall. The transit came howling in like a dive-bomber, and ploughed to a stop as I began to clamber up. With the stink of burnt rubber in my nostrils, I twisted round.

The vehicle was rocking on its wheels; the doors were opening already. Even as my stomach braced itself for the kick of bullets, someone dodged across the street behind the van, and tossed something small into its rear.

Brendan: I glimpsed his beard. Then he was over a wall and into a neighbouring garden, his threadbare coat-tails flying. I looked back at the transit, and my stilted mind put two and two together.

Grenade.

I was still rolling over the hedge (like in school PE, only minus the run-up) when the thing exploded. The bodywork contained most of the blast, but the smoke and noise burst free from every seam. Falling back into the garden, I clearly saw the driver's body blown out through his steel mesh screen, disintegrating in a haze of gore. Then the hedge reared up to block my view, and the ground crushed the breath from my lungs.

For a stunned instant I just stared at the colourless sky, and wished I could lie here for ever. Shattered panes of glass were still collapsing, somewhere close. Then the transit exploded again.

Petrol tank, this time. The fireball rose like a raging sun, and burned itself black within seconds. Cringing from the heat, I forced myself to crawl away. Spots of burning oil drifted past on the breeze as I reached the low wall between this garden and the next, and dragged myself over it. The transit was a furnace now, the street cloaked with shadow and stench. The hedge beside it was on fire as well: hydrangeas crackling orange in the heat.

I slumped onto the paved path, gasping. Had any of them got out? Was Morris still in there? Was the blue-eyed bastard burning where he sat?

The snarl of a sub-machine-gun cut across my thoughts. Bits of brick exploded from the front of the house, raining dust into my hair. The lamp on the doorpost exploded like a wine-glass. Glancing back in panic, I saw a yellow jacket advancing through the murk.

I scrabbled across the garden like a whipped dog. The oncoming Peeler fired again, blowing holes in a plastic wheelie-bin between us. I rolled aside as the flowerbed was raked. The blaze of his gun was terrifying: a flaring asterisk of foot-long flames.

The smeared, pockmarked mess we'd made of someone's neat front garden seemed to shrink around me. I kept crawling, but with nowhere to go: the four-foot wall ahead blocked my path like a mountain range. And all the time he was coming down the pavement, closing the gap. I squirmed around, wriggled back against the bricks, to watch him taking final aim.

Razoxane rose from behind the wall – seeming to loom at a crazy angle – and fired across me. In the smoky gloom, the Tinderbox's blast glowed orange, like a shovelful of coals. They ploughed through the Peeler's face and chest and flung him backwards. His sub-machine-gun clattered in the gutter.

Numbed, I heard the scuff of trainers on tarmac, and turned my head: saw Jackie crossing quickly towards us, backing and sidestepping like a defending footballer. Her gun was up and ready.

A flicker of movement in the roiling smoke, and then another Peeler appeared, walking briskly down the middle of the street. On fire.

It was the deliberation of his progress that really froze me. He didn't flail around, arms waving, like they do in films; just strode towards us, blank-faced – an almost ghostly figure, sheathed in flame. His yellow jacket had started melting. So had his expression.

Razoxane hauled out her Astra with her left hand, fired, and he crumpled up quite suddenly – like a Guy toppling off a bonfire. Bits of burning uniform flecked the tarmac.

Someone else opened fire from across the street: the *crack-crack* stung my eardrums. I glimpsed a spatter of sharp light by the rubbish skip. Jackie almost stumbled – then fired furiously in return, her pistol extended in both hands. Razoxane joined in: working her trigger with steady, confident pulls. The noise was appalling.

The hollow, retching roar of a shotgun came from deeper in the fog; I guessed that it was Brendan's. The saturation crossfire found a chink in the barricade. I glimpsed an outflung cloud of something dark, and the Peeler slumped into view and down onto the pavement.

A sudden, ghastly silence filled the street. Even the traffic on the main road seemed to have stopped. All I could hear was the distant sound of dogs barking, all across the neighbourhood.

The transit burned thickly. No one else could have got out.

The sub-machine-gun in the gutter was that round-magazine Russian job. It was Wotan we'd just stopped. Morris . . .

Razoxane leaned down and seized my collar. 'Let's go.' I tried weakly to resist. 'No . . . more . . .'

'Oh yes there is,' she insisted grimly. 'Another vanload. And they're back in their element now . . .'

Jackie was backing warily away along the pavement:

still aiming with both hands towards the bodies, even though one was half-way to cremation. And then Brendan came ducking through the acrid fog, brandishing his shotgun. He turned this way and that, tracking his aim across the houses. But the street remained lifeless. Not even a curtain twitched.

Razoxane gritted her teeth and hauled me upright.

'You won't save yourself by staying, Rachel,' she hissed in my ear. 'This isn't London any more; it's every Bosnian village they've ever fought through. We're under the Ace of Swords now. Under the gun.'

There was an alley to our left and we retreated down it – fetching up in an unmetalled lane between the backs of houses. The shadow was denser here already.

'McCain . . .' murmured Jackie, her voice full of battened-down panic. 'What do we do . . . ?'

'Scatter,' came the cold reply. 'Soon as we can.'

We hurried onwards, past back gates and dustbins; jostling each other in the narrow space. Brendan, panting drily, snapped his shotgun open and fumbled a fresh round in. Jackie grasped my sleeve with her free hand – whether to encourage or constrain me, I couldn't tell. But most of her attention was directed behind us: staring over her shoulder, her gun half-raised.

Had Nick come awake when the shooting started? I could picture him sat upright, blinking – perhaps with that rootless dread you feel, waking up in the middle of the night . . .

Razoxane slowed to scoop up some gravel, feeding a fistful down the blunderbuss's maw; then strode back into step with us.

In another moment we'd come to the end of the lane.

Razoxane pushed her hat back: it slipped down behind her neck. Cocking the Tinderbox with the heel of her palm, she peered out around the corner.

'We're clear.'

And with that we were back in the open, fanning out as we crossed the road: jaywalking through gaps in the traffic. There were still plenty of them, but the rush-hour rhythm was beginning to build. People too keen on getting home to notice much about the dark, dishevelled beggars who crossed their path. Brendan muffled his shotgun beneath his coat; Jackie kept her gun down, breathing hard. Razox-ane carried the Tinderbox sloped across her shoulder, as if daring passers-by to notice. I stuck with her.

The burnt-rubber stink of the Wotan transit had carried this far already. The scream of sirens would surely follow. Whether real or fake didn't matter much. Either would be the death of me in present company.

As we reached the far pavement, I glimpsed movement to the left, and turned my head. There was a pedestrian crossing some twenty yards down; the traffic had stopped for a straggle of uniformed schoolkids.

Two Peelers were walking with them.

They were weaving forward through the group rather than using them as cover, but the sight was no less frighten-ing: like unmuzzled dogs among toddlers. They carried their weapons at waist-height: carbine and shotgun on a level with those smiling heads. The boys stared with undis-guised interest. The girls, knowing better, kept on chattering.

A hand snatched at my sleeve: Jackie again. I found I'd faltered almost to a stop.

The Peelers reached the kerb and turned towards us, still coming at the walk. A third yellow jacket slid out of the crowds to join them; I saw the grim face of the woman called Miller. That came as a real jolt. If she hadn't been riding with the vanguard unit, maybe neither had Morris.

'*Rachel*,' Jackie hissed.

Heart thumping hard, I followed: we pushed on down the next street, fast. My final backwards glance found a mother and child in their path, the little one reaching up to hold hands. Miller swerved around her, scarcely breaking her stride; raising her radio handset to her mouth. Then the corner blocked her.

Streetlamps were beginning to come on above us, lurid pink against the sky.

We were running out of space and time. A T-junction lay ahead, with a newsagent's facing us across it. Several people stood at the bus-stop outside its well-lit window, as heedless of impending danger as a bread-queue about to get shelled.

Our pursuers were on the street behind us now, and spreading out.

Brendan's shotgun was half-drawn. Jackie, beside me, raised her pistol. Firearms in plain sight; but this was a London suburb at tea-time, and the people who saw just stared.

Razoxane crossed the intersection calmly, glancing behind her. Jackie walked it backwards, staring the way we'd come. The people at the bus queue watched us coming, unable to believe it.

It was going to end here. The four of us had drifted apart, and I felt as exposed as someone caught in the middle of a motorway. I tried to shout at the people in the firing-line, and found I hadn't the breath.

Then Jackie yelled a warning, and I saw figures scuttling up from the right, using lamp-posts and litterbins as cover. Shots filled the air like a string of fireworks going off. The bus queue ducked as one, then dropped grovelling to the pavement. Jackie backed towards them, firing: I couldn't help noticing how she blinked with every blast.

A passing car lost its windscreen – I saw it freezing over – but kept on going. The newsagent's window behind us crashed. A Peeler toppled backwards, shooting, his face doused in blood. The racket of Razoxane's pistol blended with the double thump of Brendan's shotgun. Another yellow jacket spurted scarlet.

The last of the snipers fell, and flooded the gutter.

I'd reached the pavement by now, and was stumbling

between cowering bodies. For a moment back there, the air round my head had come viciously alive – like when you poke a hornet's nest and it bursts in your face. Some of those bullets had knocked chunks out of the bus-stand.

That could have been my skull . . .

Razoxane was backing with me, her blunderbuss tucked under her arm; reloading her pistol from up her sleeve with a black magician's sleight-of-hand. Brendan ducked behind us, side-stepping away. Jackie was still in the road, reloading too: but her hands were shaking so much she almost dropped the magazine.

Sirens were on their way towards us now: screaming like things possessed.

The second round erupted a moment later: four seconds of ear-slamming noise. Jackie fell with a shriek. Razoxane snapped her blunderbuss up at arm's length and let it roar, raking the far pavement like a meteor shower. The leading Peeler took the brunt, and did a grisly backflip. Miller, still aiming a revolver, crumpled bloodily sideways. The last man ducked behind a car.

Another stunned silence. Glowing cinders settled on the road. Jackie was still with us, and trying – despite her shock – to struggle up; leaking ketchup from the leg. The whole intersection was spattered with gore. It seemed like more than I'd seen in all my years of nursing . . .

Miller, in the opposite gutter, was moving too; even though Razoxane had crippled her arm, put holes in her side. Like Jackie, she'd kept hold of her handgun. Her bloodless face was fierce with concentration.

The first police car appeared around the corner, away to the right; came racing down towards us, headlamps blazing.

Razoxane felt my collar like a copper herself. 'Come on.' But I was transfixed by the contest on the road: the two women straining to get the drop on each other, one final time.

Jackie had made it to one knee: was steadying her aim

when the police car skidded between them, slewed around and broadsided a stalled van. Glass shattered, and tinkled to the road.

I felt myself hauled bodily backwards. Jackie single-mindedly renewed her aim. Two men with carbines struggled out of the car.

'Armed police, STAND STILL!'

Miller grinned behind her wavering gun — and in that instant Jackie must have known she was trapped. Trapped into pulling her own trigger. In despair she did so. The SO19 coppers opened fire.

It was like watching someone getting beaten up by ghosts. Jackie jerked and shuddered — half-raising her arms in a uselessly defensive gesture. Blood slopped out of her like soup. As I stared in horror, she fell back against a car and slithered down it, her legs splaying wide.

Murderer or no, I moaned aloud. If Razoxane hadn't held me by a fistful of coat, I might even have darted back to try and help. Nurse's honour, maybe . . .

Another shot: and the smack and splatter of the bullet gave the instant impression of a rotten-soft tomato flung hard into her face.

The last Peeler turned his shotgun on the armed response car. Another volley of bullets blew him open. He collapsed quite close to Miller: squirmed spinelessly for a moment, and was still.

Razoxane had me back against the corner: like a human shield to conceal her gun. There was no sign of Brendan.

Miller twitched. The nearest officer fired down into her body, and she bounced against the road. Her ripped-up yellow jacket was completely crimson now.

The shroud of silence fell once more. The whole scene froze in the flicker of police lights, still spinning on the roof of the car. There were bodies everywhere: living ones hugging the pavement; dead ones drenched in blood and gore. People outside the field of fire had scampered clear . . . then stopped to stare.

The copper who'd finished Miller off was peering down at her corpse. His bloodless face looked ghostly in the dusk. The other bloke was onto his radio. Neither saw Razoxane and me melting back into the side-street.

'Don't run,' she murmured calmly, and I didn't. Just shoved my hands into my pockets, put my chin on my tight chest, and walked. She followed like a second shadow, hugging her evil antique gun beneath her coat. We were out of their sight-line now – but someone else might see, and point us out. Every step begged a bullet in the back. My ears itched for the first shout from behind us.

'Ere, I want a word with you . . .

'You know what I like about your policemen?' Razoxane asked from the corner of her mouth.

I swallowed. 'What . . . ?'

'They may be firm; but nobody can say they're not fair . . .'

The street ahead was empty; Brendan had already beaten his retreat. We reached the next corner, turned it – and found the Wampir transit waiting in the middle of the road.

For a moment longer it sat there, like a lifeless hulk; then came suddenly to life. The headlamps snapped on like opening eyes. The engine, ticking over, snarled into gear. It surged towards us.

Razoxane *screamed*.

It was like no sound I'd ever heard: a high-pitched, horrifying shriek of hate that made me want to block my ears. But all I could do was watch as her mouth opened wide and wider to let it out, until I thought she'd dislocate her jaw. Her whole body was shuddering with the effort, and still the scream came, rising, her mouth a maw as dark and depthless as the shades above it.

The oncoming van exploded.

The balloon of blazing petrol scorched my eyes shut; I felt my eyebrows singed in the instant before I jerked my face away. When I looked again, it was to see Razoxane swaying, like a tramp with a noseful of solvent fumes. I guessed that what she'd just done had drained her of power: she looked about to fall. But her grin and filtered gaze were still turned upwards – watching the fireball soar into the darkening sky.

I felt dazed enough myself. She'd stopped the transit ten yards short. The heat washed over us in waves.

She recovered herself as I watched, and looked back down towards the burning wreck. Her lip curled in grim satisfaction.

'Vampires should wait until full dark ... or they end up as ashes.' She took a heavy breath; and nodded. 'Come on, then. Nearly there ...'

We fell back from the inferno, and ran on down the first side-street. I could scarcely believe the trail of destruction we'd left behind us since emerging from the flat. And how long ago had that been? Ten minutes? It seemed an age.

The street was a cul-de-sac, but it gave onto a lane. A narrow, gloomy footpath, overshadowed with trees. Razoxane looked behind her, then dropped the Tinderbox over the fence. It thudded down into the undergrowth.

'The right person'll find it ...' she muttered, gesturing me onwards. 'And stow it safely away for the next pilgrim in need ...'

The lane veered round behind houses; the fence became iron railings. There was a railway line on the other side: two tracks in a shallow cutting. The ground slid away towards them, under bushes and brambles.

'This way, now,' she breathed.

I'm not much of an athlete, but the adrenaline today was working wonders. She gave me a boost, and I swung myself over. The landing was awkward: I started to roll. Thickets of brambles clawed at my coat. I was halfway down the bank before they brought me to a halt. Scratched and breathless, I began to struggle up – and heard a rustling noise from further down. Not something I'd dislodged; it was coming up towards me, out of the dusk. I was about to really panic when I realized it was Brendan.

He rose from a crouch, his shotgun aimed – at me. His face was bleached and bony with the aftermath of shock. For an instant I thought he was going to fire. My heart spasmed in my chest.

You can't shoot me; I'm a nurse.

Then his gaze switched to a point above and behind me. Razoxane scrambling down. 'Move,' she snapped.

'Where's Jackie . . . ?'

'She didn't make it.'

I glimpsed a flicker of something in Brendan's eyes, though he tried to mask it. Maybe the two of them had had something going. Whatever, there wasn't time to brood on it. We followed in Razoxane's wake.

It was already twilight on the tracks, shot through with the glow of signals. To our left, a tunnel opened wide, like a gateway to the depths beneath the city.

Razoxane led us straight towards it. I turned my ankle on the trackside ballast, and almost fell; but caught myself and kept going. Running on into the darkness. Fleeing deep into the grave.

Chapter 35

Brendan paused at the gate, and glanced around him –
then beckoned us on. The dusk was deep now; he was little
more than a shadow by the garden wall. The house loomed
above him, looking ominous and haunted. The place that
Nick and I had once called home.

I could feel its emptiness as we approached along the
pavement. The ground-floor windows were boarded up
where the bullets had smashed them, giving it the appearance of a gutted old squat. The first floor was dark and
silent. Blackness pressed against our bedroom window.

We slipped in through the gate like ghosts coming home;
Brendan stepped aside, still watching the street. His gun
was barely concealed beneath his coat.

I dug deep in my pocket and fished out the door-key –
complete with its teddy-bear fob. I'd carried it round for
days without a thought. With Razoxane's sombre presence
at my side, I fitted and turned it. The lock slid open. The
police had secured the scene of the crime, but they hadn't
thought of this.

The door swung open onto darkness. Razoxane eased
past me; I followed her in. My heart was thudding; this
wasn't anywhere I knew. The house felt derelict, as if
nobody had lived here for ages.

Brendan came after us, and shut the door behind him.
Apart from the gruel of twilight oozing in through the
frosted pane above, the gloom in the hall was almost
tangible.

Razoxane opened the door to the lounge. The windows
were still intact in there. Grey light lay over everything,
like a year's worth of undisturbed dust.

She glanced back at Brendan, and nodded towards the stairs. He seemed reluctant for a moment; then went trudging up into the dimness. Razoxane went on into the lounge, turning to face me as I followed. Even by the half-light, I could see how tired she looked. But her slow, sardonic grin was just the same.

'Well, we're back.'

Rage filled my mind like a snow storm. I slapped her hard across the face.

The blow skewed her head aside, and knocked off her shades. For a moment she just stood there, staring after them. Then her face came round again: her unmasked eyes as calm as moonlit pools.

I went for them with all my fingers, lunging forward across the room. The blizzard of hate was blowing though my head, obscuring thoughts and fears. All I could fix on was Razoxane. I had to hurt her.

She fended me off so casually it was insulting. Incensed, I flailed and swiped at her smiling face, breaking through her half-hearted defences and forcing her back. My memories boiled over, spurring me on. All the blood on her conscience came bubbling up: all the butchery and suffering she'd caused. Right back to that first, burned victim in our ITU bed.

She let me slap her around for a moment longer; then reached out, grasped my jaw and shoved me backwards off my feet. I slumped down onto the sofa, staring up at her wide-eyed. My rage ran out, and fear rushed in behind it.

Razoxane seemed to tower over me – but made no move to take advantage. She just reached up and straightened her hat. Her smile had scarcely wavered.

'You set me up,' I whispered. 'Didn't you? You bloody set me up.'

She didn't have to answer. As I gaped at her, it dawned on me that she might even have left that scribbled address lying round for me to find. Knowing that I'd run like a frightened hare . . . and lead the hounds right into her trap.

I shook my head, quite helpless. 'You utter *cow* . . .'

'You're so ungrateful sometimes, Rachel,' she chided drily. 'I did just save your life.'

'I don't know why you bothered,' I sneered.

'Oh, it was quite a challenge,' Razoxane murmured. 'Set Morris onto you . . . then see if I could get you out alive.'

I thought of Jackie's face exploding. Saving her had obviously not been part of the package.

Could *I* have saved her? Even from herself . . . ?

'And Morris?' I ventured – still feeling the heat of those blazing vans. 'Is he dead now?'

Razoxane stooped to retrieve her shades. 'We'll see.'

Brendan's footsteps were creaking back downstairs.

Little did he know, of course; and far be it from me to bloody tell him. I just sagged back, and tried to meet her Machiavellian smile.

Brendan appeared in the doorway, carrying the sports bag Jackie had brought round. Sealed and concealed here by Razoxane's power: the bomb I'd been living with. The very sight of it made me push myself away along the sofa.

'The guns and ammo too?' he asked, ignoring me.

'Just that,' Razoxane told him.

He seemed to hesitate again – then shrugged. He was probably as shell-shocked as I was; disillusioned by disaster. But Razoxane still had him hooked. She'd spun him a tale on our way here, explaining the state of the house in terms of a brutal Brit search. The hit-and-run reprisal team had wrecked the place, but overlooked the arms cache. It sounded a bit unlikely to me, but pandered to his prejudice. And besides, he hadn't had the nerve to question her further.

'Jackie . . .' he said, after a pause. 'You're sure she's . . . ?' His eyes strayed to me as he said it, as if I could tell him different.

But all I could do was nod my head. I was sure, all right.

He breathed slowly out, his expression blank. 'Jesus, I need a drink,' he murmured.

'I think there's some beer in the fridge,' I offered meekly. I doubted anyone had thought to turn off the electricity.

He nodded and went back out; I heard him dump the bag on the breakfast room table on his way through to the kitchen. I looked back at Razoxane.

'What do you need that for?' My voice was low and nervous.

'I'm tying up loose ends.'

I felt the weight of cold dusk in the room. The streets outside were filling up with darkness. Hostile country. 'You think Morris is still alive, don't you?'

'It's best to be safe,' she said, and wandered out.

I sat back once more, and tried to suppress the nervous itch inside me. The lounge felt lifeless; there was the same musty whiff in the air that used to welcome us back from holiday. The phantom damp we'd never quite tracked down . . .

Then something went click inside my head. I jumped to my feet and bolted for the kitchen.

By the time I got there, Razoxane was done. Brendan, his throat sliced wide, was slumping floorwards with her fist still in his hair. The blood spilt here before had been mopped up; but now the cooker and fridge were freshly coated – dripping dark.

She let him go, bending down to clean her switchblade on his coat. Then straightened up, and saw me watching.

I leaned sideways against the door-jamb, my hand to my mouth.

'Don't look so shocked,' she said calmly. 'He was a terrorist, remember? The one who bombed Liverpool Street. And a murderer's sins will always find him out . . .'

'*Murderer?*' I almost squeaked: outraged despite myself. 'What about *you*?'

'Me? I'm just on the sidelines, Rachel. Watching ignorant armies clash by night.'

And only scavengers and grave-diggers stood to gain from such encounters. I cringed as she came past me – unable to drag my eyes off the shadowy slumped corpse. One more player she'd dealt out of the game. I wondered, shakily, why I was still in it.

When I turned, she was picking up the sports bag from the table.

'Now where are you going?' I asked hoarsely.

'Your hospital – where do you think?'

I felt as though she'd punched me in the stomach. '*What?*'

'You heard. I can't wait any longer, Rachel. I'll summon the Ankerite tonight, and then expel it. Cast it out of this life. And then it'll all be over . . .'

'Summon it . . . where?' I faltered; knowing the answer even as I spoke. And the prospect of that was so appalling that it left me numbed. When I spoke again, my voice was surprisingly calm.

'Not the kids' ward, Razoxane. You can't. You just can't.'

A simple plea, addressed to a reasonable woman: and it reached her. For a moment she looked almost hurt; then chuckled softly – as if amazed that I should think her capable of this.

'Oh, *Rachel*. What kind of girl do you think I am?'

I never saw her left fist coming: a backhand smash of bone and muscle that almost knocked me senseless. My legs flew from under me and I fell back against the wall, collapsing to a heap in the corner.

Razoxane stepped over, and craned forward. Her knife was suddenly in her hand again, unlocking with a sound like a man-trap springing. The blade poked down towards my cheek, gleaming faintly in the dimness.

'You're right,' she whispered. 'A girl with no soul.'

I peered up at her, saucer-eyed.

'It's all for the best, you know,' she went on softly. 'When this is finished, I can leave *Razoxane* behind. This world behind. I might even remember my own name.'

I didn't dare reply. The sports bag dangled from her free hand. I thought of all that pent-up force and flame – shot through with twisted nails – bursting free in Sandra's ward. In Sandra's *face* . . .

She rose back upright, staring down. 'There won't be time to tame it; that's why I'll need the bomb. After midnight, when the moon is down. You can ring them up if you want to, Rachel. It won't stop me. Nothing will.'

I didn't doubt that. They could double the security and she'd slip right through it. Then the screams would start, from behind the locked doors. Before the ward was blown wide open . . .

'Razoxane. *Please* . . .'

She didn't bother answering; just turned towards the door. She paused as she reached it, and looked back at me again.

'Believe me, Rachel: if you come after me, I'll kill you.'

Then she was gone, a shadow into shadows. The front door opened and closed again. And I was left behind in this haunted house, with only a dead man for company.

I sat where I was for a long while, my head throbbing in my hands. My jaw ached sharply where she'd hit me. My legs felt like strings of liquorice.

There seemed no point in getting up. Calls to the police or the hospital would get me nowhere.

If you come after me, I'll kill you.

Her voice had chilled and hardened as she'd said it, and left me in no doubt. She'd spared my life till now, whatever her reasons; but this time she meant what she said.

I hauled myself up to sit on my heels, my back still braced against the wall. Contemplating the darkness round me – and the dismal gulf that opened up inside.

I could sit here all night, of course. Turn on the radio in the morning, or venture out to buy a paper. Find out the worst that way. But the thought of waiting was unbearable. The hours would take forever to crawl by – with nothing at the end but despair. And behind the horrified headlines, the strained voices of presenters, I'd see Sandra's pleading face, and those of all her fellow patients.

It was like Judy's house all over again. I couldn't just stand by and let it happen. I'd rather not live at all, than live with that.

I squatted in shadow for as long as I could, but the decision was made already. It was almost a relief, in fact: to know my future, however short. All I was doing now was putting off the first move – because once I'd started, I knew I wouldn't stop until I'd caught her up.

And then she'd kill me.

Dry-mouthed, I climbed to my feet and went upstairs. Our open bedroom was a murky blur, but I was past being scared of the dark now. A touch of the light switch, and it was there before me in all its detail. Our bed still rumpled and unmade, just as Nick had left it.

I realized I'd never sleep with Nick again. Or see him smile. The thought made me ache inside.

Drawing the curtains, I carefully undressed; catching whiffs of the day's perspiration as I did so. Then I went to the wardrobe and slipped one of my uniforms off its hanger. Sister's blue. Mary's blue. It wouldn't save me – but I'd feel better facing her in it. Not just anyone; a *nurse*. The strongest statement I could think of. And besides, there were worse things to be seen dead in.

My stomach was still sore with apprehension, but I had a momentum going now. With the last stud snapped together, I smoothed the dress down; then got a matching navy ribbon from the drawer and tied my hair back. My rosary still lay on the dressing table in a black and silver heap. I picked it up and fingered through it for a moment; then tucked it down into my breast pocket.

Pray for us sinners. At the hour of our death.

Time to get going. Despite my resignation, I was feeling more keyed up with every passing minute. In an effort to

405

calm myself, I forced myself down onto the bedside, and picked up my Bible. There had to be a verse I could take with me: something I could hold in my head. Then I remembered the reference I'd read this afternoon, in Razoxane's black book. *Matthew 12:43.* It seemed as good a place to start as any.

I flicked through, and found the place.

When the unclean spirit is gone out, he walketh through dry places, seeking rest, and findeth none.

Then he saith: I will return into my house from whence I came . . .

I lowered the book with a little shiver – and almost glanced behind me. Some reassurance that was. Maybe Razoxane had even taken it as a reference to herself.

Perhaps she'd been right, as well.

I came despondently back downstairs, and pulled my coat on. I could feel the dark night waiting on the other side of the door. I was just about to switch the hall light off when I caught a glimpse of something gleaming, back in the dimness of the lounge.

A step across the threshold, and I saw it was that weird pocket compass, lying before me on the carpet. Razoxane must have dropped it when I started laying into her. I stared down at it, undecided; then stooped to pick it up. The case felt icy cold against my fingers. I was on the verge of dropping it again when my thumb touched the catch and sprang it open.

By the light from the hall, the needle sat motionless – for a moment. Then it quivered, and began to turn.

The road to your destiny . . .

I stood frozen, eyes fixed on the thing in my outstretched palm: watching the sprawled pentagram rotate, as though it were a living spider I'd just picked up. Just as I'd guessed, the downward point was creeping round towards the east and south. Showing the way to the hospital. The road she'd be following already . . .

Except it didn't stop there; it kept on turning. From

south to south-westward, away from the City. And *then* it came to a halt.

Even as the map came together in my head, I knew which landmark it had fixed on. King's Cross. Three times I'd dreamed of Razoxane in that district. There was a link there, somewhere. One part of the puzzle she hadn't seen fit to share.

The needle-star was still now: as if it had been nailed into place. Its lesser points had aligned with various runes and symbols on the inner rings. Perhaps there was a message there, but it wasn't one I wanted to read. Convulsively, I closed my hand. The silver lid snapped shut.

She needn't have gone straight to the hospital; there were hours to midnight yet. Most likely she'd slip in past the skeleton staff, some time after one or two. The thief in the night that nobody expected.

In the meantime ... perhaps she needed to focus her power, one final time, in preparation. In olden days, a witch would withdraw to a blasted heath or somewhere. But tonight, in this city, she'd need a different kind of wasteland.

I'd known it in my nightmares; now the compass in my hand confirmed it. King's Cross was where I'd find her, this frosty night.

And King's Cross was where they'd find me, come daylight tomorrow. By which time I'd be well past caring.

Chapter 36

I paused beneath the streetlamp, and forced my fingers open. The compass lid flipped up. The pentagram was upright now – the needle pointing right across the road.

Reluctantly I raised my eyes. The construction site was hidden by screens of chipboard, the wall already a montage of peeling posters. No obvious way in; but I knew, with a sinking certainty, that I'd find one if I really looked.

All through the bus ride south, I'd kept the compass in my grip: holding it as tightly as a talisman. Once or twice I'd sneaked a look, and found the needle edging round with every mile. At the Angel, it was already pointing westward. As we sped downhill along Pentonville Road, it slowly swung towards the north.

I'd got off at King's Cross Station, and – heart in mouth – turned northwards, wrapped up in my thin, dark coat. Heads turned here and there, I felt them; but I really didn't care. Getting picked up or pestered was the least of my worries. In a weird way I almost felt safe.

My appointment's with the Angel of Death. I'm hers, and no one else's.

I even had her witch's compass to find my way. The feel of its coldness in my hand was like a link to the wider world she'd shown me, beyond these drab surroundings. London's lost corners – much darker than shadows and dirt. Her unreal city.

And at length it had brought me here, to a side-street just off Goodsway. Close to where the railyards were being cleared.

An unseen train passed, rumbling, in the distance; but the empty little street kept silent. I leaned back against the lamp-post, feeling a bit like the last prostitute in a ghost town. The buildings behind me were all in darkness: slums ripe for demolition. Old, dirty brickwork seemed to soak up the lamplight. It occurred to me that Whitechapel in 1888 would have had an atmosphere just like this. All we needed was the fog.

The Ripper we had already.

Dry-mouthed, I straightened up. Crossing the street, I started along the chipboard wall. The lamps along this side were out, their circuit broken; the pavement here had silted up with shadows. Glancing up, I saw orange clouds moving on the high night wind, breaking up to give me glimpses of the stars.

My toe clipped a discarded drinks can, and sent it rattling into the gutter. I froze at once, and listened to the stillness. Time dripped by; but nothing stirred. Steeling myself, I kept on going.

A minute later, I found a gap in the defences. Two misaligned screens, with just room enough for someone slim (like me) to squeeze between them. Beyond, there was only blackness. The nearest dead streetlamp craned up against the sky, marking the place like a burnt-out beacon.

The numbness of resignation was beginning to wear off now, like a dental anaesthetic. Nerves were tingling. Fear was coming back to life. With my heart pummelling in my chest, I edged my way in.

At first the only light was that from the sky. It looked huge above this sprawl of open ground: a panorama of cold winter stars and luminous cloud. As my eyes grew accustomed, I made out the contours of the desolate site around me. Ploughed-up sidings; heaps of spoil. Tarpaulin-shrouded shapes that looked about to move. And over to the left, a sudden flicker of vivid orange light.

Fatalism and fright renewed their struggle; but I'd come too far to stop now. Much too far. Warily I picked my way towards it, hearing the squelch of dark mud under my shoes. Round the dim bulk of a JCB, I came upon an oil-barrel, belching flame.

There was no one there to watch it.

After a pause, I ventured closer: drawn by the light and the promise of warmth. But the fire was dying: guttering for long moments before the wind sucked it upwards, drawing sparks. Even as my cold cheeks tingled, I realized that it hadn't been tended for a while now. Looking round, I saw crumpled blankets and the glint of beercans. Some of them unopened.

Someone had tried to make a night of it in here, and left in a hurry. Maybe there were security guards around to chase them off ... but then why had the fire been left burning?

No; something else had come this way, and cleared it. Maybe even the security had scarpered.

I sensed movement on my palm, and looked quickly down at the compass. The star was turning again. Not showing direction this time, though; just spinning slowly around and around. As if whatever I was approaching was now so close, the proximity was sending it haywire.

I tried swallowing again; but my throat was so tight I couldn't.

Beyond the site perimeter, the lights from King's Cross Station cast an afterglow like mist. The clock face in the tower of St Pancras Cathedral, lit dimly from within, made me think of a cloud-smudged moon. The cars on Euston Road were close enough to hear; a lorry came rattling down Goodsway. Evening life was happening all around; but it couldn't breach this enclave of silence and darkness. Here it was the witching hour already.

My gaze moved to the nearest gutted building, some ten yards off. As I moved out of the circle of firelight, I saw the faintest phosphorescence at one of its windows, like the glimmer of decay.

I faltered closer. The place was big, it might have been a goods-shed. The wreckers had already smashed some of it in, but the bulk of it was standing. It was too dark to read the signs that were posted around it, but I could guess what they said. *Dangerous building. Do not enter.*

Undeterred, I crept towards it. A shadow on the wall became a doorway, its panel missing. Beyond, I glimpsed more of that dim, diffused light. It flickered faintly.

Almost choked by my rising dread, I crossed the threshold, into an ante-room that smelt of plaster and old, splintered wood. The glow was seeping through from somewhere deeper inside the building; there was another open doorway across the room. I walked towards it, still holding the compass out in front of me. I could almost feel the needle whirring round.

This close to a climax, I was suddenly calm again. Razoxane would be waiting, just a few feet away. My arrival might even screw up one of her spells. With that spark of bitter hope in mind, I stepped through the doorway – and into a church.

The impression lasted only an instant, but left me short of breath. The way ahead was crammed with candles: a galaxy of glowing yellow flames. Their light stained the shadows and kept them back; but I still got a sense of the space in here – the draughty cathedral darkness. The building had been gutted all right: all its inner walls were gone. The gloom among its rafters hung like storm clouds overhead.

Razoxane sat waiting at the centre of the vault: there in a circular clearing amid the candles. Lit from below, her welcoming smile was like the face of all evil.

'Rachel,' she greeted me drily. 'How nice to see you here. I knew you'd come.'

I had no way to go but forward. Picking my path between the candles, I came to the circle's edge.

Its circumference was laid out in chalk and ashes. There were candles set at points around it, but only one of them inside, towards the centre. Lines criss-crossed its disc, forming a weirdly three-dimensional design that seemed to shift perspective even as I stared.

I felt like I'd come to the edge of a pit: the mouth of an open grave. Sudden vertigo snatched at my stomach, as if to pull me in. Razoxane watched, unmoving, from the furthest quarter. Her spinner was whirling like a gyroscope before her.

The needle of the compass was spinning too: almost a blur now. Abruptly I clenched my fist around it. The lid snapped closed. The hum of motion stopped at once.

Razoxane tipped her head back, regarding me with grim amusement. I suddenly noticed that her iron hat band was now a fillet of gleaming silver, as if the rust had peeled off like a snakeskin. It made me think of a Celtic crown.

'No need to stand on ceremony. Just step into my circle.'

. . . *said the spider to the fly*. I shuddered, and shook my head.

'You'll be safer inside than out,' she murmured, wafts of pale breath drifting from her lips.

'I'm remembering what happened last time,' I spat back at her. She'd lured me into a magic circle then, as well. And used it to open the Void . . .

Razoxane shrugged, in a *Don't say I didn't warn you* sort of way.

I flexed my throat, and ran my gaze around the circle. Her entire pack of Tarot cards was there, maybe seventy or more: set down just inside the rim. And the edge had been further fortified by interwoven words – traced by her finger in the ashes and dirt.

The whole design was fifteen feet across at least. In the centre, at the heart of that many-pointed star-shape, the blade she called the Scramasax lay inverted within a triangle of chalk. A single candle glowed at the apex.

'So what about . . . the last Ankerite?' I ventured.

Razoxane snorted faintly. 'The last Ankerite can go and pick *blackberries*, for all I care.' Her smile became a grin.

'Your hospital can sleep in peace now, Rachel. There'll be no further nightmares.'

I gave her an unconvinced look, and slowly began to walk around the circle – keeping well clear of the brink. Her head turned casually to follow my progress. Candle-light waxed and waned in the black pools of her shades.

The inner ring of words was (naturally) in Latin. The sense of *age* was what unsettled me the most. Not just a dead language. The language of the dead.

In Articulo Mortis Solum Mea Secreta Revelo.

By the time I'd read that far, I'd passed behind her; she scarcely bothered to turn her head. I fed the words through the mental mill, but didn't come up with much beyond the obvious. I cleared my throat, and tried it aloud.

'I reveal my secrets . . .'

'. . . only at the point of death,' finished Razoxane softly. 'The word of the grave.'

I kept on walking carefully round the rim. It still felt like a balancing act. I remembered my dream – remembered teetering on the edge of that violated grave, as it crumbled to sludge beneath me.

'Razoxane . . .' I said in a shrunken voice. 'What are you *after*?'

'Come in from the cold and I'll tell you.'

It was such an affable invitation, I almost forgot her parting shot back at the house. Almost; but not quite. So had this been a test or something? A way of seeing if I really would put my life on the line for someone else? If so, I'd presumably passed; and the hospital was safe now – or so she said.

I knew it couldn't possibly be that simple.

The candle-flames shivered briefly, as if a breath of night wind had found its way in here after us.

'Come on, Rachel,' she cajoled. 'One small step.'

Into the abyss. But where else was there to go?

I tossed her compass aside: the only act of defiance left to me. It bounced and rattled among the candles. Fixing

413

her shades with my naked stare, I fumbled in my pocket and brought out my rosary: clasping it just as tightly. Then I stepped forward, across the rim.

Nothing changed – not even the air. The rational part of me tried not to feel surprised: patterns on the floor, that's all they were. The rest of me waited, tense with dread, for something horrible to happen.

Razoxane just sat there, head inclined; setting her spinner going again. I hadn't the nerve to approach any closer – and certainly not to venture out across the pentagram. Like a larger version of her compass needle, it made me think of a sprawled and sleeping spider.

I was in its web now. A lost little fly.

'Well?' I prompted: half-afraid to break the silence.

Razoxane smiled to herself. 'I'm afraid I haven't been entirely honest with you, Rachel.'

Well, what a surprise. I rubbed a rosary bead hard between forefinger and thumb. 'Haven't you now?' It came out too shakily to be a sneer.

Now she raised her head, and shared her smile with me. It wasn't the mocking expression it might have been; more the indulgence of an older, wiser sister.

'I told you as much as you could bear, you know. Sometimes, when my dreams are clearest, I can scarcely take them in myself. I wasn't cast out of Paradise, you see: I realize that now. I left of my own free will. My spirit was one of the first to seek its fortune in the world of men.

'I remember the centuries of searching; but never finding. Chasing the wind and the rainbow's end. I thought there'd be no way back. But, like friend Gary used to say, there's someone always waiting. For you. For me.

'I'm going home, Rachel. But on my own terms.'

She paused. I waited.

'After vanquishing the Clinical Judges, I thought . . . *surely* . . . He'd receive me back. But He didn't. I was washed back up on this stinking shore. Which made me realize I'd have to pay my own ransom . . .'

The fat white candle at the point of the Scramasax flickered. Even as the movement drew my eyes, the flame grew firm again.

'I needed power,' said Razoxane simply. 'Power that could raise me up once more. On one of my journeys, I met a man who told me where such power could be found. And then I learned about the Ankerites.'

I moistened my lips with bitter spit. 'To set them *free*, you said . . .'

'Which I did,' was her mild response. 'I gave them peace. But there was a price for that, of course.'

'What price?'

'Knowledge.'

I didn't feel up to prompting her further: I knew I wouldn't like what must come next.

'You remember me telling you about how they came to be?' She smiled afresh at my wary nod. 'The sacrificial victims of Boudicca's druids. So I just reasoned it out. In what remained of each one's mind, there might be clues to the whereabouts of . . .'

'Her grave,' I blurted suddenly: surprising even myself. 'Boudicca's grave under London.' The memory had sprung from nowhere – the legend about the burial site at King's Cross. It all came together like the jaws of a trap.

Razoxane nodded, looking pleased. 'You *are* a clever girl, Rachel. One of the many things I like about you. You're not quite there yet; but close enough.'

I pulled a face at her.

'That was the legend, yes,' she continued, unperturbed. 'After her defeat and suicide, she was buried at the place which became King's Cross. I suspected there was a folk-memory wrapped up in that, and so it proved. A memory that no one dared remember in its original form.

'Boudicca wasn't buried here; but her darkest secrets were. The Romans defeated her up in the Midlands, and that's where she died; but some who survived that massacre fled back here. Things were hidden, and left to recharge their power in the earth. And people said that one day the Queen would arise again, and drive the invaders out of Britain.'

I peered down at the concrete under my feet. Perhaps there'd be a cellar beneath it, and then the foundations; and then . . . what?

'There were holy relics buried here,' she said, as if in answer. 'Holy to their old religion. Bones and blades. Coins and cups. Runestones and magic charms. For twenty centuries it's lain forgotten – but its wealth of power has not diminished, nor will it. Ever. It'll still be crackling with energy long after the last of your nuclear waste has turned to dust.'

Despite my awe, I had a giddy urge to giggle in her face. 'So what're you going to do now?' I demanded. 'Dig it up? What with – a bloody excavator?'

She calmly shook her head. 'No need. The hoard's somewhere under this building – and it can stay there. The power can be drawn up from it.'

Like oil, I thought numbly. Black gold. Black.

'So those were the deals I made,' she concluded. 'If you could call them deals. In communion with the things we now call Ankerites. I promised to unbind them, if they let me dig into their senses. That was . . . a harrowing experience, Rachel. Like telepathy in a lunatic asylum. But I gleaned enough from their nightmares to piece the truth together. Where the hoard had been buried; and how it could be accessed.'

Was it my imagination, or . . . was it getting darker in here? With Razoxane studying her spinner again, it was easier for me to glance away and around. The forest of flames was still alight: but the gloom of the gutted building seemed closer now, as if the outermost candles had been quenched.

I looked at Razoxane again. My heart gave a caught-out leap to find her looking right back at me.

'What about the last one, then?' I asked quickly.

'I realized I knew enough; I didn't need to mesh with that one too. It can continue its wanderings. I'm not its keeper.'

I had a flashback to that unnerving reference in St Matthew. 'But sometimes they come back . . .'

'That won't matter to me,' she murmured, watching the spinner wobbling before her. 'Or to you,' she added as an afterthought.

I wasn't quite sure how to take that. Even as I opened my dry mouth to query it, the flames around us began to turn blue.

It means the snow is coming: that's what my dad used to say, when I was small and we still had a fire. Weird bluish flames among the coals: I'd stare, and he'd nod sagely.

Snow is coming.

The tinge crept round the circle, staining the gold, though never quite suffusing it. We were bathed in a ghostlier light now, as though this place was open to the moon. Razoxane's face, still glowing yellow, seemed stained by blue; intoned with green. She grinned, and bared her teeth.

I hugged myself, the rosary in my fist clenched tight against the palm. 'What's *happening*?' I hissed in fright.

'What always had to happen,' she answered drily. 'The lines are drawn now. It's time to open the tomb.'

The candle before her grew suddenly brighter, greasily blue, as if feeding on a waft of marsh gas. It flared against her shades and her naked teeth; went glimmering down the Scramasax blade. And behind me, in the darkness, something stirred.

My whole back seemed to prickle with static, but I dared not turn to see. Whatever demon she'd conjured up this time, I could only pray that the power of her circle would keep it out.

Footsteps advanced across the floor: sounding solid and real. Razoxane's gaze moved past me. I searched her face for some glint of reassurance – but there was only a wintry satisfaction there.

'I was wondering where you'd got to,' she said – and closed her hand around her spinner, stopping it dead.

And as I turned my head, with a rising sense of horror and betrayal, Inspector Morris drew near from the darkness, and stepped into the circle.

Chapter 37

He came hatless: his short fair hair awry. Some of it looked singed, and there was a long burned patch across the stubble of his cheek, but otherwise he seemed unscathed. His face was pale, his jaw set. His deep-set eyes were the blue of gas flames, roaring in the window of a boiler. The silence here just emphasized their pent-up rage.

He paused just inside the rim: his black revolver levelled in his gloved right hand. Pointing right at Razoxane.

'I wasn't sure you'd pick the signal up,' she told him, looking casually back up the barrel; rolling the spinner between her fingers and thumb. I recalled how she'd spun it all through our conversation – and imagined a lighthouse beam, going round and around. A beacon in the night. She'd *brought him here*.

My feet had taken root. I couldn't even back away. But Morris ignored me, his eyes still fixed on Razoxane. His eyes and his aim.

'I could kill you now, McCain. So very easily.' His voice was calm but tight.

'So you could.' She spread her hands. 'I have no gun. But it would profit you nothing. You know that, now.'

He seemed to consider her point for a moment – while I just wondered what the bloody hell she meant. Then he reached a decision: and swung his pistol round to aim at me.

Jesus.

I sucked in a gasp of air: my hand went to my mouth as if to keep it in.

'I wouldn't do that either,' she added, infuriatingly calm. 'We need her.'

And that was no comfort. Rather, a sickening confirmation of what I'd already guessed. It wasn't *us and them* any longer. It was *them and me*.

But perhaps he hadn't heard. There was the slightest waver in his aim: like the tremble of someone on the verge of losing control. Behind the gun, his gas-jet gaze was entirely without pity.

'How many men have you got left?' Razoxane asked conversationally.

'None.' His eyes didn't leave me as he spoke the word; his gun stayed zeroed on my face.

I sensed Razoxane look him over. There were scorch marks on his sombre coat. 'You tried saving one of them?'

Morris shook his head; and now, at last, that cold, familiar smile wormed its way across his features.

'No; I shoved one of them back in.'

And with that he let his pistol droop aside, and eased the hammer down. *Cl-ick*.

The lungful of air came seeping back out between my fingers. The whole of my upper body seemed to sag.

His smile grew colder as my shivers set in. 'We'd come far enough together, Rachel. They'd be a burden to me now.' He glanced back at Razoxane. 'The three of us, then?'

I made a break for it at once.

As my foot touched the boundary, my innards caught fire.

It felt like heartburn fuelled with napalm; sulphuric acid indigestion. Then a horrid gynae pain that made me double up and crumple in a heap, to writhe and retch against the ashy concrete. The source of the agony stopped at once; but its blazing echoes faded only slowly. By the time my head had cleared, I found that I was sobbing.

I was still inside the rim. Squirming round, I saw Razoxane shake her solemn head.

'The circle's closed now, Rachel. There's no way out.' A flicker of regret crossed her features. 'I did warn you, remember. If you came after me, I'd kill you. That much was the truth.'

Helpless, I spat out bile. Propped up on my elbows now, but still too weak to find my feet.

'The ritual is very old,' Razoxane went on: addressing both of us this time. 'Three people meet in the circle of destiny – but only one can leave it alive. We're all of us here of our own free will, for our own good reasons. Rachel came out of love and duty – however misguided. Whereas Morris came searching for *dunamis on eortham*: power on earth. And I . . .'

She paused there: looking inwards now, as she'd looked to each of us in turn. An enigmatic smile brushed her lips. 'And I need an angel's ransom, to set myself free . . .'

I struggled up onto my knees, still panting for breath.

'In order to gain access to the spoils, the ritual must be observed absolutely,' Razoxane continued, her voice stern. 'The test is of strength, but also of cunning. So we fight hand to hand – and blinded.'

A pause. Then Morris tossed his gun away, out into the shadows: the gathering gloom. I realized then that the candles around us were going out.

'How?' he enquired flatly.

She nodded at the flame before her. 'We wait for it to die.'

Razoxane rose; I stumbled up. She began to back away, towards her side of the circle – and I saw how the three of us had aligned with the points of that central triangle. Southwest. Southeast. North.

'The Scramasax cannot be touched,' she added, still retreating. 'It holds the ring in focus. *Strong* magic.'

Candles everywhere were guttering, choking, dying – as if the air outside our circle had ceased to exist. Their smoky ghosts rose upwards, and faded to the smell of wax and wicks. The three of us were equidistant now, as the shadows crept up on us: embraced us. Only the tall flame at the centre still held them at bay. And in our long, dark coats we looked like shadows ourselves, about to be reclaimed by the murk.

Razoxane's switchblade snapped open in her hand.

Morris smiled thinly, and reached up his left sleeve. As I watched, wide-eyed, he drew out a length of piano wire, and wrapped the ends round his knuckles: drawing it taut. His own eyes had lost their livid flare; they were calm as pilot lights now.

'Wait a minute . . .' I wheezed, as the central candle too began to quiver. 'What about *me*?'

'Well, Rachel,' Razoxane said softly from the dimness. 'You'll just have to scratch my lying eyes out.'

And even as she said it, the last flame wilted and went out – and the dark slithered in like a slag heap, engulfing us all.

For more than a minute, no one moved.

I stood as if frozen solid: but my heart was still alive in my chest, and hammering to get out. I had to pinch my lips tight shut, to stifle my breathing.

The darkness was deeper than water; thicker than blood. And I was suddenly, horribly certain that the two of them were whispering together, out there in the murk. Conspiring, mind to mind. They'd kill me off first, before settling things between them . . .

I began to move: out across the circle, with small, scared steps. Razoxane would surely be creeping in on my left, while Morris edged around towards my right – but if only I could slip between them, they'd run right into each other. And then . . .

But what if I dislodged the Scramasax? Or stepped into its triangular field? I stopped again.

Strong magic. Do not touch it.

From somewhere in the distance, beyond the walls, I heard the sound of a shunting train. The outside world. Tantalizingly near. Impossibly far away.

There was a stirring of air against my cheek: as if

someone had just slipped by me in the dark. I flinched, I couldn't help it – surely giving my position away. The train noises faded, leaving my ears hissing with the silence. I turned round slowly, straining my eyes against the void ... and realized, with a plunging sense of dread, that I'd disoriented myself.

Darkness in all directions. I'd no idea which way I'd come, or where I should be headed. And somewhere, maybe feet away, Razoxane and Morris were waiting, with open arms – to gut or garrotte whoever stumbled into them.

Oh, how I wanted to just lie down and *die*.

Something moved before my face: something I sensed as much as heard. Stifling a whimper, I backed away.

Straight into the bear-hug of the person behind me.

I squealed aloud with the shock of contact – then gawped as his arms crushed the breath from my lungs: squeezing my chest like an ageing set of bagpipes. The discordant wail I made was quite similar, as well: same principle, really. I threshed and kicked, but all to no avail. My hand jerked open, and the rosary slipped out of it and was lost. A moment later I ran out of air.

I knew it was Morris, of course: even before the cold, taut wire touched my naked throat, and began to wind around it. With the pressure on my chest released, my head still swimming, I gulped in my final lungful of life ...

And suddenly my support was gone, leaving me teetering: my legs gave way a moment later. I dropped to my knees, and began clawing at the loop around my neck – but it was loose now, no longer a threat to my breath or my vulnerable flesh. I gasped and gagged. Behind and above me, the ferocious sounds of struggle filled the dark.

There were no words; just rasps of breathing. Clothing rustled: something tore. Boots scrabbled for a purchase. I knew they'd be fighting over Razoxane's knife, trying to force it back or forward: staring each other sightlessly in the face. And maybe Morris was stronger than Razoxane;

but she was surely mad enough to make it an even match.

All I could do was cower.

Then someone – either one – gave a gravelly, guttural yell, and I sensed them break apart. More hoarse breathing; and the sound of an awkward collapse. The fallen body stirred, quite close beside me . . . and was still again.

Now the gasps for air were coming from one mouth only.

I crouched where I was, all sheened in cold sweat. As I listened, the breathing slowly passed from right to left. It lingered for a moment; then ended in a sandpaper rasp. A match-flame grew like a miracle in the darkness – and glinted off Razoxane's shades.

I let my own breath go whooping out as she re-lit the central candle. It glimmered and caught, pushing a dim-edged halo back against the gloom. After a moment, I was able to pick out the dark shape slumped near the edge of the circle.

This time Morris didn't stir again.

When I looked back at Razoxane, she'd risen to her feet and was contemplating her knife. In this light it seemed to ooze with black gore, as if she'd dipped it in molasses. Then she raised her gaze to me.

For a moment I couldn't understand why she looked so grave. So very nearly sad. Then, as she started towards me, I remembered why we'd come here.

'Oh, God . . .' I began to scramble backwards. '*Razoxane* . . .'

'Don't struggle, Rachel,' she countered, almost pleading. 'It will go easier for you.'

I gathered my feet beneath me. 'You can't . . .'

'I can.'

'In the *dark*, you said . . .' I whimpered – really clutching at straws now.

She shook her head: still coming. 'The outcome here is not in doubt. It would just be prolonging the agony. And I wouldn't do that to you.'

You *bitch*, I thought back wretchedly, retreating. But I was up against the circle's rim now – my guts already tingling with the proximity of its force field. I edged away along the brink, and she came stalking round the candle after me.

'You can't leave the circle,' she chided patiently. 'There's nowhere to run.'

'Oh . . . *please* . . .'

'It won't hurt,' she whispered. 'I promise . . .'

Something caught my eye then: a glimmer in the dimness. My rosary, lying heaped where it had fallen.

. . . I'm going to die unconfessed . . .

Strange. In the warm light of day, the prospect wouldn't have made me turn a hair. This icy night, it sent me cold with terror. But then what it articulated was what every-body feels, religious or not. Death is here, and *I'm not ready*.

Instinctively I moved to scoop it up. And Razoxane lunged.

Her boot reached the beads a moment ahead of my fingers, and sent them skittering away across the circle. I went after them on hands and knees, and she kicked out again. This time the target was my ribcage.

All the breath I'd won back went spurting out of me. The force of her boot flipped me over; I rolled back onto my stomach. My emptied lungs felt ready to collapse – or catch fire. But the rosary was still in sight, and with a frantic effort I stirred my leaden limbs and resumed my crawl towards it.

Razoxane kicked me again, her face expressionless. I screamed without sound, and went limply belly-up. This was the end, I knew that: I couldn't move another inch. But even as I peered at her through squinted, smarting eyes, a part of me found time to register its puzzle-ment. Razoxane, of all people, wasn't scared of a cross. It had no power over her. So why keep it out of my grasp?

'Don't be *stupid*, Rachel,' she scolded softly. 'Just lie quiet, and I'll make it quick . . .'

She started to bend forward — and I realized that someone else was with us in the circle.

An instant later she felt it too, and twisted round; I rolled my head to look. And there, on the far side of the candle, Inspector Morris was climbing grimly to his feet.

One hand was pressed to his stomach, the black glove slimed and glistening; his body was hunched around its pain. But he had his balance now, and was swivelling towards us. The candlelight flowed up his face, and disfigured it with shadow. From my low angle, he looked monstrous.

Razoxane snarled, and straightened up. She went for him at once, doubtless aiming to get her knife back in before he was fully braced; but he was ready for her. His free hand shot out and seized her wrist, arresting her overarm thrust in mid-air. Then he twisted brutally, sideways and down, until her grip on the knife spasmed open and it clattered to the floor. Razoxane almost followed, fighting for balance — and a backhand blow from his bloody fist nearly wrenched her head from her neck.

Her shades went flying; she arched her spine. Morris let her wrist slip clear of his fingers, transferring his grip to his punctured gut. His right struck out again, an openhanded blow this time: flipping her head around the other way. Stunned, she went stumbling back.

I watched from the floor, struggling to draw air into my aching chest. Morris prowled forwards, pressing home his advantage: hitting her forehand and backhand with a metronome rhythm. Even with his left hand holding his guts in, his face was terrifyingly without expression. Razoxane had recovered herself sufficiently to block some of the blows, but the onslaught was wearing her down.

Tearing my gaze away, I dragged myself towards where

426

my rosary had come to rest, right at the circle's edge. The very fact that she'd tried to stop me reaching it was reason enough. I couldn't think any further ahead – still less speculate on how my worry beads could possibly save me from whoever won the struggle.

Round the ring they came, with Razoxane still on the defensive. Glancing back in fright, I glimpsed blood on her pale face: whether hers or his, I couldn't tell. She'd lost her battered hat along the way. It lay where it had rolled, outside the rim.

Eyes front again: the beads were almost within reach. My outflung fingers brushed them. I squirmed another foot – and scrabbled them back into my grasp. As my fist closed around them, I heard Razoxane fall.

Rolling over, I raised myself to see. She'd gone down close to the centre: the candle was spluttering, the darkness poised to swoop again. As she tried to struggle up, Morris stepped in for the kill, his dripping fingers splayed. And as he loomed over her, she grasped the Scramasax and thrust it upwards, deep into his lacerated stomach.

Strong magic, she'd said: but it carved like any other butcher's blade. Morris wasn't spirited out of existence or set ablaze; he just jack-knifed forwards, his breath hissing out between gritted teeth. No reason for the foreboding that forked through me and was gone, like winter lightning. But the chill of its passing still lingered in my *bones*.

Razoxane jerked free the knife, stumbled back and let it fall, watching as Morris collapsed to his knees. She looked more ravaged than I'd ever seen her; and I read the unease that filtered through her features. In desperation she'd transgressed the code of her own magic circle. Even she wasn't sure what the consequence might be.

I clambered painfully up, still clutching my fistful of beads.

Morris had begun to drool.

It was a yellowish gunk, like curd – or pus. He sagged

back, and coughed up some more. And then his face began to melt.

Disgust almost gutted me. I groaned.

Flesh became pulp as we watched: like cheese under a hot grill. His eyeballs popped and oozed. The whole mess began to drip and slither downwards, soaking the front of his coat like fresh vomit. I glimpsed whitish bone amidst the goo. Cheekbone. Angle of jaw. The bile in my own throat was ready to overflow.

Razoxane was faltering backwards, her pale eyes fixed on this mutation; I'd already retreated as far as I could go. And as we both of us stared, the once-handsome Inspector Morris bowed his ruined head, fumbling inside his collar with greasy fingers – and drew a thin, elastic sheet up and over the remnants of his face.

For more than a moment I didn't understand. It looked as if he was finishing himself off with a plastic bag. And then, with utter horror, I realized that he'd hooded himself with living tissue. A moist, translucent membrane. It shrank stickily to fit.

'Oh . . .' I began, almost spewing '. . . God . . .'

But he'd already pulled it tight over his whole sagging skull, and was raising his head once more. The muffled, malformed features were dreadfully familiar. Eyeless hollows; the gaping impression of a mouth. This was the face of a ghost made flesh.

It was an Ankerite that confronted us now.

I could sense – and even see – the movement behind the mask as the transformation ran its course: soft bone and liquefied flesh, remoulded by the hood, becoming solid once again. As he lowered his hands, his gloves split open, like surgical rubber. More pus and pulp came oozing through the rents.

I pressed my fist against my mouth; my eyes were huge above it. My mind was screaming that I should have known – but of course how could I? Razoxane hadn't. She'd made only throwaway mention of Ankerites and incarnation.

Her confident theories had proved horribly wrong. The creature she'd been tracking wasn't the one from Moorgate: that had probably expired long since.

This was the thing that had once dwelt under Aldgate.

I knew that now: as surely as I knew what that scholar had meant when he'd cited St Matthew. An image of Evil, wandering free – as far as Sarajevo; further. Venting its hate against the living. Avenging its own murder, again and again.

And then coming back. Coming *home*.

Razoxane looked as stunned as I was: no way had she expected this unmasking. She took another wary step – and the Ankerite's head swung round towards the movement.

It was blind again now: I realized that too. Morris's blue eyes had melted in their sockets, sloughed off with the rest of its human guise. But it could sense us right enough. And how long before it cast off the flesh completely, and reverted to icy spirit, like the Ankerite at Bank?

Razoxane glanced towards me, and gestured for me to move around. To distract the bloody thing. I shook my head.

'No choice, Rachel,' came her venomous hiss. 'You can't get out. You have to help me fight it.'

The rosary was still crushed inside my fist, so tightly that it hurt. I could feel every contour of the crucifix. She'd fought to keep it out of my grasp; and yet . . .

The Ankerite, perhaps still gathering its strength, began to crawl across the floor. Its raw skull glistened in the candlelight: turning her way – and then mine.

Three may enter the circle, but only one gets out alive. Those were the rules. Two had to die before the third walked free. Unless . . .

Something was quivering inside me: a bubble of thought about to burst. A secret on the brink of revelation. An idea whose time had surely come.

The questing beast between us paused.

Suddenly I opened my fist, the beads spilling out between

my fingers: dangling. The cross lay in my upturned palm, its silver gleaming in the dimness. I raised my stare from it to her.

'*Razoxane.*'

Her narrowed eyes flicked back towards me. 'What . . . ?'

'You can't keep me here,' I said.

Razoxane gave a small, tight smile. 'Oh no? What's *your* way out?'

'Someone died in my place,' I told her – closed my fist around the cross and took one pace backwards. And in that moment – *believing* it – I stepped over the edge, and clear of her closed circle.

It didn't relinquish its hold so easily. I felt fresh agony stab through me, enough to bring me choking to my knees. But when it had faded, I was still outside the ring; Razoxane stared after me in disbelief.

Despite the ache in my belly, I almost laughed.

She couldn't follow. It took *belief* to breach the force field. In closing the circle she'd sealed herself in, with an enemy far older than she'd dreamed.

The Ankerite was creeping forwards again. It made a noise like somebody gargling puke.

Razoxane dodged round it, and ran towards me. Pain flared across her face and she stopped in her tracks. The barrier between us was invisible still – but no less real. She hurled herself against it. It repulsed her. She backed off, panting: an *appeal* in those cold eyes.

I grimly shook my head.

'Rachel . . .'

'It's your game, Razoxane,' I bit back, with unadulterated bitchy pleasure. 'And your rules. Even in Hell they'll be laughing at this one. Even in *Hell.*'

I began to back away, towards the outer darkness of the room; and as the Ankerite clambered to its feet behind her, she tried one final shot.

'What if I *lose*? Rachel! Think what it could do with the

power here. There'll be a fire of London like no other; not even the *rats* will survive it . . .'

But once more I shook my head. It had all come together with chilling clarity.

'It doesn't want power, Razoxane: can't you see that? It wants *you*. It came back to stop you, and make sure it all stays buried.'

And even as she gaped at me, the groping creature behind her knocked over the candle, and the blackness flooded back. They were both of them blind now.

I turned and fled towards the doorway, just discernible through the murk: a ghostly smudge. As I reached it, her cry came racing after me – but only her cry.

'*Rachel . . .*'

It echoed behind me as I blundered on through the ante-room beyond; and then I was out under the stars, the huge night sky, in headlong flight from that hideous place.

Chapter 38

When I came back from cleaning my teeth, Nick was sitting waiting on the bed. His smile was almost hesitant.

God, this was like our first night together.

The thought – and the memory – helped me relax a little. I walked over and ruffled his hair. It was clear how relieved he was to have me back; but he wasn't about to push his luck and say so. This was a truce on equal terms.

I'd gone back to Jean's last night – apologizing profusely for not having rung. It was late, and she'd been worried. I managed to keep my coat closed over my uniform until I could slip upstairs and change. The flurries of reaction had been harder to hide. I'd spent ages nursing a coffee at King's Cross Railbar, waiting until the shakes had subsided; but my breath was still short. And something was buzzing in my belly, too. A glow of life and liberation, so rich it could have made me drunk . . .

'I love you, Raitch,' Nick told me softly. 'Did I ever mention that?'

I'd come back to him this morning. The street was still partly cordoned-off; the mess of yesterday's massacre being carefully cleared up. A terrorist hit-team had been cornered and destroyed here, at least if the TV news was to be believed. They'd been posing as policemen, which could explain a lot of the confusion over recent days. Men in white overalls had been crawling round looking for clues. I wondered what they'd make of Razoxane's grapeshot, if they found it.

The burnt-out transit still sat there on its naked wheels. A tarpaulin shroud had been tied around it, the corners flapping eerily in the breeze . . .

I shrugged out of my dressing-gown. Nick made room beneath the duvet.

I'd almost forgotten how good he felt.

This afternoon I'd made one further journey. Back to the hospital. Back to see Sandra. And Sandra had been beaming, full of the prospects of her imminent release. I was so glad to see a cheerful little girl again: her clouded sky had cleared. Last night she'd slept like an angel.

No more nightmares, Razoxane had said.

By the time I'd got back, the transit had been carted away, leaving just a shadow scorched into the tarmac to mark the place.

Already it seemed unreal: my journey into horror these past few weeks. Too bad to be true. Nick's warmth and weight were so much easier to believe in.

We made love cautiously at first . . . then with growing confidence. By the end I was quite breathless, and my mind had all but melted. I fell asleep with my arms round his neck, and a long-lost smile on my weary face.

When I woke it was still full dark; the alarm clock's red readout said three a.m. For a woozy moment I thought the rain had brought me awake . . . then realized that the night outside was silent.

That wet, hissing noise had been inside my head.

I knew I'd just been dreaming, but the details were slipping away already. All I could grasp was an impression of the sounds. Rain. A squelching like boots in mud. And the bump and slither of something heavy, being dragged in their wake.

I snuggled uneasily closer to Nick. The sound of his gentle snoring rose and fell, but failed to soothe me.

The image was gone, beyond recall. I could only guess at someone labouring through a mire. And some bulky thing being dragged away, towards a bleak, unseen horizon.

Whatever, it had just been a dream. No vision this time:

no symbolic showing. Just my overwrought mind getting straightened out at last.

That's what I told myself – firmly. But it was a very long while before sleep came again.

Night Sisters
John Pritchard

The first novel from a talented new horror writer

YOU'LL NEVER FEEL SAFE IN HOSPITAL AGAIN

CLINICIANS

A word that will come to haunt Casualty Sister Rachel Young through the dark nights ahead. A word she hears from a terrified patient, brought dying into her department after driving a stolen car straight into a brick wall. Still trying to escape from someone who has surgically mutilated his brain.

He isn't the first; he won't be the last. People are disappearing into the darkness; the lost ones, with no shelter from the night. Those that are found again have hideous post-operative injuries.

For centuries they have pursued their cold and merciless quest for knowledge, leaving death and mutilation in their wake. And tonight they have come for Rachel Young. For here they have a special role . . .

'A good old fashioned tale of battling evil, which turns into a roller-coaster ride to heights of gut-churning suspense and real terror'   Ramsay Campbell

'A taut and fast-moving tale with bags of authentic detail and a slam-bang finale'   Stephen Gallagher

'*Night Sisters* is one of the creepiest and most shocking novels I've read in a long, long time. The writing is superb. The story brilliantly eerie, marked by stunning shocks of violence'   Richard Laymon

ISBN 0 586 21769 X

Beauty
Sheri S. Tepper

Brilliant, unique and unforgettable. The first great fantasy achievement of the 1990s.

Winner of the Locus Award for Best Fantasy Novel.

On her sixteenth birthday, Beauty, daughter of the Duke of Westfaire, sidesteps the sleeping-curse placed upon her by her wicked aunt – only to be kidnapped by voyeurs from another time and place, far from the picturesque castle in 14th century England. She is taken to the world of the future, a savage society where, even among the teeming billions, she is utterly alone. Here her adventures begin. As she travels magically through time to visit places both imaginary and real she eventually comes to understand her special place in humanity's destiny. As captivating as it is uncompromising, *Beauty* will carve its own unique place in the hearts and minds of readers.

'*Beauty* lives up to its name in all ways. It is a story of mankind and magic, fairies and fairytales, future and fantasy all intertwined into a complex collage about the downfall of Earth . . . It is a story you can float away in. The writing is beautiful and the storytelling immaculate, so get it' *Time Out*

ISBN 0 586 21305 8

Night Relics
James P. Blaylock

'Thoroughly satisfying, memorable, and the best thing that James Blaylock has ever written.' Dean R. Koontz

In a blend of the supernatural, the magical, the fantastic, *Night Relics* continues Blaylock's progression towards a magical-realist literary style with thoroughly convincing elements of horror.

When Peter Travers moves into an old house in a remote canyon to try to separate himself from his old existence, his wish becomes reality . . . all too literally. For his wife and son vanish and the people of the idyllic rural town begin to relive the horrors of a nightmarish crime committed one windy autumn, sixty years earlier. Against a backdrop of murder and midnight terror, Peter must contend with the abandoned relics of his own past before he can overcome the dark forces that haunt the canyon and the people he loves.

'Blaylock is better than anyone else at showing us the magic that secretly animates our world' *Tim Powers*

ISBN 0 586 21780 0

Weaveworld
Clive Barker

Weaveworld is an epic adventure of the imagination. It begins with a carpet in which a world of rapture and enchantment is hiding; a world which comes back to life, alerting the dark forces from which it was hiding, and beginning a desperate battle to preserve the last vestiges of magic which Humankind still has access to.

Mysteriously drawn by the carpet and into the world it represents are Cal Mooney and Suzanna Parrish, two young people with no knowledge of what they are about to live through and confront. For the final conflict between the forces of good – the Seerkind – and of evil, embodied by the terrible Immacolata and her ravening twin wraith sisters, is about to take place.

Weaveworld is a book of visions and horrors, as real as the world we live and breathe in, yet opening doors to experiences, places and people that we all dream of, but daren't hope are real. It is a story of quest, of titanic struggles, of love and of hope. It is a triumph of imagination and storytelling, an adventure, a nightmare, a promise . . .

'Graphic, grotesque, and yet compellingly readable . . . its energy is unstoppable.' *Washington Post*

'A powerful and fascinating writer with a brilliant imagination. *Weaveworld* reveals Clive Barker as an outstanding storyteller.' J. G. Ballard

ISBN 0 00 617489 2

Imajica
Clive Barker

AS MYSTERIOUS AS THE FACE OF GOD, AS SECRET AS THE HUMAN SOUL

The Imajica – five Dominions, four reconciled, and one, the Earth, cut off from them, her inhabitants living in ignorance on the edge of a sea of possibilities, an ocean of mystery and magic. Only a few know of the Imajica, and many of them are frightened, for a shining mystical moment is approaching, a time when the Earth can be reunited with the other four Dominions – a time of Reconciliation

Racing to capture that moment are three memorable characters: Gentle, a master forger whose own life is a series of lies, Judith Odell, a beautiful woman desired by three powerful men, but belonging to none of them, and Pie'oh'pah, a mysterious assassin who deals in love as well as death. Together they embark on an epic journey through all five Dominions to the very border of the greatest mystery of all: the First Dominion, on the other side of which lies the Holy City of the Unbeheld, where their greatest hopes, or their deepest fears, will be realized.

'The tears and blood and nightmare imagery are passionate and ingenious. *Imajica* is a ride with remarkable views'
Times Literary Supplement

'Barker's fecundity of invention is beyond praise. In a world of hard-hitting horror and originality, Clive Barker dislocates your mind'[1]
Mail on Sunday

'An astonishing feat of the imagination, immensely engrossing, running riot with ideas, fantastical inventions, soul-terrors and emotional and intellectual resonances. Barker's best yet'
Kirkus Reviews

ISBN 0 00 617804 9